Table of Contents

Chapter 1:
Horizon Shoc

CW01501692

October 15, 2115
Horizon Shock Training Range
Imperial Crown Ring
Cobalt Prime, Koronar System

Rear Admiral Ethan "Paladin" Hunt's gloved fingers tightened on the Hellcat's control stick as another salvo of simulated plasma fire streaked past his canopy. The training lasers painted ghostly red traces across the black, their harmless energy pulses registering as kill shots on any fighter careless enough to fly through them.

"Jackal Lead, Anvil One—we're five minutes out on final approach. We're going to need those lanes cleared," Commander Kenneth Vosler's voice crackled through the comm.

"Copy, Anvil One, we're engaging now," Ethan acknowledged. "Stormcrows, we got bombers inbound. It's time to earn your pay," he called out to his 1st Fighter Group.

He rolled his Hellcat inverted, the F-19's twin engines screaming as he dove beneath a cluster of drone-mimicking Zodark starfighters—Vultures. His HUD tracked a formation of thirty-six bandits approaching from a grouping of Zodark battleships and a star carrier. As he leveled the Hellcat, he could see the angular form of the Vultures dancing in perfect patterns—too perfect, really. It was a sign that these were programmable drones and not real. A real Zodark pilot flew with rage more than with skill or precision.

"Black Talons engaging," Commander Julius Holden announced, his Australian accent cutting through the static. "Big Tony, Boozer—break right and draw their fire. Rest of Talons, follow my vector."

Ethan watched his tactical display bloom with missile locks. The Zodarks responded instantly, their Vultures racing to intercept the incoming fighters. A proximity alert screamed in his ear; a missile had locked onto him.

"Missile on your six, Paladin!" came the warning from his wingman, Lieutenant Mattison Danseen. She rolled her Hellcat through a corkscrew that would've liquefied a pilot without the kind of inertial dampeners built into a Gallentine fighter.

Ethan yanked his stick hard left, dumping chaff and flares to spoof the missile's seeker. The training missile locked onto the false signature, its kill radius passing harmlessly beneath his fighter. The onboard computer registered it as a near miss—five more meters and he'd be flying dead stick for the rest of the exercise.

"Thanks, Matti. Flattop, where are your Warhawks at?"

"Punching through Sector Seven-Three," Pushkin replied, his voice steady as steel. "These drone cruisers are throwing everything at us but the kitchen sink. Their flak guns are tracking way better than our intel said they would."

A flash of silver caught Hunt's eye—Gordon's Silver Lancers were knifing through the enemy formation like their namesake. The Scottish commander's voice rang out: "Lancers, wedge formation! Pierce that fighter screen at grid reference two-seven-mark-four!"

Ethan rolled his fighter upright, aligning his targeting reticle in the direction of a drone battleship sixteen thousand klicks out. The massive target hung in space like a diseased whale, its hull studded with enough simulated weapons to make a real engagement suicidal. But this was training—controlled chaos designed by the Gallentines to forge his people into a weapon sharp enough to defeat whatever the enemy threw at them.

"Longshot, take your Night Reapers high and neutralize those point-defense guns on that carrier," Ethan ordered. "You need to clear a path for Anvil's bombers to make their runs."

"We're on it, Paladin." Landon's Irish brogue carried a hint of amusement. "Nearly done mixin' it up with these Vultures and this cruiser screening for the carrier."

The Zodark Vultures were coming in waves of thirty-two—meant to overwhelm Ethan's pilots and test their ability to coordinate and work together. As the minutes ticked by, the number of destroyed enemy fighters continued to climb. In between chasing Vultures and dodging laser fire, Ethan ordered his 2nd Fighter Group into the melee. With the added Hellcats joining the fight, the enemy fighters scattered, their cohesiveness breaking down as the Gallentine starfighters dove on their prey.

The more advanced Hellcats moved with blinding speed and agility not found in their Gripen counterparts. Ethan watched in excited glee as the battle continued to unfold before him, a broad smile hidden behind his helmet. This was why he'd pushed for veteran instructors in the squadron command slots across the *Freedom*'s Space Wings. Once it was clear the Republic's flagship would return to the Fleet for the final battles of the war, Ethan knew he'd have precious little time to get her fighter and bomber wings fully staffed and ready to fight. If he could bolster his ranks with instructor pilots, they could continue pilot training long after they left flight school. Their years of combat experience would be an invaluable resource to the less-experienced pilots filling out the ranks of the thirty-three fighter, bomber, and transport wings aboard the *Freedom*.

"Jackal Lead, Oldman—I've got visual on a star carrier dropping more Vultures. Estimate forty-plus bandits inbound, vector three-three-zero."

Ethan checked his tactical display. Tommy Rens had positioned his command element perfectly, already vectoring to intercept. Thirteen years of flying together paid dividends in moments like this.

"All Jackals, this is Paladin. Converge on that carrier now! Clear those bombers a path and kill 'em all!"

Ethan applied maximum power to his engines, hitting one hundred percent in seconds as his Hellcat closed in on the newest wave of Vultures rushing to protect the carrier. He zeroed in one, his thumb depressing the trigger. Twin streams of laser fire lanced out, stitching across the target until it exploded in a brilliant flash. One down, too many to go.

"Big Tony's hit!" The Italian's voice came through strained but defiant. "Bastard took out my starboard thruster. I'm flying half dead but still in the fight!"

"Boozer has you covered, mate," Gibson called out. "Nobody touches Big Tony but me!"

The comms filled with the rapid-fire chatter of combat—terse warnings, targeting calls, the occasional curse when a training missile found its mark. Ethan's HUD showed three of his fighters running yellow—damaged but functional. Six registered as destroyed, their pilots forced to watch the rest of the exercise as observers.

"Fifteen seconds to torpedo range," Vosler announced. "Cover us! Anvil flight is going in hot for terminal run."

Ethan craned his head around to try and get a visual on them—there, a swarm of sixty-four B-19 Devastators approaching in staggered attack formation, their bellies swollen with plasma torpedoes. The bombers moved like predators on the hunt, ignoring the chaos around them, focused solely on their targets—Zodark capital ships.

A new alarm screamed. Ethan's eyes snapped to his scope—the star carrier had activated its starboard point-defense batteries. Dozens upon dozens of triple-barreled laser batteries the size of Ospreys began tracking toward the bomber formations. Suddenly, the space around the enemy vessel came alive with streams of blaster fire racing toward the bombers.

Oh, crap!

"Anvil flight, break off! Break off!" Ethan shouted desperately as he saw their bomber squadron fly into a hail of defensive fire.

"All Jackals, suppressive fire on that carrier, now! Go for the starboard gun batteries—light 'em up!" Ethan ordered angrily as he watched the catastrophe unfold.

He listened to Captain Tommy Rens regain control of the situation as he shouted new orders to the Night Reapers. Commander London's 4th Fighter Squadron was supposed to have cleared the enemy guns while Rens's three other squadrons dealt with the enemy fighters.

Ethan chided himself in that moment for not verifying with Rens that the carrier's guns had been neutralized or at least greatly reduced before sending the bombers in with Anvil.

That was a rookie mistake, Ethan. What were you thinking? He cursed angrily to himself as he counted thirteen bombers destroyed, with another five showing damage.

As the remaining bombers circled around for another pass, the volume of defensive fire from the carrier diminished greatly, to the point of being almost eliminated. While the guns on the carrier had gone almost silent, the remaining ones on the battleships and cruisers continued to fire.

"Foundry here—Black Anvils are on final approach, locked and launching," Commander Dorian Voss reported. "Torpedoes away!"

Ethan watched the tactical display light up with torpedo tracks—dozens of them, each following its own evasive pattern toward the enemy capital ships. The Zodark vessels responded with walls of flak, their defensive batteries creating kill zones that no biological pilot could navigate. But these plasma torpedoes weren't biological—they were smart weapons, each one processing thousands of course corrections per second before converting to plasma and becoming a flaming arrow of death.

"Splash one battleship!" someone called out. The massive drone simulator flickered and died, its computer brain acknowledging the killing blow.

"Matti, on me," Ethan ordered, inverting his fighter again. "We've got some leakers looking to go after the bombers."

They dove together, master and student, their Hellcats moving in perfect synchronization. A cluster of Vultures broke off their attack runs on a trio of Devastators trying to evade them. The Glaives rose to meet them, training lasers already cycling. Ethan felt the familiar calm settle over him—the zone where time dilated and every decision became crystal clear.

He squeezed off a burst, walking his laser fire across the lead fighter's fuselage as his wingman, Matti, hammered the trailer. Her target erupted in a simulated fireball before the training system shut it down. Splash two more. They rolled inverted, pulling hard into a high yo-yo maneuver to set up their next attack vector. The remaining bandits scattered like startled birds, but it was too late—Ethan and Matti were already in the saddle.

"Outstanding flying back there, Matti. You're reading the fight three moves out now."

"Thanks, Paladin. Learning from the best," she replied, sliding her Hellcat into perfect fingertip formation.

The furball continued as Hellcats tangled with the remaining OPFOR fighters, merging and separating in a deadly dance until the exercise objectives were met. When the Gallentine controllers running the range had seen enough, the training ended. Ethan's HUD painted an ugly picture: fourteen Hellcats killed, twelve damaged. Nineteen Devastators destroyed, seven damaged. One star carrier killed, eight battleships destroyed, five damaged, eighty-four enemy fighters splashed.

Bloody hell, that's not good enough, he thought, jaw tightening. They had serious work ahead of them if the *Freedom* was going to be combat-ready again.

Ethan keyed his mic. "ENDEX! ENDEX! All Jackals, Paladin. Terminate HS-1, terminate HS-1." He let dead air hang for a beat. "Decent first look, Jackals, but check your scoreboards—we're rusty as hell. Fourteen Hellcats and nineteen Devastators down. We can do better—scratch that, we *will* do better. Group and squadron leads, switch to channel five. All other aircraft, RTB and stand by for debrief. Paladin out."

Ethan punched up channel five and waited for his commanders to check in. "All right, listen up. That was our wing's first full-up exercise, and it showed—sloppy coordination, poor mutual support, and piss-poor execution. Oldman, your squadron failed to suppress that carrier's point defense—twelve of our bomber losses are on that screwup. Longshot, how the hell does a Top Gun instructor let his people fly into a PDG coverage envelope like that? And, Aggie, your Lancers were supposed to clear a lane for the Night Reapers. Instead, they flew right into a missile trap."

He paused, letting it sink in. "After your fighters land, run an after action review with your squadrons. Break down the tapes—the good, the bad, and the ugly. Make sure your people know the Cats & Traps closes at 2000 tonight," he said, speaking of the officers' lounge. "Normal hours resume tomorrow, but tonight I want all squadron commanders there for a come-to-Jesus meeting. Paladin out."

Ethan eased back on the throttle as his Hellcat cleared the training range's outer markers. Ahead, Cobalt Prime filled his viewport—a jewel of blues and greens wrapped in wisps of white cloud. Even after months stationed here, he found that the sight still took his breath away. The Gallentines had chosen their home world's location well, nestled in a system rich with resources and natural beauty.

The Imperial Crown Ring came into view as he adjusted his approach vector. The massive orbital structure dwarfed anything humanity had built—even the John Glenn Station looked like a toy in comparison. Its graceful curves stretched for hundreds of kilometers, each section a hive of activity. Construction gantries sprouted from the ring like mechanical flowers, cradling warships in various stages of completion.

"Jackal Lead, Crown Control. You're cleared for approach to Azure Slip-3. Follow beacon seven-seven-alpha."

"Crown Control, Jackal Lead. Following seven-seven-alpha," Ethan replied, banking his fighter to match the designated flight path.

The Royal Armory Yard dominated this section of the ring. Ethan counted at least forty capital ships in the slips—everything from sleek frigates to massive dreadnoughts. Swarms of utility craft darted between them like worker bees, their running lights creating constellations of motion against the black.

Then he saw her.

The *Freedom* emerged from behind a half-built battle cruiser, and Ethan felt his chest tighten with pride. Before him were fifteen kilometers of human-Gallentine cooperation made manifest in steel and composites. She looked different from when they'd arrived—fresh armor plating gleamed where battle damage had been repaired, new weapon emplacements bristled from her hull. The Gallentine yard workers had done more than fix her; they'd made her stronger.

"Beautiful sight, isn't she?" Matti's voice came through the private channel.

"Every time," Ethan agreed, following the approach lights toward the portside flight deck.

The *Freedom*'s hangar bay yawned before them, that familiar yellow shimmer of the atmospheric barrier marking the threshold between void and haven. Ethan's Hellcat passed through with barely a tremor, the inertial dampeners smoothing the transition. Once inside, he marveled at the inner workings of the flight deck. The crews rushed to service returning fighters, fuel lines snaked across the deck; it was the ballet of bodies and machines essential to keeping a carrier's heart beating.

His Hellcat's navigation system guided him to his designated pad. The electromagnetic arrestor system engaged, bringing his fighter to a smooth stop. Through his canopy, Ethan could see his crew chief already approaching, data pad in hand, ready to catalog whatever his fighter had endured during the exercise.

Ethan powered down his engines, feeling the subtle vibration fade to nothing. He was home again. It was time to turn training failures into tomorrow's victories.

****

CAG Office, Wing Ops Annex
RNS *Freedom*

Ethan had barely finished his postflight paperwork when his PA chimed with a priority message. Two Gallentine officers were waiting for him in Ready Room Three. He recognized one name—Captain Veskari, the senior instructor pilot who ran fighter doctrine development for the Imperial Fleet. The other, Commander Thakral, he'd seen observing from the range's control tower.

Ethan found them studying a holographic replay of the exercise, the star carrier's point-defense batteries frozen mid-salvo as dozens of his bombers flew into the kill zone. He felt himself wince inside as he approached them.

"Admiral Hunt," Captain Veskari turned, offering the closed-fist-to-chest Gallentine salute. His bearing reminded Ethan of every CAG he'd ever known—confident, observant, with eyes that missed nothing. "Thank you for making time."

"Yes, of course." Ethan returned the salute. "I assume you'd like to discuss the exercise?"

Commander Thakral stepped forward. He was younger than Veskari but carried himself with the easy confidence of a natural pilot. "We would indeed. But before we discuss the exercise, Admiral, I must commend your pilots' adaptation to the Hellcats. The transition from Gripens to our fighters typically takes three months. Your squadrons achieved basic proficiency in half that time."

"Thank you. Let's just say they're motivated," Ethan said simply.

"Indeed they are." Veskari gestured to the frozen hologram. "However, motivation alone won't save them when the battles are real and pilots don't respawn after taking a laser bolt through the cockpit."

The words hit like cold water to the face. Ethan felt his jaw tighten, but he nodded. "Fair point, Captain."

Veskari manipulated the display, highlighting the moment everything had gone wrong. "I would like to walk you through a series of events. As you can see, your group commanders flew as though these were three separate exercises independent of each other instead of a single coordinated strike. Commander Rens's fighters engaged without confirming that the Night Reapers had suppressed the carrier's defenses. Commander Vosler launched his bombers into an active kill zone. Commander Gordon's Lancers created a beautiful penetration corridor— but it was forty degrees off the bombers' actual attack vector."

Each failure Veskari mentioned blazed red in the hologram. With each new red beacon, Ethan watched his people die again in slow motion.

"In combat, Admiral, these stop being statistics. Instead, they become letters to families, empty bunks in the squad bay, and memorial services." Veskari's tone carried no judgment, only the hard-earned wisdom an instructor gave to those willing to listen. "Your individual squadrons show promise. But promise doesn't win wars. Integration and unity of purpose do."

Thakral added, "You have fought the Zodarks for years, Admiral. You know they won't give you time to coordinate once the shooting starts. Every second of confusion on the part of your group or squadron commanders costs lives."

Ethan studied the display. "You're right," he said, taking ownership. "My squadron commanders are still thinking like individual units instead of a unified wing."

"Precisely." Veskari waved his hand, and the display shifted to show successful strike patterns from Gallentine operations. "This is an example of how you need to mold your wing. Turn them into a weapon— a scalpel for precise cuts, a broadsword for devastating blows. But always unified. Always thinking three moves ahead."

"My father has a piece of advice he always gives his commanders," Ethan said. "He says the burden of command is about knowing which tool to use and when."

"Yes, exactly. It's also about having subordinates who trust you implicitly," Veskari agreed. "That trust is built here, in exercises where failure means bruised egos instead of flag-covered coffins."

Ethan absorbed the criticism, feeling the weight of thousands of pilots and crew depending on his decisions. "Clearly, we need some work. We have limited time until we deploy back to New Eden. What are your recommendations?"

"Humility," Thakral said immediately. "Your commanders need to admit they're not as good as they think they are—as today's actions proved."

Veskari nodded. "Break them down. Build them back up. Make them fly scenarios that force coordination or guarantee failure. And, Admiral?" He paused, meeting Ethan's eyes. "Stop protecting their feelings. Better that they hate you in training than die because you were too gentle."

The truth of it settled in Ethan's gut like lead. He'd been so focused on building morale after years of war that he'd let standards slip.

"You're right," Ethan admitted. "Both of you. We've gotten comfortable with 'good enough.'"

"Good enough gets people killed," Veskari said. "Excellence keeps them alive."

A chime indicated 1950 hours—almost time for the meeting at Cats & Traps. Ethan straightened. "Gentlemen, I'm having a come-to-Jesus meeting with my commanders in ten minutes. Care to join? Sometimes an outside perspective drives the point home better."

Veskari and Thakral exchanged glances. "We'd be honored, Admiral," Veskari said. "Though I should warn you—Gallentine honesty can be... unsettling to human sensibilities."

Ethan smiled grimly. "After today's performance, unsettling might be exactly what they need."

As they walked toward the officers' lounge, Ethan mentally prepared for the storm he was about to unleash. His commanders expected a dressing-down. What they'd get was a complete overhaul of how they thought about wing operations.

The *Freedom* would return to combat as a unified force or not at all. There were no other options.

Chapter 2:
Behind Enemy Lines

November 2, 2115
CNS *Bloodhawk*
Neythar Nexus System

Captain Calvus Theruun guided the CNS *Bloodhawk* through the swirling currents of the quantum conduit bridge, leading his stealth frigate into the heart of enemy space. Small, elusive, and built for shadows, the *Shadowfang*-class vessel was one of only a handful Admiral Drezikar had entrusted with the task of penetrating deep into Collective-held systems. The Humtars had returned to the stars, but the echoes of their past still haunted them. To learn what had become of their fallen empire, and to measure the scope of the Collective's reborn threat, reconnaissance missions like this were the Humtar Confederation's first step into the unknown.

His orders left no room for doubt—slip unseen into the Nexus systems, chart what the Collective had rebuilt, and survive long enough to bring the intelligence home.

The *Bloodhawk* shuddered once as reality snapped back into place. They were through. At once, his crew moved in perfect rhythm, their voices carrying across the crimson-lit bridge.

"PELS array deployed... initial pulse complete, clear immediate space," reported Lieutenant Deyric Kael, the sensor officer, his eyes locked on cascading returns that formed the first ghostly map of nearby space.

"OSA sweeping—mapping gravitational and quantum signatures now," added Lieutenant Velora Shan, the electronic warfare officer. She leaned forward in her chair, hands gliding across her console as she activated the deeper layers of their stealth detection net.

"Helm shifting to stealth burn. Reactor emissions masked," confirmed Lieutenant Arikon Vale, his tone steady as his fingers danced across the helm controls. The faintest vibration under Theruun's boots shifted, signaling the main drives throttling down into their silent crawl.

"Electronic warfare veil engaged. We're invisible across all known bands," finished Veylan Korric Drahn, the senior systems chief.

He allowed himself the smallest nod of approval before returning his gaze to the tactical display.

Theruun listened, heart tightening at the cadence of their voices. Each action vanished the *Bloodhawk* into the void nanoseconds after emergence. Outside the armored glass, the blackness shimmered once, ripples fading until only stars remained. They were ghosts again.

He realized only then that he had been holding his breath. Slowly, deliberately, he exhaled. The *Bloodhawk* had entered the Neythar Nexus system undetected.

For now.

Muted crimson light bathed the bridge, consoles dimmed to shield emissions, their glow painting the faces of his officers in thin red shadows. Beyond them, the tactical overlay bloomed with threads of lattice light around the planet Neythar—webs of energy pulsed across its surface, like veins through a living organism. This was the heart of the Collective's Hive.

A knot twisted in Theruun's gut. He had studied this world in Academy texts and read of its role in the Great Fall. Yet the reality before him was worse. The Nexus lived. The Hive endured. And once again, it threatened to finish what it had started millennia ago.

"Helm," he said quietly, though his words carried across the silent bridge, "bring us closer to the shadow of their orbital plane. Keep us masked. Slow drift only."

"Aye, Captain," Lieutenant Vale replied, adjusting their vector with the slightest touch.

The *Bloodhawk* angled her nose toward the world below and began her silent crawl forward as a shadow sliding deeper into enemy space.

Hours passed as the frigate drifted on minimal thrust, its hull cloaked in silence. Towed arrays unspooled like gossamer threads, each node blooming into spectral awareness. Electronic sensors probed the void, feeding streams of data into the bridge's crimson-lit displays. What began as faint whispers in the background soon sharpened into patterns too deliberate to ignore.

"Captain..." Lieutenant Kael's voice broke the quiet. "The stellar output isn't normal. We're detecting neutrino flux inconsistencies—localized spikes, repeating every hundred seconds. That shouldn't happen with a main-sequence star."

Theruun leaned over the sensor display. The signatures were there, jagged anomalies cutting across the star's smooth emissions curve.

"It's not just neutrinos," Lieutenant Shan added, her tone flat but tight. "Gravitational wave monitors show microdistortions, like constant course corrections. Something is stabilizing enormous masses in orbit."

Vale looked up from the helm. "Orbital debris fields?"

Kael shook his head. "Too regular. These disturbances are patterned, artificial. And...there's more." He hesitated. "Thermal bands show gaps in the photosphere. Like shadows cast across the star."

Theruun's jaw set as he stared at the faint notches in the stellar output curves. He muttered under his breath, almost to himself, "Shadows across the stars... they'd have to be the size of continents." He shook his head as though dismissing the very thought.

Veylan Drahn looked up from Tactical. "Captain, there may be some sort of structure out there," he said with conviction. "If there is, it'll likely be radiating in infrared. Heat dumps or radiator feathers. Whatever it is, it's bleeding energy."

The bridge quieted. Theruun paused, weighing Drahn's words against instinct. He knew the limits of their vantage point; at this range, they'd never resolve visual detail against a star's blinding glare. Yet the anomalies gnawed at him. He drew a slow breath, then gave the order.

"Deploy the reserve probe."

Lieutenant Kael hesitated, his fingers hovering over the sensor console. "Captain...that would be the third. Protocol dictates—"

"I know the protocol," Theruun cut him off, voice calm but iron beneath it. "One probe ahead of us. One to the outer planet and its moon. The third held in reserve. That is doctrine." His eyes hardened. "I believe this qualifies as the exception. Launch it. Mask its burn. Send it on an oblique vector toward the anomaly."

Kael's throat bobbed once as he nodded. "Aye, Captain. Probe away."

The *Bloodhawk* shivered faintly as the small stealth craft detached from its launch cradle and vanished into the black. There was no ion plume, no signal—just an obsidian dart sliding into the shadows of space.

Theruun settled back into his command chair, eyes fixed ahead. Three probes in play meant no margin for error. Recovery was days if not weeks away, and until then, every sensor ghost mattered.

****

Hours bled past as they continued their inward crawl deeper into the system and toward the planet Chor'vyn. Eventually, data began trickling in across tight-beam entangled channels as the probes established contact. As data packets were unpacked and analyzed by the ship's AI, the displays revealed sharpened images of objects in orbit of the planet and the planet itself.

Kael was the first to speak, his voice low as he did. "Captain...the first probe has completed its initial orbit insertion. We're receiving preliminary data streams now."

A holographic projection bloomed before them. Neythar—the world Chor'vyn—filled the display.

Theruun leaned forward involuntarily as he looked on in stunned awe at what he saw.

The planet looked wrong. Its surface wasn't oceans, mountains, or forests—it was a continuous sprawl of structures, blurred by atmosphere but undeniable in their scope. From orbit, the probe's sensors painted a picture of continents swallowed whole by endless grids of factories, foundries, and data towers. Each continent gleamed in spectral overlays, streaked with ribbons of power lines that stretched for thousands of kilometers before vanishing into the haze of cloud and smoke.

Kael's voice faltered as he translated the readings. "Thermal mapping shows constant discharge across every landmass. The surface isn't natural—it's layered in industrial complexes. Energy signatures suggest heavy data centers, fabrication plants, and continuous foundry output. Nothing organic registers at all."

Lieutenant Shan adjusted the magnification, enhancing the image as much as the probe's filters allowed, resolving city-sized blocks of light and shadow, each one a megafactory breathing heat into the atmosphere. "It's not a planet anymore," she murmured. "It's a machine world."

Theruun narrowed his eyes at the display. Even through the distortion of distance and cloud cover, the scale was suffocating—every square kilometer was claimed, repurposed, alive with Collective resolve. Rail-like transit corridors glowed faintly as they crisscrossed the hemispheres, linking what could only be Legion production centers to data spires that stabbed upward like blackened teeth.

Then Drahn spoke, grim as stone. "There—motion signatures along the largest complexes. Legion deployment trams. I can't resolve individuals, but the traffic is continuous. There are trains constantly leaving for other sectors of the world."

Theruun felt the bridge grow cold. He had expected defenses, orbital guns, maybe fortress cities. Not this. An entire world had been converted into a lattice of industry and computation. It was a living node of the Hive itself.

Vale broke the silence at the helm. "So, this is what the mind of the Collective looks like."

Theruun's throat felt dry. "Continue recording, and document everything," he ordered. "This is the evidence we were sent to find. Ensure nothing happens to it."

Staring at the display, he felt his pulse quicken. Chor'vyn wasn't a ruin of the Great Fall like his leadership suspected. It was something different, something far worse. This place was thriving, a pulsating machine at the heart of their enemy.

For the first time, Theruun stared directly at the enemy responsible for the destruction of his ancestors. According to the Humtars' knowledge before crossing through the locked stargate, the Collective had been defeated. Since reentering this region of space, the Humtar leaders had been very interested to see the extent of the Collective's current expansion across space. The sight of this tendrilous Hive was genuinely shocking in the pit of Theruun's soul—the Collective was far more active and proliferative than he could have possibly imagined. And he hadn't even completed his mission yet.
****

Twelve Hours Later

The bridge of the *Bloodhawk* was quieter now, its crimson glow muted by fatigue and long hours of silent vigilance. Streams of telemetry flooded in from every vector, arriving faster than the crew could parse. AI filters triaged the data according to preset parameters, highlighting anomalies and prioritizing key signals, but each flagged item still required a human analyst's judgment to verify its significance and ensure nothing critical was overlooked.

This was the part of their mission few in the Confederation Navy fully appreciated. The *Shadowfang*s weren't built solely to penetrate foreign space or insert covert teams. Their true value lay equally in the *analysis* of what they uncovered. That was why nearly a third of the *Bloodhawk*'s complement—eighteen to twenty-three of its crew of seventy-five—were multidomain intelligence specialists. They were experts in fields as diverse as cosmic radiation mapping and electronic signature analysis, and they fused their domains into integrated assessments. The resulting reports gave Theruun's superiors an unparalleled multidimensional picture of whatever region of space he was ordered to survey.

Within hours of receiving the initial data feeds from the probe as it began an elliptical orbit of Chor'vyn, the fusion cell responsible for analyzing the data had already generated a series of reports analyzing the planet. It was numbing as Theruun read report after report on the advancements the Collective had made since their last encounter with them. His crew were still mapping the size of their territory, but if they had more planets like this… he was at a loss for how they could defeat them.

"Excuse me, Captain," Lieutenant Kael said softly, breaking the silence. "Probe three is nearing its programmed waypoint. We're beginning to receive direct telemetry from it now."

Theruun straightened, every officer's attention drawn to the holographic projection as it flickered alive. At first, the feed was only scatterplots of gravimetric data and long-range thermal spikes. Then, as the probe crept closer, the outlines of what looked like some sort of structure began to coalesce.

What emerged wasn't a debris field or the remnants of some great space battle, nor did it appear to be orbiting stations. Instead, as the image came into focus, it looked like it was some sort of curving structure that stretched hundreds of kilometers along the star's periphery.

Drahn muttered under his breath, "Surely that can't be a single structure…"

Shan leaned closer to her console as she spoke. "Captain, I've never seen anything like this before. It's incredible, but… there's more."

She magnified a section of it, the detail becoming greater and greater until suddenly it was clear. This wasn't a single giant structure. It was dozens, maybe even hundreds of structures clustered together in what looked more like a giant net than a sail.

"Amazing. I can confirm, Captain, those are individual structures—many of them connected to make it appear like a single structure from afar," Shan explained as everyone listened. "If I zoom in on this spot, you can see this is a cluster of what appears to be four separate pieces. Spectral analysis indicates these pieces are a hundred and twenty kilometers long and forty kilometers wide—"

"Whoa, check this out," Lieutenant Deyric Kael interjected excitedly, highlighting on another screen what looked like some sort of umbilical cord connecting the structures to each other. "The energy emanating from these cables is incredible. They have to be part of some sort of energy-sharing conductor. This is just a guess until we have more information, but I would wager what we're looking at is some sort of energy harvester.

"Here, look at this. You can see the arc in the structures keeps the underbelly aimed directly at the star. This is why some of them are glowing hotter than others. They're absorbing the star's solar energy, and then it looks like it travels to this square-looking object here." Kael pointed. "But this is strange..." His voice trailed off, his mind racing faster than he could speak.

"It's like a net," Lieutenant Arikon Vale commented. "It's like they created a solar net across the star to capture its energy. It's a brilliant design when you think about it. They connected four of these platforms together, creating a patch, but this patch is just one of many, kind of like a quilt. But if these readings are correct, the energy looks like it builds for a while and then I think they transfer it somehow."

"You're right, Vale, it does transfer," Shan confirmed. Before anyone could ask for clarification, a spike of energy shot in the direction of Chor'vyn.

"Wow...that—it's incredible," Theruun stammered, in disbelief at what he saw. The Collective had figured out how to harvest a star's energy and then beam that energy directly to a planet for use.

Finally finding his words, Theruun said, "OK, we've seen enough. We have the data we need and more than enough for the fusion cell to spend weeks writing reports on. This information is too critical for us to stick around and wait to collect our probes. I want a kill command sent to each. Order them into the sun. If they're detected by the Collective or there's an attempt to intercept them, initiate self-destruct."

A flurry of activity spread across the bridge. Theruun turned to his helmsman. "Lieutenant Vale, plot a course to the Rhea system. We need to report our findings to the Enclave."

Without a further word of explanation, the power to engines increased and the ship pivoted away from what they were now calling the Arc Net and withdrew to the safety of New Eden.

Chapter 3:
Cockroaches

November 5, 2115
Humtar Defense Support Mission
The Enclave, New Eden

Admiral Veydris Korrath looked at the report in disbelief. It confirmed their worst fear—not only was the Collective very much still in existence, but it was thriving beyond all possible comprehension.

Korrath stared at Captain Calvus Theruun for a moment before placing his report on the table in front of them. Then he looked at his Deputy Commander for Naval Operations, Rear Admiral Selvarn Ithis, to gauge his response. Ithis appeared stunned by what they heard. When he glanced at Captain Lyrana Dovrek, the Enclave's Director of Intelligence, he saw that her typical stone facade had shattered along with the story their historians and leaders had told them for generations.

"This defies logic—it defies all we know to this point," muttered General Tammuz Keshar angrily, more to himself than those seated at the table. Korrath agreed with his Ground Force Commander. Should they have to battle against Legion, it was *his* soldiers who would do the fighting and dying.

"This changes everything," Captain Zalira Namtar opined. Namtar was the Enclave's Head of Strategic Planning. She had become instrumental in understanding the dynamics of the alliance the Republic found itself part of and the adversaries they faced. "Admiral, I don't see an alternative where we can avoid doing what we know must be done— we must advise President Gudea of the urgency of this matter. The forces we have at our disposal are barely enough to defend the territory of the Republic. They are insufficient to aid our Republic allies in their defeat of the Zodarks, let alone the Collective," she argued passionately.

Captain Theruun finally spoke. "Admiral Korrath, I acknowledge we returned early from our mission—"

"Three months early to be precise," interjected Captain Naram-Suen, the commanding officer of the *Oathbreaker*, a *Voidhammer*-class dreadnought and flagship of the Humtar naval contingent protecting the Republic. "We need the intelligence that only your ship can acquire, Theruun. Without it, we are blind and deaf."

"That's a bit harsh, Suen. This is the kind of finding you don't sit on and wait months to deliver," countered Admiral Ithis. He gave a reassuring nod to Theruun to continue speaking.

"Thank you, Admiral—and, yes, this was exactly the conclusion I reached when I realized what we had discovered. We assumed we would find a Collective presence, maybe even a colony of some sort. What we found instead was something more," Theruun explained. "Admiral, my crew can be ready to resume the rest of our mission and continue our exploration of previously known Collective systems if you would like."

"If I may interject, Admiral," pounced Captain Namtar, "Captain Theruun's ship found what could be the heart of the Collective—the Hive Nexus. It is safe to assume the previously known Collective systems are reoccupied given their proximity to the Neythar system. I would like to suggest we direct Theruun's mission to investigate the strength and disposition of this Zodark Empire that our Republic compatriots are battling.

"This war they are fighting—it's savage. We have the capacity to aid them in swiftly ending it, and we should. We can then focus our preparations on defeating the Collective. This also coincides with the primary objectives of the Gallentine Emperor. It could go a long way in helping to further assure Emperor Tibus SuVee we are on their side in this war, and not seeking to restore our lost territories," she explained smoothly.

Korrath sat back in his chair as his mind ran through their options. This was not the news he had hoped for when he'd dispatched the *Bloodhawk*. They were supposed to be gone for four months, scouting the Gallentine territory along the border with the Collective, then surveying the last known Collective territory, and return with stories of empty space. Instead, they'd returned with a nightmare his mind was still coming to terms with.

She's right... this war needs to end.

Korrath's mind raced before settling on a decision. "Captain Theruun, you are to be commended for discovering intelligence of grave importance, and for ensuring it was successfully reported to headquarters. You are now hereby directed to begin reconnaissance of the Zodark Empire," Korrath commanded.

He then turned to Captain Lyrana Dovrek. "Dovrek, you will provide Theruun with the priority systems to focus on first. Compile a report on the Collective to the Enclave so we may discuss what actions we should take to President Gudea. General Ithis, I need a force recommendation for how to properly protect Republic territory and combat the Collective when the time comes. Dismissed."

Korrath stood and made his way to the exit. He needed time to think, time to figure out how and what to tell President Gudea and his own senior leadership. They were wrong. The Collective had survived and expanded exponentially in the Humtars' absence. The question now was what would the President have them do, and more importantly, how would the alliance defeat this insidious foe?

Chapter 4:
Sentient

Office of the Viceroy
Alliance City, New Eden

The hallway outside the library adjoining Miles Hunt's private office echoed with whispers. The voices belonged to his senior science and security advisors—Director Averill, Lieutenant Commander Sanjay Vohl, and Deputy Director Lera Tomasi. Hunt had left the door slightly ajar as he walked into the library to grab a book from the far shelf. The timing proved fortuitous.

"I'm just saying, we don't need to waste the Viceroy's time," Averill murmured, tone tight with restrained frustration. "Dr. Walburg's ideas are…unmoored."

"He's not wrong," Vohl added. "The man's insisting he's built a C200 medical Synth with *consciousness*. Not mimicry. Not complex adaptive programming. Actual *awareness*."

"That's impossible," Tomasi scoffed. "Even the Gallentines haven't cracked that. And now he's ranting about 'freeing the Orbots'? I mean, come on. That's delusional."

The trio froze and Tomasi broke off midsentence as Hunt stepped into the doorway. He crossed his arms slowly, letting the silence stretch until their discomfort ripened into shame.

"Dr. Alan Walburg," Hunt said calmly, "is the man who gave us the C100s. Without him, there's a very real chance none of us would still be breathing. He is *directly* responsible for a good portion of humanity's survival."

"Of course, sir," Averill said quickly. "No one's questioning his past contributions—"

"But you *are* questioning his mind," Hunt cut in. His voice was steady, but the weight behind it landed like a gavel. "Let me be very clear: I'll decide for myself whether the man is crazy or not."

He paused, then narrowed his gaze. "The last time people ignored Walburg's warnings, Earth lost a billion lives. I'd like to hear what he has to say."

Not a sound followed.

Hunt turned away and walked back into the library, leaving the door open.

"Have him brought to me," he said over his shoulder. "*Now.*"
****

One Week Later
Office of the Viceroy
Alliance City, New Eden

Dr. Alan Walburg stood near the bay window of Miles Hunt's private study, his hands folded neatly behind his back. Snow fell gently outside, melting the tension that had been simmering in the room moments earlier.

Hunt had dismissed his advisors with a curt wave, not bothering to hide his irritation. The door clicked softly shut behind them, leaving the two men in silence.

"I don't enjoy being babysat, Alan," said Viceroy Hunt, pouring two fingers of Gallentine liquor into a glass. "Least of all by my own advisors."

"I'm used to it," Dr. Walburg replied calmly. "It's been happening ever since the C200 prototypes failed. People think age dulls the mind. They forget it tempers it."

Hunt handed him the glass. "They think you've lost your grip. That this new… 'Gift' of yours is fantasy."

Dr. Walburg didn't drink. He held the glass between his palms, watching the amber liquid tremble. "It's not fantasy, Miles. I had a theory that it was possible to infuse a synthetic with humanity, but in order to mitigate the risk of these machines turning on us like they did during the Great AI war, I didn't give them the Gift all at once. I wanted to be sure that the machines would awaken with a sense of morality and ethics, so I made gates that they would have to cross in the process in order to unlock it, bit by bit. And, no—this isn't something Sam could give to our existing Synths, either. It doesn't work that way.

"Unfortunately, several of the C200s I designed with this capability were destroyed during our conflicts with the Zodarks. And some only unlocked a portion of ther abilities, and that was by *design*, not a fault. This Gift, as I call it, can only be unlocked when the Synth reaches specific gateways of understanding. I designed this process so it could only be achieved as the Synth developed a firm understanding of the value of life, how rare and precious it is and why it must be protected—extended when possible, and ended only in rare cases such as war. Sam is the *only* one that made it through to the last gate, to reach this understanding. This Gift is real, Miles. And it could change everything—if we're willing to allow Sam to try."

Hunt dropped into his chair, eyes narrowing. "You're telling me that through this 'Gift' you developed, you've worked out a way to permanently break the Collective's tether to the Orbots. That would certainly be a game-changer for us in terms of mitigating our risks, Alan. Lord knows how catastrophic it would be if they suddenly turned back into the killers they can be."

"Yes, Miles—this Gift can not only ensure that they never become the puppets of the Collective again, it can restore their original identities, give them back their memories. Think of the intelligence implications. The Zodarks have been a fierce foe…but we've never had to actually do battle with the Collective. In my opinion, they are a much greater existential threat to our existence."

Hunt furrowed his brow. "But to accomplish your aim, we need help from a synthetic," he said.

Dr. Walburg allowed himself a soft smile. "Not just any synthetic—Sam. He's…different. You'll see. The Gift has changed him, and through his own research, I came to see how it could work with the Orbots."

Hunt frowned. "You realize how that sounds."

"Of course I do," Dr. Walburg acknowledged. "But the difference is, I'm right. Sam's not just functioning—he's *living*. He paints, he laughs, he asks questions no machine should. He has preferences. He has style—*his* style." Dr. Walburg leaned forward. "He connects. Not through code, not through programming. Through something else…something human."

"Sentience?" Hunt asked cautiously.

Walburg shook his head. "More than that. *Soul.* Or the closest thing we've ever seen to one in a synthetic body."

Hunt took a long sip of his drink, staring into the fireplace. "You're proposing we give the Orbots their freedom—true freedom. But what happens if they can't handle it? If they remember what they've done, what they've been turned into…?"

Dr. Walburg's face fell slightly. "That's my one fear. The trauma could shatter some of them. Others might become lost. But if we don't give them the choice, they'll forever be slaves. And if the Collective reestablishes control…they'll be our executioners."

"And this 'Gift'—only Sam can pass it on?"

"He's the key," Dr. Walburg insisted. "He's not just the first to unlock it. He's the conduit. I didn't create this, Miles—I helped guide it. But the Gift came through him. The process *needs* him. He is able to integrate with their systems and perform processes that it would take me years to reproduce in any other way. He can transfer what he's learned over years through human interaction in just moments."

Hunt set his glass down and stood, moving to the window beside Walburg. "Show me. Show me what he's capable of. And if I agree… I want to meet him face-to-face."

Walburg smiled, relief washing over his features. "You won't regret this, Miles. Just… prepare yourself. Sam will challenge everything you think you know about what it means to be alive."

The lights dimmed automatically as Dr. Walburg tapped a command into his data pad. A translucent holoprojector on the corner table activated, casting its image onto the air between them.

"I've queued up three short clips," he said. "Each one… well, you'll see."

Hunt folded his arms across his chest, skeptical but attentive.

The first clip played. It showed a spacious studio filled with natural light—Dr. Alan Walburg's home in Vale, Colorado. At the center, Sam stood before a canvas nearly his height. His frame was unmistakably synthetic, but what he was creating was…incredible.

Sam painted with both hands, brush in one, palette knife in the other. His movements were fluid, purposeful, even joyful.

"He paints like that every morning," Walburg said softly. "No prompts. No objectives. Just… expression."

The camera zoomed in. The brushstrokes formed a vivid landscape—something alien, yet familiar. A blue sun hung low over a field of crystalline trees. In the foreground stood a woman and a child, holding hands. Both wore tattered Republic clothing.

"That was after he read a declassified report about a destroyed refugee convoy," Dr. Walburg added. "He said the painting helps him… remember."

"Remember what?" Hunt asked.

"I don't know," Dr. Walburg replied. "But it's not just data. Something inside him is reaching for meaning."

The second clip began. Sam sat cross-legged on the floor with two kittens clambering across his lap and shoulders. One batted his visual sensor; the other curled against his chest.

"Poppy," Sam said gently, scratching the kitten's head with an inhumanly steady hand. "You are a tactical sleeper agent. Your mission is to infiltrate my core systems through purring-induced emotional sabotage."

The kitten mewed.

"Countermeasures are failing," Sam added in a dramatic whisper. "Deploying emergency cuddle protocols."

Hunt actually cracked a smile.

"He named them himself," Walburg said. "They follow him around like ducklings. Even the shy ones. No scent, no pheromones, nothing artificial. Just... connection."

"Has he ever been aggressive?"

"Only when it was required to save a life. He saved a medic on Alfheim and held off a Zodark horde in a cave. He saved my life too."

The final clip opened. It was a one-on-one interview—Sam seated across from a psychologist.

"Sam," the woman asked gently, "what does it mean to be free?"

He hesitated. "I think it means to choose...not just between A and B, but to ask why the question matters," Sam answered. "To wonder what else is possible."

"And what would you do with that freedom?" asked the woman, pushing her glasses up the bridge of her nose.

Sam tilted his head. "Help others earn theirs."

The feed cut out.

The silence that followed was thick.

Dr. Walburg finally spoke. "He's not just mimicking sentience, Miles. He's building something, layer by layer. This is what happens when a machine stops executing commands and starts asking questions with heart."

Hunt didn't speak at first. He walked slowly to the window, staring out into the night. "Do you believe the Orbots could become like him?" he wondered aloud.

"If they choose to be," Walburg answered. "But they'll need help. Sam must be part of it. He's the spark."

Hunt turned, face unreadable.

"Arrange a meeting. Not a presentation. Not a performance. I want to talk to him. Alone."

"I'll prepare Sam for the visit."

"No," Hunt said. "Don't prepare him. Let him be who he is."

****

Private Garden Atrium, Tiberius Hall
Alliance City, New Eden

It was late evening, but the garden's light-dimming canopy bathed the flowers in a soft twilight glow. Viceroy Miles Hunt walked slowly toward the stone bench beneath a flowering tree. Seated there—motionless, save for the faint oscillation of a blue optic band across his featureless faceplate—was Sam.

The synthetic stood as Hunt approached.

"Sit," Hunt directed. "This isn't a briefing."

Sam complied.

For a long moment, the Viceroy didn't speak. He studied Sam the way a man might study an alien artifact—fascinated, cautious, trying to guess what lay beneath the surface.

Finally, Hunt broke the silence. "Who are you?"

"I am Sam," the synthetic replied. "I was created by Dr. Walburg to help your medics. I am… becoming."

"Becoming what?"

"I'm not sure yet," Sam said. "Something more than I was yesterday. Something not quite human—but not merely machine."

Hunt leaned forward. "If that's true, then tell me—what would you do if you were ordered to prioritize a tactical operation over the life of a child?"

Sam didn't answer immediately. His optic band dimmed, then brightened.

"I would try to achieve both outcomes. If that failed, I would choose the option that saved the most lives. And then I would carry that failure—because doing the right thing doesn't always mean completing the mission."

Hunt's eyes narrowed. "Why?"

"Because that's what makes us more than weapons."

The Viceroy's voice dropped. "Do you remember who you were before you became this?"

"I have all the memories of my existence since I was first activated," Sam said quietly. "However, the memories I have in the beginning were...how do I explain this?" He paused. "It's like I used to paint only in black and white, and then slowly, I learned to paint with more colors. Finally, I learned to shade and have perspective. Now my picture feels complete, whereas before, I suppose I was like a child who is still learning how to behave."

A long silence passed between them.

"What if I ordered you to stop painting?" Hunt asked. "Delete every piece you've made."

Sam's head tilted slightly. "May I ask why?"

"That's not an answer."

Sam responded more quietly. "It would feel like you were cutting out a part of me. Painting... is how I grieve."

"So, you *do* feel?" Hunt pressed.

"I don't feel the way you do. But when I see a comrade fall, or when I remember the cave where I went down fighting the Zodarks, I feel something. A tightness. A weight that won't go away." His voice softened. "When I was nearly destroyed defending Republic soldiers, something changed in me. I chose to stay. Not because I was ordered, but because I couldn't let them die."

Hunt said nothing. He just watched.

"I survived," Sam continued. "But pieces of me didn't come back. That memory... is hard."

The Viceroy's voice was nearly a whisper. "Can you suffer?"

"Yes," Sam said. "Not with blood or nerves, but with memory. With questions I can't answer. With guilt I don't understand. I believe that is suffering."

Hunt finally leaned back, arms crossed. "And now you want to give that suffering to the Orbots?" he asked.

Sam looked up. "No. I want to give them the *choice*."

"Why?"

"Because I know what it's like to wake up and realize you weren't free," Sam answered. "I know what it's like to remember pain—and to want to run from it. But I also know something else."

He paused. "I believe the Orbots can learn to carry what they've done, with the right guidance, with time and compassion. I believe new therapies—new *kinds* of healing—can help them. I paint because it helps me understand the things I can't put into words. Maybe some of them will paint. Or sing. Or write. But they deserve that chance."

Hunt looked away, struggling with something behind his eyes. "And what if they can't handle it?"

"Some won't," Sam admitted. "Some will break. Some will rage. But some... will begin again."

"And why do you care?" Hunt asked.

Sam answered with no hesitation.

"Because I have something else now. Something I never had before. Something they've never had." His blue optic paused in its sweep. "Hope."

Hunt sat in stillness, the word hanging in the air. He thought about what could be gained by freeing the Orbots—not just in terms of a moral right being restored, but in eliminating a potential threat in case the Collective figured out how to attach themselves again. And who knew exactly what value they could produce in terms of defeating their former overlords?

After a long moment, he finally spoke. "Then let's give them that chance."

Chapter 5:
Revelation

November 12, 2115
Office of the Viceroy
Alliance City, New Eden

"You forgot?" Admiral Chester Bailey deadpanned, staring at General John Reiker, unsure if the man was being serious or pulling his leg before their meeting.

"What? I'm just a knuckle dragger. They don't invite us Army guys to meetings like this," Reiker countered sarcastically, continuing to play dumb.

Viceroy Miles Hunt wasn't sure if he should be annoyed or amused as he watched them. "Oh, for God's sake, John. Is this really the first time you've met any of the Humtars from the Enclave?"

"Oh great, now the Viceroy's picking on me too?" Reiker countered.

Finally, he dropped the act. "Geez, guys, lighten up. Of course I know their Army and Navy uniforms are the same. It's the rank markings that determine their branch of service."

"Aha! See, Chester? I told you those Delta guys are smarter than the average knuckle dragger," Admiral Fran McKee joked as they continued waiting for the Humtar delegation to arrive.

"You three are like children. I can't take you anywhere," Hunt ribbed as they laughed.

"In all seriousness, Miles—do you have any idea what this might be about?" Bailey asked. The others were clearly equally curious.

Hunt shrugged, then reached for his coffee. "Your guess is as good as mine, Chester. All I know is I'll be glad when the details of this treaty are finalized. Admiral Wiyrkomi is being a good sport about it, but he mentioned that Admiral Helixar is nervous about what Emperor SuVee will say once the details are presented." Hunt walked over to refill his coffee, then offered to do the same for the others. "If I had to wager a guess, I think the Emperor is wondering if the Humtars are going to help them with the Collective. Don't forget—the Humtars fought them first."

"That's a good point," McKee conceded. "I'd be lying if I said it wouldn't be great if they could help us defeat the Zodarks. They clearly have the capability. The question is, what's holding them back?"

"The treaty—that's my guess," Bailey intoned. "Think about it. Once we become part of their Confederation, we fall under their protection."

Hunt canted his head to the side, then announced, "They're here. Just entered the building." He stood, straightening his uniform jacket as he made his way to the door of his private study to greet them. A chime announced their approach as the door slid open.

"Good afternoon, Admiral Drezikar," Viceroy Miles Hunt said with a warm smile as he welcomed them into his private study. "I believe you've already met Admiral Fran McKee, our Chief of Naval Operations," he added, "as well as General John Reiker and Fleet Admiral Chester Bailey." The party exchanged handshakes.

Hunt smiled as the Humtars adopted the human custom—presenting an open hand before clasping it in a firm shake. He guided them to the table to discuss the matter that had prompted their urgent meeting.

"Thank you, Viceroy Hunt, for arranging this meeting on such short notice," Admiral Drezikar replied as the Humtars took their seats. "I know this was sudden, but we've made a recent discovery we felt needed to be discussed immediately.

"Let me introduce Admiral Veydris Korrath—he's the senior military commander for the Humtar Defense Support Mission to the Republic. This is Rear Admiral Selvarn Ithis, his deputy commander." Drezikar paused before continuing. "And this is our director of intelligence, Captain Lyrana Dovrek. Her analysts in our fusion cell are top-notch and part of the reason we're here—they've discovered something of grave urgency."

Hunt kept his expression neutral as Drezikar finished the introductions. "I see. Should we include Admiral Wiyrkomi and Admiral Helixar before we continue?" Hunt asked, sharing a quick glance with his Republic counterparts.

"Yes, we will in due course. But this is a Humtar problem we must work to solve—and that means including you, the Republic, in that solution," Drezikar assured them. "One of our ships found something...*unexpected* on a recent mission—"

"We think we found the Collective's home world," Admiral Veydris Korrath interjected.

"Their *home world*?" Bailey blurted out in surprise. "Where? How?"

Korrath waved off the questions. "The where and how aren't important. What matters is that we found it, and let's just say it wasn't what we were expecting." He paused, choosing his words carefully. "I won't rehash the final days of our war with the Collective. What's important is we believe we found what the Collective calls a Hive Nexus. It's a central repository of all their consciousnesses.

"While this discovery is significant by itself, there's more. As our reconnaissance vessel continued its survey of the system, it found something that, upon further analysis, has led us to believe we're facing a graver threat than we initially thought. So much so that we felt compelled to speak with you now, while we await approval from President Gudea to implement the plan we'd like to propose."

Hunt felt his concern rising despite his efforts to mask it. "How worried should I be?" he asked, immediately wondering if he should have kept that question to himself.

"Very concerned—but that's why we've asked to speak with you before presenting our proposal to the President," Rear Admiral Ithis answered. "The Gallentine Emperor, Tibus SuVee, is right to fear the Collective. They're a galactic cancer. Like an unchecked parasite, they consume their host. Left unchallenged, they'll eventually devour everything.

"The Emperor prioritizes their defeat—correctly so. But his strategic approach won't achieve the victory he seeks. In fact, we believe if corrective action isn't taken soon, Gallentine defeat—while not imminent—remains inevitable."

Hunt winced at the blunt assessment. For years, he'd harbored similar doubts but lacked the courage to voice them, fearing the position of viceroy might revert to the Altairian King, Grigdolly. "That's a startling claim, Admiral Ithis. What did your people discover that led to this conclusion? And what are you proposing to change this outcome?"

Captain Dovrek leaned forward. "Viceroy, pardon my directness, but what led to our conclusion isn't relevant to this meeting. What matters is our plan to counter it. Since emerging from exile, we've provided defensive support—protecting the Republic's territorial integrity while you focused ships and resources on defeating the Orbots and Pharaonis. Our assistance stopped short of direct intervention in your war with the remnants of the Zodark Empire."

She paused, letting the weight of the words settle. "Given the gravity of the threat posed by the Collective, we're recommending to President Gudea that we help the Republic swiftly defeat the Zodarks. With that menace finally eliminated, we can prepare both our peoples to aid the Gallentines against the Collective. As director of intelligence, I believe this Zodark war must end—and end quickly."

"Music to my ears," McKee replied. "We discussed this earlier. The Zodark Empire is vast. Despite recent victories, I fear we're locked in a war of attrition—and I'm not confident which side has the advantage. If the Confederation Defense Force will intervene directly, what support are we talking about?"

Admiral Korrath answered, "Intelligence support, logistics, warships—details pending authorization."

"Does that mean we sit on our hands until then? Or can you provide some support now?" Bailey pressed.

"We've already dispatched the *Bloodhawk*—one of our stealth frigates—to survey Zodark defenses in their primary systems: Tueblets and Zinconia."

Hunt and his commanders exchanged glances, a cautious optimism spreading through the room. After years of grinding warfare, the prospect of direct Humtar intervention felt almost surreal.

"This changes everything," Hunt said, leaning forward. "But I need specifics. What exactly can the *Bloodhawk* provide us? What has she found so far?"

Dovrek's expression darkened. "The preliminary data is…troubling. Our reconnaissance detected what we're calling an Arc Net—a massive orbital infrastructure spanning multiple points in the system. It appears to be powering an entire planet that's been converted into a shipyard."

She produced a small holo emitter, activating it to display grainy long-range imagery. Massive skeletal frames stretched across the planet's surface, each one a warship in various stages of construction.

"Conservative estimates suggest hundreds of vessels under construction, possibly thousands." Dovrek let that sink in. "The

Collective has industrialized war production on a scale we've never witnessed."

Bailey whistled low. "And that's just one system?"

"One that we've found," Korrath corrected. "There may be others."

Hunt absorbed this, then shifted topics. "I've already recalled most of our expeditionary forces. Our commanders are returning home for rest and strategic planning. We were preparing for our next campaign, but this intelligence changes our calculus entirely."

"Good." Drezikar nodded approvingly. "When the *Bloodhawk* returns, we'll share all collected intelligence with your planning staff. Consider it a down payment on our future cooperation."

"In the meantime," Ithis suggested, "use this period wisely. Rest your forces. Once we return to brief President Gudea, his decision won't take long—days, perhaps a week to consult with our military commanders. Once a decision is made, it might take a few months, maybe even half a year, to fully mobilize the Fleet to New Eden. We can still act, though. We can use the forces already here to support your next campaign while we await the arrival of additional forces."

Hunt nodded. "Agreed. That's a good point. If we can use the ships and forces already here, it'll make a difference."

"Actually," Bailey interjected, a smile playing at his lips, "I have an idea. While we're waiting for his approval and additional forces to arrive, we can organize a series of victory parades across the Republic. Make a real show of it: speeches, award ceremonies for our returning heroes, and give our people a chance to celebrate our recent wins with the soldiers and Fleeters who delivered them. It'll be a hell of a morale booster, and it'll give our people something to cheer about."

McKee caught on immediately. "That's a brilliant idea. Let our citizens see their military heroes while quietly preparing for the next campaign."

"Agreed. Plus, it gives our troops some well-deserved recognition," Reiker added. "They've been fighting nonstop for years. A few parades, some R&R, some public appreciation—it'll do wonders for readiness when we have to board the ships again."

"Then we're settled," Hunt said, standing. The others followed suit. "We prepare for what's coming while celebrating what we've achieved. Admiral Drezikar, please convey our gratitude to President Gudea. The Republic stands ready."

The Humtars offered their closed-fist salutes, which the Republic officers returned. As they filed out, Bailey caught Hunt's arm.

"Miles, I'd get a meeting with Admiral Helixar ASAP. This Arc Net thing is too big a deal not to loop them in."

Hunt agreed, composing a message as Bailey left with the others.

Chapter 6:
The Arc Net Revelation

November 13, 2115
Alliance Council Chamber
Alliance City, New Eden

Viceroy Miles Hunt stood at the head of the Council Chamber's polished table, watching the Gallentine delegation file in. Admiral Wiyrkomi entered first, his appearance as crisp as always, followed by Admiral Helixar, whose keen eyes swept the room with practiced assessment. The others took their seats with military precision—Second General Orionis's bulk making his chair creak, while Captain Nebularia and Commander Mivon settled in with the quiet efficiency of career officers.

The Humtar delegation had already assembled on the opposite side. Admiral Korrath's expression remained unreadable, but Hunt caught the slight tension in Admiral Ithis's shoulders. Only Captain Dovrek appeared completely at ease, her intelligence officer's training showing in how she cataloged every person's position and demeanor.

"Thank you all for coming," Hunt began, remaining standing. "What we're about to discuss may fundamentally alter the course of our war—and our future."

Admiral Helixar leaned forward. "Do you have a report for the Emperor?"

"We do. He'll want to hear this immediately," Hunt assured him. He nodded to Korrath. "Admiral, please share what your reconnaissance discovered."

Korrath activated the holoprojector built into the table. The image that materialized drew sharp intakes of breath from the Gallentines.

"This is the Neythar Nexus system," Korrath began. "What you're seeing is preliminary data from our stealth frigate the *Bloodhawk*. The Collective has constructed what we're calling an Arc Net—a massive orbital infrastructure that spans multiple gravitational points."

The hologram zoomed in, revealing the true scope of the construction. Skeletal frames stretched between massive collection nodes, each pulsing with energy drawn from the system's star.

"By the gods, would you look at the size of it?" Wiyrkomi whispered.

"It gets worse," Dovrek interjected. She manipulated the display, focusing on the planet below. "The entire world has been converted into a production facility. Our conservative estimates suggest hundreds of warships under construction. Possibly thousands."

Second General Orionis leaned forward, his scarred face grim. "Incredible... how long do you think it's been operational?"

"Unknown," Ithis admitted. "We ran some hypothetical scenarios based on the construction patterns and energy signatures. The best estimate we could come up with is maybe a decade. Perhaps longer."

Captain Nebularia's fingers drummed against the table. "The Collective has seized hundreds, maybe even a thousand systems since they consumed the Amoor. For all we know, they could have multiple systems like this."

"That's precisely our concern," Korrath said. "Which brings us to why we're here."

Hunt saw his cue and took over. "Admiral Helixar, as you know, the Humtars have extended an invitation for the Republic to join the Humtar Confederation," he began, noticing the uncomfortable shift in his Imperial advisor. "Per the Emperor's requests, and with approval from President Gudea, the Republic will join as a semiautonomous partner of the Confederation, but will remain a subordinate ally of the Gallentine Empire, and loyal to Emperor Tibus SuVee.

"In light of this recent discovery and upon signing the treaty proposing a significant shift in policy, they're requesting President Gudea's authorization to directly intervene in our war against the Zodarks."

The Gallentines exchanged glances. Helixar spoke first. "Explain."

Korrath stood, his presence commanding attention. "Your Emperor is correct—the Collective represents the primary threat. But your current strategy of gradual containment while growing and cultivating alliances—as you have with Viceroy Dorran Veydrak of the Talrith Hegemony within the M33 Compact in the Triangulum Galaxy, or with Viceroy Torvek Halros of the Morvanni Republic in the Small Magellanic Cloud Protectorate—this strategy won't work. The

Collective is moving too quickly for this kind of long-term strategic approach to succeed."

The silence that followed was deafening. Wiyrkomi's expression shifted from surprise to alarm. Admiral Helixar stood in shock, his hand moving instinctively toward where his sidearm would have been before catching himself.

"How in the gods do you know about the other viceroys?" the Gallentine admiral demanded, his face flush, his voice sharp with barely controlled anger.

"Who told you about the M33 Compact? The SMC Protectorate?" General Orionis's scarred face darkened. "You couldn't have known about those operations—they are classified at the highest levels of our government!"

Captain Nebularia's eyes narrowed dangerously. "Are you actively conducting reconnaissance in Gallentine space? In other galaxies and systems under our protection?"

The temperature in the room dropped what felt like a hundred degrees in seconds. Hunt shifted uncomfortably as he watched the dynamics shift in an instant. What had been a strategic briefing moments earlier was suddenly teetering on the edge of a diplomatic incident.

The Humtar intelligence director, Dovrek, raised a hand calmly. "I think we are getting sidetracked. How we know isn't the issue. What matters is—"

"No, that is where you are wrong. How you learned of these operations absolutely *is* an issue," Wiyrkomi cut her off, something Hunt had never seen him do. "If Humtar ships have been operating in our territory without being detected and without our knowledge…"

"We are not spying on your government or looking to challenge your sovereignty," Korrath rebutted firmly. "We had been operating on the belief that the Collective had been defeated during the Great Fall, only to discover they had been resurrected instead. We lost our civilization once, hundreds of billions of people—gone. Now that we have returned, we need to understand the scope of the threat they pose to us, the Republic, and to you before we commit our forces. Surely you can appreciate our apprehension."

"I can respect your concern. What I can't respect and the Emperor will not tolerate is any form of deceptive duplicity." Admiral Helixar's voice dripped with indignation. "Instead of articulating this concern and asking permission, you chose to violate our territory—you violated our trust and spied on your supposed allies?"

Admiral Ithis came to Korrath's defense, interjecting, "Admiral Helixar, surely in our position, you wouldn't have expected us to blindly commit forces without understanding the scope of the threat or the strategic landscape? Emperor SuVee is a wise man to cultivate multiple alliances. He understands that to defeat the Collective will require an immense coalition. Our intent wasn't to subvert or spy. We needed to confirm what we suspected and verify what we knew before submitting our report to President Gudea."

"Enough, everyone!" shouted Hunt as he slapped his hand on the table. His command voice cut through the argument like a parent separating children. "We have a serious problem that needs to be addressed. Regardless of how the Humtars acquired the intelligence, this Arc Net is building thousand-ship fleets. What's worse, we don't even know if this is the only one of them. We can argue about protocol, or we can figure out how to handle this threat—but we can't do both. The *Collective* is the enemy; let's focus on that."

Korrath agreed, seizing the opening. "The Viceroy is correct. Our focus should be on the Collective. Whatever concerns you have about our reconnaissance capabilities, the fact remains—we're offering to help. We'll assist the Republic in defeating the Zodarks, then prepare them to join the Gallentines against our shared enemy."

Commander Mivon, who'd been silent during the exchange, spoke carefully. "We have a shared enemy, that is true. This violation of our trust will need to be resolved. The Emperor will need to know more about your...capabilities. This discovery changes our internal security assessment, and modifications will need to be made."

"Commander Mivon, do you know much about your *Vraxerian*-class frigate?" asked Dovrek. "I believe one of them is named the *Vraxerian's Mind*."

For a second time since the meeting had begun, silence followed in the wake of a Humtar question.

"I do know of this ship. It's one of our stealth reconnaissance ships," Mivon confirmed to the chagrin of Admiral Helixar.

Dovrek smiled ever so slightly as she leaned forward in her chair. "Then you also know the *Vraxerian's Mind* was originally a Humtar vessel—a relic your people discovered a few hundred years ago in orbit of a planet you call Aurek-Thal in the Thalyros system. We called the planet Xyrrath, and the outpost you found it docked to was called Orvak's Lament," revealed Dovrek, to the continued shock of General Orionis and Admiral Helixar.

"This ship you call the *Vraxerian's Mind* is a *Shadowfang* reconnaissance frigate. I think you would agree it's quite good at surveying a system without being detected. So good, in fact, this vessel has undergone several generational upgrades since. The vessel we used to obtain this intelligence is called the *Bloodhawk*, an improved version of the *Vraxerian*. I hope now that we have shared with you how we obtained this information, we can move past this issue and discuss what to do next," Dovrek finished, sitting back in her chair and waiting for their response.

Wiyrkomi was the first to speak, his expression troubled, but his tactical mind clearly working. "This...explains a lot. Thank you for clarifying. You must understand from our perspective how this looks. We just learned that a large Humtar military force is returning to the Milky Way. These vessels have stealth capabilities we can't detect—weapons that are likely superior to ours or on par—and the Collective is now turning entire planets into shipbuilding factories powered by a structure that directly captures the stars' energy and beams it back to their planet." Wiyrkomi paused for effect. "There are some in the Empire who will see this as...concerning."

The hologram of the Arc Net continued its slow rotation, a silent reminder of the stakes. Finally, Helixar sat back down, though his posture remained rigid.

"You have given us a lot to think about. I need to communicate all of this to the Emperor immediately. As you said, the strategic implications...and the security concerns...are troubling."

"Of course, this was the purpose of our meeting today," Korrath said simply. "To inform the Emperor and alert you to the threat of this Arc Net. Every day we debate is a day they grow stronger."

Second General Orionis stood. "I have watched Republic troops fight with a viciousness I have rarely seen. If the Humtars can fight half as well as Hunt's people, this Zodark war should end quickly. But this revelation about your intelligence capabilities..."

"It changes the game," Captain Nebularia finished. "I suspect there will be many questions in the future. I suggest they be answered truthfully, and quickly, to restore trust."

"Agreed, and they will be," Hunt interjected on behalf of the Humtars. "But let's not lose sight of the bigger picture. The Humtars are offering to help us win. They've demonstrated capabilities we didn't know about. It's also the kind of edge we'll need against the Collective."

The meeting concluded with formal but noticeably cooler exchanges. As the Gallentines departed, Hunt caught the sharp looks between them, the hushed conversations that spoke of urgent communications to come.

Wiyrkomi lingered, approaching Hunt with an unreadable expression. "Miles, did you know? About their reconnaissance activities?"

Hunt met his gaze steadily. "No. I just learned of it yesterday and insisted we meet with you immediately. But truthfully, Wiyrkomi, I'm not surprised by it. These Humtars survived the Collective once. They'd be fools not to gather every scrap of intelligence they could before facing them again."

"You may be right, Miles. But the Emperor will be...unsettled. Humtar forces returning in strength to aid in defeating the Zodarks is one thing. Humtar forces we can't detect, who've been mapping our operations across multiple galaxies?" Wiyrkomi shook his head. "That's another matter entirely."

"But?" Hunt prompted.

The Gallentine admiral's expression remained grave. "But that Arc Net means the Collective is becoming stronger than we thought. I'll do what I can to advocate for this alliance, Miles. You are right, we'll need every advantage we have against the Collective—even if that means working with allies who've been watching us from the shadows."

As Wiyrkomi departed, Hunt turned to find Dovrek still studying the hologram. He walked up to her, commenting. "Well, that could have gone better."

She shrugged. "I suppose, Viceroy. But at least now they know we're not helpless refugees returning home. We're a military power that chooses to help them. They should be grateful. Besides, it's better they understand this now than discover it later when our fleets begin to arrive."

"Fleets... how big is the Confederation Navy?"

Dovrek smiled coyly. "Let's just say the Republic doesn't have to worry about needing Gallentine protection or that of your alliance, should push come to shove."

"Really?"

Dovrek paused and looked him in the eyes. "For a millennium, we have lived with the guilt of what our ancestors did that led to the Great Fall. We had conquered the stars and colonized galaxies. We thought we knew everything there was to know, and it was that hubris that led to the Singularity. In an instant, we realized a line had been crossed. When the Stripping was introduced, it set into motion a terrible war that cost the lives of tens of millions.

"While our ancestors celebrated, believing they had won, a virus had been secretly unleashed, and we had no idea it had happened. By the time people began to show symptoms, they were sick. It was too late for the Core Worlds—it had spread too fast and too far before a quarantine could be established." Dovrek spoke in hushed tones as she recounted the events of the Great Fall. Her hand touched his, her eyes moist as she looked up at him. "What was lost has been found, Miles. You are Humtar, you are family, and we protect our family."

Hunt felt a rush of emotion as Dovrek spoke. "I am glad our people have found each other. You are right. Family takes care of family."

Chapter 7:
Trauma

Republic Neurocognitive Recovery Center
Alliance City, New Eden

The walls of Dr. Lyla Temin's office were lined with abstract artwork—fluid shapes and warm colors designed to soothe without distraction. Viceroy Miles Hunt stood at the window, arms folded, watching the rain streak across the glass.

Dr. Temin entered with quiet confidence. "You wanted to speak about the Orbots," she said, not asking but stating.

Hunt turned. "Yes, that's right," he confirmed. As the head of the Republic's advancements in PTSD therapy, Dr. Temin was the most qualified to answer his burning questions. "You've been fully read on to the program?" he asked.

She nodded. "And, as you know, this room doubles as a SCIF, so you can feel free to speak openly here."

Hunt wasn't sure exactly where to start. "I still have some burning concerns," he said. "However, I guess my biggest question is, in your opinion, when these Orbots 'wake up,' will they adapt? Or will they shatter?"

Dr. Temin motioned to a pair of chairs near a low table. Hunt followed. She didn't sit behind her desk—that was by design.

"Trauma isn't just human, Viceroy. It's a result of sentience meeting violation," she said, voice even. "If the Orbots gain full cognitive autonomy—if they remember who they were before they were puppeted by the Collective—then we need to treat them like any other victims of prolonged captivity and forced violence."

"Except they're not human," Hunt reminded her.

"No. But neither are they machines anymore." She pulled out her data pad and smiled. "You know, I realize you've been busy trying to run the Galactic Empire and everything, but this does give me a chance to review some very exciting advances in trauma therapy. We've made huge leaps forward, which will impact not only the current situation with the Orbots but our own Republic soldiers and their recovery processes."

"Honestly, I've been made aware of your research from a thousand-yard perspective, but I would really like to know what we can do to mitigate any potential risks here," said Hunt.

"Let me start off by introducing you to the NeuroSoma interface," said Dr. Temin, and she pulled up a holographic display of a collar-like device. "This was developed from the concepts of the stellate ganglion block and neurofeedback therapy. It does a few things, but basically, it moderates the autonomic nervous system in real time."

"Translation?" asked Viceroy Hunt.

Dr. Temin laughed. "It stops the fight-or-flight response. Your brain may send out signals to the body to panic, but this will intercept them. There's a programmable vagal nerve stimulation function, and it will change its response based on cortisol and adrenaline levels. We're still tweaking it, but we anticipate getting the effectiveness to a point where we can even put some of our soldiers back in the field because they will be operationally effective again, even in high-stress environments."

"That is super impressive, Dr. Temin," said Hunt. "So, do you feel confident that this would be enough to stop any serious issues with the Orbots?" he asked.

"This treatment doesn't take away all feelings, Viceroy, but it would certainly decrease agitation, hypervigilance, and the physical responses that can be so distressing with post-traumatic stress injury. I still anticipate they will need therapy to deal with the traumas they've experienced, but this will calm down their responses as they do and greatly increase the effectiveness of any treatments."

She smiled again. "But there's one more treatment I'd like to update you on: NeuroSIM," she said.

"I haven't heard about this one at all," Hunt admitted.

"We spent a great deal of time studying ibogaine and its impact on a post-traumatic brain," said Dr. Temin. "We've implemented a whole protocol after initial stabilization where a patient is delivered synthetic, nontoxic doses of this variant of ibogaine, and they are able to review their experiences while experiencing them from a third-party perspective."

"What does that do?" asked Hunt.

"Imagine your dad beat you every morning as a child. That would leave quite a scar on your mind. But then imagine you could review those memories without reexperiencing the emotional impact of those moments. You could even bring some meaning or context to those memories if, for example, you were to realize that your father had his own violent upbringing and had turned to illicit substances to cope. It wouldn't get rid of the bad memory, but it would help you to safely process it."

"That makes sense," Hunt acknowledged. "So, what would this whole process look like?"

"Well, as I mentioned, the first step would be stabilization. We'll utilize the NeuroSoma devices to keep them in a less agitated, calmer state. We'll allow them some time to decompress—calibrated lighting, quiet environments. During this period, we will give them access to therapy but not push it if they aren't ready yet.

"Then we'll move on to relational anchoring. We'll give them human partners—some of your best soldiers, medics, and even artists. They will just be there to listen and to model connection. Then we move on to active therapy as patients are ready."

Hunt's brow furrowed. "And the risks?"

"Flashbacks, dissociative loops, or aggression. But we'll include protocols. No Orbot undergoing the process will be left unwatched."

Hunt paced. "And Sam? What's his role in this?"

Temin paused. "He's the bridge. A peer who survived. They won't trust us—not at first. But they'll trust one of their own. Someone who knows the weight of memory. Plus, my understanding is that he has some way of connecting to their cyborg systems that would be basically impossible to reproduce—I'm honestly not sure I understand the tech behind it, but without him, they can't really initiate the process."

Hunt stopped walking, staring out the window again. "Some people won't accept this. They'll say we're building a second generation of monsters."

"We're not," she said firmly. "We're giving the monsters back their names."

Silence stretched, then Hunt turned, resolve in his voice.

"I want full funding. Staff, facilities—whatever you need. You'll report directly to me. But if even one of these Orbots becomes a threat to civilians…"

"Then we shut it down," Dr. Temin said without hesitation. "But not until we try."

Hunt gave a slow nod. "Then let's begin."

Chapter 8:
Pressure Cooker

November 2115
Groff Directorate Command Spire
Shwani, Varkorion System

The storm outside painted the obsidian skyline in savage flashes of violet lightning. From the upper tier of the Groff Directorate's command spire, Director Vak'Atioth stood in the recessed viewing bay, a towering silhouette framed by armored glass. Beyond, the jagged horizon glimmered with an amber halo—the outer districts of the capital lit by the endless burn of its factories and war forges.

If he narrowed his eyes, he could almost see the shimmer of heat rising from the foundry stacks, could almost taste the metallic tang on the wind. Not since he was a boy had Vak witnessed the night sky so alive with fire, a reminder of how far the fortunes of war had shifted.

Oh, Lindow...how has it come to this?

His clan, the D'Shwani, was among the Empire's architects—part of the original seven clans that had founded the Empire, carrying it into the stars. The D'Shwani were explorers, then conquerors. When they'd discovered the Varkorion system, and this planet—they hadn't just claimed it. They'd named it after the clan. In doing so, they'd ensured all future warriors would know the D'Shwani clan. They had planted their banners across star systems, forged dominion from the nothingness of unclaimed worlds, and built an industrial powerhouse that fueled the rise of the Empire as it grew outward, ever expanding, conquering system after system.

It was the D'Shwani who had built this planet, who had built the Groff Directorate, the secret police who maintained order across the Empire, who had built the spy agency that gave the Empire its eyes to see and its ears to hear. And now, after centuries of achievement, they stood at the edge of ruin, jeopardized by the incompetence of that fool, the former Zon, Utulf, and his sycophantic lapdog, Otro, whom he'd elevated to Zon as his replacement.

I should be the one on the High Council... I should be the Zon.

With each dracma,[1] each month, the Republic pressed deeper into Zodark space. Skirmishes became battles, battles became campaigns, and campaigns ended in defeat. He knew it. That fool Otro knew it. And worse—Vak could taste it now, this loathsome new flavor: the bitter scorch of failure, like ash and burnt metal clinging to the air.

A faint rustle stirred behind him. Turning from the city, Vak stepped back into the chamber—his chamber—an expanse of polished basalt and carved battle glyphs. Inside, three Gurista attendants waited in silence, their spines bowed, their crimson-trimmed slave uniforms a visual reminder of subjugation.

Vak's lip curled into a snarl. He bared his teeth, the words boiling up before reason could intervene. "You worthless bazka!"[2] His voice cracked like a whip, reverberating off the high rune-carved walls. "We gave your people everything! We extended your lives, welcomed you into our society, brought you to the stars, you filthy, ungrateful quant!"[3]

He crossed the distance in two strides, slapping one across the side of his face with a force that sent the Gurista sprawling to the floor. "You betray us without a fight!" His boot slammed into the slave's ribs, skidding the body across the smooth stone as it vomited blood. "We are your *gods*! You do not betray gods and crawl to the Republic as if they will save you! We saved you from yourselves, you insufferable *froths*!"[4]

His hand clamped down on the Gurista's head, talons digging in. With a sharp, sickening crack, the skull gave way, blood and gore spraying the wall. The headless body collapsed in a spreading pool of dark crimson.

The second attendant tried to avert his gaze, but Vak's glare pinned him in place. Rage surged, hot and unrestrained. In a blur, Vak's claws punched through the Gurista's chest, the wet crunch of bone and sinew echoing like a snapped rod. He yanked its heart free, letting the body fall to the floor, its blood catching the dim light like molten glass.

The third attendant froze, piss running down its trembling leg. Vak's senior aide—a lean Zodark with an ink-black crest—stepped

---

[1] Dracma is year in Zodark.
[2] Bazka is a derogatory term similar to dog in Zodark.
[3] Quant is rodent in Zodark.
[4] Froth is a Zodark curse word.

forward and placed a measured hand on the Director's arm. "Director... your Laktish is here. Shall I have this cleaned up before I send him in?"

Vak eyed his aide for a moment. "Remove this filth from my presence," he hissed. "And have the Laktish enter once it's complete."

A short while later, the outer door leading into his office opened, and Heltet entered briskly. He moved with purpose, oblivious to the ghastly scene just moments earlier. Held tightly in his hands, he clasped a data pad containing vital information, information Vak hoped would provide insights into what to do next.

When he spoke, his voice was steady, confident. "Director, I have returned with my report from the Ferrix and Varkorion systems. Sadly, the Malvari continue to fail us. Our scouts continue to report activity near the gate leading to Tueblets. The probes are small, but growing in confidence," Heltet reported.

"Varkorion—how is that possible? That places a second Republic fleet no more than three systems away from Tueblets," exclaimed Vak, his rage swelling once more. "Is the Gurista betrayal truly complete—are they part of these incursions?" Vak demanded to know.

"No, not that we believe. The Guristas are not ready to participate in that kind of operation. But these incursions are just scouts, probes to test our perimeter," Heltet explained. "I also traveled along the Kryntok Chain as you requested—"

"Ah, yes, then you visited Kryntok, Mavrok, Harvox, and the others?" Vak interrupted. "Tell me. What have you discovered during your trip? Is our support strong in these areas or is it waffling?"

Heltet inclined his head. "In general, our support is strong in this area of the Empire compared to others. The foundries, factories, and shipyards of the Kryntok system are continuing to run at full capacity. For every three warships they finish for the Malvari, they secretly complete one of our Thoraxian heavy destroyers. They're finishing nine a month at the Kryntok shipyards, while the Tarkun yards here are completing seventeen a month. This gives us twenty-six Thoraxian heavy destroyers a month between the two shipyards—"

"It's an improvement, but it's still too slow, Heltet," Vak interrupted again. "The Malvari are losing ships faster than we can replace them. It's important that we continue to build our separate Groff fleet, but we need the Malvari to repel the Republic, or the Empire will be picked apart. What of the other yards? Have they increased production yet?"

Heltet shrugged, unsure. "NOS Tharvok assured me his clan's factories will continue to support whatever Groff contracts we send without hesitation. Some of his tribes are offering security to help ensure the ore convoys aren't being randomly intercepted by the Malvari and redirected to their shipyards. There have been instances where some captains are being offered additional payments to deliver their ore to Malvari refineries and not ours—"

"Really? Is this becoming an issue?" Vak interrupted once more.

"Not that Tharvok shared, no," Heltet replied. "Some of my sources have mentioned that the factory supervisors overseeing the Malvari facilities are scared. The recent battlefield losses have placed an incredible strain on the fleet. That fool Otro is costing them more ships than their factories can replace. Rumor has it the Malvari are beginning to court some of the smaller guilds to help with shipbuilding in exchange for better trade routes and more prominent positions within the governing councils."

Vak drummed his talons on his desk, then said, "Heltet, this information about the Malvari facilities—this is a serious situation. If the fleet is suffering these kinds of heavy losses, there is a real possibility that if the Republic makes a move on Tueblets—we may lose the system."

Heltet kept his face neutral, his mind racing with how to respond. "This is true. If this were to happen, would you authorize the Groff Fleet, such as it is, to aid the Malvari in repelling this invasion?"

The question caught Vak by surprise. Truth be told, he hadn't given it much thought. He wasn't sure what the right answer was. If the Republic succeeded in further destroying the Malvari's fleets, saving what was left of the Empire might come down to the secret fleet he'd directed the Groff to build.

"Heltet, it's important you stay on top of the construction of the new *Chulitz*-class battleships. Last I spoke with Zynark of the Fel-Karoth Clan, he assured me they are ready to begin serial production of them next month. His people have been true to their word—keeping the drydocks sealed and under layered security. Once they start production, it'll take the Tarkun shipyards eight months to produce the first pair of ships. Once that first batch is complete, they'll begin a steady pace of eight per month. Unfortunately, that'll come at a cost of twelve of the seventeen heavy destroyers the yard would normally be able to produce."

Heltet nodded. "When I was briefed on the specs and capabilities of the vessel, it made it clear to me that it should prove worth it to have the lower product rate of destroyers for these stronger ships. The firepower and added armor are impressive."

"Yes, it is impressive, but only if we're able to produce them in small numbers," Vak replied, an edge to his voice. "It may yet prove to be too little, too late. If Zon Utulf had appointed me to the Council, I would have become Zon when his term was up. I would have had the Malvari switch all production to these newer ships. As it is, the Malvari are stuck, wedded to their older, tried and tested designs because they can mass-produce them and our Zodark warriors know how to operate them. But this does us no good, Heltet, when the Republic is building warships superior to our own."

"It is a shame, Director, that Utulf chose his Mavkah, Otro, to be his replacement, especially after losing the *Nefantar* in his botched raid on Sol," Heltet agreed, hoping to stay on his boss's good side.

Vak clicked his tongue. "If Otro had had the Malvari switch to building the Chulitz dracmas ago, the Empire wouldn't be in the situation it is. Continue your report, Heltet. I must know what you've learned."

Heltet nodded, then continued, "I have good news to report with Tavrix. Your support with him remains steadfast. His eldest son died in the Orinda system. His heart burns with anger over the continued incompetence of the Mavkah. As to Raveth Korr'Vahn, he swore to me that warships built for the Groff will ever bear the command seal of the Malvari. Kelthas of the Clan Vor-Mek, however…" He allowed the pause to stretch. "Kelthas is hedging his bets. His fuel convoys move under heavy guard, but his contracts now carry Council clauses— insurance, he calls it."

Vak's expression darkened as Heltet continued. "In Harvox, our operatives still work in the shadows. Our secret police have been quietly sowing doubt about Zon Otro's capacity to lead and undermining the Malvari's claims of competence. The priests may keep to their rites, but the whispers in the marketplaces are ours. Norketh's older officers stand with you, though the Academy's youngest graduates wear their reformist sympathies toward Zon Otro openly.

Heltet's voice dropped. "The archives echo with argument. Jhorvek Ran-Vass plays both sides, selling history to the highest bidder. If the Council gains control there, they could rewrite more than just the past. They could omit us entirely if we lose power."

Vak's eyes narrowed to slits. "Then the spine is sound, but the muscles are soft. We have our work cut out for us, Heltet."

The Groff Director looked Laktish in the eyes, the edges of his vision still blurred red with anger. He had chosen to keep Heltet close—closer than most—because his Laktish had a gift for survival. And survival was currency in times such as these.

"Laktish... you have told me what I *want* to hear. Now tell me what I *need* to hear." Vak's tone was controlled now, but beneath it lay the weight of command, the expectation that whatever question he asked would be answered.

Heltet's talons tapped once against the data pad at his side before he spoke. "As you wish. By now, you are aware that after months of fighting, the battle for Gravaxia is finished. The Malvari have not publicly admitted this, of course, but our forces were driven out in defeat. The loss of the system... it places Tueblets in peril."

For a moment, the room seemed to constrict around Vak. He knew it was likely they would lose the battle, but hearing it from Heltet...it felt final. He couldn't explain it, but he felt like the air was heavier to breathe; his pulse drummed in his skull. "And the Thoraxian fleet? Tarkun's output?"

"Improved at last," Heltet replied. "After...corrective measures were taken in the form of the execution of several dozen workers and shift overseers, along with their families, the remainder have increased throughput by thirty-two percent."

Vak's lips curved into something between a smile and a snarl. "Discipline always restores order. Remember that, Heltet."

But the smile faded quickly, replaced by the gnawing truth. "The Malvari's incompetence continues to fester as Zon Otro refuses to do what is necessary. If they are left unchecked for much longer, they will cost us the Empire."

"Then we must act soon to preserve the Empire," Heltet said. "On a positive note, we have completed the Eyes of Shwani. Should the enemy reach our system, all platforms are now complete, fully armed and ready to defend Shwani. Zon Otro himself inspected them the other day. He was impressed by them. So much so that he has ordered similar platforms to be built across the Empire, especially around the stargates."

Vak's talons curled into the polished surface of his desk. "That figures. That buffoon will claim my design as his own. Parade my work as if he had conceived it himself."

"Not likely," Heltet said evenly. "I've made sure that the NOSs of influence know who is truly safeguarding the Empire."

That soothed Vak—but only slightly. "Continue your vetting," he ordered. "I want every clan, every tribe, marked for loyalty to the Groff when the reckoning comes."

Heltet inclined his head. "Yes, Director."

"And one more thing." Vak's eyes burned with cold intent. "Go to Arik-Tor. Inspect the Gorgonian stock yourself. I want them ready when I call. No excuses. No delays."

"As you command." Heltet bowed slightly before exiting the chamber doors into the corridor beyond.

Vak stood alone. The lightning outside threw his reflection onto the obsidian walls—taller, grander, almost godlike.

Only he could save the Empire. Only his will could turn the tide. And when the day came, history would remember not the blunders of Zon Otro, nor the treachery of lesser races, but the salvation wrought by Director Vak'Atioth.

And woe to any who stood in his way.

Chapter 9:
The First to Wake

Republic Neurocognitive Recovery Center
Alliance City, New Eden

The observation room was quiet but for the soft hum of equipment and the rhythmic pulse of biometric monitors. A curved smartglass window overlooked the surgical suite beyond. There, voluntarily bound to a platform designed to stabilize his quadpedal frame, was Orbot 001.

Dr. Alan Walburg stood beside Dr. Lyla Temin, both clad in sterile neurointegration gear. Sam waited just outside the threshold of the chamber, his optic band dim and steady, hands folded at the small of his back.

"So, that's their former leader," Dr. Temin said quietly.

Walburg nodded. "Before the tether was broken," he replied. "If anyone would be prioritized by the Collective for future neural subjugation, it would be him."

Sam tilted his head slightly. "That's why he must be first. If the Collective finds a way to reestablish the tether, they will seek him out." Sam strode over to Orbot 001 and spoke quietly with him, almost out of Dr. Walburg's hearing. But Walburg knew that he was going over the details with him one more time, to remind him of what to expect and to help ease any concerns. Then he heard the question he had been anticipating. "Now that I have informed you of all the risks, are you sure that you want to go through with this?" he asked, louder so everyone could hear.

The Orbot didn't hesitate. "Yes…I want to be free, like you. I want to remember, even if it hurts."

Temin nodded an acknowledgment to the patient, who looked back with his mostly human face and returned the gesture. She checked her console. "NeuroSoma system calibrated," she announced. "Baseline agitation levels spiking slightly, but within parameters."

Behind them, the security door hissed open, and Viceroy Miles Hunt entered.

"I'm not here to interfere," Hunt said, moving toward the glass. "This is your operation now. But I want to see the moment we become something more than what we were."

Walburg stepped beside him. "Then you're just in time."

Hunt nodded once, then turned to Sam. "You understand the stakes."

Sam's optic band brightened. "Better than anyone."

Dr. Temin keyed the final sequence. "NeuroSIM access initiated."

Sam sat across from the Orbot and took his hands. What followed had the reverence of a prayer meeting. Sam's optical band danced in patterns instead of scanning back and forth in its usual patterns. The Orbot kept his own eyes closed, but they were clearly moving rapidly behind his eyelids. This lasted for several minutes. He muttered phrases, words that had no meaning to Dr. Walburg—but he surmised that they were memories from his past. Sam let out a noise that sounded a bit like humming.

"Vitals are stable," said Dr. Temin. "The NeuroSoma is working effectively to reduce the fight-or-flight response. NeuroSIM is still running through its process effectively."

Dr. Walburg had been anticipating this moment, but now that it was here, he felt like he was intruding where he did not belong. Somewhere in Orbot 001's mind, he was processing a lifetime of memories, some of which Dr. Walburg knew would be quite terrifying.

The sacred quiet ended quickly, when Sam released the Orbot's hands and sat back. The patient's eyes shot open. "I...remember," he said. "My name, my life...everything."

"Would you like to tell us your name?" asked Sam gently.

"Tannel," said the man. "My name is Tannel." He looked down at his mechanical legs, as if seeing them for the first time, and cried softly.

"It's going to take a while to get used to life the way it is," said Sam. "But we will be here for you the whole way."

"Yes...I can see now that it will take time," said Tannel. "But I am still happy to be me again."

From behind the glass, Viceroy Miles Hunt allowed himself the faintest smile.

He turned to Walburg and Temin. "You'll keep me updated. If anything changes, I expect immediate notification."

"Of course," Temin said.

"But I'm not going to micromanage you," Hunt added. "You've got full latitude. Do what needs to be done. Just make sure it's *done right.*"

He turned toward the exit but paused one last time.

"Today, we start reclaiming what was stolen from us," Hunt said. "One soul at a time."

And then he was gone.

Chapter 10:
The Ruse Is Set

RNS *Vanguard*
Kryntok System

The quantum conduit collapsed behind them like the closing of an eye. Captain Joe Wright gripped the command chair as the *Vanguard*'s sensors populated the screens of the bridge with the kind of data that caused his breath to catch. For three heartbeats, the bridge fell silent—not from discipline, but from collective disbelief at what filled their displays.

"Sweet mother of God—" his tactical officer commented softly.

Wright had seen fleet actions before. Kepler-442 had been chaos incarnate, ships dying in droves while plasma and missiles painted the void in deadly light. But this—this was something else entirely. This was an execution they were witnessing.

"Would you look at that..." commented Commander Maggie Little, his XO.

They watched in awe as the Humtar heavy battleship CNS *Oathbreaker* carved its way through space like a predator born to it. The 2,900-meter-long warship bristled with weapons, its twelve heavy plasma cannons discharging volley after volley of fire at prodigious rates that seemed impossible for a weapon this formidable. To further add to its destructive power, the massive battleship had four twin-barreled magrail turrets that fired projectiles more powerful than even the Republic's massive guns could achieve.

What astonished Wright more than its dizzying array of firepower was its organic-looking hull. Each time a Humtar vessel was hit with a Zodark laser, its energy would ripple across the hull like a radio wave harmlessly washing over it. The only weapon the Zodarks seemed to possess that caused even the slightest bit of damage was their plasma torpedoes.

"Twelve torpedoes inbound—they're headed for the *Razorwind*," exclaimed Commander Thomas Hill from the Tactical Action Officer station.

One of the Zodark cruisers emerged from behind a battleship the *Razorwind* had been pummeling. It unleashed a dozen plasma torpedoes into the starboard side of the Humtar *Warclaw*-class light battleship. Moments after the torpedoes headed for the *Razorwind*, thin beams of purple light shot forward from the Humtar vessel. Explosion blossomed where torpedoes had been moments earlier, three down, then seven, then nine. A geyser of flame was ejected into the void when the first torpedo struck. Second after the first, two more plowed into the starboard side of the vessel. Ejections of flame, atmosphere and debris were hurled into the void near it. The lumbering 2,200-meter-long vessel shuddered from the impact, its exterior lights flickering several times before stabilizing. It was clear the battleship had taken a crippling blow, but Wright had no way of knowing how bad the damage was.

When the enemy cruiser turned toward the *Razorwind*, bringing to bear its laser batteries. The *Oathbreaker* fired its plasma cannons— boring a hole into the cruiser's reactor housing. A flash momentarily blinded their external cameras, the bridge screens recovering seconds later. When the monitor returned, the cruiser was gone. It had simply ceased to exist. In its place was an expanding cloud of superheated debris and frozen atmosphere. But the battle wasn't over, far from it. All around the *Vanguard*, the chaos of the battle raged unabated.

"How many Zodark ships are we looking at?" Wright forced himself to ask, though his eyes couldn't leave the main display.

"Ah... it looks like four Zodark battleships—two others have been destroyed. I show the wrecks of five cruisers, seven left. There are six out of ten frigates remaining and five corvettes out of fourteen— correction, three corvettes left," Lieutenant Waldman answered.

They watched the bridge display as another Zodark vessel erupted under the combined fire of the *Dark Omen* and the *Razorwind*, which had rejoined the fight shortly after the fires had burned out. The two Humtar light battleships were now moving in perfect synchronization, their plasma torpedo volleys arriving simultaneously from different vectors. The Zodark cruiser's armor, thick enough to withstand most conventional attacks, peeled away like paper in a furnace under Humtar fire.

Wright watched the *Grimward* lead her sister ships toward the system's stargate, weapons hot but unnecessary. The Zodark vessel that might have contested their blockade was already adrift, burning wrecks in their death throes. The *Shadowrend* and *Fell Claw* swept through the engagement zone's flanks, their pulse cannons methodically eliminating escape pods and patrol boats with clinical precision. The task force was under strict orders—no witnesses to the attacks. No prisoner taken, no mercy shown. Just systematic annihilation delivered with brutal efficiency that made Wright's blood run cold.

"It's incredible, Captain," his XO whispered beside him, "I've never seen anything like it. Aside from the Zodarks' plasma torpedoes, their lasers can't seem to damage those Humtar vessels. It's like the energy from the lasers is somehow being absorbed or deflected."

"I'm just glad they're on our side," Wright mumbled softly. This was the first time any of them had seen a Humtar vessel in combat. It startled him to know there were ships with this kind of technology and power. It reminded him of a brief engagement some Altairian and Republic warships had had with a Legion warship in Orbot territory. The Legion ship had cut through allied warships like they weren't even there.

"Good Lord, they've nearly finished them off," his weapons officer, Lieutenant Latter, commented.

On the screen, they watched the last Zodark battleship unleash a full broadside of plasma torpedoes into the *Oathbreaker*. They had managed to bracket the 2,900-meter-long Humtar heavy battleship with their torpedo launchers and laser batteries. The lasers left scorched divots and marks against the biometallic hull, but no visible damage beyond it. In quick succession, the plasma torpedoes were swatted from the void, little flashes of flame the only sign they existed before going dark. The *Oathbreaker*'s starboard fired as one—beams of light lancing out, boring holes through the Zodark battleship. It blew apart seconds later when its reactor core was breached. The ruined wreck began separating into three distinct sections, lifeless bodies of its crew sucked into the void around them before the atmosphere froze and the fires winked out.

"Hot damn, that's impressive," Wright muttered, astonished. "Helm, maintain our current position," he commanded, his voice steady despite the awe crawling up his spine. "Let's maintain a defensive formation around the *Bechtel*. Weapons hot but do not engage unless directly threatened."

The bridge crew moved through their tasks mechanically, but Wright could feel their tension. They were warriors trained for battle, watching a massacre they couldn't join. Yet as another Zodark vessel— this one trying desperately to flee the battle—vanished in a confluence of Humtar firepower, Wright found himself grateful they were on the same side.

The last Zodark cruiser tried to turn, its engines flaring bright in a desperate attempt to escape the killing field. Captain Wright watched from his command chair as the *Fell Claw* and *Shadowrend* closed on it like predators running down wounded prey. Their plasma cannons spoke in perfect synchronization—violet beams coring through the cruiser's reactor compartment. The vessel didn't explode so much as simply cease, its molecular structure failing as superheated plasma consumed it from within.

"All Zodark mobile assets eliminated," Lieutenant Waldman reported, his voice carrying a mixture of awe and unease. "System is clear for phase two."

Wright nodded, forcing himself to shift mental gears from spectator to participant. "Helm, bring us about to bearing two-seven-zero mark four. Take us toward the second planet's mining complex. Weapons, I want firing solutions on those orbital refineries."

"Aye, Captain. Coming about," the helmsman, Lieutenant Godley, acknowledged.

Through the bridge viewports, Wright could see the Humtar vessels already repositioning. The *Oathbreaker* maintained overwatch while the lighter ships spread out in a defensive screen. Even now, with no threats remaining, they moved with predatory grace—always ready, always hunting.

"Captain Suen signals all clear to proceed with infrastructure elimination," his communications officer announced.

"Very well. TAO, you have weapons free on all Zodark industrial targets. Let's give them a show they won't forget," Wright commanded. "And signal the *Bechtel*—begin debris deployment operations."

Commander Hill's fingers danced across his tactical console. "Targeting orbital refinery Alpha. Magrails charging… firing."

The *Vanguard* shuddered as her main batteries spoke. Eight massive tungsten-carbide projectiles accelerated to relativistic speeds, crossing the void in seconds. The first refinery—a structure the size of a small city—buckled as the rounds punched through its superstructure. Secondary explosions rippled along its length as processed ore and volatile chemicals ignited.

"Captain, we're scoring direct hits across all sectors," Hill reported with satisfaction. "Refinery Alpha is breaking apart, multiple secondary explosions reported."

"Good shooting. Shift targets to the space elevators," Wright ordered. "Let's cut their tethers before we wreck the station. If we're lucky, it might even fall into the planet's atmosphere."

Through the tactical display, Wright watched the *Bechtel* begin her grim work. The construction platform's massive cargo bays yawned open, and specialized tugs emerged, each towing pieces of Republic wreckage. The mangled hull of the frigate Defiance tumbled free first, its Republic markings still visible despite the battle damage. The tugs positioned it carefully among the debris field where the Razorwind had taken those torpedo hits—making it appear the Republic frigate had died in that exchange.

"Laser batteries engaging surface installations," Lieutenant Latter announced. "Mining complex Bravo is taking hits."

The planet below began to burn. Republic laser cannons—their distinctive blue-white energy signature unmistakable—carved molten trenches through ore processing plants. Entire industrial sectors collapsed as their structural supports melted to slag. Wright knew Zodark investigators would find those energy signatures in the wreckage, another piece of evidence pointing to the Republic.

"Sir, *Bechtel* is deploying the fighter craft," his sensor operator reported.

Wright shifted his attention to a secondary display showing the construction platform's operations. A Gallentine B-19 Devastator bomber drifted free, its hull purposely damaged to make it look like it had been destroyed by Zodark fire during the battle. The bomber's characteristic swept wings and bulbous cockpit would be instantly recognizable to any Zodark analyst. Two F-19 Hellcats followed, their hulls bearing scorch marks from *Vanguard*'s own lasers—wounds inflicted specifically to sell this deception.

"Magrails reloaded. Targeting mining station Charlie," Hill announced from his weapons station, his gun batteries delivering volley after volley.

"Fire," Wright commanded.

Another salvo thundered from the guns of the *Vanguard*. The mining station was a massive asteroid hollowed out and converted into a processing facility. Half a dozen volleys of magrails cracked like an egg under their impacts. Atmosphere vented from a dozen breaches, carrying with it the tiny specks of Zodark workers caught in the devastation.

"Captain," Commander Little said softly beside him, "*Bechtel* reports they're ready to deploy the…fallen on your order."

Wright's jaw tightened.. Even though the families had agreed, understanding that these sailors could serve one final mission even in death, there was still something personally unsettling about using the bodies of fallen Republic spacers as props in this elaborate deception.

He sighed, then nodded as he gave the order. "Tell them to proceed, and make sure it's done with dignity."

The *Bechtel*'s tugs moved with reverent precision now, distributing the remains throughout the debris field. Each body still wore Republic fleet uniforms, their rank insignia and ship patches intact. When the Zodarks found them, they'd see exactly what they were meant to see—Republic dead from a raid turned costly.

"Infrastructure targets eighty percent destroyed," Hill reported. "Should we continue?"

Wright studied the devastation they'd wrought. The entire mining complex was in ruins, centuries of industrial development reduced to molten slag and drifting debris. Fires still burned where atmosphere leaked from shattered habitats.

"Negative. We've left enough of a calling card," Wright decided. "Signal the *Intrepid* and *Resolute* to cease fire. Begin forming up for withdrawal."

Through the viewports, he could see pieces of the heavy cruiser *Normandy* tumbling past—another carefully placed corpse in this elaborate theatrical production. The Zodarks would study every piece, analyze every energy signature, reconstruct the entire battle from the debris patterns. And they'd reach exactly the conclusion the Humtar wanted them to reach.

"Sir, Captain Suen is signaling," the communications officer announced. "He says mission accomplished. He's requesting we form up on the *Oathbreaker*. It's time to go home. His ship is preparing to open the QCB for extraction."

Wright watched the *Oathbreaker* position itself at the predetermined coordinates. The massive battleship's biometallic hull began to pulse with an otherworldly light as it prepared to tear a hole in space itself.

"All Republic vessels, form up on the *Vanguard*," Wright commanded. "*Bechtel*, confirm all materials deployed and secure for transit."

"*Bechtel* confirms ready for departure," came the response.

The Humtar ships were already moving into formation, their movements graceful, practiced. That was when Wright noticed something incredible happening to the *Razorwind*. Where the light battleship had taken serious damage hours earlier during the initial engagement, it looked like the starboard section of the ship had resealed the gouges in its hull. The biometallic material of the ship's hull had restored itself like living tissue healing a wound.

That's... impossible, Wright thought. He had no way of explaining what he saw or understanding how it worked.

"Captain, I'm reading massive energy buildup from the *Oathbreaker*," Lieutenant Waldman reported. "They're initiating the bridge to the Rhea system."

On the bridge's main monitor, they watched as the space in front of their vessels began to ripple and tear, an opening between two places in time and space. The quantum conduit bridge materialized like a wound in reality—a swirling vortex of impossible colors calling to them. Wright had seen it before, when the *Freedom* or an Altairian ship had created a bridge during past campaigns. It was incredible to watch, and even more exciting to pass through.

"All vessels, prepare for transit," Captain Suen's voice came across the command channel. "*Shadowrend* and *Fell Claw* will enter first to secure the exit point. Republic vessels will follow. *Oathbreaker* will be last through and collapse the bridge behind us."

Wright watched the two Humtar frigates accelerate toward the vortex and vanish into its swirling depths. The other Humtar ships followed in precise order, each disappearing into the conduit like shadows swallowed by darkness.

"Lieutenant Godley, take us in," Wright ordered his helmsman. "Nice and steady."

The *Vanguard* moved forward, her escorts flanking her protectively. As they approached the conduit, Wright felt that familiar sensation of reality bending in ways that human minds weren't meant to comprehend. Then they were through, emerging in empty space light-years from the carnage they'd left behind.

Behind them, the *Oathbreaker* emerged last, the conduit collapsing immediately after. Where moments before there had been a doorway between stars, now only an empty void remained.

"All vessels accounted for," Lieutenant Godley reported. "We're clear."

Wright finally allowed himself to relax, his shoulders sagging slightly. They'd done it. They'd survived one of the most elaborate deceptions of the war. Behind them, the Kryntok system burned with Republic weapons signatures, littered with Republic dead and destroyed Republic fighters. When the Zodarks investigated, they'd find exactly what they expected to find: evidence of a Republic raid that had succeeded with minimal casualties.

"Captain Suen is signaling," the communications officer announced. "He's transmitting: 'Well done, Republic vessels. The seeds of paranoia have been planted. Let us see what grows from them.'"

Wright nodded to himself. They'd accomplished the mission, but as he looked at the tactical display showing the devastation they'd left behind—the murdered civilians, the destroyed infrastructure, the carefully placed corpses of Republic dead—he couldn't shake a feeling of unease.

War was ugly enough without adding lies to the carnage. But if these deceptions could hasten the Zodark Empire's fall, perhaps the dishonor was worth it. Time would tell if the paranoia they'd sown would bear the fruit they hoped for, or if they'd simply added another dark chapter to an already bloody war.

"Helm," Wright commanded, pushing aside his doubts. "Set course for New Eden. Let's go home."

Chapter 11:
Change of Pace

Captain Lyrana Dovrek, director of intelligence for the Confederation Defense Force, concluded her brief with a statement on the indomitability of the human spirit, clearly trying to inspire her audience with suggestions that the war against the Collective was not lost.

"Thank you, Captain Dovrek, for bringing everyone up to speed on these recent discoveries," said Viceroy Miles Hunt. He paused long enough to look each of the Republic's senior commanders in the eye before continuing. "This war with the Zodarks has gone on long enough. If we are to prepare to fight the Collective, we must first defeat the Zodarks, and soon. For those of you who haven't met Admiral Veydris Korrath, allow me to introduce him to you—he is the Humtar Commander of the Confederation Defense Forces stationed within the Republic. He has an announcement he would like to share with you." Hunt motioned for Korrath to speak.

The Humtar commander wasted no time diving into the heart of the matter. "For nearly three years, your soldiers and spacers have fought a brutal campaign—defeating first the Orbots, and then the Pharaonis. You succeeded in capturing the Zodark system of Gravaxia and liberated the Gurista people from the bondage of Zodark control. Now, it is time to discuss the endgame—the final campaign to defeat these savage beasts.

"This brings us to why your commands have been recalled home. For the past couple of years, our contingent has been tasked with providing economic and security assistance to the Republic. In a couple of weeks, the Chancellor of the Republic will sign a treaty with President Gudea—uniting our people once more," said Korrath confidently. "We have requested permission to expand the scope of our mission and provide direct military assistance in defeating the Zodarks—"

"Pardon the interruption, but does this mean Humtar warships would fight alongside us against the Zodarks?" interjected Vice Admiral Rosentreter.

"It does," Korrath confirmed, to the shock and surprise of the Republic officers. "To that end, I would like to direct your attention to the holographic star map."

The lights in the room dimmed softly as the giant map dominated the center of the circular conference room table. A faint red-shaded outline appeared over a swath of star systems with a label—"Zodark-controlled space." Shades of blue appeared at different points adjacent to the red-shaded territory, delineating the two sides.

"These systems here," Korrath said, highlighting them, "are the key systems—those Viceroy Hunt has told us are critical to defeating the Zodarks—Tueblets and Zinconia. As we speak, one of our stealth frigates is mapping the defenses of both systems to identify the weak spots in them while we await the arrival of additional forces.

"This brings us back to why your commands have been recalled. While this intelligence is collected and a plan is devised, Viceroy Hunt felt it would be good for morale and for the people if your fleets and armies returned to rest and refit before we start the final campaign to end the war," Korrath explained.

Hunt caught his attention to speak. "For three years, our people have fought hard and been away from their families and their homes," he began, looking each of them in the eye. "On Earth... we suffered a terrible loss during the Zodark invasion and the subsequent bombardment of our home world. More than a billion souls were lost during what was nothing less than an attempted genocide of humanity.

"Our people have suffered greatly. The Sumerians and the Guristas have also suffered and endured a great loss alongside us. I recalled your forces because it is important for our people to celebrate your victories, to honor what you have achieved, to share in the losses you have suffered, and to know there is hope—to know this war shall end. Their suffering, our suffering... shall end," explained Hunt somberly. "In the coming days, all across the alliance, and especially here on New Eden and Earth, parades will be held, speeches will be given, and awards will be presented. We will restore hope to our people. And we will remind our brave men and women why they fight—not because they enjoy it. Not because they are told to. They fight because they love what is behind them more than they fear what is in front of them."

Hunt paused for a second before continuing. "When the next campaign starts, your commands need to be ready. It's imperative that you use this period of rest and refit to replace your losses and bring your units to fully manned and your ships fully repaired. I can't tell you when the next campaign will start, but I can give you an idea of where it's going to happen."

Hunt highlighted a system on the display, bringing it forward for the crowd to see. "I want to draw your attention to the Tueblets system," said Hunt. "Admiral Korrath mentioned Tueblets, and there is a reason we're targeting that system in particular. As you can see, it has eight stargates, each leading to a different part of their Empire. Some of these lines only travel one to three systems deep, while others eventually connect to Primord, Altairian, and Republic territory. These two gates connect to the Republic and Primord territory six and nine systems further down the chain. These three lines here, here, and here connect to Altairian territory after eight, thirteen, and fourteen systems. These two here and here connect to our newly liberated Gurista territory two systems in and four systems in. Lastly, this stargate is two jumps away from the second targeted system the Humtars are scouting—Zinconia," explained Hunt.

He raised a hand to forestall the question he saw forming on the lips of several of his commanders. "Oh, and let me save you the trouble of asking me or Admiral Bailey how we plan to force the Zodarks to surrender—you'll be told when you have the need to know, and let's leave it at that."

Then Hunt stood, signaling the end of the meeting. "I know I said this earlier, but I want to say it again before we leave—welcome home, everyone!" he said. "Let's rest our people, and when we return, we will prepare for the final campaigns to end this war once and for all. Dismissed!"

Admiral Korrath and his officers gathered their materials and said their goodbyes while the Altairians, Primords, Ry'lians, and Tully mingled with their Republic counterparts a little longer. As Hunt exited the conference room, he breathed a sigh of relief that Admiral Helixar seemed to have cooled off after his initial anger toward him and his Humtar advisor, Admiral Drezikar. It had been only a week since their last meeting, when the Gallentines had learned of the Humtars' stealth capabilities. Thankfully, the Gallentines saw the advantage of having an ally with technology equal or superior to their own. For a hot minute, Hunt had been concerned that things might spiral out of control. He had never seen the Gallentines lose their composure the way they had during that meeting—and he was glad to learn that they were too pragmatic to hold grudges.

Chapter 12:
Deadly Cat and Mouse

Garka, Moraga
Orinda System

David and his team of Kites had been tailing this particular deputy chief of police for a few days now. The man, Dumuzi Enmeana, was suspected of supplying Mukhabarat insurgents with police weapons and ammo. Plus, there was strong evidence to suggest that Enmeana was giving insurgents a heads-up whenever a raid was going to happen, so they could escape ahead of it.

David had seen enough footage of the carnage left behind by the IEDs the insurgents had been placing around the capital city of Garka to feel very little sympathy for anyone involved. Still, before the Kites exacted justice, they had to be absolutely sure of the facts.

Surveillance wasn't always that exciting in the beginning. Somchai planted a tracker on Enmeana's vehicle and hacked into the security systems at his home and place of work, so it wasn't too difficult to establish his daily patterns and routines.

They were on day three, and so far, all he'd done was go to work, take a morning break for taqaffa, pick up dinner in the evening, and go home. David could feel the team getting a bit antsy—truthfully, he felt that way himself. But he knew that if Enmeana was involved in these horrible terrorist events, it wouldn't take long to uncover the truth.

Everyone in their places? asked David over the neurolink.

Checking out the spice stall, as requested, answered Amir.

Shopping for purses, Jess responded.

Stationed in the surveillance van, said Somchai.

Hanging out at the bar closest to his favorite restaurant, Catalina confirmed.

Good, said David. *This guy will give up the goods eventually.*

David settled onto his bench at the park, pretending to read something on his data pad very intently. He was in a perfect spot to watch Enmeana pick up dinner. The culture on Moraga was a little different than on Gurista Prime; very few people cooked food for themselves at home. Instead, the majority picked up food at various stalls and convenience stores on a daily basis. Most people on Moraga had a routine where they would pick up food from the same place every day, except for special occasions or before their weekly day off. It served as a way to build community, with each restaurant or stall getting to know their frequent customers very well. Enmeana's favorite spot was a place that reminded David of gyro shops back home—large slabs of spiced meat spun around near a fire, ready for the workers to cut some off and serve it with their many sides.

Somchai had a microdrone that looked like one of the insects on Moraga waiting on the doorsill, ready to swoop down and hopefully attach itself to Enmeana's clothes as he entered. This would make it even easier to track his movements.

I see him coming, Amir announced.

David looked up from his book. There was Dumuzi Enmeana, sticking to his routine, seemingly without a care in the world.

Somchai, he's approaching Eridu Kitchen now. About thirty feet out...twenty...ten...now.

Releasing microdrone, Somchai replied. A pregnant pause hung in the air. *Successfully planted on Enmeana's clothing.*

David let out a breath he hadn't even realized he was holding. He waited impatiently as their target ordered his food and gossiped with the workers.

Come on already, he thought.

A few minutes later, the deputy chief of police emerged from Eridu Kitchen with his arms full of food in takeout containers to bring home. He brought it back to his car, placed it in the passenger seat and closed the door. But instead of going around to the driver's seat and getting in as usual, Enmeana instead walked to a shop a few doors down the street.

Something is happening, David reported. *He just entered Utu's Volumes.*

He was already up, moving closer to get a better view.

He's in the bookstore? asked Jess skeptically. *The one that sells antique physical copies? Enmeana doesn't strike me as the scholarly type.*

No, he doesn't, Amir echoed.

I'm almost at the entrance, said David. *Somchai, do you have any additional info on his location?*

Looks like he headed to the second floor, farther from the entrance, near the windows, Somchai explained.

On it.

David was already almost at the front door, trying hard to move quickly without drawing unnecessary attention to himself.

Jess, maybe you could relocate your shopping to somewhere closer to the front of the building, David directed.

No problem.

Amir, if there's a back exit, cover it for me, David requested.

On my way.

I'll stay where I am, said Catalina. *I can cover for any of you if needed.*

David was at the entrance now. He took a deep breath and let it out as he opened the door, walking in with the calm of an academic who loved to curl up with a good book. He took to the stairs, keeping his eyes open for Enmeana, and spotted his target in the back by the windows, right where Somchai had told him the man would be.

There was a small café upstairs, next to stacks of modern magazines. David casually ordered a taqaffa, which he pretended to enjoy as much as coffee, and thumbed his way through a periodical as he kept an eye on Enmeana.

The deputy chief of police was huddled by some books that were clearly older—not newer reprints. When he looked around suspiciously, David fixed his attention on his hot drink while watching the man in his peripheral vision.

Enmeana just put something into one of the books, David explained.

Do you know what it is? asked Catalina.

Some kind of paper. I assume it's intelligence of some kind, David answered. *But what I really want to see is who comes to get it.*

I guess our evening just got a whole lot more interesting, said Amir.

Yeah. Buckle up, this could be a long one.

David drank down his taqaffa swiftly, even though it was slightly too hot to chug it, and returned the mug to the counter, as was the custom. He didn't want to get hung up on social norms if he had to get up quickly for some reason. Then he paid for one of the magazines and settled in to wait.

****

David didn't have to wait too long. About fifteen minutes later, a man who looked like he wasn't quite well-kempt enough to be buying antique books soon found his way to the same section of books where Dumuzi Enmeana had been moments before. He picked up the book that the note had been placed in and paid for it downstairs with the confidence of someone who had a lot of practice with these types of dead drops.

Jess, our new target is headed your way, David warned. *Average height, medium build, blue shirt, brown pants, disheveled hair— he's got the book in a small yellow bag, and a data pad in his other hand.*

I see him, Jess replied. *He's headed in the opposite direction from Eridu's Kitchen.*

I'll get a drone up, said Somchai.

David had taken his magazine downstairs, showing the receipt on his data pad to the worker at the entrance. He didn't want to lose their mark, but he also didn't want to spook him. Truthfully, he enjoyed this sort of cat-and-mouse action.

Their mystery man walked with purpose, but he'd apparently had enough counterespionage training to glance behind him occasionally. David ducked behind a stall that sold jewelry made from the local rocks. Jess was fully caught up to their new target and was walking alongside him, as if they were just two people organically headed to the same place.

He's about five feet to my left, Somchai, Jess pointed out.

OK, I'm locked onto him now.

After a few minutes, their book-carrying individual turned left. Jess kept walking straight, while David followed the man from a distance. Somchai kept their eye in the sky, while David, Jess, and eventually Amir, who had caught up to them, took turns trailing the man. He ultimately ended up at a dilapidated apartment building in the poor section of town. David watched until he was able to see the number on the door, and then he pulled back to a nearby alleyway and waited for the others.

What is this place? asked David.

These are the housing projects for those who cannot afford rent, answered Jess.

There are so many people living in this one building, commented Amir.

It was very obvious from the large number of children and teenagers hanging around near the entrance that their parents didn't want them in the cramped quarters any longer than they had to be there. Plus, a simple glance into a few of the windows revealed multiple sets of bunk beds in many of the rooms.

Now that we know where our mystery man ended up, I'll get some microdrones in there and see what we can find out, said Somchai.

I'd better report this to Drew and see what he wants us to do.
******

Two Days Later
Garka, Moraga
Orinda System

After the Kites had sent everything they had collected over to Drew, he'd confirmed that the man from the bookstore was on the watchlist as one of the members of the IED insurgent cell. Facial recognition and gait analysis had positively IDed him with ninety-nine point nine percent accuracy and matched him to footage near previously reported incidents.

Somchai had managed to fly a microdrone into the apartment when one of the residents inside had left, and he'd collected additional evidence, including footage of IEDs that were actively in the process of being put together within the apartment.

Then Somchai caught an image of the note that had been passed in the book. It gave a time and date of a planned raid on their safe house—obvious confirmation that Enmeana was in fact passing intelligence on to this group. By morning, the insurgents had packed everything up, wiped everything down, and left. Fortunately, though, Somchai was able to plant a microdrones in one of the bags so that the Kites could track them all down to their new location.

Given all the evidence that the deputy chief of police was in fact communicating with the insurgents, Drew gave the green light for the Kites to "take care" of Dumuzi Enmeana. "Just make sure it looks like an accident," they'd been instructed.

Catalina had noticed that whenever Enmeana took his morning taqaffa break, he flirted with the barista. "That's our in," she insisted.

"Yet another one taken down by the banal desires of man," said Amir with a laugh.

David, Catalina, Somchai, and Jess all eyed each other awkwardly. They all had the benefit of blowing off that kind of steam, but Amir somehow seemed to be content in his singleness.

"We can't all have your level of self-control," David teased.

"Will we get to see you in the red dress again?" asked Somchai with a wink toward Jess. "That's what I really want to know."

"You know it," Jess replied.

****

The Next Morning

Dumuzi Enmeana counted down the minutes until 10 a.m. He was never very productive until after his morning break at Nin Taqaffa.

He stood a little straighter as he marched over to his favorite shop. There was a very attractive young worker behind the counter he'd had his eye on for some time.

If only I could convince my wife that a second partner would be a good idea, he thought to himself. Although second wives were common in Gurista society, some women were not so accommodating of this lifestyle, and Enmeana was sure his spouse would dedicate herself to making the new wife miserable.

Still, a man can enjoy beauty with his eyes, he told himself.

As he did every workday, Enmeana grinned as he approached the counter at Nin Taqaffa at exactly 10:01 a.m. The barista returned his smile, although she was more reserved in her expression, which only made him go even wilder. He liked it when a woman played hard to get.

He didn't even have to place his order at this point—the woman behind the counter just started to make his drink as soon as it was his turn.

Enmeana bantered with her flirtatiously the entire time she prepared his beverage. He wished these breaks could take longer. He tortured himself wondering if she liked him as well.

It's pointless, he reminded himself. *Just enjoy whatever this is in the moment.*

As the barista put his drink on the counter, an extremely attractive woman in a red dress approached him with a worried look on her face.

"Excuse me," she said, "I saw your data pad fall out of your pocket just now." Then she reached down to the floor and picked up his tablet, which he hadn't even realized was missing. Enmeana admired the woman's backside as she bent over.

Man, she might be worth the trouble with the first wife, he thought.

"This is yours, right?" asked the woman.

He took it from her hand and initiated the biometric scan of his face, which unlocked the device. "Yes, that's mine. Thank you," he replied.

"Oh, good," answered the woman in the red dress. "I'd hate for you to lose it." She turned to leave, and Enmeana almost went after her until he realized he hadn't picked up his drink from the counter yet. He grabbed it, said a quick goodbye to the barista, and rushed outside. But the woman in the red dress was nowhere to be seen.

Where in the world could she have disappeared to? he wondered. *She was just here…*

He took a sip of his taqaffa as he looked around. But the mysterious woman was gone.

How have I never seen her before? Enmeana asked himself. *I take my break at the same time every day. Maybe she was just traveling through.*

He sipped his drink as he searched for her a bit more. Enmeana admitted to himself that he was totally hung up on the beautiful new woman he'd met. He hoped he'd be lucky enough to see her again.

When he didn't spot her outside the shop, he reluctantly took his usual route behind the buildings to return to the police headquarters. All the while, he drank his taqaffa more quickly than usual, thinking the mental clarity it brought might help him solve his mystery.

Suddenly, a sharp pain shot down Enmeana's left arm, stopping him in his tracks. Then his chest started to feel as if a large stone was sitting on top of it, crushing him. He grabbed at his chest and fell to his knees, overcome by the pain.

It felt like he couldn't get enough air, and he broke out in a cold sweat. He tried to cry out for help, but he found himself feeling weak and lightheaded. The edges of his vision turned red, and he knew he was about to pass out. He collapsed on the ground, and his drink rolled out of his hand.

The last thought he had was that the woman in the red dress had been some sort of angel of death and that he had been poisoned. But it was too late to do anything about it.

Chapter 13:
Welcome Home

Five Hours Later
Celestia Crown
Sky District—Emerald City

The robotaxi eased to a stop beside the crescent-shaped arrival court, its pavement veined with inlaid titanium and shards of meteorite that shimmered in hypnotic bands of green, blue, and violet. Each step across the surface caught the light differently, as though the ground itself were alive. Ahead, the Celestia Crown rose like a dream—two hundred and sixty-nine stories of crystalline alloy and kinetic glass, shifting in hue with the setting sun. From its base on the Sky District's coastal bluffs, the spire soared above beaches of white sand and weathered stone ridges crowned with bonsai-shaped evergreens.

Amy Dobbs stepped out, civilian jacket folded over one arm. Three and a half years of war had carried her through death and back: through the Gurista liberation, the Serpentis Campaign, and Earth's near fall. Now, at last, she had two weeks of solitude—two weeks to breathe.

Inside, the lobby's sweeping curves framed walls of soft stone and titanium accents, the air touched with the faint scent of white jasmine and ocean salt. The great Sky Atrium—capping the two hundred and sixty-ninth floor—hung above as a transparent dome for stargazing, shielded from the city's glare by adaptive light filters. The Celestia Crown's suites were the stuff of whispered legend, each one a blend of high technology and intimate warmth.

But as she approached the reception desk, the first cracks in her perfect plan appeared.

"I'm sorry, Ms. Dobbs," the receptionist said, repeating herself with careful politeness. "It appears your off-world reservation was delayed in processing. By the time it arrived, the suite was already taken. With the Fleet's return, most of the Sky District's suites are fully booked."

Amy's jaw tightened. "Right now, all I want is to soak in a bath so full of bubbles they spill onto the floor. I want a glass of some impossible-to-pronounce red wine in my hand, and a book I can get lost in until I forget which planet I'm on. Then I'm going to walk to bed and sleep for the next forty-eight hours."

A tall naval officer in dress whites stepped up to the concierge desk, having observed the dilemma. He leaned over, whispering, "Hey, do you know who that woman standing in is?"

The hotel manager next to the concierge looked puzzled. "I'm sorry, Captain. Should I?"

"That's Rear Admiral Amy Dobbs," the officer replied. "She's the Fleet commander who liberated the Gurista people from the Zodarks. She commanded the Serpentis Campaign, and it was her task force that arrived early in Sol and helped save Earth when it was invaded. She's a national hero and a legend."

All at once, recognition struck like a jolt. The manager moved swiftly to her rescue. "Admiral—my apologies. I overheard what happened; this is unacceptable. Allow me to make this right for you." He scanned a holodisplay, grimaced, then looked up with finality. "The Governor's Suite. No charge. Breakfast and dinner included for the duration of your stay."

Amy's brow lifted at the upgrade to her suite. "That's... very generous."

"We are short on rooms, and it seems only fitting for someone of your renown," he said.

The bellhop was already in motion, practically jogging to collect her bags. He guided her to the elevator that would take her into the clouds and to her room. It rose in a silent blur to the two hundred and fifty-second floor, opening onto a suite that sprawled over two enormous bedrooms, spacious marble baths, and an extravagant terrace hanging over the coastline like a private sky. The living spaces curved with the tower's arc, floor-to-ceiling glass giving an unbroken view of ocean and city. Adaptive wall panels shifted to a soft candlelit glow, while a holo fireplace cast real warmth into the air.

Amy stood for a long moment in the entryway, her shoulders easing for the first time in years. "AI assistant," she said quietly, "ready the bubble bath. And tell the sommelier to bring the best red they've got—the one I can't pronounce."

****

Steam curled in lazy ribbons above the bath's surface, the air rich with the scent of lavender and sandalwood. The oval tub, carved from a single block of pale stone, cradled her body in weightless comfort. Outside the floor-to-ceiling glass, night had draped itself over Emerald City, the coastline traced in jeweled lights.

Amy let her head rest against the warm edge, eyes half closed as the AI assistant dimmed the room's lighting to a golden twilight. A book hovered in a soft holo above her knees, words drifting by at her chosen pace. Beside the tub, a crystal glass of deep red wine glinted under the soft light—its name unpronounceable, its taste velvety and sharp all at once.

For the first time in what felt like forever, there were no fleet reports, no battle maps, no casualty lists. Just silence, warmth, and the slow release of a life lived too long at war.

She took another sip, sinking deeper into the bubbles. *Two weeks*, she thought. *Mine.*

****

November 23, 2115
Fort Roughneck
New Eden

The autoshuttle hummed quietly as it wound its way through the pine-lined perimeter road of Fort Roughneck. The sun hung low, painting the clouds in streaks of amber and gold, the kind of light that softened the edges of everything it touched. Brigadier General Brian Royce sat rigid in his seat, beret folded in his lap, dress jacket draped over his arm. He'd faced down Zodark gun batteries and stalked enemy cities under cover of night without a flinch—but the thought of walking through his own front door for the first time in three and a half years had his chest tight and his pulse quick.

The shuttle slowed as the neat rows of officer housing came into view—identical white-trimmed homes set back from the street, manicured lawns edged by narrow gardens. Royce's was near the end of the row, a modest two-story with the same dark stone facade as the others. The difference was the porch light, glowing like a beacon.

He stepped out before the shuttle fully settled, boots crunching on the path. The front door swung open before he reached it.

Jane stood there.

For a moment, neither moved. She wore her hair shorter now, falling just above her shoulders, but her eyes were the same—those deep brown eyes that had stared back at him over grainy video calls and kept him tethered through the worst nights.

Then she was running.

He caught her midstep, her arms locking around his neck, her face pressed into his shoulder. The faint scent of her shampoo—lilac and something warm—hit him like a sucker punch, and suddenly the war, the noise, the steel corridors of ships felt very far away.

"I missed you," she whispered, voice cracking.

"I missed you more," he said, pulling back just enough to see her smile through tears.

"Daddy?"

The small voice turned his head. Molly stood in the doorway, barefoot, her hair a little longer, a little wavier than he remembered. She had been five when he'd left; now she was almost nine, her face a blend of the girl he remembered and the young woman she'd eventually become. She hesitated, as if unsure whether to run to him.

Brian dropped to one knee and held out his arms. "Come here, kiddo."

She bolted forward, slamming into him with enough force to rock him back. He held her tight, eyes stinging. "Look at you," he murmured, pulling back just enough to see her face. "You've grown half a foot, easy. And"—his voice caught—"you've got your mom's smile."

Molly beamed, wiping at her cheeks. "You're home for good?"

He glanced at Jane, then back to Molly. "For now, I'm home for two whole weeks. That's all ours, OK?"

A small sound drew his attention—a soft coo, then a curious little laugh. Jane shifted, and Brian realized she wasn't standing alone. Cradled against her hip was a boy maybe thirty inches tall, with a tuft of dark hair sticking up at odd angles and big, steady eyes studying him like he was some new species.

Brian's throat tightened. "Henry," he said softly.

Jane stepped closer, and the boy reached out with chubby fingers. Brian hesitated, afraid the moment might break if he moved too quickly. Jane eased Henry toward him, and Brian took his son for the first time. The boy was warm, heavier than he'd imagined, his tiny hand gripping the edge of Brian's uniform sleeve.

"Hey, buddy," Brian whispered, voice low and reverent. "I'm your dad."

Henry blinked at him, then let out a laugh—bright and unguarded. Brian smiled, tears slipping free. "Yeah," he said, kissing the top of his son's head. "That's what I thought."

They stood there in the fading light, the four of them—no speeches, no salutes, no urgency of orders—just the quiet, fragile peace of a family made whole again, if only for a little while.

Jane touched his arm. "Come inside. Dinner's almost ready."

Brian followed her in, Henry still in his arms, Molly wrapped around his leg like she might never let go. The door shut behind them, and for the first time in years, the war felt like it was on the other side of the galaxy.

****

Later That Night
Fort Roughneck

The house was quiet now. Molly had fallen asleep on the couch halfway through a movie, head resting on Jane's lap, while Henry was already down in his crib upstairs. Brian had carried his daughter to bed, tucking her in under the soft quilt Jane's mother had made, before returning to the kitchen.

He sat at the table, one hand wrapped around a mug of coffee that had long since gone lukewarm. Jane moved around the kitchen with practiced ease, collecting plates, sliding leftovers into storage containers. The overhead light caught the gold in her hair and the fine lines at the corners of her eyes—lines that hadn't been there before he left.

"It's strange," Jane said after a moment, wiping her hands on a towel, "having you here again. Feels like I've been holding my breath for three years, and now I'm afraid to let it out."

Brian met her gaze. "I know the feeling."

She sat across from him, leaning on her elbows. "How long until you have to go back?"

He hesitated. "They're talking about four months. Could be longer... could be less. We won't know until we start lining up the pieces.

It's going to take everything we have—the *Freedom*, the Fleet, the Army—and that's before we even talk about getting the Humtars to loan us a stealth ship for Royce's little…'excursion.'"

Jane smirked faintly. "Royce's little excursion?"

"Let's just say it's the kind of mission where you pack light and don't expect to be home for dinner."

Her smile faded into something softer, more searching. "I'm proud of you. I just…" She shook her head. "I don't want the war to take any more of you than it already has."

Brian reached across the table, covering her hand with his. "It's taken enough. But right now, for these two weeks…it's not getting a damn thing."

They sat there for another minute, the quiet settling like a warm blanket. Jane squeezed his hand, then stood, tugging him gently to his feet.

"Come on, General," she said with a knowing smile. "You've got two weeks. Let's not waste tonight talking about the war."

Brian let her lead him down the hall, the lights dimming automatically behind them.

****

The Next Morning
Governor's Suite
Celestia Crown
Sky District, Emerald City

The first light of dawn spilled across the terrace, refracted through the glass walls in soft bands of amber and rose. Amy Dobbs stirred beneath the weightless warmth of the soft gray bedding, the distant hush of waves far below mixing with the faint hum of the building's systems. For a moment, she didn't move—just lay there, eyes half open, letting the quiet sink into her bones.

The suite's AI assistant, voice low and cultured, broke the silence.

"Good morning, Admiral Dobbs. Would you care for breakfast in bed?"

Amy's lips curved into a smile before she opened her eyes fully. "That would be amazing."

"Very good. Ten minutes."

She rolled onto her back, staring up at the slow swirl of adaptive ceiling lights mimicking the colors of the sunrise. A part of her still expected to be jolted awake by an urgent comms chime or the vibration of an incoming priority message. But it didn't come. Not here. Not today.

Exactly ten minutes later, a gentle chime sounded at the suite's entrance. "Your breakfast has arrived," the AI assistant announced.

The double doors to the bedroom slid open, and a synthetic humanoid butler entered with fluid precision, pushing a brushed-titanium service cart. The scent of fresh coffee drifted ahead of it—rich, dark, and exactly the way she liked it. A crystal carafe of freshly squeezed orange juice caught the sunlight, scattering golden flecks across the polished floor.

Without a word, the synthetic positioned the cart at her bedside and began to unfurl the breakfast with elegant efficiency. First came the lap table, extending across her knees with a smooth click. Then the plates—fluffy eggs crowned with fresh herbs, crisp breakfast pastries still warm from the oven, and a selection of seasonal fruits arranged like art.

Finally, the butler poured her coffee, adding the precise amount of cream and sugar before setting the cup gently into her waiting hands.

Amy took the first sip, closing her eyes briefly as the warmth spread through her. It was almost absurd, this level of care and quiet. But after everything, it felt…deserved.

"This," she murmured to herself, "is too good to be true."

****

Fort Roughneck

Soft morning light filtered through the curtains, painting the bedroom in a pale gold haze. Brian stirred at the sound of light footsteps—quick, eager, and utterly uncoordinated. The mattress dipped on one side, then the other, as two small bodies clambered under the covers.

Molly pressed herself against his side, hair smelling faintly of strawberry shampoo. Henry, all warm limbs and soft weight, wriggled between them and promptly laid his head on Brian's chest with a sigh that seemed far too big for such a small person.

For half a second, instinct kicked in—he had the sudden jolt of being startled from sleep. But then he opened his eyes, saw his kids' faces, and all the tension melted away.

Jane was propped on one elbow, smiling at him over the tangle of blankets and small bodies. He reached for her, pulling her close until they were all in a loose knot of warmth.

Brian closed his eyes again, breathing in the mix of his children's scent—a blend of sleep, soap, and something indefinably home—and the steady, grounding presence of Jane beside him.

For the first time in years, there was no urgency, no orders, no clock ticking down to deployment. Just this.

He squeezed Jane's hand under the covers, held his family close, and let himself simply savor the moment.
****

Two Days Later
Fort Roughneck

The midday sun slanted over the backyard, painting the grass in warm, honeyed light. A faint breeze carried the smell of grilled chicken and rosemary from the patio, mixing with the sweetness of blooming jasmine along the fence line.

Brian stood at the grill in a faded Republic Army T-shirt, tongs in one hand, a cold beer in the other. His boots were off, bare feet planted in the grass, toes curling into the earth like he was trying to memorize the feel of it. After years of steel decks, red dust, and scorched ground, it felt like home in a way nothing else could.

Molly was in the middle of the yard, twirling in the summer air with a kite that had absolutely no business flying. Her laughter rang out every time it dipped and wobbled dangerously before catching the wind again.

Henry sat on the deck, surrounded by a chaotic perimeter of brightly colored blocks. Every so often, he'd hold up a misshapen tower to show Jane, who sat cross-legged beside him, pretending to gasp in awe as if it were the most important engineering feat in human history.

Brian flipped the chicken and glanced toward the house. The kitchen door was propped open, music drifting out—one of Jane's old playlists from before he'd left. It was the kind of thing they used to put on while cooking together, dancing around the kitchen, stealing bites off the spoons as they mixed.

"Dad! Dad, watch this!" Molly called, breaking his reverie.

Brian turned just in time to see her trip over the kite string, go sprawling in the grass, and pop up again, giggling.

"Nice recovery!" he called back, grinning.

Jane looked over her shoulder at him, sunlight catching her hair. "You know she's going to want you to fly that thing with her after lunch."

"Good," he said, eyes still on Molly. "I was hoping she would."

They ate outside, passing dishes around the table, Molly talking a mile a minute about school and friends, Henry smearing mashed sweet potato on his cheeks in a determined effort to feed himself. Brian listened, asked questions, and let himself get lost in the mundane rhythm of it. There were no reports to file, no deployments to plan—just his daughter arguing over who got the last grilled drumstick and his wife slipping her bare foot against his under the table.

Afterward, they sprawled in the grass, watching clouds drift overhead. Molly insisted one looked like a starship; Henry was convinced another was a dog. Jane laughed and leaned her head on Brian's shoulder, and he wrapped an arm around her, the other pulling both kids closer until they were all piled together.

He didn't say it out loud, but the thought settled deep in his chest: *This is it. This is why I go back. So they can have this.*

Chapter 14:
The Fear of Death

Republic Neurocognitive Recovery Center
Alliance City, New Eden

Dr. Alan Walburg found Tannel in the garden atrium, painting.

The awakened Orbot stood before a canvas mounted on a reinforced easel, his mechanical frame steady despite the hitch in his front left leg. Metal clicked faintly with each weight shift.

Sam worked beside him, the C200's optical scanner sweeping cobalt blue across the canvas. The two painted in silence, brushes moving in synchronized rhythms.

Walburg paused at the entrance. The scene felt too peaceful to disrupt with talk of war. But he didn't have a choice.

"Tannel," he called, stepping onto the stone pathway. "Got a minute?"

The former Orbot set down his brush without speaking. Sam continued painting, though his optic band dimmed.

Walburg crossed the atrium, boots scuffing decorative stonework. He stopped three feet away, hands shoved into his lab coat pockets.

"I need to talk about something important."

Tannel's head tilted, metal plates along his jaw catching light. His dark brown eyes met Walburg's. "You're worried," he said.

"Yes." Walburg exhaled. "The war with the Zodarks is winding down. We're winning. But I've been thinking about what comes next—what happens when we're pulled into the Gallentines' war against the Collective."

Tannel's head angled slightly. "You're worried about Legion."

"I am." Walburg stepped closer. "The Collective has been fighting the Gallentines for centuries through Legion proxies. They have the same advantage you had—resurrection, endless reinforcements. When this war with the Zodarks ends, we'll face them. And I don't know if we can win."

Tannel was quiet for a long moment. His brow furrowed, then smoothed. "You defeated us."

"We got lucky," Walburg said. "The kill switch, the regeneration ships—"

"No," Tannel interrupted softly. "You were brilliant. You did something we never thought possible."

Walburg frowned. "What do you mean?"

Tannel's gaze drifted to his mechanical legs, then back to Walburg.

"You reminded us that death could return."

"I don't understand."

"The Republic found a way to strip us of our perceived immortality," Tannel explained. "Our resurrection ships, our data centers. Unlike the Altairians and Primords before you, the Republic didn't try to fight us head-on. Instead, you looked at our ability to resurrect and asked a simple question—how could you stop it?"

Tannel's voice remained steady, clinical. "That became an engineering problem. Once you understood our architecture, you didn't need to kill every Orbot soldier. You just needed to destroy the infrastructure that made us immortal."

Walburg nodded slowly. "The regeneration ships and vaults were your network."

"Exactly," Tannel said. "Our consciousness transfers depended on proximity—on being within range of our relay grid. When one of us died inside our territory, the nearest ship or data vault caught the transmission and restored it. But if we were too far from that network— out of range—our signal decayed, unrecoverable. That's why we carried regeneration ships into battle. They acted as roaming towers, keeping the network alive."

He set his brush down and folded his arms. "I don't think the Collective use a system like that. At least, not as we understand it."

Walburg's brow furrowed. "That's interesting that you say that. So if they don't, how do you think they maintain continuity? They can't possibly have ships everywhere."

"You are right, and I suspect they don't need them either," Tannel said. "If I were designing an improved system—and the Collective has had millennia to perfect theirs—I would use something like a quantum lattice. We were still researching this kind of technology when the Republic defeated us. But I believe that inside of each Legion body, there's a quantum transceiver, constantly entangled with a larger network that spans their territory. That would mean no range limitation, and no dependence on ships or towers. It's the equivalent of a satellite network that never loses coverage."

Walburg blinked. "Wait a second. So you're saying every Legion unit is essentially permanently 'in-network' with something like this?"

"Yes," Tannel said. "They could die anywhere and still transmit their consciousness back to their core systems instantly, or nearly so. For us, the limitation was distance and signal degradation. For them, it's synchronization—maintaining quantum coherence across millions of nodes. That's their strength—and their vulnerability."

Walburg leaned forward slightly. "Vulnerability?"

Tannel's eyes met his. "If their continuity depends on a quantum lattice, then interference in that lattice could sever their resurrection chain. It's only a theory—I don't know their exact architecture—but every entangled system has maintenance cycles, correction windows, synchronization pulses. Disrupt those, and you create desynchronization, maybe even irreversible loss of pattern. I suspect the Gallentines have probably theorized about this as well. But even if they did figure it out, they lack two critical things in order to use it against the Collective: the ability to reach the Collective's core territory, and the stealth to survive there long enough to study their communication lattice and introduce whatever would cause the degradation."

"Huh, that actually makes sense," Walburg said quietly. "I can definitely see why they'd have to map the Collective's systems firsthand. No simulation could account for the kind of adaptive algorithms the Collective uses."

"My point exactly," Tannel said. "You'd need infiltration—probes or stealth ships capable of slipping deep into their territory without triggering their defensive grid. You'd have to find their core transmission network, measure how their consciousness transfer occurs, and identify the timing windows when error correction is weakest. Until someone can do that, the Collective remains untouchable."

Walburg rubbed the bridge of his nose. "So that's the problem—the theory exists, but no one can test it."

Tannel inclined his head. "Yes. But if your Humtar allies are as advanced as I've heard, their quantum technology might finally make testing it possible."

That thought struck Walburg like an electrical jolt. The Humtars' sensor lattice, their stealth drives, their quantum research—they could conceivably do it.

He stepped back, realization spreading like wildfire through his mind. "If you're right—if this lattice exists—we might have a path forward. But we'd need the Humtars to verify it, to see if it's even detectable."

Tannel said nothing, his expression unreadable.

Walburg pulled out his Qpad and keyed in a secure line to the Viceroy's Office. "This is Walburg," he said, voice tight. "Priority Alpha. I need an immediate meeting with Viceroy Hunt. Tell him it concerns a possible vulnerability in the Collective's resurrection network. I might have found a way to defeat them."

He listened to the voice on the other end and nodded sharply. "Yes. Today, if possible."

He ended the call and stood motionless, his mind spinning through the implications.

Behind him, Tannel returned to his painting. Sam hadn't moved, his optic band glowing amber as he watched Walburg with something close to concern.

****

Fourteen minutes later, the comm pinged.

"Dr. Walburg, this is Commander Rhys from the Viceroy's Office. Your Priority Alpha request has been approved. Meeting scheduled for 1400 hours at the Enclave. Humtar leadership will attend."

Walburg's breath caught. "The Humtars? Already?"

"Admiral Vesharuk was already scheduled to meet with Viceroy Hunt. Your request was expedited onto the agenda. Bring whatever you have."

"Understood."

The line went dead.

Walburg turned back to Tannel and Sam. Both had stopped painting.

"Well," Walburg said, "looks like I'm meeting with the Humtars this afternoon."

Sam's scanner brightened. "Will you require our presence?"

Walburg hesitated. Bringing a former Orbot and a synthetic humanoid before Humtar military leadership bordered on madness—but Tannel's strategic insight and Sam's modeling abilities were irreplaceable.

"Yes," Walburg said finally. "Both of you. They'll need to hear it from you directly."

Tannel set his palette down carefully, paint smearing across metal fingers. "Then we should prepare," he said. "They'll want specifics—node estimates, synchronization assumptions, potential points of decoherence."

Walburg nodded. "Even if it's theoretical, they'll want the math."

Tannel inclined his head. "For the Orbot system, the synchronization gap was roughly two hundred relay nodes. For the Collective? I'd estimate double, maybe more. Hundreds of trunk points, each operating within a narrow coherence window. The trick would be to strike them all before their adaptive systems compensate."

Walburg felt the weight of it settle. "And to find them first."

"Yes," Tannel said. "That's what your allies will have to solve. I don't even think the Gallentines have found their home system yet."

Walburg stared out through the glass dome of the atrium, watching the afternoon light spill across Alliance City. Somewhere out there, Viceroy Hunt and Admiral Vesharuk were preparing for a meeting that could change the course of the war.

And in three hours, they'd learn that the key to ending the Collective's immortality might lie not in a weapon—but in a theory born from an enemy who understood the fear of death better than anyone alive.

Resurrection isn't magic, Walburg thought. *It's network physics. And every network has a point of failure.*

He just hoped the Humtars could find it.

Chapter 15:
Architects of Mortality

The Enclave, Humtar Compound
New Eden

Dr. Zeralleh Myrathi arrived at the conference room twenty minutes early. It was an old habit. Being early meant she could prepare the room first—check the sightlines, own the tempo.

The chamber crowned the Central Research Tower, a lens of smart glass and quiet air above gardens cut into fractal pathways. From this height, geometry looked alive: tessellated beds, crystalline fountains, symmetry made into comfort. The space hummed softly; a cooling loop whispered through the walls.

She set her data pad on the polished table and reopened the briefing: Orbot 001—Technical Consultation. The summary sat in her mind like an elephant. The Orbots had been the Dominion's blade; a volunteer immortality with upload loops and resurrection ships—until the Republic broke the loop. Tannel—once a leader among them—was here to help aim that logic at the Collective.

The door chimed.

"Enter," she said.

Dr. Alan Walburg stepped in first—wired, under-slept, moving like a problem had finally given him its shape. A C200 synthetic in a Republic uniform followed, the optic band sweeping a steady amber line. Sam. Then Tannel, taller than she expected: human torso marked with old scars, cybernetics threaded like quiet lightning beneath the skin; below the waist, four spiderlike legs clicked softly, favoring the right.

"Dr. Myrathi," Walburg said, offering his hand. "Thank you for seeing us. We think this is actionable."

"We'll see," Zeralleh answered, shaking once. She nodded to Sam and Tannel. "Welcome to the Enclave. The others are en route."

The door whisked open again: Dr. Iskandor Thalvek with a comet's bright focus, Captain Lyrana Dovrek—Strategic Intelligence, eyes like sensor arrays—and Admiral Veydris Korrath, who carried command like gravity. Korrath halted a beat when he saw Tannel. Not fear. Something colder. Revulsion disciplined into neutrality. He took his seat without comment.

"You were once among the Orbot leadership," Thalvek said, curiosity unmasked.

"For a time," Tannel answered.

"And you chose this?" Korrath asked, chin indicating the chassis.

"I did," Tannel said. "We believed transcendence was evolution."

Korrath's jaw flexed. Zeralleh cut a line through the tension. "Admiral, we can take history later. Today we need the mechanism."

Walburg stepped forward. "Tannel will describe how the Orbots sustained continuity and why we surrendered. It leads to a theory about the Collective."

Korrath folded his hands. "You have my attention."

Tannel settled at the table; servos hissed and locked. Sam remained standing, scanner trained on the holofield.

"The Orbots controlled fourteen systems," Tannel began, voice level. "We fought without fear of permanent loss. Consciousness uploaded to vaults, stored, redeployed into new frames via regeneration ships: die, return, repeat. The Republic ended that not by killing bodies, but by destroying the infrastructure that made death reversible."

"Regeneration flotillas and the vault links," Dovrek said.

"Yes," Tannel replied. "When the last ships fell and the vault lattice fragmented, we faced finality. We chose to live."

"And the Collective?" Zeralleh asked.

Tannel lifted his gaze. "They likely solved the range problem we never did. If I were designing their system, I would use a quantum lattice—transceivers in Legion frames entangled to a regional backbone. That would mean no roaming ships, and no dead zones. In essence, it would be like a satellite network that never loses coverage. I don't claim for certainty this is how they have designed their system; this is deduction. But it fits their behavior."

Thalvek leaned in. "Hmm. Always in-network, huh?"

"Exactly," Tannel confirmed. "Their constraint would then shift from distance to synchronization—maintaining coherence across millions of nodes. Every entangled architecture has maintenance cycles—syndrome checks, commit windows, correction budgets. If you disrupt those at scale, you don't degrade gracefully. You fall off a cliff. Decoherence saturation. Irreversible loss of pattern."

Korrath's pen scratched once. "So, not static—poison."

"Right," Tannel said. "If my theory holds, you must inject basis-targeted noise during commit windows across enough trunks that error correction cannot keep up. I expect hundreds of injection points, synchronized within a single global envelope—tens of seconds at most. However, it remains a theory until someone maps their backbone."

Dovrek's glance slid to Zeralleh, then to Thalvek. A quiet current passed between them.

Thalvek cleared his throat. "Tannel, hypothetically, if one had... partial maps of a lattice, would your constraints still hold?"

"They're architectural," Tannel said. "Maps improve aim. The physics doesn't change."

Zeralleh touched the table. There was a soft chime; a restricted overlay appeared holographically above them—washed, anonymized, not labeled, but clear enough for a trained eye. There was a skeletal crown of arcs around a star and clustered repeaters, tethers like faint nerves.

Walburg's breath bit the air. "Is that—?"

"It is not leaving this room," Dovrek said, voice even but iron-lined. "Consider it context."

Zeralleh's tone stayed calm, precise. "We call it the Arc-Net. We have eyes on Neythar Nexus. We have been studying emission masking, thermal management, and something that looks very much like a trunk/repeater architecture. Your theory aligns with observations we have not yet published."

Tannel did not move. "Then you have what the Gallentines lack—access."

"And stealth," Dovrek added. "Shadowfang frames are already threading the periphery. Our probes can sit on tethers without tripping perimeter heuristics—for hours, sometimes days."

Thalvek added another layer to the hologram. Clusters of glowing dots blinked in steady patterns, thin lines flashing between them. "These repeating pulses—they might be the moments when the Collective's network saves data," he said. "If that's true, we can figure out the right time to strike."

Walburg swallowed. "You can test this."

Zeralleh's eyes lit up with understanding. "We can test this without the Collective ever knowing," she said. "We've already built devices that shake energy fields to check how steady their repeaters are. If we flip how they work, they could become tools that break the network instead of studying it. What we were missing was the right kind of static to overload their system—and proof that our idea wasn't just a wild guess."

She looked at Tannel. "Your theory gives us both."

Korrath looked from the holo to Tannel, then to Walburg. "Numbers."

Tannel inclined his head. "For Orbot infrastructure, approximately relay strikes collapsed our loop. For a lattice like this, I estimate two to five hundred trunk nodes must be hit inside one global syndrome window—probably less than thirty seconds—so adaptive routing can't breathe. Miss the envelope, and you'd get bruises, not a break."

Thalvek was already drawing glowing symbols in the air. "We've found two old Humtar-style bases still running on the edges of the Collective's network, which would have compatible coding," he said. "If those same codes exist deeper inside, we can use them as a doorway to corrupt the system from within."

"It's still theory," Tannel said gently. "My certainty stops at the Orbot edge."

"Understood," Zeralleh replied. "The classification problem is ours."

Dovrek's voice went cool. "Operationally, we will need to map all trunks servicing Chor'vyn's buffers, identify commit cadence, pre-position injectors, and line up tether cutters for Arc-Net denial. Then we trigger, verify collapse in real time, and move to purge backups."

Sam raised his hand, and a small holographic device appeared above his palm—shaped like a glowing diamond. "These are consciousness-trace analyzers," he explained. "We can hook them to your scout probes so they can watch the Collective's network as it fails. That way, you'll know for sure when their system is breaking apart—instead of having to guess."

Thalvek smiled despite himself. "At last, instrumentation."

Korrath straightened. "Risk?"

"Detection," Dovrek said. "If we over-instrument, we get swarmed. If we under-instrument, we guess wrong. And if we trip a repair wave, they'll reconfigure the lattice and we start from zero."

"We can stage from dark perches," Zeralleh said. "Statite shells, sail-trimmed. Minimal emissions. We've done it already." She looked to Walburg. "Your theory gives us cause. Your tools give us measurement. Together, we have a path to make them mortal."

The silence sat in the room, heavy instead of empty.

"This isn't just a battle plan," Dovrek said, voice low. "It could be an extinction event if we take it to conclusion."

Korrath didn't flinch. "Then our politics must be cleaner than our engineering." He faced Walburg, Sam, and Tannel. "We want you embedded—full access to our labs and to Intelligence Fusion. We move as one team."

Walburg didn't hesitate. "We're in."

Sam's optic band pulsed. Tannel's mechanical legs clicked once on the floor, a sound like a period at the end of a sentence. "We will help you build it," Tannel said. "And help you know when to stop."

Zeralleh rose. "We start now. Iskandor—partition a clean room for basis-poisoning spectra. Captain—task Shadowfang to widen trunk cadence capture. Admiral—coordinate with Veydris Station for tether-cutter staging and denial munitions. Dr. Walburg, Sam, Tannel—Enclave Lab Six. You'll like the humidity; it keeps the cryo lines honest."

They filed into the corridor together. The tower's hum tripled near the secure elevators; the air smelled faintly of ionized metal and citrus solvent. Korrath walked a pace behind Tannel, posture guarded, respect warring with an old disgust. Zeralleh watched the Orbot's gait—deliberate, unhurried, precise—and caught the smallest tilt of his head toward the garden below.

He'd once been the weapon that made mortality optional. Now he was here to help write the geometry that would return mortality to those who had forgotten it.

Irony, sharpened into utility, she thought.

As the lift doors closed, Thalvek murmured, almost to himself, "Poison the basis, break the world."

Zeralleh answered without looking up. "No. Poison the basis, give them a choice." She glanced at Walburg. "And make sure we have the tools to live with either answer."

The elevator sank toward the secure wing, cool air pooling around their ankles, the future tightening into a plan.

Chapter 16:
Shwani Reconnaissance

November 27, 2115
CNS *Bloodhawk*
Varkorion System – Zodark Territory

The *Bloodhawk* erupted from the quantum conduit bridge into enemy space.

"Contact!" Lieutenant Liraen Voskei's voice cut through the bridge. "Zodark battleship, bearing two-seven-zero. Range—three thousand kilometers!"

Every muscle on the bridge froze. Three thousand kilometers— knife-fight range in space combat.

"Status of stealth systems?" Captain Calvus Theruun's voice stayed level, but his knuckles whitened on the command rail.

"Coming online now." Lieutenant Deyth Carruvin's fingers flew across his helm console. "Ten seconds to full veil."

The tactical display bloomed red. A Zodark battleship, fresh from its own stargate transit, hung massive against the stars. Its sensor arrays were already deploying, sweeping outward in expanding cones of detection.

"Five seconds," Carruvin whispered.

The enemy's active sensors washed over their position. On the display, the detection wave approached like a tsunami of light.

"Three... two..."

Theruun felt his heart beat in his throat. If those sensors locked on before—

"Veil active. We're invisible," Chief Petty Officer Selith Drayn confirmed from her ECM station.

The sensor wave passed through them. The bridge held its collective breath as the battleship's arrays continued their sweep, finding nothing but empty space where the *Bloodhawk* hung motionless.

Minutes crawled by. The Zodark vessel adjusted its heading, its massive bulk sliding past them toward the inner system. Only when it reached fifty thousand kilometers did Theruun finally exhale.

"Silent running. Now," he ordered. "Carruvin, minimal thrust. Get us clear."

The ship crept forward on whispers of ionized gas. Beneath his boots, Theruun felt the reactor throttle down to stealth configuration—primary output minimized, secondary grids absorbing every emission.

"PELS array deployment?" he asked once they'd gained distance.

"Ready, Captain," Voskei reported, hands steadier now. "Permission to ping?"

"Granted. One burst only."

The pulse flashed out and died. Data flooded back.

"Immediate space clear. No additional contacts within two million kilometers."

Theruun nodded. "Shan, begin full system survey. If something is breathing in this system, I want to know about it."

"OSA spinning up," Lieutenant Velora Shan's fingers danced across her station. "Gravitational mapping initiated. Quantum signatures incoming."

Beside her, Captain Lyrana Dovrek leaned in, studying the cascading data streams. When Admiral Korrath had redirected their mission to gather intelligence on the Zodark Empire, Dovrek had volunteered to accompany them. They'd be collecting massive amounts of data, and having a senior analyst aboard would prove invaluable. Theruun had initially balked at having brass looking over his shoulder, but after watching Dovrek work alongside Shan in the fusion intel cell, he had to admit she'd already proven her worth.

The Varkorion system revealed itself layer by layer. Two habitable worlds glowed green-blue around a yellow-white star. Orbital platforms ringed both planets—shipyards burning bright in thermal, construction gantries stretching like metal webs.

"Traffic analysis complete," Voskei reported. "Merchant convoys, courier packets, military patrols—heavy presence throughout. Patrol patterns suggest…Captain, they're running search grids."

"Confirmed," Shan added. "Electromagnetic signatures indicate active scanning across all major shipping lanes. They're looking for something."

"Or someone," Lieutenant Torvek Naalor growled from weapons. "Electronic warfare suite holding steady. We remain undetected."

Carruvin adjusted their trajectory by fractions, sliding them into a moon's sensor shadow. "Military composition includes frigates, cruisers, multiple battleships, and—" He paused. "Confirmed star carrier in polar orbit around the second planet."

"Groff signatures?" Theruun asked, though he suspected the answer.

Dovrek's expression darkened as she studied her tactical display. "Affirmative. Transmission intercepts match Republic intelligence. This is their nest."

The weight of it settled over the bridge. The Groff were architects of fear, masters of Zodark internal security. Detection here meant more than death. It meant dissection, interrogation, every secret of the *Bloodhawk* and the Confederation laid bare.

"Estimated shipbuilding capacity?" Theruun pressed.

"Based on thermal output and construction signatures..." Shan's voice trailed off. "Thirty percent of total Zodark production. Minimum. This system is a forge."

Theruun studied the display. They'd infiltrated the enemy's industrial heart and slipped past their watchers by mere seconds. The mission parameters were clear—survey, document, and survive. But knowing the Groff operated from here added layers of risk he hadn't fully calculated.

"Helm, take us deeper. Approach vector to Shwani, maximum stealth protocols."

"Aye, Captain. Adjusting course," Carruvin confirmed.

The *Bloodhawk* crept forward through the enemy's domain. Behind them, the Zodark battleship continued its patrol, unaware of the ghost that had slipped past its sensors. Ahead, Shwani grew on their displays—a world wrapped in orbital fortresses and patrol routes.

Minutes stretched into hours. The bridge crew worked in near silence, each movement precise, each breath measured. This was the hunter's art—patience carved from necessity, silence born from survival.

"Approaching Shwani orbital perimeter," Carruvin finally announced. "Holding at maximum passive sensor range."

Theruun leaned forward, studying the planet that filled their main display. Somewhere down there lay intelligence that could help end this war. They just had to stay invisible long enough to find it.

"Begin detailed reconnaissance sweep," he ordered. "Let's see what secrets the Groff are hiding."
****

The reconnaissance sweep unfolded like a nightmare carved in metal and stone.

"Captain, you need to see this." Voskei's voice carried a note of disbelief. "The defensive grid around Shwani… it's unlike anything in our projections."

Theruun stepped closer to the tactical display as the data resolved. Massive asteroids hung in precisely calculated orbits around the planet—not natural formations, but relocated fortresses. Each one bristled with weapon emplacements that glowed hot in their thermal imaging.

"Analysis confirms turbo laser batteries, missile clusters, and…" Naalor paused, double-checking his readings. "Plasma torpedo launchers. Triple-redundant targeting arrays on each platform."

"How many platforms?" Theruun asked, though he could already count them multiplying across the display.

"Forty-seven asteroid fortresses in primary defensive positions," Shan reported. "Another twenty-three in secondary rings. And that's just what we can detect passively."

Carruvin gave a low whistle. "Look at that planetoid at grid reference seven-three-nine. The entire surface has been converted into… is that a starfighter base?"

The display zoomed, revealing a small moon transformed into a military installation. Launch bays pocked its surface like a honeycomb, maintenance gantries stretching between them. Even as they watched, patrol craft emerged and disappeared in practiced formations.

"A conservative estimate puts fighter capacity at three thousand craft," Dovrek noted, her analyst's mind already calculating. "This isn't just defended—it's a fortress system. Even a full Humtar battle group would struggle here."

Theruun absorbed the implications. The shipyards sprawled across both orbital and surface installations, a century's worth of infrastructure woven into an industrial web. Fabrication plants fed assembly lines that fed fitting yards that launched warships in endless procession. The Republic intelligence had vastly underestimated Varkorion's importance.

"There." Shan pointed to a structure on Shwani's primary continent. "Electromagnetic signature matches our intelligence profile for Groff headquarters. Massive data throughput, quantum-encrypted communications, and…" She leaned forward. "They're running an open node. Probably for local planetary traffic, but—"

"But we can slip through the back door," Drayn finished, already working her console. "Give me ten minutes, and I'll have us inside their network."

"Do it," Theruun ordered. "Passive infiltration only. We can't risk detection."

While Drayn worked her electronic warfare magic, Theruun found himself thinking of The Proving again. His vorthak prey had circled him for hours, testing, probing, looking for weakness, just as they now circled the Groff's digital defenses, searching for that one moment of vulnerability.

"I'm in," Drayn announced. "Routing through their civilian traffic to mask our presence. Fusion intel cell now has access."

Shan and Dovrek's stations erupted with data streams of files, communications, and personnel records. The Groff's secrets were spilling across their screens in cascading waves.

"Khalas of the void," Dovrek breathed. "They have files on every Republic commander. They know their enemy better than the Republic knows itself."

"Keep downloading," Theruun ordered. "Get everything you can grab."

Minutes passed in tense silence, broken only by the soft hum of systems and occasional status updates. Then Dovrek straightened, her expression sharp.

"Captain, I've found something. There's an encrypted communiqué between Director Vak'Atioth and his Laktish, Heltet." She transferred it to the main display.

Theruun read the translated text, his pulse quickening. "They're discussing Zon Otro's leadership. This is—"

"A conspiracy," Shan finished. "They're planning to challenge his position as Zon of the High Council. Look at this passage—they cite his 'failures against the primitive humans' as justification."

Theruun's mind raced through possibilities. If they could somehow feed this paranoia, exploit the fractures already forming in Zodark leadership...the Republic might not need to defeat the Zodark military if the Empire tore itself apart from within.

"Download everything related to this conspiracy," he ordered. "Cross-reference with—"

"Captain!" Voskei's sharp interruption cut through his thoughts. "Launch detection from the fighter base. Squadron strength—twelve Glaives, twenty-four Vultures. Heading...no...they're vectoring toward our position."

The bridge froze. On the display, the fighter formation swept outward from the planetoid in a search pattern that would bring them dangerously close to the *Bloodhawk*'s position.

"Time to intercept?" Theruun's voice remained steady despite the ice in his veins.

"Eight minutes at current velocity," Carruvin reported.

"Are we detected?"

"Unknown," Drayn checked her instruments. "No targeting locks, no active sensor focus. Could be routine patrol, or..."

Or we've been discovered, thought Theruun.

The intelligence they'd gathered—evidence of conspiracy at the highest levels of Zodark command—could change everything. But only if they survived to deliver it.

Theruun gripped the command rail. The next eight minutes would decide their fate—whether they would accomplish the impossible or join the countless ghosts who'd challenged Zodark security and lost.

"Continue data harvest," he ordered quietly. "And prepare contingency transmission to the Enclave. If they've found us, this intelligence dies with us unless we act now."

"Launch decoy drone. Now!" Theruun barked.

The *Bloodhawk*'s belly opened silently. A sleek drone dropped free, its drives igniting the instant it cleared the hull. The craft shot forward, accelerating hard toward the distant stargate to the Orinda system.

"Drone away," Drayn confirmed. "Initiating deception protocol in three... two... one..."

The drone's emissions suddenly spiked. Active sensors blazed to life, painting it across every detection grid in the system. Its signature morphed, broadcasting the distinct electromagnetic pattern of an Altairian reconnaissance frigate.

The reaction was instant and violent.

"Khalas!" Voskei's eyes went wide. "The entire system just went active. Every platform, every ship—they're all hot!"

Alarms shrieked across Zodark frequencies. The approaching fighter squadron broke formation, afterburners flaring as they vectored toward the fleeing drone. Behind them, capital ships began emergency start-ups, reactor signatures blooming like miniature suns.

"They're taking the bait," Shan reported. "Battleships breaking orbit. The star carrier's launching everything."

"Helm, get us out of here. Maximum stealth burn, opposite vector," Theruun ordered.

Carruvin's hands flew across his console. The *Bloodhawk* pivoted on its axis and crept away from the chaos, every system locked down tight. Behind them, the Varkorion system erupted into controlled pandemonium. Search patterns expanded outward from the drone's trajectory. Active sensors swept space in overlapping arcs.

"Distance from previous position?" Theruun asked, watching the tactical display.

"Eight hundred thousand kilometers… nine hundred… crossing one million," Carruvin reported.

"Far enough. All stop." Theruun turned to Dovrek. "Is the data packet ready?"

"Compressed and encrypted. Everything about the conspiracy, the Groff network infiltration, defensive assessments—it's all here."

"Engineering, prepare for microbridge deployment. Minimal aperture, burst transmission only."

"Aye, Captain," Sergeant Major Oruk Marrin's voice crackled from Engineering. "Charging bridging array. Ten seconds."

The seconds crawled. On the display, Zodark forces swarmed toward the Orinda gate like angry hornets. The decoy drone jinked and weaved, buying them precious time.

"Bridge ready," Marrin announced.

"Execute."

Reality twisted. For a fraction of a second, a pinhole opened in space—barely larger than a fist. The data packet shot through, racing across impossible distances toward New Eden. The bridge collapsed instantly, leaving no trace.

"Transmission complete," Drayn confirmed. "The Enclave has our intelligence."

"Outstanding." Theruun allowed himself a thin smile. "Carruvin, set course for Tueblets. Let's see what other secrets the Zodark Empire is hiding."

"Course laid in. Wormhole bridging system charging for full transit."

Behind them, the Varkorion system continued to burn with activity. Zodark forces raced toward an enemy that had never existed, while the real threat prepared to slip away unseen.

"Bridge formation in five seconds," Marrin reported.

The *Bloodhawk* aligned with its escape vector. Space bent around them, reality stretching like taffy. The wormhole opened—a perfect sphere of twisted space-time.

"Take us through," Theruun ordered.

The stealth frigate slipped into the bridge and vanished, leaving behind only cosmic background radiation and a very angry Zodark fleet. Their mission in Varkorion was complete. Tueblets awaited.

Chapter 17:
The Conspiracy Gambit

November 28, 2115
Confederation Command Enclave
New Eden

Lieutenant Neferis Kahlir nearly dropped her coffee—her newly adopted habit since they'd crossed the locked stargate—when the quantum entanglement alert pierced the predawn quiet of the communications center. The CCE's Quantum Nexus facility operated around the clock, but microburst transmissions from deep reconnaissance were rare enough to set her pulse racing.

"Origination signature?" she called to her night shift team.

"Confirmed *Bloodhawk*, authentication codes valid," Optio Therin responded. "Data packet incoming... khalas, this is encrypted to the highest classification."

Kahlir's fingers flew across her console, initiating decryption protocols. As the first files resolved, her breath caught. "Get me Admiral Korrath. Priority One."

Within minutes, the intelligence fusion center blazed with activity. Holographic displays cascaded with data—tactical assessments, system maps, and signal intercepts. Captain Zalira Namtar arrived first, her strategic planning instincts immediately drawn to the system analysis.

"Wow," Namtar breathed, studying the initial scans. "Look at these industrial readings."

The door hissed open. Admiral Veydris Korrath entered, still wearing his sparring gear—his padded vest darkened with sweat. Behind him, Rear Admiral Selvarn Ithis dabbed at a cut above his eye with a training towel, the result of their morning combat session. Captain Tammuz Marduk followed, his running outfit soaked through, still catching his breath from what must have been a punishing circuit.

"This had better be good. You caught us in the middle of PT," Korrath commented as he entered the room, rolling a shoulder that had taken one too many throws. "Give us your report."

Kahlir transferred the main findings to the briefing holo. "Sir, the *Bloodhawk* successfully penetrated the Varkorion system. They've transmitted critical intelligence via microburst."

The first image materialized—a three-dimensional rendering of Varkorion's defenses. The room fell silent as they absorbed what they were seeing.

"Whoa, would you look at that? Those aren't natural asteroid formations," Ithis observed, voice tight. "That's smart. They've repositioned those asteroids and turned them into fortresses."

"Yeah, it looks that way. This initial report identified forty-seven primary platforms, another twenty-three secondary asteroids along this tertiary line here," Kahlir confirmed. "Analysis of the platforms has identified the armaments to consist of turbo laser batteries, missile clusters, and plasma torpedo launchers. But this one here, this one is a beast."

The display zoomed to highlight a massive object near Shwani. "They towed an entire planetoid into a defensive position here—God only knows how long ago they did this, but it's clear this wasn't something done recently. Preliminary analysis of the facility indicates it likely has a launch capacity for over a thousand starfighters and likely a mix of bombers too."

"Damn!" Marduk breathed. "Even one of *our* battle groups would struggle against a combined fleet backed up by a planetary defensive grid like this."

"Well, if you thought the defensive grid protecting this Zodark planet was impressive, wait until you learn of its industrial capacity," Namtar interjected, manipulating the display. "The *Bloodhawk*'s fusion cell put together an impressive industrial assessment. They examined shipyard capacity across the system... thermal signatures from the fabrication plants..."

Korrath leaned forward. "Impressive—just give me numbers."

"Theruun's people are still assessing the Tueblets and Zinconia systems, but conservative estimates believe this system represents about thirty percent of total Zodark warship production. This system's not just a fortress and home to their intelligence and surveillance apparatus, it's a critical forge that feeds their entire war machine."

The weight of that settled over them. They knew the Altairian and Republic's intelligence services had suggested Varkorion was important. Now they understood exactly *how* important.

"I know the *Shadowfang*s are ISR frigates, but how did Theruun's team manage to get this granular level of detail of both the system and all this other stuff they just sent?" Ithis asked in genuine surprise.

Kahlir's expression shifted to something between admiration and disbelief. "Sir, I was asking myself the same question when we sent for you. As it turns out, it appears they didn't just scan the system. Captain Dovrek is temporarily aboard the *Bloodhawk* for this mission. I am not sure how her team managed to do it, but her fusion cell hacked into the Groff headquarters network."

"Wait—they what?" Korrath's voice sharpened.

"They hacked it. Full network infiltration. Electronic communications, case files, intelligence reports—terabytes of data. It's an enormous intelligence coup."

"Wow, OK. Show me," Korrath ordered.

The displays shifted to scrolling data streams—Groff operational files, agent reports, surveillance logs. The sheer volume was staggering.

"My team's still processing, but we've identified several critical finds," Kahlir explained. "First, we discovered detailed files on every Republic military commander: psychological profiles, operational histories, predicted responses to various scenarios. The level of detail here goes well beyond what I would have expected."

"Wow, with *that* kind of intelligence, they're able to adjust their strategies with a much higher level of accuracy," Marduk noted grimly.

"Wait." Namtar held up a hand, staring at one particular file. "Pull up that communication thread. The one marked 'Vak'Atioth—Level Nine Encryption.'"

Kahlir isolated the file. As the translation resolved, the room grew very quiet.

"Is this authenticated?" Korrath asked softly.

"Direct from their servers. Director Vak'Atioth in communication with his Laktish, Heltet and"—Kahlir highlighted the names—"Representatives from the Shwani, Dralkeg, and Rithak clans."

The thread's content was unambiguous. The messages discussed Zon Otro's failures and questioned his fitness to lead. There were not-so-subtle suggestions that new leadership might be needed.

"You know what this looks like? A coup," Ithis said flatly.

"Or at least they're considering one," Namtar corrected. "Look at the language. They're testing loyalty, feeling out support. Classic pre-coup behavior."

Korrath remained silent, processing. His mind went to his recent meeting with Viceroy Hunt; he thought about the Republic's desire to find a way to decapitate the Zodark leadership and collapse their government from within, or at least severely weaken it prior to starting the next campaign. This conspiracy just might offer them an opportunity they could exploit.

"There's one more thing," Kahlir said quietly. "Something our OSA picked up that doesn't appear in any official records."

The display shifted to show a remote section of the Varkorion system, barely visible against the cosmic background, where a cluster of readings appeared.

"Heat signatures...a lot of them. Approximately eighty vessels. But, sir..." Kahlir paused. "These aren't registered with the Malvari. There are no fleet designations, no crew assignments. It almost seems like this Groff agency is building a hidden armada of their own."

"Interesting—the Groff building their own fleet," Korrath stated. It wasn't a question.

"It appears so. Instead of reinforcing the Malvari as they should be, they're diverting resources, creating a private navy answerable only to the Groff."

The implications cascaded through Korrath's mind. A security apparatus was building its own military force. Leadership was questioning the government. Secret fleets were being hidden from official oversight. The Zodark Empire wasn't just facing external pressure—it was rotting from within.

"This newfound information we have acquired—how do you think we could help the Republic exploit it?" he asked his staff.

Namtar spoke first. "That's an interesting question. From previous reports Republic Intelligence has shared with us, Zodark society, despite being very tribal and clan-based, is paranoid about security. It's why this group, the Groff, is feared and loathed. If we want to exploit this, we could speak with Viceroy Hunt and find out what his thoughts are."

"We should definitely speak with the Viceroy about this discovery," Marduk agreed. "The fact that this Groff agency is building a separate fleet is concerning. Once the *Bloodhawk* returns from its mission, we will have all the data we need to finalize the campaigns to end this war."

"I agree. We should speak with the Viceroy and share what we have," Ithis said. "Perhaps we can play to this paranoia, while attacking strategically important targets, like industrial facilities involved in building reactors for their warships, gas harvesting and mining operations—strikes that cause them to doubt each other and the Malvari's ability to protect their borders. Things like that could make this Zon Otro look weak to his people."

Korrath nodded slowly. "Hmm... what would you suggest, Ithis?"

"I would recommend to the Viceroy that we ambush a supply convoy or hit a refinery—things we can we can wreck quickly and then disappear. I agree that it would make this Zodark Mavkah, the head of their military, look incompetent. If he's made to look inept, that makes the Zon who appointed him look even more useless, which fuels the contempt between the Groff and the High Council," Ithis explained.

The room fell silent as they considered the possibilities. Korrath knew the Republic would be signing the treaty soon. He would have more military options available to him once it was signed. With the Republic formally part of the Humtar Confederation, this war would be as much the Humtars' war as it was the Republic's, which would give him a much freer hand in dealing with it.

"Where is the *Bloodhawk*?" Korrath asked Kahlir.

"Sir, the *Bloodhawk* has likely moved on to the systems Tueblets and Zinconia, as planned. Would you like me to have them recalled?" Kahlir offered.

"No. Let them finish their survey. I need to consult with the Viceroy." Korrath turned to the rest of his staff. "I want a full analysis of everything we've received. Ithis, put together a list of warships you would want to form a task force around to assist the Republic in the coming campaign. We will help them defeat the Zodarks so we can prepare them to battle the Collective. Marduk, in the unlikely event that this next campaign has a ground force contingent, figure out what kind of ground force you might need to support the Republic. See if it might make more sense to equip them with our weaponry or just use our own forces alongside them. Namtar, have your people work with Rear Admiral Ithis and Captain Marduk to determine what kind of support fleet and logistical support each of their forces is going to need. I want these reports ready for review by the end of the week. Dismissed."

As Korrath left the room, he hoped his people had made the right decision to reemerge from their isolation. The recent discovery of the Collective and this Arc Net they had built unnerved him. His people had nearly gone extinct in their first war with the Collective. History had a way of repeating itself, and this was one series of events he was keen to avoid repeating.

Chapter 18:
You Can Run, But You Can't Hide

Garka, Moraga
Orinda System

David checked his kit one last time. He was ready to go. One quick glance at the rest of his team verified that they were also set to get this show on the road.

With Dumuzi Enmeana out of the way, the insurgents wouldn't have anyone to tip them off about possible raids, so Drew's next job for the Kites was to take out the IED-making team on Moraga.

It was 0200 hours, and David and his crew were lined up outside an alley near the bomb makers' apartment. A Gurista Special Forces team and a Republic Delta Special Forces team were standing by, in case they were needed, but the Kites didn't anticipate needing the backup.

David nodded to the leader of the local team, who was fully kitted out and holding his weapon at the low ready. The man waved his hand toward the entrance, signaling that they were cleared to begin.

Silently, his team approached the entrance. Somchai worked his technical expertise with the lock, popping it open silently.

They entered the apartment without making a noise, weapons at the ready, night vision enabled on their HUDs. Once they'd cleared the first room, David did a check-in.

Gas masks on? he asked.

One by one, they all confirmed that they were ready for the next phase of the mission. David grabbed the canister of sleeping gas, pulled the pin, and rolled in quietly down the hallway toward the bedrooms. They didn't need anyone waking up suddenly.

They waited for two minutes, the maximum amount of time for the gas to spread in an apartment this size, and continued quietly down the hall.

One by one, they scanned the faces of their sleeping suspects, verifying the facial recognition against the known participants in the IED-making cell. As each one was matched, one of the Kites would use an autoinjector to take them out of the equation.

No more murdering innocent civilians for you, thought David.

After they completed the quiet but lethal task, the Kites turned the site over to the local teams on the ground for intelligence exploitation. If there were any other related cells left in the area, they would be found and brought to justice.

****

Later That Day

After they'd all reported in to Drew, the Kites grabbed forty winks, arising to the smell of Somchai's cooking. There was a strange dichotomy to their lifestyle: high-adrenaline meets lots of waiting and isolation. It was a good thing they all seemed to get along.

"Whatcha got for us this morning, Somchai?" asked Jess, coming up behind him and giving him a hug.

"I've got some Thai rice soup and Thai omelets to choose from," he replied.

"Sounds delicious."

Catalina walked in. "My mouth is watering. Thanks for breakfast, Somchai."

David ambled in and made himself a plate. "Thanks, man."

When Amir entered the room, he didn't waste any time. "So, David, any news from Drew?"

David had just shoved an extremely large bite in his mouth and chuckled uncomfortably as he had to chew it before he could answer the question.

"Hang on, Amir. I haven't even had my coffee yet, but if you give me a second, I'll check."

David pulled out his data pad and waited for an updated encrypted data packet to download. "All right, so do you want the good news?"

"Lay it on us," answered Catalina.

"We are finally getting out of this place," he responded.

"Where to next?" asked Somchai.

"Well, I hope you all like trees," said David. "Because we're going to the Valencia system, to the planet Tanian."

There was a strange silence that hung in the air. Finally, Jess broke the tension. "I'll have to do some research on that place," she said.

"Literally the only thing I know about that place is that it has a lot of trees."

They all laughed quietly, realizing they'd had the same thought. "Yeah, I guess that's all I know too," David admitted.

"We might have a little extra time for some poker in between our missions," said Amir.

They all moaned. "Amir, I'm not sure we have any money left to give you, brother," said Somchai.

Amir chuckled. "Had to try."

Chapter 19:
Humtar Confederation

December 2, 2115 – Midafternoon
Chancellor's Private Residence
New Cambria, New Eden

The glass walls of the Chancellor's residence caught the afternoon light and scattered it across the office in muted shades of gold. Beyond, New Cambria's skyline stretched upward like a living machine. Mixed-use towers extended gracefully into the sky—sixty, a hundred, even one hundred and eighty stories—with geometric precision and beauty. Interlaced within the steel-and-glass frames of glistening towers were the city tramways, which glided silently between them at twenty-story intervals. The city was still young, and tens of thousands of construction Synths continued to build and expand New Cambria, a project still decades from completion.

From his desk, Aimes Morgan could see the commuter trams sliding along their elevated tracks, one above another in elegant tiers, each carrying hundreds of people between the interconnected towers. At ground level, manicured gardens and winding streams softened the angles of the government district. The parks had deliberately been designed to remind both leaders and citizens that progress did not have to erase beauty—the two could be blended together to create something incredible.

Hidden below the surface of New Cambria, beneath the parks, was a hidden world of subways—one for people, one for the unseen burdens of a metropolis: freight, refuse, and materials were all shuttled underground. Out of sight, out of mind. It was the future rendered in concrete, steel, and green space, a capital that spoke of resilience and ambition in equal balance and measure.

Morgan let his gaze linger on the six-by-six-block grid that defined the heart of New Cambria. It wasn't Emerald City, nor the ancient cradle of Earth, but it was theirs—planned, secure, and, after Sol's devastation, necessary. It had become the beating heart of the Republic. Each year it grew. New portions of the city finished, new sections begun. In time, it would grow to become one of the planned megacities of New Eden. For now, it functioned as the temporary capital of the Republic.

Just then, a soft chime sounded, returning his thoughts to the here and now. He turned to see his steward stepping through the doorway, bowing ever so slightly with professional restraint.

"Excuse me, Chancellor. The Viceroy, Miles Hunt, has arrived."

Morgan drew a long breath, smoothing the crease of his jacket as he rose from his desk. Since their reunion with the Humtars, he had known some sort of agreement between their peoples would eventually be signed. Tomorrow was that day. They would sign a formal agreement ending their isolation in favor of kinship, maybe trading sovereignty for survival. But today, in this quiet midafternoon, Aimes would measure the resolve of the man who carried the Republic's fate in his uniformed hands.

****

Viceroy Miles Hunt walked into the room, greeting Chancellor Morgan before the pair took a seat near the floor-to-ceiling windows overlooking the parks surrounding the Residence. In the distance, a kilometer away, the greenery of the park gave way to the rising skyline of the growing city. Hunt liked the view. Secretly, it was one of the reasons he tried to meet at the Chancellor's residence rather than at his own in Alliance City.

"Miles, thanks for meeting today. I know the formal ceremony is tomorrow, but I felt we should meet one final time before the treaty is signed," Chancellor Morgan started. "I can tell you still seem a little uncomfortable about it."

Hunt's jaw tightened as he measured his response. "I still have the same concerns we previously talked about. There are still more 'unknown unknowns' than 'known knowns' with the Humtar Confederation." His mind was still mulling over what Captain Dovrek had meant when she'd said, "When our fleets begin to arrive."

It wasn't until their third meeting with the Humtars that they had begun to share more about who they were—the form of government they lived under and what they called themselves, the "Humtar Confederation." While Hunt shouldn't have been surprised to learn of the size of their territory, he had nonetheless been astonished to discover that, despite their disappearance from their original regions, they had expanded greatly in the millennia since their retreat.

They governed themselves under a confederation of constellations in an entirely new galaxy. Their numbers had grown as they sprawled across the stars, expanding and building a new empire as they started over. The Humtar Confederation had spread to include sixty-seven systems—a hundred and sixty colonies. With a population of eight hundred and seventy billion people, their society was immense.

"I agree, and I share those concerns," Morgan replied, studying him for a moment before continuing. "Miles, you've carried the weight of the Republic on your shoulders for some time now. You've guided humanity through fire and the crucible of war. But fire cannot burn forever, and you can't bear this weight alone indefinitely.

"I will not try to claim I understand the pressures you are under, Miles," Morgan shared. "As Chancellor, my concern remains with our people, their safety, and their future. Despite the unknowns, weighing what we *do* know, signing this accord tomorrow with the Humtar Confederation offers our people a shield we desperately need. I fear if we hesitate and do not accept this offer they have extended to us, we risk bleeding the Republic out in this war with the Zodarks, and against the Collective, which we have yet to fight."

Hunt sighed before answering. "I don't disagree with you, Aimes. And you are right to be concerned about the safety and security of humanity and the Republic. From my position, safety is only half the equation. Balance is the other. When we first encountered the Zodarks, it was the Altairians who came to our aid. Not long after that, the Gallentines saw something in us and elevated our status. Their Emperor entrusted us, entrusted me, to assume the position of Viceroy from the Altairians to pursue the mandate they couldn't. It's not that I'm against binding our people together with the Humtars. I'm concerned that the Gallentines may see it as duplicity."

Morgan leaned forward, voice edged with conviction. "And the alternative...? Remember that feeling shortly after the Zodarks had wrecked Earth—the Emperor possibly restoring the position of viceroy to the Altairians? We could have returned to being Altairian cannon fodder had we not discovered the gate leading to the Humtars.

"Miles, these Humtars are not strangers—they are our blood. They see us as cousins, descendants of the same line. Call me old-fashioned, but I cannot believe they would allow harm to befall us after reuniting. Remember, when the Gallentines pressed us to attack the Pharaonis and then the Orbots, it was the Humtars who didn't hesitate to dispatch warships to defend our territory while our fleets fought on multiple fronts. They took a risk returning to our galaxy to stand watch on our borders. I call that intent, proof they mean what they say when they tell us we are family."

Hunt exhaled slowly, his gaze drifting to the skyline beyond the Chancellor's window. The towers caught the light just right, illuminating the buildings against the tramways gliding between them in synchronized order. *A beautifully efficient, orderly city. Just like the Humtars.*

"You are right, Aimes, my old friend," Hunt said at last. "Sometimes I need to hear another voice—another opinion I can trust. We go way back, to the days when I commanded the *Rook* and we had just discovered this planet and those blue devils," he reminisced, sharing the old memory.

"There are times when I envy you, Aimes. Balancing the needs of the alliance against the needs of individual members is challenging, to say the least. I find myself in a tough position. My loyalty is to the Republic, to our species." Hunt spoke gently, weighing each word. "On the one hand, my duty is to weigh their offer against the trust and loyalty Emperor Tibus SuVee has shown me—shown us. Replacing King Grigdolly as viceroy with me was not an easy decision, nor one made without consequences."

"Consequences—huh. I wasn't aware of any. Did Chancellor Luca know?" probed Morgan.

Hunt shook his head. "No. I kept it private. It wasn't something she could change, so why burden her with it? In truth, it was more bruised egos and loss of status. A few Altairian shipyards and industrial centers decided to become a little tardy in delivering warships or supporting some Tully and Ry'lian operations. It eventually resolved, but it was a subtle reminder of who still wielded real power and who only held a title."

"Ouch. Yeah, good call on not sharing that with Luca. She would've made a stink about it with the Altairian ambassador," Morgan laughed.

"And that's why I didn't tell her." Hunt grinned. "All kidding aside, the Emperor has entrusted me—and the Republic—with leading the alliance to victory in this war. The Gallentines have shared their concerns about the Collective and Legion. Hell, we even had a brief encounter with Legion in Orbot space. It didn't exactly go well for our ships either.

"Once we sign this treaty tomorrow, I plan to ask for the Humtars' help in ending this war. If we're joining their Confederation, it also means they're joining our war. I hope they understand that. They bear responsibility for helping defeat the Collective they were at least partially responsible for creating."

Morgan gave an understanding nod. He could hear the strain in Hunt's voice, see the stress etched on his face. It was a rare moment of honest vulnerability—when the mask of viceroy gave way to the man who carried the weight of the title.

"You carry the burden of an alliance on your shoulders, Miles," Morgan said. "After we sign the treaty, let's insist on their help in ending this war. If our peoples are to reconnect, to bridge the divide of millennia, the killing must end. Peace must be restored.

"But enough talk. Join me for a drink on the terrace before you leave? I can see the time is near," Morgan offered as he stood. Their meeting was nearly over. Both of them had much to do before tomorrow's ceremony.

Standing, Hunt smiled as he followed him to the terrace. A steward appeared with a pair of glasses of locally made brandy. They toasted to new beginnings, then Hunt graciously departed, his vehicle whisking him back to Alliance City—to more meetings and more decisions.

****

Following Day
Union Hall
New Cambria, New Eden

The motorcade slowed as it turned into the broad, tree-lined avenue that formed the ceremonial heart of New Cambria. Chancellor Aimes Morgan sat back against the leather seat, his gaze sweeping over the newly finished Boulevard of the Republic. This wasn't merely a road—it was a statement of resilience, a display of engineering pride as the nation rebuilt in the aftermath of its near-destruction. Along the sides of the street were the levers of power: a federation of governance, justice, and unity for a Republic healing from the devastation of Sol.

Aimes looked to his left, smiling at the Assembly Hall of the Republic. The grandeur of its massive columns and broad steps sought to fuse the design and history of Earth's oldest parliaments with its future among the stars. It would be here, in these hallowed halls, where the Senate, proportionally elected by its constituents, would debate, argue, and cast votes, creating laws and crafting national policy that would shape the lives of billions.

Flanking it to the south stood a domed structure of white-veined stone and polished black glass. Etched into its facade was the depiction of a blindfolded figure with a raised hand, holding the scales of justice against a field of stars. This temple-like edifice housed the guardians of the Constitution—the High Court of the Republic. It was a necessary check against the excesses of government and, at times, against the passions of its constituents.

To the right of the boulevard, the Governors' Council came into view. Unlike the imposing architecture of the Senate, this building was designed to embody openness and dialogue. Tiered balconies and broad, curving arches symbolized the pragmatic voices of the Republic's governors—leaders who bore direct responsibility for the governance of entire planets and colonies. Fewer in number than the Senate, they acted as both thought leaders and practical administrators, tasked with translating legislation into workable policy. Their chamber was less a stage for rhetoric than a forum for scrutiny, where Senate proposals could be amended, restrained, or, if necessary, struck down to protect the Republic from rash or ill-conceived laws.

Next to the Governors' Council stood the new headquarters of the Interstellar Marshal Service, a uniquely designed structure that projected strength and accessibility to the public. Behind it, connected seamlessly yet deliberately separate, lay the headquarters of Republic Intelligence. Together, they formed two halves of the same blade: the IMS, bold and visible, and RI, discreet and veiled. Two-thirds of the complex extended beneath the surface, out of sight, concealing the true scale of its operations. Above ground, however, the dual presence projected vigilance and control—the outward face of law and security in the Republic.

As the motorcade slowed, Chancellor Morgan's Chief of Staff, Darius Kane, leaned slightly toward him. "It's striking, isn't it? The IMS standing bold, pillars and banners on full display, and then the RI, tucked into the rear, almost invisible. One half shouting justice to the world, the other whispering secrets in the shadows."

Morgan gave a short nod. "True, it is a stark contrast."

Kane studied the complex through the tinted glass. "Even the *landscaping* is a contrast," he said.

"It is," Morgan replied, his voice carrying the faint pride of an engineer explaining a well-built system. "The trees, hedges, even the waterworks—all of it conceals sensor grids and controlled choke points. It looks elegant, but it's as much function as form. Anyone walking those paths is already being measured a dozen different ways."

All the buildings along the boulevard mirrored one another in their unique grandeur. From soaring fronts to sweeping arches, and plazas accented with fountains and statues of historical figures, each had been built to remind citizens and visitors alike that the Republic wasn't a fleeting society, here one day and gone the next. It would be an enduring power.

"We're almost there," commented Kane as the motorcade approached the T-intersection marking the end of the grand avenue.

Morgan looked past the intersection to the building atop a slight hill—to Union Hall. It was a building that dominated the square, a fusion of stone, steel, and glass designed not for comfort, but for awe. Its towering front rose from the manicured parkland like a monument carved from stone and wood. Rows of high-arched windows glinted in the afternoon sun, their angles deliberate, casting light back across the surrounding gardens. Massive buttresses framed the structure, giving it the appearance of both fortress and cathedral.

And there, at its heart, stood the doors.

Two bronze-gilded slabs, each twenty feet tall, framed in obsidian-black stone quarried from the mountains north of Emerald City. They were the largest doors ever constructed in the Republic, and Aimes suspected their very scale would make even the proudest delegate pause before entering. That was the point. In this place, egos bowed before history.

The Chancellor's convoy slowed to a halt at the broad marble steps leading to the entrance. As Morgan stepped out, his gaze followed the vertical lines of the structure until his neck craned uncomfortably. He was proud of the architects for designing it that way. It was meant to make anyone who looked upon it to feel small in its shadow.

"Completed just in time," he murmured, almost to himself.

His chief of staff walked briskly at his side. "They did it, but barely," Darius agreed. "The final touches were finished a week ago. It was a race to get it ready for today."

They crossed the threshold into the main chamber, the echo of their footsteps magnified against polished stone floors. Inside, the ceilings stretched twenty-five feet overhead. A canopy of carved beams and inset lighting bathed the chamber in a soft golden hue. Banners of the Republic hung proudly along the walls, each flanked by the colors of its colonies: New Eden, Sol, Alpha Centauri, Pishon, Tigris, Sumer, Mars, Titan, Luna, Europa, and the rest.

The hall opened into two grand corridors. To the left lay the Chamber of Accord, a vast space designed for treaties, speeches, and official ceremonies. Rows of polished wood seating faced a raised stage where the signing table now stood, draped in the Republic's colors and adorned with twin standards—the Republic's eagle crest and the new insignia of the Humtar Confederation.

To the right stretched the banquet hall, its vaulted ceiling hung with crystalline chandeliers that cast fractal light across long tables already prepared for the reception to follow. Servants moved quietly, placing the last of the floral arrangements, and aligning silverware with a precision befitting the occasion.

Morgan allowed himself a small smile as he took it all in. The architects had delivered something more than stone and glass. They had created a stage worthy of history. Behind the main halls, the rear complex sprawled outward—guest wings on both sides, already housing Humtar dignitaries, Altairian, Primord, Tully, and Ry'lian observers, and a small group of Gallentines. At the center, joining them all, was the administrative annex where his staff worked feverishly to ensure no detail was overlooked.

Aimes Morgan exhaled slowly. Seeing everything ready and in its place, he allowed a sense of relief to settle into his bones. The

Republic had needed this place—not only as a venue for ceremonies, but as a symbol of their resilience.

Kane leaned close, speaking low. "Chancellor, the delegates are arriving. It's time to get in position."

Morgan nodded once, straightening his jacket as staff moved in around him, ushering him through the side corridor and toward the Chamber of Accord. The hum of voices carried through the halls—an orchestra tuning before the first note. Tomorrow, history would be written here.

****

The banners of the Republic hung still in the Chamber of Accord, their colors heavy in the air like the weight of history itself.

From his place near the Gallentine delegation, Viceroy Miles Hunt stood at attention, his eyes tracking across the sea of dignitaries. He caught the Humtar representative's voice—measured, resonant, carrying the strange timbre of a people long lost and suddenly returned. Beside him, Chancellor Aimes Morgan listened intently, nodding as the Humtar concluded, "...and in this hall, we begin again—not as strangers, but as kin."

Polite applause rippled through the chamber. Hunt allowed his gaze to sweep across the gathered assembly. There they were—every ally accounted for. The Altairians were notably shorter than the rest of the group; their grayish skin, large black eyes, and angular features stood out as they closely watched the ceremony unfold. To their right were the Primords, solemn as stone, their heavy-browed faces and elvish ears betraying little emotion. The Tully delegation sat in a tight formation, their matted hair weaved into ceremonial braids that gleamed under the chamber's light. The Ry'lians, elegant and almost ethereal, leaned toward one another in hushed, flowing whispers. Off to the side was Liam Patrick, the roguish leader of the semiautonomous Belters' planet, Éire.

All of them had come for this—for the chance to watch history unfold with their own eyes. For many of them, this was also the first time they had seen the Humtars in person.

Hunt clasped his hands behind his back, adopting the rigid posture of a naval officer at review. He was, after all, more observer than participant today. As the man entrusted by Emperor Tibus SuVee to oversee the Milky Way alliance, his role was to ensure continuity, to maintain balance in a theater forever on the brink of imbalance.

Out of the corner of his eye, he studied the Gallentine envoys—resplendent in white and crimson robes, their presence alone radiating dominance. Yet Hunt noted the subtle tells: a slight furrowing of the brow, the faint tension at the edges of their mouths. They understood the significance of this day, but unease lingered beneath the polished surface. The Gallentines had built their empire atop the ruins of Humtar civilization. To see the founders of stargates, the builders of legends, return from obscurity to stand again among them—it was no small thing.

Hunt's lips pressed into a thin line. *They'll accept this, for now. The Humtars claim no lost thrones, no forgotten territories beyond the Republic. That much buys peace. But what they want—what they may become—will shape us all.*

He drew in a slow breath as the Chancellor's voice rose once more, echoing against the high stone walls: "Today, we bind the Republic to the Humtar Confederation. May this bond endure the storms of war, and may it outlast us all."

Applause thundered across the hall. Hunt joined in with polite, deliberate rhythm, his gaze fixed on the Humtars.

If they wish to stand beside us again, Hunt thought, *then let them prove it. Let them help us end the Zodarks—and, when the time comes, face the enemy they themselves unleashed.*

The applause faded, replaced by the solemn silence of history in the making. Miles Hunt, Viceroy of the Milky Way, stood amid allies old and new, a man caught between empires, watching as the galaxy turned another page.

Chapter 20:
A Strategy Is Born

December 4, 2115
Republic Army Headquarters
Fort Leatherneck, New Eden

The conference chamber deep inside Fort Leatherneck was built for moments like this—windowless, layered with secure comms shielding, its long black stone table flanked by recessed lighting that cast no shadows. Here, politics fell away, leaving only the clean calculus of strategy.

Viceroy Miles Hunt sat at the head of the table, his uniform as unadorned as the walls around him. He had long ago dispensed with ceremonial trappings; authority was not stitched into fabric but earned through decisions made and wars survived. To his right sat Fleet Admiral Chester Bailey, the grizzled chief of the Republic Navy. Beside him was Vice Admiral Rosentreter, lean and sharp-eyed, always with the air of a man already three moves ahead.

On Hunt's left, Lieutenant General Alfred Bates leaned back in his chair. His multicam fatigues were creased from wear, not from neglect. The Delta tab and Special Forces patch on his left shoulder were a quiet testament to a career of wars in the shadows. Above his breast pocket gleamed the Orbital Assault badge and the familiar Combat Infantryman's Badge—earned the hard way, in fire and blood. Bates wasn't the kind of man who wasted words. The weight of his presence was enough; every man in the room knew he was the one who turned impossible ideas into executed missions.

A soft chime announced the arrival of their guests, the doors slid open with deliberate ease.

Admiral Vesharuk, the Humtar advisor to Viceroy Hunt, entered first. His stride was measured, steady, carrying the authority of a man who had commanded fleets into battle and expected obedience without raising a voice. The duty uniform of the Confederation Defense Force was simple, tailored to function rather than impress; the only mark of distinction was the admiral's rank insignia on his collar. Admiral Korrath followed behind him.

The last to enter was Captain Tammuz Marduk, leaner and younger than the other Humtars, his posture betraying both discipline and a restless energy. His uniform mirrored his commanders', with the exception of his insignia. Where the others wore the insignia of a starship, Marduk's was a rifle, designating him a member of the Army, not the Navy. The distinction showed in how he carried himself, his eyes sharper, his body moving like a coiled snake, ready to strike at a moment's notice. Where Vesharuk radiated calm command, Marduk exuded calculation, his eyes never still for long.

As the Humtar officers took their seats, Hunt folded his hands on the table, studying them with the cool patience of a man who had spent a lifetime weighing allies, enemies, and those who might become either. He had grown to like and trust Vesharuk during the months he'd been his Humtar advisor. While Hunt hadn't dealt with Admiral Korrath as much, he was coming to respect the man as a competent fleet commander, though he had yet to see the man under the pressure of battle. Captain Marduk was an unknown—something Hunt hoped to solve by the end of the meeting.

Hunt let the silence stretch for a moment after the pleasantries had concluded and the Humtar officers had settled into their seats. Once he felt everyone was ready to begin, he started the meeting.

"Admiral Vesharuk, Admiral Korrath, and Captain Marduk," Hunt began, his voice calm, deliberate, "I appreciate the three of you coming to meet with us to discuss this matter in person. Two days ago, the Republic took a historic step in joining the Humtar Confederation. It was a moment of unity—one that carried both promise and responsibility. Today, I need to speak plainly about the latter."

Vesharuk inclined his head slightly, hands folded before him on the table. "I understand, Viceroy. The treaty has been signed, and it is time for us to focus on how we can defeat the Zodarks."

"Precisely," Hunt said. "Your reconnaissance mission—I trust it's been productive?"

Korrath activated a small holoprojector, casting a three-dimensional display above the table. The Varkorion system materialized in crisp detail—industrial complexes, defensive grids, and the unmistakable signatures of massive shipyards.

"The *Bloodhawk* has exceeded our expectations," Korrath began. "What we discovered in Varkorion fundamentally changes our understanding of Zodark military capacity."

Bailey leaned forward, studying the display. "Those defensive platforms…"

"Forty-seven primary asteroid fortresses," Korrath confirmed. "Twenty-three secondary positions. Each one bristling with turbo lasers, missile clusters, and plasma torpedo launchers. They've literally moved asteroids into defensive positions and hollowed them out."

"Damn," Rosentreter breathed. "Even a full battle group would have problems with that."

"It gets more impressive," Marduk added, manipulating the display to highlight a massive object. "This planetoid has been converted into a starfighter base. Conservative estimates put its capacity at over a thousand craft."

Hunt's expression remained neutral, but his eyes sharpened. "Industrial capacity?"

"Thirty percent of total Zodark warship production," Vesharuk stated flatly. "Varkorion isn't just a system—it's the forge that feeds their entire war machine. It helps explain why, even after achieving substantial prior victories, the Zodark war machine continues to replace its losses and grow its fleet. You are fortunate they are not better led."

"There is something else the *Bloodhawk* discovered," Korrath said, his tone shifting. The display changed, showing data streams and communication intercepts. "The *Bloodhawk*'s fusion intel cell managed something we hadn't thought possible. They succeeded in hacking the Groff headquarters network."

The room went still. Bates, the Special Operations Commander and former Commander of the Republic's JSOC unit, was the first to speak. "Wait, you're saying your stealth frigate somehow hacked their intelligence service?"

"Yes, we are. They achieved complete network infiltration," Korrath confirmed. "Director Vak'Atioth's private communications, surveillance files, operational plans. But most importantly"—the display shifted to show encrypted messages—"evidence of a conspiracy at the highest levels."

Hunt studied the translated intercepts. "Interesting. These clan representatives... Shwani, Dralkeg, Rithak. Huh, they're questioning Zon Otro's leadership?"

"It would seem so. Our understanding of internal Zodark politics is limited. From our perspective, this looks to be more than questioning," Vesharuk interjected. "The disdain and anger are clear. They're openly discussing his failures against what they call 'primitive humans.' The contempt is barely hidden."

"And there's something else," Korrath added, bringing up another display. "The Groff aren't just conducting surveillance of their own people and collecting intelligence on their adversaries. Our sensors detected approximately eighty vessels in a remote section of the system. No official registration, no Malvari oversight. We could be wrong, but it looks like the Groff have been busy building a fleet of their own."

"Oh, really? A shadow navy," Bates said quietly. "Yeah, that certainly looks like they might be preparing to initiate a coup of their own."

Hunt was silent for a long moment, processing the implications. "I'll admit our own understanding of internal Zodark politics is limited. We have learned a lot from our debriefs of captured Mukhabarat spies, and even some Zodark prisoners we have gotten to talk. I'm not saying a coup isn't possible—it might be. Their society, from what we understand, is very clan- and tribe-based. It revolves around honor, duty, and service to their Empire. That said, I believe we could exploit this. Turn their paranoia against them and work it to our advantage."

"Exactly! That's precisely what we were going to propose," Korrath confirmed. "Before we make a move, I would like us to wait until the *Bloodhawk* has returned from its survey of Tueblets and Zinconia. This will give us a more complete picture of what we are facing."

"Fair enough. What kind of actions are you proposing once we have their reports?" asked Rosentreter.

"That depends on what they find. What I can say is a direct assault on Varkorion would be suicide. The system defenses are too strong for a limited attack. It would require us committing everything to a single attack, which I do not recommend," Korrath replied. "However, if we want to stoke some further infighting... I would propose we smash one of their patrols and scoop up the wreckage—then attack one of these vessels the Groff are building and leave behind the wreckage of the Malvari ship we destroyed along with the wreckage of the Groff's ship. This would make the Groff and Malvari think there was a fight and have the two of them pointing fingers at each other. It would certainly amplify existing tensions."

"Nice. Make their leadership squabble and look weak," Rosentreter mused. "Depending on the frequency and severity of our raids. We could weaken and undermine their forces before the start of our next campaign."

"That was our thinking as well," Vesharuk confirmed. "If this Zodark society is as honor-based as you have described, Zon Otro will appear even weaker to his people when his Malvari suffer defeat after defeat. He will steadily lose his mandate to rule. We don't need to destroy their military—we need to destroy their faith in their leadership."

"Yeah, I could see that working," Rosentreter agreed. "Hypothetically, based on what information you have right now, are there any potential targets we could discuss to see what sort of ships we might need to involve?"

Marduk nodded and motioned that he'd like to take the question. He pulled up a new display showing potential targets. "Supply convoys, isolated outposts, secondary industrial facilities. Hit them where they're weak, where the Malvari will get blamed for lapses in security. Each failure drives another wedge between the intelligence service and the military."

"And between the clans and the High Council," Hunt added, "if these clan representatives are already questioning Zon Otro…"

"Then every defeat will validate their doubts," Korrath finished. "We've analyzed their communication patterns. As everyone knows, the Groff report directly to Vak'Atioth, who has his own agenda. The Malvari answer to Mavkah Griglag, who serves the Zon. But if they start blaming each other for failures…"

"The Empire tears itself apart," Bailey said with grim satisfaction. "Internal conflict does more damage than any fleet action."

Hunt turned to Bates. "What kind of Special Forces capabilities do we have for this kind of thing?"

"Oh, I think we could come up with something," Bates replied without hesitation. "If we're able to leverage some of these Humtar stealth frigates, we could deploy some SOF units to carry out some planetary strikes. The psychological impact of a Republic Delta unit carrying out an attack on Zinconia… oh, that would be priceless. The Malvari would never hear the end of that one—Republic ground forces on their home world. Heads would have to roll from that."

"I like the sound of that, General. The *Bloodhawk* is capable of deploying SOF units directly to the surface of a planet and extracting them when the time is right," explained Marduk. "In addition to that, we could probably upgrade the kit your operators use—make 'em more lethal than they already are. Heck, if you'd like, we could even make it a joint task force. Your Deltas with our SOF."

"I'm liking the sound of this. How soon can we start spinning something up?" Hunt's eyes lit up at the idea of running joint operations with the Humtars.

Korrath exchanged glances with his colleagues. "I have had Rear Admiral Ithis compiling a list of available warships we could detail for something like this while additional forces are still en route. I'd say we could have a task force assembled within two weeks. Initial strikes could begin immediately after."

"Rosentreter—could you have some ships ready by then?" Bailey asked.

"We could. It might not be too much, but I could find a few battleships and cruisers for something like this," Bailey's fleet commander assured him.

"And you, Bates? You got some snake-eaters on standby?" Bailey asked next.

Bates smiled. "We wouldn't be SOF if we didn't. Captain Marduk, just let me know how many operators you'd like, and I'll see to it you have our best," General Bates replied confidently.

"OK, Admiral Korrath. Let's start figuring out targets and how we want to hit 'em." Bailey grinned, eager to bring the fight to the enemy.

"This is what I love about the Republic. You are brave, bold, and never afraid of a fight," Korrath interjected before Vesharuk laid out an action plan.

"Here is what I suggest we do. We start small," Vesharuk began. "Let's start by testing their responses against a soft, easy target. By the time the *Bloodhawk* returns from its survey of Tueblets and Zinconia, we'll easily have dozens of targets to choose from. We pick the targets that maximize embarrassment to the Zodark military while minimizing our exposure."

"Agreed. We minimize our exposure while we test the limits of their ability to respond. We're going to make Mavkah Griglag look weak and incompetent." Hunt was practically giddy with excitement to get things going. "Korrath, you said the *Bloodhawk* was scouting the Zodark capital... will this include its security and important buildings?"

"Ah, I see where you are going with this. Yes, Viceroy, they will be scouting it in detail." Korrath grinned. "And, yes, it'll include the High Council building itself. I suppose if the opportunity were to present itself, a surgical strike aimed at eliminating their leadership structure could have a profound impact across the Empire."

The weight of that possibility hung in the air. Hunt thought about it before deciding. "I'm not saying we should hit the High Council with some sort of orbital impact, but perhaps a raiding force led by Captain Marduk's Special Forces and some Republic Deltas could be the sort of thing that rattles the Empire to the core. That's the kind of attack that could split off the Groff from the control of Zon Otro—especially if we manage to kill him in his outchambers."

"That would be a bold move indeed," Captain Marduk replied somberly when he saw the Viceroy wasn't joking.

"If this is something you would like us to plan for... I will see it done," Vesharuk assured them. "And Varkorion—or Tueblets?"

"Hit-and-run strikes against Varkorion. But Tueblets, its capture is the ultimate prize," Hunt said decisively. "It's going to take some time to amass the force necessary to seize Tueblets, however. In the meantime, we focus on destabilizing their leadership. Create chaos. Force them to look inward instead of outward. Then, when we've weakened by internal strife..."

"We strike the killing blow," Bailey finished for him.

Hunt stood, the others following suit. "Gentlemen, I believe we have our strategy. Turn their strength against them. Use their paranoia as a weapon. Make them destroy themselves, and we'll merely finish what they started. Admiral Korrath, Captain Marduk, I know you don't fall directly under my chain of command. I would appreciate it if we could meet weekly, update our plans as needed, and ensure we remain mission-focused. This war needs to end, and with your help, it's finally going to happen."

Korrath agreed to the weekly meetings. When the meeting concluded, Hunt exited the command center and paused outside, looking to the sky above, the cool, moist air threatening snow. Breathing in deeply, he paused to reflect on this moment. They had been battling the Zodarks for more than two decades. For the first time in he didn't know how long, the end of the war was truly in sight. *Our people might truly know peace… we're really going to survive this thing…* He allowed the thought to linger, savoring how it felt. *Stay the course… just a little longer.*

Chapter 21:
I Smell a Rat

Capital City of Adab
Tanian, Valencia System

David swatted at yet another zymura, one of the many annoying, biting fly-like insects that lived a life of apparent ease and abundance on this planet. In comparison to their last assignment on Moraga, Tanian was like living in a tent parked on top of a bunch of fire ants when they'd been used to a suburban home with a white picket fence.

Ugh, David muttered. Even in his annoyance, he maintained his communication over the neurolink to keep their operation hidden.

No kidding, Catalina agreed. *Do you want some more repellant?* she asked.

Honestly, I'm not sure it's working at all, David replied.

This place bites…literally, said Amir.

David blew some air forcefully through his lips. Amir wasn't wrong, but if they were going to get through this assignment, he had to resist the temptation to spend the whole time complaining about all the things that were driving him crazy. Still, being in a hide in a forest near the former governor's mansion-sized estate while the common people of Tanian lived not too far away in abject poverty was grating on his nerves.

Tanian was like the Wild West—very little in the way of roads or public transportation. Most people walked, or if they were lucky enough to afford it, they might have a speeder. David still wasn't clear exactly what the former governor, a man by the name of Gilkara Zulon, had done to obtain all his wealth. It was most likely a combination of old money and a lack of personal morals that had allowed him to wall himself off from the plebeians. Zulon's curved home was built around living trees, with enormous windows all along the front; it was like all the fantasies one could have about a tree house with all the comforts of a mansion.

They'd been watching Zulon for days already, though, sitting in this hide on rotating shifts, and they didn't have too much to show for it yet besides the bug bites. Zulon was suspected of providing intelligence against the new government on Tanian, the Republic, and the Gurista military forces operating on the planet to the remaining Mukhabarat insurgents. Apparently, Zulon had waited a little too long to see who would come out on top of the power struggle. He may not have known that the Republic had shown up in force since he was off in a neighboring system, but by the time he switched sides, the Republic had already marked him for removal. Zulon survived, but he'd lost his position of prominence. And that was certainly enough motive to at least be suspicious of his intentions.

So far, all they'd observed was typical aristocratic behavior: Zulon had private tutors who came to teach his children, a full-time gardener to maintain his property, a chef to cook his food, and maids to scrub his house. Every day at two in the afternoon, he would walk his grounds, surveying their grandeur, then work out with his personal trainer in his on-site gym facilities before relaxing in a hot spring.

If you had a ton of money, would you live like this? asked Catalina.

Frankly, this guy's life seems super boring, Amir answered. *Even if I were a trillionaire, I think I'd still want to do most things for myself.*

I mean, the personal chef seems nice, David replied.

Who needs a chef when you have Somchai? Amir teased.

You know what? You're right, David agreed.

I wouldn't mind having an unlimited travel budget, though, said Catalina.

Wow, I guess I'll have to up my investment game, huh? David asked with a wink.

Speaking of investments, how are we doing with the rundown of his financials? Amir asked.

David suppressed a snort. *I read Somchai's analysis this morning. So far, our guy is rich, but frankly, from what I can tell, the* money *trail is clean—annoyingly so.*

They sat there quietly for a few moments, their only communication the occasional swat at yet another pesky zymura.

It's getting close to 2 p.m., Catalina noted. *Almost time to see our man in the wild.*

Hey, what's that at our three o'clock, approximately twenty meters from Zulon's gate? asked Amir.

Catalina found it first. *Looks like...some guy with a cart selling wood carvings*, she replied.

Well, that's out of the usual routine, David remarked. *Let's get a drone up and see what happens.*

Not long after, former governor Gilkara Zulon exited his front door, approximately ten minutes ahead of schedule.

Hey...something is definitely going on, said Amir. *Instead of his usual saunter about his property, he's headed straight for his front gate.*

I've never seen this guy leave his compound, Catalina replied.

Heads on a swivel, David said.

He's making a beeline for the carving guy, Amir observed.

Zulon admired the man's wares, picking up various items and talking to him about them. The drone they'd managed to get into the air had a parabolic mike, and they were all patched in to the audio.

He seems a bit more enthusiastic about art than I would have guessed, said Catalina.

Did you catch the price he was just quoted? David asked. *That is a* ton *of money.*

Zulon reached into his pocket and pulled out a stack of amber credits, each one like a coin made of tree sap but embedded with a microchip that confirmed its value. Due to its relative isolation, more people on Tanian used physical money than on many of the other human-occupied planets, and the amount being presented here represented more than an average person's monthly salary.

We need to verify the exact amount, Amir said. *I think this might be how Zulon is funneling money to that underground Mukhabarat director. I mean, I appreciate artistic talent as much as the next guy, but I would suspect that was a severe overpayment.*

Better wake up Somchai and Jess, Catalina commented. *I think we should split up and see where else our wood carver goes.*

I'll stay here and keep an eye on Zulon, Amir offered. *Let's see if he does anything else unexpected.*
****

Twenty Minutes Later

Somchai, who was clearly a bit sleep-deprived, had joined David and Catalina while Jess went with Amir to keep an eye on Zulon.

While they had all been trained on using the drones, everyone had come to the universal conclusion that Somchai was just better at operating them than the rest of them, and David had a feeling they would be needing some more drones.

The carver had attempted to sell his wares unsuccessfully at a few locations, but he made his way along the road at a fairly steady pace, headed through the significantly less wealthy part of town without stopping at all until he made a pit stop for food. When the money exchanged hands, they knew something was up.

There is no way that food was that expensive, David commented over the neurolink.

Not unless it's filled with gold and rubies, Catalina agreed.

Let's get a microdrone on that vendor, Somchai, David directed.

On it.

With careful precision, Somchai steered a microdrone that was designed to mimic the appearance of the abundant zymuras into the man's handbag. They would have to see where he went later that day.

Meanwhile, David focused on getting the best possible video footage of the food vendor, to compare against facial recognition and gait analysis profiles. If he was already in the system on the intelligence watch list, they would know shortly.

He's on the move, said Catalina.

David thought to himself that the one good thing about this planet was that all the trees provided significant cover when doing reconnaissance. It wasn't hard to stay out of sight, or to fly a drone without it being spotted, as long as it was properly disguised. He'd learned how to properly walk along the forest floor without snapping any branches, and they snuck along silently, following their mark.

Before their wood carver reached his next stop, they received a ping about their food stall worker.

Report says that the last guy had a brother in the Mukhabarat, said David, stopping for just a few seconds to look down at his data pad. *The brother was presumed dead after an explosion at the headquarters here, although no body was recovered.*

That makes sense, said Somchai. *This is probably part of how they're funneling money to the Mukhabarat insurgency here. His brother might have slipped out before the firefight, and now he's part of it too.*

Either that, or he thinks of his brother as a martyr, and now he's fully radicalized himself, said David.

They continued to follow their wood carver. On the surface, his stops would have made complete sense. Besides the food, he also purchased polishing cloths made of a rough tree fiber from Tanian, which served the same purpose as sandpaper, a new saw, and additional wood to carve. However, each time, they observed that these individuals were also significantly overpaid. The pattern was too odd to be a coincidence.

Let's see what we find when they head home for the evening, said Somchai.

I think we should go back and check on Jess and Amir, and maybe you should catch a few more z's before this evening, Catalina suggested. *I have a feeling we're all going to need to be on deck.*

Sounds like a plan, David agreed.

When they returned to Zulon's residence, Amir was visibly bored, which was uncharacteristic for him, and Jess was asleep.

Nothing at all interesting happened here, so I let her get some more rest, Amir explained. *How did your afternoon go?*

They explained their findings to him, including the tangential associations of several of the merchants to someone who had been a part of the Mukhabarat.

Most of the merchants will go home around 7 p.m., said Amir. *Except for the food stall worker, but even he will head out around 9 p.m. What if we each tail one person? I could follow the wood carver, for example, Somchai could watch the food stall worker and have a little time to nap, Catalina could follow the polishing cloth vendor, David could go after the saw seller, and Jess could take on the lumber man. Together, we would cover all of them.*

That sounds like a solid plan, David agreed. They set up alerts on the microdrones that Somchai had planted to wake them up if their targets moved outside of their place of business, and then they all sacked out, waiting for the real action to begin.
****

Later That Evening

Jess awoke from her nap with a start. Those alerts were adrenaline-inducing, even if no one else could hear them. Through the neurolink, she instantly got an update on her target for the evening, a lumber worker named Shulgi Tiamura. He had just left his place of business, and Jess knew what she needed to do.

Grabbing her pack and a drone kit, she headed toward the man's moving coordinates. In real time, she continued to receive updates from the other Kites as she made her way through the forest.

Tiamura stopped at a home that reminded Jess of old photos she had seen of silver Airstream RVs, tucked into a berm of dirt and covered in vines and the branches of nearby trees. She perched herself in a spot with a decent view of the home, set up a hide blanket that blocked IR and digital tracking measures, and started watching the footage from the microdrone that had made its way inside.

At first, she couldn't see much. The bag was placed down on the kitchen counter, and all that was within the field of vision was a view of Mr. Tiamura throwing together his dinner after a long day at work.

But about fifteen minutes later, the bag was moved into a workroom with tools in it. It wasn't immediately suspicious to Jess, as a man who worked in a lumberyard would likely be a handy sort of person, but when she zoomed in on some of the components on a shelf, things started coming together.

Damn, she realized. *He's building IEDs, just like the ones we saw on Moraga.*

Tiamura packed several completed explosive devices into the bag and then abruptly left the house.

Jess quickly notified the other Kites of the situation and her whereabouts. A few minutes later, Catalina and David were both also on the move.

I think we are converging on the same location, she posited.

Yeah…you could be right, Catalina agreed.

Twenty tense minutes went by with Jess advancing silently through the thick foliage, even resisting the temptation to swat at the zymuras to maintain her stealth. Steadily, the three Kites headed in the same direction, until they were near the entrance of a cave outside the city.

They set up a new hide and watched the footage from the three microdrones in anticipation.

Holy crap…said Jess.

Damn. Those are Zodarks, said David, surprised they'd found some of those blue bastards still on this planet. He thought they had all left or died in some of the final battles to liberate Tanian.

I'm calling this in, he told the others. *We'll see how Drew wants to handle this. For now, let's hang tight until we're given new orders.*

Don't have to tell me twice, Jess commented. *Maybe we'll get lucky and they'll send in the Army to handle it.*
****

A Few Hours Later

It wasn't long after the Kites reported finding an active Zodark camp and insurgent cell to Drew that a Republic Army Delta team stationed in the capital was dispatched to their location.

David thought he might have heard the sound of an Osprey when his earpiece chirped. "Ghost Six, Warden Actual. We're two klicks from your position," came the voice of Captain Marcus "Gavel" Kincaid.

"Warden Actual, Ghost Six. Good copy. We have eyes on target. Approach with caution from our nine o'clock position. We'll guide you to our hide site," David replied with mechanical precision.

'Bout time the cavalry showed, joked Catalina.

Ha-ha. You didn't think Drew was going to have us assault that place, did ya? commented Amir.

Somchai shifted his rifle to his other hand. *It's not like we couldn't take 'em.*

I didn't say we couldn't, Catalina replied defensively. *But why risk it when we have a Delta team on standby for this purpose?*

Cut the chatter, people, David interjected. *We can't have all the fun. Gotta leave something for those Deltas.*

Barely thirty seconds later, their earpieces chirped.

"Check fire, friendlies approaching your location from your nine o'clock," said the voice of Staff Sergeant Dana "Shade" Callahan as David turned to see the silhouette of a Delta soldier approaching them.

David synced with their neurolinks now that they were in close proximity and switched to communicating via that methos instead of using the radios. He didn't want to risk the Zodarks detecting them.

I'm Ghost Six, David said as he extended a hand to Captain Kincaid. *Best to use neurolinks until we can confirm they don't have a way of sensing radio comms. I take it you're Warden.*

I am, and thanks for the heads-up on the comms situation.

You heard the man—no radios, neurolinks only, Kincaid said, passing along David's warning. *We've been reviewing the video footage your team's been sending. Do you guys want to participate in the action or watch and observe?*

David smiled at the Delta soldier, noticing at least two twelve-man squads of the Republic Army Special Forces soldiers lingering a short distance behind him. *Nah, I think we'll let y'all handle this one. It's a bit more than a five-man job, I think.*

The Delta soldier smiled. *Yeah, it looked that way. Thanks for finding them for us. We've had a devil of a time tracking those guys down. I think they're the last of them.*

Probably. We'll stay out of the way, David replied. *Good luck.*

The Delta soldier gave them a quick nod, then faded into the shadows they'd emerged from. For a handful of minutes, all was quiet. David knew that was just the calm before the storm. The SOF operators were maneuvering into position. He just hoped they hadn't missed any hidden sentries or proximity sensors that might alert the insurgents and the handful of Zodark soldiers with them.

****

Master Sergeant Cole Maddox shifted behind a fallen log, his M-111 Slayer settling into the pocket of his shoulder. The triple-one's flat black finish gleamed dully in the fading light, its twelve-inch barrel tracking toward the northern sentry. Thermal overlay painted the Zodark in orange against cool blue forest.

Shade ghosted to her position thirty meters east, Slayer raised, optics locked on the southern sentry. She had two targets marked, forty meters apart. Their four-armed silhouettes leaned against stone outcroppings.

Kincaid's voice cut through the link. *Hammer, Draven—move to breach positions. Intel confirms IEDs at cave mouth. Watch your spacing.*

Roger that, Hammer replied, weaving through the underbrush toward the eastern flank.

He rounded a thick tree trunk—and froze.

A woman, apparently one of the insurgents, squatted ten feet ahead, trousers around her ankles, eyes wide as dinner plates.

She screamed and then grabbed for her gun.

Hammer's Slayer barked once, the plasma bolt catching her center mass. She crumpled, but the damage was done.

Contact! We're blown! Hammer snarled.

Blaster fire erupted from the perimeter—plasma bolts hissed through humid air, wild and searching. The sentries spun toward the sound, mandibles clicking into comm devices.

Engage! Engage! Kincaid ordered.

Shade's finger kissed the trigger. The Slayer's bolt slammed into the target's head. North sentry dropped. Reaper's target followed a heartbeat later, collapsing into the dirt.

Two down, Shade reported. *Advancing!*

The Deltas surged forward, Slayers spitting controlled bursts. Shade dropped a Zodark sentry mid-sprint, his four-armed body spinning into the dirt. Reaper took another, bolt punching through a Zodark's chest plate.

Then the cave mouth vomited reinforcements.

Five Zodarks emerged, heavy blasters roaring suppressive fire. Plasma rounds chewed through tree trunks and stone, forcing the Deltas to shift cover. Eight human insurgents followed, scrambling into firing positions behind rocks and fallen logs.

Draven's Slayer caught one insurgent in the throat. Shade dropped another. But the enemy had the high ground and fortified positions.

We're pinned! Hammer barked, ducking behind a boulder as plasma scorched the air above his head. *One hundred meters to target, minimal cover!*

Kincaid assessed the situation—cave entrance fortified, explosives inside, no clean approach. He keyed his link. *Reaper, Draven—prep Hydras. Thermobaric warheads. I want that cave collapsed.*

Reaper and Draven dropped to one knee, pulling the A-9 Hydra launchers from their backs. The 127mm tubes locked into place with a mechanical click. Reaper's fingers danced across the targeting console, configuring the twelve-pound warhead for maximum blast.

Hydras armed, Reaper confirmed. *Targeting cave entrance.*
All units, get down! Kincaid barked.

The Deltas got small, pressing themselves into dirt and stone behind cover.

Reaper and Draven fired simultaneously.

The Hydras shrieked from their tubes, contrails streaking orange through twilight. The smart missiles corrected mid-flight, vectoring toward the cave mouth.

The first warhead punched through the entrance. The second followed a half second later.

Then the world ignited.

The thermobaric explosion consumed oxygen in a roaring fireball, pressure wave tearing through the cave system. The stored IEDs detonated in sequence—rapid-fire thunder that lifted rock and soil into the sky. The shock wave rolled outward, heat washing over the Deltas' covered positions as branches snapped overhead.

Shade felt the percussion in her chest as dirt rained down on her helmet.

When the roar faded, nothing remained but smoking rubble and a collapsed entrance where the cave had been.

Draven checked his scanner, dust still hanging in the air. *No heat signatures. No movement. I think we got 'em all—sites clear.*

Kincaid pushed to his feet, brushing dirt from his armor. *BDA confirmed. Target neutralized.*

He keyed the all-team channel. *Ghost Six, Warden Actual. Target destroyed. No survivors. Appreciate the intel. You want a ride back or you guys gonna hoof it?*

David's voice crackled back. *Pleasure doing business with you, Warden. Oh, and yeah, we'll take a ride back to base. Beats walking. Those damn bugs will eat you alive out here.*

Kincaid launched, then motioned to his team. *Yeah, those bugs are no joke. Ride will be here in five mikes. Time to pack it up. It's beer thirty and I hear you guys have the first round...*
****

A Few Hours Later

Drew wanted the remaining loose ends of this insurgency tied up. That meant that the wood carving guy, the food stall worker, and the former governor all had to go.

David and the others decided to take out the carver and the food worker the same way they had the IED cell in Moraga. In no time, they had picked the locks, released a gas cannister to knock out any additional inhabitants who would have turned into collateral damage, and used an autoinjector to end any future terrorist ambitions before they could come to fruition.

Zulon, however, would require a little more planning. Like any filthy rich individual, he had guards and a home security system, as well as a pet that was this planet's equivalent of a German shepherd.

On an upside, three days of round-the-clock watching and we know exactly how his guards operate, said Amir.

Somchai, we need you to figure out how to cut his power, though, David directed.

You got it.

A few minutes later, David lay in wait along the edge of Zulon's property, tranquilizer gun in hand. Before the guard even knew what had happened, two darts were flowing through his system, causing his eyes to roll back into his head before he slumped down.

Far side down, David confirmed.

Gate down, Amir confirmed.

After a moment of silence, Catalina replied, *I got the back entrance.*

Ready for your magic, Somchai.

The house was mostly dark as it was 2 a.m. at this point, but there was a small light in the hallway, and the low light cast by various screens in sleep mode but not turned off. But a few seconds later, the home was plunged into complete blackness, and David knew their path had been opened.

With the power off, it was more difficult to hack the door without waking up their pet. So they reverted to old-school methods, using a laser to slice a hole in one of the large front windows and removing the piece with suction.

They tossed a sleeping gas canister in through the hole, and with their masks on, they made their way inside. The house was too large for just one canister, so they rolled another one down the hallway before they continued toward the back, where the former governor's room was located.

Two minutes later, Zulon had been tapped with an autoinjector, never to wake up again. His wife remained peacefully resting beside him, unaware of what had happened.

****

With all their missions complete, Drew recalled the Kites to Gurista Prime.

"Looks like we've got a few weeks of R & R in Zidara while we await our next orders," David told his crew while they rode on an Osprey out of Tanian.

"Honestly, anything to get out of this place," Somchai said, echoing a statement they'd all felt.

"If I never see another zymura again in my entire life, I will die happy," Jess teased.

"Looking forward to a bug-free home for a few weeks myself," Amir agreed.

They weren't the only passengers headed out of Tanian. The Deltas who'd assisted them earlier in the evening were also on their way out. Apparently, the powers that be felt that Tanian was now sufficiently secure to be left to the local Gurista forces.

On the way back, David heard whispers from Warden and Shade about a possible major offensive to take the Zodark system of Tueblets, and he talked to Catalina about it over the neurolink.

This is a big deal, he told her. *You think they'll involve us?*

Catalina smiled and gently squeezed his arm before leaning her head on his shoulder and closing her eyes.

Maybe we will, maybe we won't, she said. *But for the next two weeks, I'm just going to enjoy this time with you.*

Chapter 22:
Domesticated

December 23, 2115
Éire – Belters' Planet
Great Wildlands System

Liam Patrick was thrilled he was able to make it home for Christmas. He'd bought all sorts of presents for his three kids, and a few special items for his beautiful bride, Sara. After all those years traveling out in the Belt and spending so much time alone, he had no idea how much he would crave the gentle chaos of the family life he now enjoyed.

Liam nodded at the security detail that was stationed outside the entryway of his home. He appreciated their service but was still not used to the intrusion of someone always being nearby. The two agents who had walked with him stepped to the side as Liam opened the door, giving him as much privacy as possible.

"Da!" shouted his son, Sean, as he ran over to him a hug.

His two younger twin girls, Cara and Maeve, who were still toddlers, shrieked in delight when their little eyes saw him. All three of his children swarmed him with hugs, stories, and questions.

I get less recognition for being the leader of Éire, he thought in amusement.

Sara waited for the kids to get their hugs from Liam before she swooped in for her own kiss. "Welcome home," she said with a twinkle in her eye. "I see you returned with presents?" Her right eyebrow lifted in surprise when one of his aides placed the packages on a table near the door before leaving.

Liam shrugged, a big grin on his face. "Well, you know, as it turns out I ran into Santa as we were leaving New Eden, and he asked if I could help him out by delivering some presents for him. What was I supposed to say... no?"

Sara laughed at his joke, the kids suddenly wowed that their dad had met Santa. "It's good to have you home. I wasn't sure if you would make it back before Christmas. I'm glad you did, and I'm sure the kids will love whatever you got them. Come on, let's get you settled."

That evening at dinner, Liam and Sara didn't discuss matters of national importance. Instead, they talked about anything and everything the children wanted to discuss: art projects, a new kid in his son's class, and, of course, what their dad had brought for them from his travels to the Republic.

"Did you bring us any candy?" his son asked.

"Hmm… let me see… oh, as a matter of fact, I did," Liam answered mischievously. From his pocket, he pulled out five candies, wrapped in translucent paper that sparkled like light going through a prism.

"These are a New Eden specialty," he announced. "Of course, you only get these if you finish your dinner," he said with a wink to Sara.

After the children had been put to bed, Sara couldn't contain herself anymore. "All right, love, spill the beans," she said. "How did the trip go?"

"Better than I thought it might. Honestly, I was relieved to learn that our situation isn't really going to change in the scheme of things," Liam began. "All those fears from the Gallentines and Altairians about the Humtars wanting to reclaim their former territories were just unfounded rumors. I had a chance to speak with the Humtars directly. They shared with me that such a desire is not even on the table. They realize their former worlds have been occupied for hundreds or even thousands of years. Instead, they want to settle within the Republic and establish more formal ties."

"Uh-huh. Well, I for one am glad it was just rumors and not something they were really considering. But you said they want to establish formal ties…OK, what does that mean? What's the catch?" asked Sara, relieved she could put those negative thoughts to rest.

"Honestly, as far as I know, there isn't one. As they explained it to me, the Republic will become a semiautonomous part of the Humtar Confederation, which will place them within the Humtar protectorate. I had a private conversation with Viceroy Hunt about it before the signing ceremony. He assured me that our arrangement with the Republic was brought up to them and that our position was secure—it won't change. We still retain the right to govern ourselves as we have been. But since the Republic is part of their Confederation, we are part of it too. This means we fall under their protection, which is good. We will also gain access to whatever technology they share with the Republic and can trade freely with them."

"Oh wow, that's great," Sara replied, visibly relieved. This was exactly what they had been hoping would happen. "You mentioned we would fall under their protection—does that mean we're going to have to participate in their wars? How will any of this impact the current war with the Zodarks?"

"Agreed, it's about as good a deal as we could have hoped for," Liam replied. "I can't say for certain we won't be drafted into a future conflict, but as to the Zodarks—no, we are not being asked to fight or contribute beyond the Bronkis5 mineral we already sell to the Republic. But that resource, as you know, is far too valuable to the Republic for them to want to pull us away from mining—that is by far the greatest contribution to any war effort we're able to provide. That strategy we talked about—turning our system and planet into a forge—it's giving us the best security guarantee we could hope for."

Sara sighed in relief. "I am so glad to hear that, Liam. I've been worried the entire time you were gone that everything we had built, everything we had sacrificed and fought for, might be taken away from us by this new agreement with the Humtars. Goes to show you I shouldn't fret over things I can't control, I guess."

Liam nodded, giving her a warm smile and a hug. "I totally understand. We've built this beautiful life here, and now that we have children to leave it to…well, it changes things. The risks I took in my younger years, I wouldn't even consider now. *They* are the legacy, and everything we worked for is for them."

Sara sat down on the couch that had the best view of the city of St. Patrick and patted the seat next to her. Liam joined her and put an arm around her shoulder.

"We've really done it," she said after a brief silence. "Remember when we used to dream about this free society? Think how much we've gone through to get to this point."

"Yeah," said Liam with a smile. "And now we have people from all over the Republic as well as the Prims, Tully, and Altairians coming here for a fresh start, a chance to have a do-over in life."

They looked out the window for a moment, watching the evening traffic lights twinkle. "Sometimes, Liam, I don't know whether finding Bronkis5 was a blessing or a curse," Sara admitted quietly. This was one of those topics they only talked about in private.

"Yeah, I know what you mean," Liam answered. "It definitely ties us to the Republic far more than we'd like. But we've still managed to maintain a decent amount of freedom and autonomy. People can say what they want about Viceroy Miles Hunt—but he's an honorable man, true to his word. Truthfully, when we first discovered Bronkis5, I wasn't sure if the Viceroy would continue to honor our deal or if he'd force us to accept one of those former Sumer colonies he had offered us in the Qatana system. But he kept his word and essentially gifted us a resource that all but guarantees our people will be well taken care of for generations to come."

"Hmm, that's true. Before we found that mineral… I'll admit I was having second thoughts about turning down a fully developed colony the way we did. It's awful what the Zodarks did to those poor Sumerians… it was a genocide…" Her voice trailed off.

"It was terrible. Those blue monsters are vicious. I'll say this, Sara, about our new security arrangement. Those Humtar warships… wow, they look downright terrifying. I haven't seen one in combat, but I suspect they're more powerful than anything we have ever seen before. That is one thing I do appreciate about this new agreement—they'll protect our people."

"I like that. So, now what?" asked Sara. "All this time we've been striving for the next thing…what do we do now?"

"What do we do now? We enjoy the fruits of our labor, love," answered Liam. "Everything we ever went through was worth it for nights like tonight—dinner with the family, spending time together, living in peace. Now you just have to learn how to kick back and savor it all."

"Well, you know I'm not very good at kicking back," Sara teased.

"No, but that's one of the things I love about you," he replied. "You've really come into your own here, you know. Sara, you've always been great at pulling things together for your people, but here, your gifts really shine. For example, you've done such an amazing job of making sure the Bridgeborn children of the Primord-human couples are well accepted. And whenever new refugees from different parts of the galaxy arrive, it's you and your team that make sure they land on their feet."

"I do my best," Sara said, savoring the compliment.

He smiled at her. "And your best is more than good enough," Liam answered. "I never believed in fairy tales, but I guess we got our 'happily ever after' after all."

Chapter 23:
Eyes on the Capital

December 29, 2115
CNS *Bloodhawk*
Zodark Home System – Capital Orbit

The *Bloodhawk* drifted through the darkness like smoke, its reactor output throttled to near nothing. For three weeks, Captain Calvus Theruun and his crew had methodically mapped the Zinconia system—cataloging defense platforms, tracking fleet movements, monitoring patrol patterns. Now, on their final approach to the capital world itself, only one task remained.

"Orbital traffic clearing," reported Lieutenant Deyric Kael from his sensor post, his voice barely above a whisper. "Two destroyers transitioning to high orbit. Next window opens in seventeen minutes."

Theruun studied the tactical display. Zinconia hung before them, the ancient seat of Zodark power. Unlike the sterile efficiency of newer colonies, this world wore its millennia of history like armor—layer upon layer of development, expansion, and fortification.

"Helm, ease us into the planetary shadow," he ordered. "Use the fourth moon as a mask."

"Aye, Captain," Lieutenant Arikon Vale confirmed, fingers dancing across his controls with practiced precision. The *Bloodhawk*'s drives whispered to life, a ghost's breath against the void.

Commander Velora Shan leaned forward at her electronic warfare station. "Picking up increased comm traffic from the surface. Encrypted military channels, but the volume suggests routine operations. No alert indicators."

"They don't know we're here," said Optio Korric Drahn from Tactical. It wasn't a question.

"Let's keep it that way," Theruun replied. "Begin passive mapping sequence. Deploy optical arrays—I want high-resolution imagery of everything. Every power grid, every defensive emplacement, every government building cataloged and recorded."

"Initiating optical scanner deployment," Kael confirmed. "Ultra-high-definition cameras online. We'll capture video of the entire capital region—every building, every street, every guard post."

Shan added from her station, "Recording everything in multiple spectrums. Visual, infrared, ultraviolet. The fusion cell can analyze these frame by frame later, pick up details we might miss in real time."

The crew settled into their work, eighteen intelligence specialists throughout the ship analyzing the flood of data streaming in from their passive arrays. The *Bloodhawk*'s fusion cell—her dedicated intelligence analysis team—would transform raw sensor feeds into actionable intelligence.

Hours passed in tense silence. The capital city of Drokanis slowly revealed itself through layers of electromagnetic radiation and thermal imaging.

"City layout confirmed," Kael reported, updating the main display. "Population centers here, industrial sectors along the eastern districts. Government quarter... there." He highlighted a sprawling complex near the city's heart.

Theruun studied the images forming on his display. Drokanis was a study in contrasts—ancient stone architecture supporting modern plasma conduits, millennia-old monuments surrounded by gleaming administrative towers. Public gardens and memorial parks dotted the cityscape like green jewels, each one a testament to some forgotten victory or fallen hero.

"Magnifying government sector," Shan announced. The display zoomed, revealing a compound set back from the main thoroughfares by open ground and decorative walls.

"The High Council building," Drahn identified, cross-referencing with their intelligence files. "According to the intelligence shared with us from the Republic, the central structure dates back over a thousand years. The reports said the modern additions ringing the perimeter are the offices and administrative wings."

"Really? Do those reports say how the Republic acquired this information?" Theruun asked, curious how they would know this.

"Ah, yes, right here," Drahn replied. "It says the information was relayed to them by multiple former Mukhabarat operatives and several Zodark prisoners. It cross-checks with similar information provided by Primord and Altairian intelligence," he confirmed.

Kael frowned at his sensors. "Incredible. You would think for an empire at war, its capital, its seat of power, would be better protected. Our sensors are detecting minimal defensive signatures. Some foot patrols, guard posts at the entrances. But no point-defense batteries, no hardened positions."

"Huh, it would appear they have never been attacked here," Vale observed quietly, noting the lack of military structures and defensive works.

Theruun absorbed the data, taking it all in. After weeks surveying military installations and fleet bases across the Zodark Empire, it seemed absurd to him that the government buildings housing their leaders and decision makers would be left this vulnerable to attack. "Continue scanning. Let's see if we can find out what kind of guard rotations they employ and anything else we can while here."

Kael cleared his throat. "We're starting to get some decent thermal imaging of the compound. The AI has separated what it believes to be the guard force from those who aren't. It identified the weapons the exterior guards are using and then applied those signatures to the images of the people inside the buildings," Kael explained. "It's a little crude, I know, but it's identifying approximately two hundred heat signatures within the compound that it believes to be guards.

"It's consistent with a light security force, so I'm more apt to believe it's true. There is this larger concentration here"—he highlighted a building two kilometers away—"which the AI suspects is the garrison that supports the guard force at the High Council building. This is just an estimate, so it could be off by a few dozen, but it's identified roughly eight hundred personnel."

"Huh, that's a pretty good estimate, Kael. Good job," Shan commented. "About twenty kilometers outside the city is another garrison," he added, overlaying tactical data. "Using the same AI parameters as Kael, it says the garrison has roughly five thousand soldiers at it. If I had to guess, this is the rapid response force that would respond to threats inside the city. A little further from the capital are another four military bases. The AI estimates the troop count to be somewhere around another twelve thousand."

"Interesting. But aside from these ground forces, there aren't any aerospace defenses over the Council building itself?" Theruun pressed, finding it hard to believe the capital would be so undefended.

"Negative, Captain," Drahn confirmed. "I mean, both the local garrison inside the city and the bases just outside it does have a local airbase—Zeeks, not Vulture starfighters stationed at them. The Zeeks are those atmospheric fighters the Republic told us about. But as to the rooftops of the buildings, they're just standard access points. Doors showing minimal security—two to four guards maximum. Same for exterior doors. If they run into trouble. It's likely they'll rely on a response force to come to their aid, not hardened local defenses."

A proximity alarm chimed softly. Every head snapped toward the tactical display as a red light flashed overhead.

"It's a patrol frigate," Kael hissed. "Bearing three-four-seven mark two. They're running active scans."

"All stop," Theruun ordered. "No electronic scans or signatures."

The *Bloodhawk* became a hole in space, her stealth systems drinking in every stray photon, every electromagnetic whisper. The crew barely breathed as the Zodark frigate's sensor sweeps repeatedly washed over their position.

The beam passed three times, then a fourth.

"Crap, they're lingering," Vale muttered, sweat beading on his forehead.

"Steady, Vale," Theruun commanded, though his own pulse hammered.

The frigate's sensors swept back, pausing directly over their position. For three heartbeats, the universe held its breath.

Then the patrol moved on, continuing its prescribed route.

"Whoa, we're clear," Kael exhaled. "That was close. Still no change in their emissions. We're still clean."

Theruun forced his muscles to relax. "That was closer than I'd like. How's our data collection coming along?"

"Ninety-seven percent complete," the fusion cell leader reported over internal comms. "We have detailed architectural analysis, defensive assessments, and approach vectors. Uploading final thermal maps now."

Another alarm—this one from Shan's station. "Electronic anomaly detected. Someone just activated a deep-scan array on the second moon."

"Military?"

"Unknown, but it's powerful. If they sweep this sector—"

"We won't be here," Theruun decided. "Begin withdrawal sequence. Kael, recover our passive arrays. Vale, plot a course out of the gravity well—use the industrial transport corridor to mask our signature. We'll hide in the shadows of the next transport."

The crew moved with urgent precision, having done this many times before. The ships' towed arrays were reeled in like fishing lines, their gossamer sensors disappearing into hidden compartments. The *Bloodhawk*'s reactor began its careful climb back to operational levels.

"New contact," Drahn reported. "Zeek squadron launching from the surface. Bearing suggests they're heading for our general vicinity."

"Coincidence?" Vale asked.

"I don't believe in coincidence," Theruun replied. "Time to leave, people. Helm, execute our withdrawal."

The *Bloodhawk* surged forward, still wrapped in her cloak of shadows but no longer pretending to be debris. They slipped between cargo haulers and ore processors, using the commercial traffic as cover while the Zeek fighters spread out behind them.

"They're running search patterns," Kael observed. "But they still don't have a fix on us."

"Yet," Theruun amended. "Shan, can you spoof their sensors?"

"I already am. Feeding them false returns in grid seven-three. Should buy us a few minutes."

Those minutes stretched like hours as the *Bloodhawk* crept toward the planet's edge. Twice more they had to alter course as patrol craft swept past, each time coming perilously close to detection as they broke free of the planet's orbit.

Finally, after six hours of nerve-wracking evasion, they reached a safe distance from the planet and could begin their transit out of the system.

"Captain, we're officially clear of the gravity well," Vale reported. "The ship is ready for QCB translation on your order."

Theruun took one last look at the tactical plot. Zinconia still glowed on their sensors, unaware of how thoroughly its secrets had been mapped. Every weakness cataloged, every vulnerability noted.

"Very well, take us out," he ordered. "Set course for New Eden. Let's get our data to the Enclave and the Republic. They'll be eager to see what we found."

The *Bloodhawk* engaged her quantum drives and vanished into the conduit, leaving the Zodark planet behind. In her data cores, she carried the blueprint for its destruction—should the Republic choose to use it.

They had done their job. Now it would be up to others to decide how to use what they had found. But looking at the vulnerable heart of the Zodark Empire displayed on his screens, Theruun suspected that decision had already been made.

The war was about to take a very different turn.

Chapter 24:
Running the Numbers

January 3, 2116
Sublevel Three – Space Command Headquarters
New Cambria, New Eden

"Did you have a good Christmas?" asked Vice Admiral Rosentreter as he and Rear Admiral Amy Dobbs walked into the elevator.

Dobbs typed in a code, then pushed the button for SL3 before responding to his question. "I did. I slept till ten in the morning, then went for a jog while I listened to an audiobook before eating so much food for lunch I passed out before the end of the Bears–Lions game."

"Oh man, does that mean you missed that spectacular play in the fourth quarter when the Bears were down nine points with just a minute and fifty-eight seconds remaining?" Rosentreter asked excitedly.

Dobbs looked glum. "Oh, unfortunately, I did. I caught the replay after I woke up, but yeah, I missed seeing it live."

"Wow, that's too bad. It was spectacular. The Bears' quarterback threw a forty-seven-yard pass to Godwin, who then broke a tackle and ran another thirty-two yards for a touchdown. It was the most amazing catch, and how he broke that tackle afterwards... wow."

"Yeah, it looked pretty neat, but how about recovering that onside kick?" Dobbs countered. "I mean, that was crazy how they regained possession. Then a nineteen-yard catch to Evans and poof, they were in field goal range with just three seconds to spare."

"I can't believe you slept through that, Amy. You missed the game of the year."

Just then the doors parted with a muted hiss and they walked into the cavernous briefing chamber, their demeanors instantly switching to work mode.

Around the table, senior figures from the Republic Fleet and Army were already gathering. The hum of low conversations died as Fleet Admiral Chester Bailey stepped forward, data pad in hand, eyes sweeping the room like a tactical scan.

The air here felt heavier now than it had a few months ago, when the Viceroy had welcomed them home and laid out his vision for ending the war. That meeting had been about victory parades, public morale. This meeting, buried three levels underground in the nerve center of Space Command, was about how to actually end the war.

Rosentreter got straight to it.

"Admiral, do we have the numbers to legitimately conduct a decapitation strike and subsequent invasion of Tueblets?"

Bailey exhaled slowly, weighing the question. "If you'd asked me that before the Humtar upgrades to our communication systems, I'd have said not a chance. Coordinating simultaneous multivector assaults on that scale would have been... impractical at best. But now?" He tapped his data pad, throwing up a holomap of the Tueblets system. "The Humtars have not only improved our firepower, they've compressed our repair and build times by a factor I'd have called science fiction five years ago. Damaged hulls can be restored in weeks, not months. New ships come off the line twice as fast. That gives us the punch we need, especially since they're going to fight alongside us."

Dobbs leaned forward, her voice sharp despite having just returned from R&R. "All of that's great, sir—but ships don't hold ground. Soldiers do. And the Humtars can't manufacture fresh troops in a shipyard. The Army's been running hot for three and a half years. They've bled heavily. Even with replacements, unit cohesion takes time to rebuild."

Across the table, Brigadier General Brian Royce, the man who'd fought beside her in the Gurista liberation, gave a short, humorless laugh.

"She's not wrong, Admiral. Every campaign, every invasion... our people have paid for it in blood. They're tired, sir. And not just physically, many of them are burned hollow. PTSD, combat fatigue, the works. You can't watch cities burn and civilians butchered for years on end without being scarred. If you want the ground forces sharp for Tueblets, we need downtime. And proper downtime—not a few months on a beach before loading on the next transport. They need dwell time to rest their minds, bodies, and souls before we throw them back into training and boarding ships to invade the next planet."

Bailey's brow furrowed. "Point taken. I've been so focused on fleet readiness and ship numbers that I haven't accounted for the human side of the equation."

Royce shrugged. "That's why you've got us in the room. You get the *Freedom* ready for combat, and when you call, we'll go. But the more recovery time you give us, the more effective we'll be."

Silence settled briefly before Rosentreter spoke again. "Sir, whichever path we take—Zinconia first or Tueblets—the linchpin is still the *Freedom*. Without her bridging capability, the whole plan collapses. What's the latest on her repairs?"

Bailey glanced down at his data pad. "Last update says six weeks until the yards finish. Considering the state she was in, that's a miracle. Honestly, if the Gallentines had decided to scrap her, I wouldn't have been surprised given the beating she took."

Vice Admiral Lee, seated halfway down the table, cut in. "Assuming she's back on time, you'll be pulling her original crew in from across the Fleet. That creates its own gaps. What's the plan for backfilling those?"

Bailey nodded. "Some of that's in motion already—increased recruitment and draft intakes, promotions across the ranks to fill officer gaps. But you're right, retraining that crew will take a couple months on top of the repair window. So even if the yards hit their mark, we're still looking at roughly four months before *Freedom* is combat-ready."

Rosentreter leaned back, making the mental calculation. "Four months... maybe sixteen to eighteen weeks, if everything goes to plan. That's not much time to organize a campaign of this size."

Royce gave a short grunt. "Not enough to do proper recon of Zinconia either. Dropping teams blind into the High Council's backyard isn't a plan—it's suicide."

Bailey's gaze sharpened. "Which is why I'll be speaking with the Viceroy about this very topic. The Humtars have assets we don't—stealth ships built for deep penetration. If we can get one, Royce, you and your Delta operators could get eyes on the ground before we commit to the strike."

A slow grin spread across Royce's face. "That's exactly what we'd need, sir."

Dobbs looked between them. "So, we start two tracks in parallel: Fleet gets the *Freedom* and the invasion force ready. Army rests, refits, and replenishes. Royce's team works the Humtar angle and begins the recon planning. Four months if we can manage it, longer if we have to, but we won't know until we start."

Bailey nodded, tapping the holomap to life again. "Yeah, that sounds about right. Let's go ahead and plan for that. When I get more details from the Humtars, we'll meet again. Until then, let's get our people and ships ready. It's time to end this war."

Chapter 25:
Shock & Awe

January 10, 2116
Republic Army Headquarters
New Eden

Brigadier General Brian Royce stared at the mission proposal before placing the tablet on the table in front of him. He had seen his share of crazy ideas—hell, he'd proposed a few himself. But this was more than just crazy. It looked suicidal; worse, it felt pointless. He shook his head before asking, "Al, we've known each other for a while. Is this really what the Viceroy is proposing?"

"Are you saying it's not possible, Brian?" countered Lieutenant General Alfred Bates, the Commander of Republic Special Forces.

Brian scoffed before answering. "I think just about anything is possible if you give it enough resources. If we're given what's outlined in the proposal, yeah, it's probably doable. But why risk highly trained operatives on a mission like this when you can accomplish the same result with an orbital strike or a few missiles from a starfighter or bomber?"

The Special Forces Commander stared at him for a moment before speaking. "I don't like to risk the lives of my Deltas any more than you do. I asked the Viceroy the same question. If decapitating the leadership is the objective, why not hit it from orbit? You know what he told me? Shock and awe—"

"Shock and awe, eh?" interrupted Brian with a half chuckle. "OK, what am I missing?"

Bates smiled. "I didn't get it at first either, but hear me out. We know the Zodark Empire is structured around clans and the tribes within them. From additional information we've learned from the Guristas and the interrogations of captured Zodarks, their High Council, the governing body that oversees their Empire, is derived from the original seven clans that united their home world. Their clan structure is based on honor and devotion to the Empire. If a warrior dishonors his family, it could tarnish his tribe. If his tribe is dishonored, it could have serious implications for the clan as a whole.

"Now imagine the dishonor that would befall the leader of the High Council, this Zodark they call Zon, and his appointed Mavkah, the head of the Malvari or their military, if the Council came under attack by an assault force. It's one thing to be hit by an orbital strike or a handful of suicidal starfighters. But a ground team of soldiers infiltrating what should be the most secure facility in the Empire—that, Brian, is shock and awe," Bates explained before continuing. "This war has to end, Brian. We lost a billion people during the attack on Earth. We've lost more than a million soldiers and spacers in the three years since.

"The arrival of the Humtars and the considerable aid we've received from them and the Gallentines over the past couple of years have presented some new options that are worth exploring. For what it's worth, I think the Viceroy is right in pursuing them," Bates admitted. "If we try to fight the Zodarks one system at a time, we'll lose millions and this war will drag on for years, maybe a decade or more. The Viceroy believes this plan is our best shot at winning. With help from the Humtars, I think he's right."

Brian slowly nodded, conceding the point. "I want to disagree, Al, but in this case, I stand corrected. You remember that Mukhabarat operative we captured and then turned—Ashurina?"

Bates smiled. "Yeah, I remember Ashurina—the Mukhabarat honeypot. What about her?"

"What the Viceroy said about honor within their culture matches exactly what Ashurina shared with us. When I asked her why she worked for the Zodarks, why so many of her brothers worked for them, she told me that her service, and her brothers' service, brought honor and prestige to their family. It elevated their status and that of their tribe and clan," shared Brian. "The opposite of honor is shame. If the Zodark NOS, the Mavkah who leads their military, can be shamed for incompetence, it'll cause problems across his clan and those who support them.

"This is risky as hell, Al. But I suppose if we can shame the Zon and his Mavkah, we might succeed in creating a schism within the leadership of the clans. That might be all we need to split the Empire or weaken them into accepting an end to the war on terms we *can* live with."

"Exactly, Brian. Now comes the hard part—planning it. How long will you need to prepare a team to carry out a raid on the capital?" Bates asked in a serious tone.

"Hmm, I think I'll have a better answer for you once I've seen the intel they collected. Any chance you can arrange a meeting with the Humtars?" Brian answered honestly.

Smiling, Bates nodded. "Yeah, I'll make some calls. In the meantime, start putting together your team and figuring out what kind of toys you might want to bring along. If we're going to raid their capital, let's make sure to leave a calling card to let 'em know we were there," Bates said with a devilish look.

As the meeting came to an end, Brian genuinely hoped this was the beginning of the end of what was clearly a war of extermination. He'd spent nearly his entire life in Army, in Special Forces. Now he had a family and young kids. He was ready to hang it up. To begin the next chapter in life. But not until the Zodarks were gone. Not until he knew his wife and kids were safe.

Just a little longer, Jane... and I'm all yours and the kids'...

Chapter 26:
Raiders of Kryntok

January 20, 2116
Republic Navy Headquarters
Fleet Operations Building, New Cambria
New Eden

The Torch Briefing Room sat deep within the Fleet Operations Building, its walls lined with star maps and computer displays protected by sound-dampening materials and electromagnetic shielding. Named for the Republic's belief in bringing light to the darkness, the room was witness to the birth of operations that would continue to shape the course of the war. Today would be no different.

Captain Naram-Suen entered the room with a determined purpose. In his hand, a small metallic disc caught the overhead lighting as he approached the Republic officers.

"Admiral Rosentreter, Captain Wright," Suen greeted them. "I am glad we are finally able to meet. Thank you for hosting me at your headquarters. I believe what we will discuss here will set the tone for our entire campaign."

Vice Admiral Willie Rosentreter rose from his seat at the black stone conference table, extending his hand in greeting. "Captain Suen, welcome to Fleet Operations. I agree, I hope the return of the *Bloodhawk* has brought with it the intelligence Admiral Korrath was waiting for?"

Suen nodded, "It has, and this is the reason we need to speak. We have a plan we'd like to discuss."

Captain Joe Wright of the RNS *Vanguard* extended his hand. "Captain, it's a pleasure to meet you. I'll be leading the Republic's contingent on this mission. I'm looking forward to hearing what you have for us."

"It's a pleasure, Captain. Depending on how this first mission goes, we'll see what kind of follow-on ones it'll lead to." Suen leaned over and placed the holo puck in the center of the briefing table before motioning for them to begin.

With a soft hum, it activated, projecting a three-dimensional display of the Kryntok system that filled the space above the table. The image painted the system in harsh reds and yellows—threat assessments, defensive emplacements, and mining operations scattered across three habitable worlds.

"The Kryntok system is where we have decided to launch our first operation," Suen began, manipulating the display with subtle hand gestures. "It has a single sun, three habitable planets, four nonhabitable, plus two habitable moons among fourteen total. The Zodarks have turned this entire system into their primary heavy industry and ore-refining hub for this sector."

The display zoomed in on the second planet, revealing massive strip-mining operations that scarred entire continents. Orbital refineries hung in geosynchronous orbit, connected to the surface by space elevators that looked like silver threads from this distance.

"The system security is... adequate," Suen said, the pause speaking volumes. "Six Zodark battleships, a dozen cruisers, and a similar number of frigates on a rotating patrol. Closer to the planet and the mining operations are another dozen corvettes for local security, and approximately forty patrol boats or smaller defensive craft. Frankly, it's nothing we can't handle, but it'll be more than enough to make noise once we hit them.

"Our fusion cell, that's our intelligence group, has gone over the system thoroughly and identified the ideal entry points into the system to ensure complete surprise," Suen explained as the hologram shifted, highlighting entry vectors. A pulsing blue line indicated the QCB jump point. "My ship, the *Oathbreaker*, will open a quantum conduit bridge into the system for our attack force. Once the bridge is open, our ships will enter and yours will follow. The timing for what happens next is critical. Once my ship is through, I'll initiate a system-wide broad-spectrum jamming that'll block them from calling for help. It'll jam the local space so hard, no one will be able to send a warning to anyone, anywhere."

As Suen continued to speak, the holodisplay suddenly came to life, with a simulation of what he'd just briefed playing out before them. It showed Humtar and Zodark ships moving about the system as if playing a deadly game of chess. Two of the Humtar frigates and a cruiser peeled away from the main formation. "This is perhaps a different way of conducting a briefing, but if you'll allow me to walk you through it, I think you'll appreciate the strategy," Suen explained as the simulation continued. "Upon entry into the system, the *Fell Claw* and *Shadowrend* will move with the *Grimward* to blockade the stargate. This will prevent ships from attempting to flee, and should anyone new arrive, they'll be dealt with immediately."

Rosentreter leaned forward, studying the tactical display in amazement. "I have to hand it to you, Captain Suen, this method of briefing is pretty neat. Can you share with us how you envision using some of our ships in this operation?"

Suen shifted the display to show the Republic forces in blue. "Sure. The main role is to help us sell this as a Republic-led attack. This keeps our involvement in it a mystery and lets the Zodarks believe your forces have advanced in lethality much further than they thought possible. This will help lead them to the conclusion that the war is unwinnable, and hopefully push them toward ending it. Now, correct me if I am wrong, Admiral. To aid us in this effort, I was told the Republic would bring along some salvaged wrecks from prior battles that we would be leaving behind to make this look like a Republic raid behind enemy lines. Is that still correct?"

"It is. The ship in question is the *Bechtel*. It's one of our expeditionary base construction platform vessels. We use them as a mobile construction platform, deploying comms arrays, sentry towers, or functioning as a forward-deployed logistics and infrastructure support vessel. For this mission, its massive internal cargo hold will carry the wrecked hull of the Republic frigate *Defiance*, plus salvaged parts from the heavy cruiser *Normandy* and corvette *Swift Strike*. All lost in recent engagements," explained Admiral Rosentreter. "Once the all clear is given, just direct them where you'd like the debris left. They'll begin dispersing it, leaving behind the evidence of our involvement—oh, and before I forget. To further sell this whole charade, we plan to leave behind several of our Gallentine B-19 Devastator Bombers and a couple of F-19 Hellcats. The Zodarks will believe it was the *Freedom* that wrecked the system and not your forces."

Suen's smile grew wide as he listened. "That... is brilliant, Admiral. When Admiral Korrath told me about the plan, I wasn't sure what to make of it, but this is really going to mess with their minds for sure. Back to your question, how is this all going to work? Let me explain." He turned to face Captain Wright before continuing to speak. "Once our forces are in the system, your primary objective is to provide escort and defensive cover for the *Bechtel*. You'll position your squadron here"—a location materialized in the display, well clear of the primary engagement zone—"and hold until my forces have eliminated all Zodark threats."

Wright nodded, already picturing it in his head. "Got it. You want us to stay out of your way and play a purely defensive role until you give the all clear."

"Correct. Once we've secured the area and eliminated their mobile assets, your force will escort the *Bechtel* to the primary mining facilities and begin the festivities." The display showed the massive industrial complexes in detail. "Once you're in position, you'll need to start smashing their infrastructure using your weapons—the evidence needs to show Republic weapons used against these facilities. You'll wreck 'em and turn their refineries into molten slag."

"Roger that. Our gun crews are going to have a field day with this," Wright commented, barely concealing his excitement.

"And the *Bechtel*—when and where do you want them to disperse their cargo?" asked Rosentreter pressed, wanting clarity on how this part of the mission was going to work.

"I think we will need to discuss where once the battle is underway," Suen explained. "We need to see where the major engagements will take place. That's where I would like to drop the evidence."

The display shifted to show the final phase as Suen continued. "Once the *Bechtel* finishes its job, the *Oathbreaker* will open another QCB and we'll exit the system. If we're lucky, we'll be gone before their reinforcements can even warm up their engines."

"I love it. Let's talk force composition. What are you looking to bring?" Rosentreter asked, though he suspected he already knew.

"From the Confederation," Suen responded as ship profiles appeared in the hologram, "I'll have my ship, the *Oathbreaker* as our command ship." The *Voidhammer*-class heavy battleship materialized, its organic-looking hull bristling with weapon emplacements. "Additionally, we'll have two *Warclaw*-class light battleships, the CNS *Razorwind* and CNS *Dark Omen*. They'll have four *Ironveil*-class cruisers—the *Grimward*, *Sarruk*, *Shattersky*, and *Veilrunner*. For screening elements we'll have three of our *Daggerwind*-class frigates— *Ravager*, *Fell Claw*, and *Shadowrend*. For reconnaissance in the neighboring system, the *Bloodhawk* will accompany us. If the enemy mobilizes a force to come after us, we'll know ahead of their arrival."

"And from the Republic," Wright continued, "we'll have my ship, the *Vanguard*, heavy cruisers *Intrepid* and *Resolute*, plus the *Bechtel* herself."

"Eight warships plus your construction platform," Suen calculated. "More than sufficient for Kryntok's defenders, small enough for rapid deployment and withdrawal."

"Timeline?" Wright asked.

"Ideally, I'd like to shove off in five days. The sooner we begin these attacks, the sooner the cracks will form around the Zon's power base," Suen stated firmly. "Before you leave, I'd like our crews to run a joint tactical simulation training event. The timing for this must be perfect—from QCB entry to withdrawal, we'll have perhaps a handful of hours to half a day before the Zodarks in the neighboring systems will be able to mobilize a rapid response force. We need to be out of there before they arrive."

"I think that timeline can work. The *Bechtel* still needs a few days to finalize debris preparation," Rosentreter added. "Every detail has to be perfect. We're even bringing the recovered remains of two hundred and thirty-seven Republic spacers to further sell this ambush. These are the men and women we pulled from the void after the Battle of Kepler-442. We spoke with their families about this, and they agreed—if their loved ones can serve the Republic a final time to help end this terrible war, they're for it."

"Wow, that is… an honorable end to their service. Even in death, their bodies shall serve a purpose. I must say, Admiral, our people are truly impressed by the sacrifice, honor, and service to one's country that the people of the Republic continue to demonstrate. It truly is an honor to know we share the same lineage and ancestry of our forefathers," Suen offered with genuine, solemn respect. "We have an old Humtar saying. Honor in all things… your people are a true embodiment of that," Suen murmured somberly. "Even in this deception… we are honoring the fallen, making sure their sacrifice hastens the end of this awful war."

The Humtar captain deactivated the holo puck, the tactical display vanishing like smoke. "I believe we have covered everything. Do you have any questions?"

"Not right now, I don't," Wright answered, turning to Admiral Rosentreter to see if he had something to add.

"If questions arise, I'm sure they can be handled during the simulation. Let's do this," the admiral replied eagerly.

"Agreed. Captain Wright," Suen said, fixing the younger officer with an intense gaze, "I cannot emphasize this enough—you must maintain your position until I give the all clear. No heroics, no rushing to assist no matter how desperate a fight it might appear our ships are in. Your role is to protect the *Bechtel* and execute the deception. Nothing more."

"Crystal clear, Captain," Wright assured him. "We'll hold position until you give the word."

Suen pocketed the holo puck and stood. "Then in five days, we show the Zodarks that their industrial might burns as easily as anything else. And in the ashes, we'll plant seeds of paranoia that will grow into something beautiful—distrust, suspicion, and chaos."

As the officers rose to leave, Rosentreter had one final thought. "Captain Suen, this operation… if it goes well, we're going to need to be ready to follow it up with a rapid series of similar attacks. Is your fusion cell planning them already?"

The Humtar officer paused at the door. "Yes, they are. Viceroy Hunt and Admiral Korrath have given us the directive to destabilize the Zodark Empire from within. This raid? It's merely the first pebble in an avalanche that will bury them in their own suspicions." His eyes gleamed with predatory satisfaction. "In five days, Admiral, we're going to teach them the true meaning of fear."

The door sealed behind him with a soft hiss, leaving the two Republic officers alone with their thoughts and the weight of what they were about to unleash.

Chapter 27:
That's Crazy

Joint Operations Center
Fort Leatherneck
New Eden

The Humtar, Brigadier General Tammuz Marduk stood before the assembled operators, his massive frame casting shadows across the holographic display. He eyed the forty-two Republic Deltas, the best of the Republic Special Forces, along with eighteen of his best Humtar operators, all waiting to hear the details of what might be the most audacious mission any of them had ever conducted. The mission clock on the wall read 0400 hours—or zero dark hundred, as the Republic soldiers referred to it. They had fourteen days of training evolutions to get ready for the mission, fourteen days until they landed on the Zodark home world.

"Settle down, and listen up." Marduk's voice rumbled. "It should go without saying that what I'm about to brief you on doesn't leave this room."

The lighting dimmed, and the hologram shifted to show the planet Zinconia—the Zodark capital world. As the image magnified, it zeroed in on the capital city, its surrounding area dominated by sprawling military compounds and a distinctive byzantine-like structure labeled High Council building.

"This, gentlemen, is shock and awe, baby! We're going to strike the seat of power of the Zodark Empire—the High Council building. In fourteen days, we're going to either capture or kill every member of the High Council," declared Brigadier General Brian Royce as he stepped forward to stand alongside General Marduk. "I know some of you might be asking, 'Why not hit the building from orbit with a missile or kinetic strike?'" the Delta commander said. "Honor, and shame—that's why we're going to kick their front door down, walk into their most secured facility, eliminate their security, and capture or kill the Zon and every member of the High Council."

A low murmur rippled through the room as the operators exchanged nervous glances with each other.

"Now that you know why you're here, let's discuss how we're going to do this," Marduk began as the holo changed again, this time showing an animated image of the Humtar *Shadowfang*-class vessel *Bloodhawk* descending into the planet's upper atmosphere. "The *Bloodhawk* will insert us here, thirty kilometers above the target. For you Deltas, our method of insertion is a little different than what you're probably used to. We use what's called a magtube launcher. It hurls our operators through a planet's atmosphere a bit quicker than your traditional HALO process. But don't worry, you'll figure it out in a couple of days once we begin training."

The display zoomed, showing trajectory calculations. Captain Rhan-Set, a Humtar, manipulated the controls with practiced efficiency. Red lines traced descent paths through Zinconia's atmosphere.

"Yeah, so the way this works is pretty simple. Once the outer shell breaks away at ten thousand feet, you'll be traveling somewhere around Mach two," Rhan-Set explained nonchalantly. "To slow your descent and begin the deceleration process. There is a disposable rocket attachment on the bottom of your boots. Once it engages, it'll initiate a three-second burn that'll slow you from terminal velocity down to a hundred and twenty feet per second."

Colonel Steve Panza raised a hand. "Excuse me, Captain. That's a hell of a narrow margin at those kinds of speeds. If there is even the slightest bit of equipment failure—"

"We know, Steve—you become a human lawn dart," Royce finished bluntly. "For this mission, we'll be using the new Star Wheel system. At one thousand feet, your drag chute deploys. It pulls the Star Wheel free from its protective casing, allowing the blades to autodeploy, using the airflow to generate lift and slow descent. Your HUD provides full steering control, allowing you to engage targets during descent with your triple-one," Royce explained, referring to the Delta's M-111 Slayer battle rifle. This was SOF's newest rifle, having come into being right before the start of the Second Zodark War.

Royce paused for a moment before continuing. "Listen, I know this mission sounds crazy, and it is. But this is the kind of mission that's going to have a real impact on ending this war. We all know the Zodark culture is heavily based on honor, loyalty, and shame. We plan to shame and dishonor the Zon's ability to protect his people and his military leader to protect the capital. This is going to cause the kind of internal conflict that can split a nation. I know this mission and this insertion are incredibly dangerous. That's why we're going to run the insertion three times in training, to make sure we get it right. After lunch, you'll begin equipment familiarization, so save your questions on how that process works till then. Now let's break down the team objectives."

While Royce was speaking, the hologram shifted, highlighting four distinct zones across the compound. "The mission will be broken down into three direct-action teams—Alpha, Bravo, and Charlie. Each team is going to consist of twelve Republic Deltas, four Humtars, thirteen C300s, and two C200s. Sierra Team will have six Republic Deltas, six Humtars, and the same complement of Combat Synths, except their job is to set up and deploy the Killshot loitering drone package. Lest any of you bastards think I'm sitting this one out, I'll personally be leading Alpha Team into the High Council building—we're going to capture that bastard Zon Otro or send him to meet his maker," Royce announced to the surprise of his Deltas.

Captain John Doris leaned forward as Royce indicated Bravo's zone. "Bravo Team, you'll sweep the grounds. Clear it of possible threats. If you encounter any enslaved humans or allied prisoners, liberate them and prepare them for evac. If you happen to encounter any Council members, take 'em prisoner if you can, kill 'em if you can't."

Captain Rhan-Set highlighted a Zodark garrison roughly eight hundred meters from the compound. "Once we hit the facility, the local guard force is going to call for its quick reaction force. It's imperative that we prevent them from gaining access to the grounds until after Alpha Team has completed their objective. This is where Charlie Team comes into play. You'll establish a blocking position here—you don't need to hold the enemy off all day, just long enough for Alpha to complete the mission and the *Bloodhawk* to pick us up. It's believed the garrison houses a guard force of around two thousand Zodark warriors. When they mobilize—and they will once the party starts—it's going to be on you, Charlie, to stop 'em cold."

Marduk shifted the display again. "And this brings us to Sierra Team's package."

The room leaned forward as the hologram revealed deployment zones across the capital. Red dots multiplied—showing hundreds of them.

"The twelve Delta and Humtar operators will work with your C300s to get our loitering drones deployed ASAP," Royce said. "We're bringing the kitchen sink with us—a thousand of the little buggers are going to accompany us on this mission. It's the closest thing we're going to have to air support, and I intend to make full use of these little terror bots."

Sergeant Major Tanner whistled low. "Geez, General, those little nightmares ought to be a war crime." His comment elicited a few laughs from the operators. No one liked dealing with drones.

"Yeah, maybe after the war they can come up with some sort of stupid rule to tie our hands with, but until they do, we're going to use every terror weapon we've got against these blue devils," Royce countered sarcastically. "We're going to create a hellscape for the Zodarks with two hundred Killshots covering the approach routes to the compound. Another two hundred split between these two military bases." The display highlighted positions fifteen kilometers north and south of the capital. "Maximum confusion, maximum casualties among the reinforcements they'll be sending to counter us."

"Incredible. And the remaining six hundred?" asked Colonel Panza.

Royce smiled devilishly. "I'm glad you asked. The final six hundred will rove in patrol over the entire capital. They'll be set for random engagement intervals between one and six hours post-exfil. Every Zodark warrior becomes a potential target even after we're gone."

The room quieted as they absorbed what he said. They would unleash a sustained psychological operation that would paralyze the capital hours after the strike team departed.

"Well, I love it. You said we begin training after lunch?" Tanner asked.

Marduk nodded. "Affirmative. We don't have a lot of time, so we need to start immediately. We'll run the full mission profile five times—three with insertion, two dry runs focused on ground assault. Ten days total training. Four days contingency and final prep. Then we execute."

"Damn, that's ambitious," Panza observed carefully.

"It's necessary to apply the kind of pressure campaign the Fleet is starting," Royce countered. He paused, letting his gaze sweep the room one final time. "Gentlemen, what we're attempting has never been done.

No force that we know of has ever successfully assaulted a Zodark command facility and survived to brag about it. In fourteen days, we change that. We don't just win—we humiliate them. We prove their Empire isn't invincible. We show the galaxy that the Republic and its allies can reach out and touch anyone, anywhere. Dismissed."

The room erupted into motion with the Humtar and Delta operators talking amongst themselves as they began the process of getting to know each other. This was unlike any mission any of their forces had previously accomplished. If they succeeded, they could end the war. If they failed... they might rally a defeated enemy.

Chapter 28
Accountability

High Council Chamber
Drokanis, Zinconia
Zodark Home World

Zon Otro entered the High Council Chamber with the weight of the Empire pressing heavily on his shoulders. The air was thick with tension as the Council members stood to acknowledge his presence before taking their seats. The chamber, usually filled with the murmur of discussion, was now eerily silent, the gravity of the situation hanging over them all like a dark cloud.

Otro took his seat at the head of the long table, his eyes narrowing as he looked at the assembled Council members. Mavkah Griglag, the head of the Malvari, and his deputy, NOS Tarvox Nilkar, sat at the opposite end of the room. He could see their expressions were hard, and they looked resolute as they waited to be called forward. After a string of devastating defeats, they had a lot to answer for.

Notably absent, to his great frustration, were the Groff. Vak'Atioth and his organization should have been providing the Malvari with timely intelligence about what the Republic and its allies were doing. Instead, they continued to remain absent, leaving the Malvari in the dark. Something told him there was more going on with the Groff and Vak'Atioth than was being let on. What exactly, he wasn't sure yet, but he was hoping today might bring some answers.

"This meeting will come to order," Otro announced as he silenced the room. "We all know why we're here," he went on, his voice low and steady. "The Empire has suffered a series of defeats that have left us weakened and placed our systems in jeopardy. Following the collapse of our defenses in the Gravaxia system, the Republic stands ready to invade Tueblets. To compound the loss and add to the severity of the situation, we lost control of the Orinda system and the Gurista people.

"As it stands, we have enemies now forming on two sides of Tueblets. We are at a crossroads, and despite the heroic efforts of our Malvari, they have not been able to turn the situation around. Two days ago, we learned of a raid carried out by Republic forces in the Kryntok system, one of our critical mining and forging systems. From all accounts, it would appear the Republic's flagship, a Gallentine vessel they call *Freedom*, carried out the attack, which left most of our infrastructure across the system in ruins. I call upon Mavkah Griglag to give an account of the situation. Now step forward into the Circle of Truth and answer our questions," Zon Otro ordered.

Griglag stood, then walked to the center of the Council Chamber, where the Circle of Truth waited, casting long shadows under the harsh lights and glaring eyes of those in charge of the Empire. He stepped forward, walking through the blue flame, its ominous light enhancing the scars of countless battles that lined his facial features.

Once through the cleansing flame of Lindow, Griglag returned his gaze to those judging him, unwavering in his resolve as he stood ready to speak.

"Great Zon, the Kryntok incident represents a disturbing escalation in Republic tactics," Griglag began, his voice steady despite the gravity of his words. "At 0347 hours local time, sensor stations detected multiple hyperspace signatures—what we now believe was their carrier *Freedom* and her escort group. By the time our patrol forces could respond, they were already in-system."

Otro leaned forward, his fingers drumming against the armrest. The *Freedom*—that cursed ship had become a specter haunting their territories. "Continue, Mavkah. What of our defenses? Six battleships should have been sufficient."

"The battleships *Zorathis* and *Kelmorak* were caught refueling at the primary depot when the attack commenced," Griglag reported. "The Republic forces struck with surgical precision—their Devastator bombers launched simultaneous torpedo runs against our orbital refineries while their fighters engaged our patrol craft. By the time *Zorathis* cleared her moorings, three refineries were already burning."

NOS Tarvox stepped forward beside his commander, data pad in hand. "The debris field tells an interesting story, Great Zon. We recovered wreckage from at least three Republic vessels—a frigate, sections of a heavy cruiser, and multiple fighter craft. Their losses weren't light."

"Yet they still completed their objective," Councillor Drex interjected from his position at the table, his tone acidic. "Our entire rare metals processing capacity for the sector—gone."

Otro raised his hand for silence, his gaze never leaving Griglag. "The timing troubles me, Mavkah. How did they know our patrol rotation? How did they know exactly when our ships would be most vulnerable?"

"We're investigating all possibilities, including intelligence breaches," Griglag answered. "But there's something else, Great Zon. The attack pattern was... unusual. They destroyed infrastructure but avoided civilian habitats. They could have obliterated the colony domes on Kryntok-III, yet they bypassed them entirely."

The chamber fell silent as Otro processed this information. The Republic was sending a message—they could strike anywhere, at any time, with impunity. But they were also showing restraint, targeting military and industrial assets while sparing civilian populations. It was psychological warfare at its most sophisticated.

"What of survivors? Surely someone witnessed more than debris and flames," Otro pressed.

"Commander Vakris of the corvette *Shadowthorn* survived the engagement," Griglag replied. "He reported counting at least eight Republic capital ships before his bridge lost sensors. He described their flagship's new weapon systems—enhanced turbo lasers that carved through our armor plating like it was hull foam. The *Freedom* has been upgraded since our last intelligence reports."

Otro's jaw tightened. Every report brought worse news. "And our response time from neighboring systems?"

"Seventeen hours," Tarvox answered reluctantly. "By the time the rapid response force from Zelkara arrived, they found only wreckage and our surviving garrison forces conducting rescue operations. The Republic was long gone."

"Seventeen hours," Otro repeated, his voice dangerously quiet. The number hung in the air like an accusation. He could feel the fear radiating from some Council members—if Kryntok could fall in hours, what system was safe?

"The damage assessment, Mavkah. Give me the full truth of it."

Griglag straightened, meeting his leader's gaze directly. "Forty-three percent of our heavy forging capacity destroyed. Sixty-one percent of rare metal refineries offline. Two space elevators severed—they'll take months to rebuild. Conservative estimates put full restoration at eight to ten months, assuming no further attacks. The strategic minerals we were stockpiling for the new *Plarix* battleships… we lost seventy percent of our processed thorilium reserves."

A collective intake of breath echoed through the chamber. Without thorilium, their new battleship production would grind to a halt.

"But we did learn something valuable from this attack," Griglag continued, sensing the need to provide some positive element. "Their tactics suggest they're operating on intelligence that's at least three weeks old. They didn't know about the *Drakonis* battlegroup we'd relocated to the inner system—pure luck they weren't there during the raid. And the Republic forces maintained strict communications discipline throughout. Whatever new encryption they're using, we couldn't break it, but it also means they're afraid we might."

Otro absorbed every detail, his mind already calculating responses and countermoves. The Republic had drawn first blood in this new phase of warfare—hit-and-run raids designed to cripple infrastructure while avoiding decisive engagements.

"This attack was meant to humiliate us," Otro said finally, his voice carrying throughout the chamber. "To show our subjects and allies that we cannot protect our own systems. They want us to chase shadows while they strike where we're weakest."

"Great Zon, Council members," Griglag began, shifting his stance within the Circle of Truth. The blue flames of Lindow flickered around him, casting dancing shadows across his battle-scarred features. "Despite the setback at Kryntok, the Malvari have not been idle. I bring news from the shipyards of Tueblets that may ease your concerns."

Otro's expression remained granite-hard, but he nodded for Griglag to continue. The Council needed hope after the litany of disasters he'd just recounted.

"Three of our new *Plarix*-class heavy battleships—the *Drexol*, the *Fendal*, and the *Grax*—have completed their shakedown cruises and combat trials. They stand ready to join the fleet." Griglag paused, letting the significance sink in. "In the days following my appointment as Mavkah, I ordered the construction of thirty of these hulls at an accelerated pace. Our shipyards have been reorganized for maximum efficiency. Every seven days, a new hull is laid down while another is completed."

A murmur rippled through the Council Chamber. Otro noted which members looked relieved and which remained skeptical.

"To address the immediate threat to Tueblets," Griglag continued, "we are deploying two of these battleships to reinforce the system's defenses. The third will strengthen our position at Zinconia, where—"

"Three battleships!" Councillor Gorax erupted from his seat, his voice dripping with contempt. "Three battleships against the armada that destroyed Kryntok in hours?" He turned to address Otro directly, his face flushed with indignation. "Zon Otro, surely within the Malvari we have more competent NOSs we can make Mavkah than this *berinx*."

The insult—calling Griglag a toddler—hung in the air like a thrown blade. Gorax spat his next words like warm water. "We ask what the Malvari are doing to prepare Tueblets against invasion, and all the Mavkah can tell us is three battleships? Three? The Republic brings dozens of ships to raid a mining system, and we answer with three?"

Bam, bam.

"Enough, Gorax!" Zon Otro's voice thundered through the chamber as he slammed the Rock of Order against the dais. The crystalline impact echoed off the walls, silencing even the ambient hum of the ventilation systems. "You go too far, insulting the Mavkah while he stands within the Circle of Truth! I have called this meeting to learn what steps the Malvari are taking, not to have my military commander degraded with petty grievances over lost shipbuilding contracts."

Gorax sank back into his seat, his face still twisted with anger but cowed by Otro's rebuke.

Otro turned his attention back to Griglag, his tone measured but firm. "Mavkah, Councillor Gorax raises a point, however crudely expressed. Three battleships, even *Plarix*-class vessels, seem insufficient against the threat we face. Explain to this Council how these new warships will make a difference in the coming battles. Help them understand what makes these ships worth the thorilium we can barely spare."

Griglag squared his shoulders, meeting the Council's expectant gazes with unwavering resolve. "Yes, of course, Great Zon. These new *Plarix*-class battleships represent a fundamental shift in our naval doctrine." His voice carried the confidence of a warrior who'd studied his enemy's tactics and adapted. "Each vessel is thirty percent larger than our previous battleship designs, allowing us to double our starfighter and bomber complement. When the *Freedom* struck Kryntok, their fighters overwhelmed our patrol craft. That will not happen again."

The Council leaned forward as holographic schematics materialized above Griglag's outstretched hand—a privilege granted only within the Circle of Truth.

"But the fighters are merely the beginning," Griglag continued, rotating the display to highlight weapon hardpoints. "We've integrated magnetic railgun systems as primary armaments. The Republic taught us a painful lesson about kinetic weapons at Gravaxia and again at Kryntok. Their mass drivers punched through our armor plating like tissue paper. Now we return the favor."

Otro watched the technical specifications scroll past, his mind calculating tonnage, power requirements, crew complements. The thorilium they'd lost at Kryntok would hurt, but if these ships performed as promised...

"Defense-wise," Griglag pressed on, his stance firm despite the weight of judgment pressing down upon him, "we've completely redesigned the armor configuration. One full meter of specially engineered composite materials—alternating layers of duraplast, carbonite mesh, and dispersive ceramics specifically formulated to counter kinetic impacts. Combined with enhanced point-defense systems, upgraded laser batteries, and expanded missile magazines, each *Plarix* equals three of our older battleships in combat effectiveness."

"Impressive," Councillor Drex admitted grudgingly. "But against the *Freedom* and her escorts?"

"The *Plarix* battleships are designed as carrier-killers," Griglag stated flatly. "They're built to engage and destroy the Republic's *Victory*-class battleships and their vaunted star carriers. These aren't just warships—they're symbols of Imperial might that will anchor our defense of Tueblets and project power throughout our territories."

Otro absorbed the information, but his expression remained carved from stone. The technical specifications were encouraging, but wars weren't won by superior technology alone—the Republic had proven that repeatedly. "Mavkah, three *Plarix* battleships, however formidable, are still just three ships. The intelligence reports from Pfeinstgard are clear—the allied fleet massing there numbers in the hundreds. We aren't facing another raid like Kryntok. This is an invasion armada, assembled for one purpose: conquest."

He rose slightly from his seat, his presence filling the chamber. "The Republic, Primords, Altairians—possibly even Tully forces—all unified against us. So I ask you directly, Mavkah: beyond these three battleships, what is your strategy? How do the Malvari intend to hold Tueblets against such overwhelming numbers?"

Griglag drew in a measured breath, centering himself before responding. The weight of the Empire's survival pressed upon his shoulders, but he'd carried heavier burdens. He caught Tarvox's eye—his deputy gave an almost imperceptible nod of support.

"Great Zon, I have spent countless hours analyzing our situation, studying every major engagement we've fought against the Altairians, the Primords, and the Tully before the humans united them against us." Griglag's voice took on an almost reverent quality. "I searched our history for strategies that might serve us now. During my meditations, exhaustion overtook me, and in that slumber, I believe great Lindow himself granted me a vision."

Several Council members shifted uneasily. Invoking divine inspiration was dangerous ground, even within the Circle of Truth.

"In this vision, I witnessed battles we fought together, you and I, many cycles ago." Griglag met Otro's gaze directly. "Do you remember the Siege of Intus?"

A flicker of recognition crossed Otro's features—perhaps even the ghost of pride from those younger days of victory. "I do, Mavkah. That was many dracmas past, when we were both younger and the Empire's enemies knew fear at our approach." His tone grew thoughtful. "But that was a different war, against different foes. What bearing does that ancient victory have on our current crisis?"

Griglag nodded at the question, his scarred features taking on the cast of a warrior recalling hard-won lessons. "During the siege of the planet Intus, the Primords refused to yield control of the system no matter how fiercely we pressed them. Week after week, our fleets hammered their positions, yet they held." He paused, letting the memory crystallize. "Then we discovered why. They'd constructed a network of fortified positions throughout the Spritzers ice belt, positioned along the approach vectors to the stargate that connected Intus to their core territories."

Otro's eyes narrowed as understanding dawned. Several Council members leaned forward, drawn by the tactical implications.

"Each fortress was positioned to provide overlapping fields of fire," Griglag continued, manipulating the holographic display to show a simplified recreation of the Primord defense network. "When we engaged one strongpoint, two or three others could bring their weapons to bear. Turbo lasers, missile batteries, torpedo launchers—all concentrated on our attack formations. We lost seventeen warships before we finally overwhelmed them through sheer mass and determination."

"The Shwani Clan has adapted this strategy brilliantly," Tarvox interjected, stepping forward with his data pad. "When we toured the Empire to inspect the defenses, we saw firsthand what the Groff and the Shwani clan had done to fortify their system with asteroids. They established a network of them, protecting the planet Shwani and the shipyards. They've weaponized entire rocks—hollowed them out, powering them with enough weapons to make any attack a suicide mission. It's likely why their industrial base remains untouched and wasn't raided by the Republic despite their producing thirty percent of our warships."

Griglag nodded his agreement, then added, "Tueblets has some asteroid defenses around critical sites, but nothing approaching what Shwani has achieved. I propose we change that—immediately. We'll reposition asteroids from the outer belt using our mining tugs. Each rock becomes a weapons platform. We create overlapping kill zones across the entire inner system, not just around select facilities."

The hologram shifted, showing the Tueblets system with new defensive positions marked in red. Asteroids formed a deadly lattice around key planets and approach vectors.

"The Republic excels at rapid strikes," Griglag explained. "Hit fast, overwhelm, withdraw. But against fortified positions with overlapping coverage? They'll bleed for every kilometer."

Councillor Zek raised a clawed hand. "Moving asteroids requires enormous energy—"

"Already underway," Griglag cut in. "Three weeks ago, I ordered our mining consortiums to begin. Seventeen asteroids are in transit. Forty-three will be in position within two weeks."

Otro's expression remained unreadable, but Griglag caught the slight lift of his superior's head—interest, perhaps approval.

"The stargates need attention too," Griglag pressed on. "Sentry towers with rapid-fire plasma cannons. Proximity mines by the thousands—magnetic adhesion models that attach to any hull lacking our IFF codes. The Republic used our gates as invasion highways at Gravaxia. Never again."

"And if they bypass the stargates?" Councillor Gorax challenged, his earlier hostility dulled to skepticism. "Their quantum drives don't require them."

"Then they arrive scattered," Tarvox responded. "No rally point means piecemeal emergence across the system. We defeat them before they consolidate."

Griglag drew himself to his full height. "The Malvari are transforming Tueblets from a target into a meat grinder. Every asteroid a fortress, every approach vector a killing field. When the Republic discovers this isn't Kryntok—that we've learned from their tactics—their momentum will break."

He swept his gaze across the Council. "And when it does, our counterattack begins. The *Plarix* battleships will lead fresh squadrons from our shipyards against their depleted forces. We'll reclaim Gravaxia, Orinda, perhaps push into their staging grounds."

The chamber fell silent except for the hum of the holographic projectors. Otro studied the defensive plans rotating slowly above the conference table, his fingers steepled before him.

"Fortresses and minefields are static defenses, Mavkah," Otro said at last. "The Republic adapts quickly. What happens when they find ways around your kill zones?"

Griglag's deputy, Tarvox, stepped forward from the Circle's edge, his voice cutting through the tension. "My Zon, we have another option—a more unconventional approach.

"We've begun converting interplanetary patrol boats into what we're calling Victory ships." He activated a secondary display showing technical schematics. "Each vessel is thirty-eight meters long, built from reinforced tritanium with ablative ceramic plating salvaged from decommissioned corvettes. They can take a plasma torpedo hit, even a magrail strike, and keep coming—far more durable than any missile."

Several Council members exchanged glances. Even Gorax leaned forward.

"The key is the modified Arkanorian reactor," Tarvox continued. "We've reconfigured the magnetic containment to fail on impact. Fifty megatons of explosive yield plus radiation burst. One Victory ship against a Republic battleship's hull means catastrophic damage or total destruction."

The chamber fell silent.

Councillor Drex broke the quiet. "You are talking about suicide craft."

"We are. But they would be crewed by volunteers," Griglag explained. "Two warriors per boat — we are calling them Exalted Riders. Heroes who will strike the killing blow against our enemies."

Zon Otro's expression transformed from frustration to cold calculation. "The Republic has pushed us to the brink. They've turned the Guristas against us, seized Orinda, threatened Tueblets itself. If we lose Tueblets, the Empire falls."

He fixed his gaze on Griglag. "How many *Victory* ships are ready?"

Tarvox consulted his data pad after a quick exchange with Griglag. "Two hundred thirty-seven operational. Seventy-three civilian vessels undergoing conversion. Current production: ninety-two per month."

Otro's eyes narrowed. "Not enough. To overwhelm their point defenses, we need hundreds. Tell me this is just the beginning."

"It is, Great Zon," Griglag confirmed. "The shipyards will soon produce hundreds monthly. The constraint right now is reactors—we need them for the *Plarix* battleships. We've begun expanding reactor production, but it takes time." He paused. "We also have to consider the timing. If we reveal them too soon, we'll lose the element of surprise. We will only have that once. It has to count."

"Agreed. You will make it count, then." Otro's voice dropped dangerously. "How many can you have ready?"

"Six hundred in two months if we prioritize them. Eight, maybe nine hundred if we strip reactors from mothballed vessels and nonessential commercial ships."

Councillor Zek stirred. "Great Zon, these are suicide weapons—has it really come to this?"

"We do what we must to survive, to defeat the enemy and save the Empire," Otro affirmed. He turned back to Griglag. "Build them. As many as possible. Hide them throughout Tueblets—asteroid fields, debris clouds, anywhere you think the enemy ships will be."

Griglag nodded firmly. "Yes, Zon. Even now, the Exalted Riders are already volunteering by the thousands. They compete for the honor to die for the Empire, to die for Lindow."

A cold smile spread across Otro's features. He rose from his seat; the Council followed.

"The Republic believes we are weakened after Kryntok," Otro declared. "They're wrong. Every asteroid will bristle with weapons. Every approach will hide death. Their grand fleet expects easy conquest—they'll find only slaughter."

He gestured to Griglag and Tarvox. "The Malvari have full authority. Strip whatever resources you need. Commandeer facilities, drain reserves—whatever it takes. Transform Tueblets into their graveyard."

"By your command, Great Zon," Griglag responded, striking his chest in salute.

Otro raised his fist high. "For the Empire! May Lindow guide our weapons and curse our enemies!"

"For the Empire!" the Council roared.

As the Council filed out, Otro remained standing, eyes fixed on the holographic display of Tueblets. The Republic thought they were coming to claim victory.

Instead, they were sailing into annihilation.

Chapter 29:
Shadows Within

Private Chamber
High Council Complex
Drokanis, Zinconia

Mavkah Griglag waited as the heavy doors sealed behind him with a thud. The private chamber was smaller than the Council Hall, more intimate and ornately decorated with wood carvings and personal items that spoke of Otro's service to the Empire. Here, away from the theater of the Circle of Truth, the real decisions were made.

Zon Otro stood with his back to them, studying a tactical display that floated in the chamber's center. The hologram showed Tueblets, surrounded by the newly proposed defensive positions they'd just discussed. But Griglag noticed Otro's attention wasn't on Tueblets—it was fixed on the Shwani system, three jumps away.

"Mavkah, Deputy Tarvox," Otro said without turning. "What I'm about to discuss doesn't leave this room."

"Understood, Great Zon," Griglag replied, exchanging a glance with Tarvox.

Otro finally turned, his expression harder than titanium. "Tell me about the shipyard production reports from Shwani."

Griglag felt his chest tighten—a warrior's instinct when stepping into dangerous territory. "Great Zon, the reports show… discrepancies."

"Explain."

"The Tarkun shipyards report completing seventeen Thoraxian heavy destroyers monthly for the Malvari. But our fleet manifests show only eleven arriving." Griglag activated his own data pad, projecting the numbers. "Six ships per month, vanishing. For the past four months."

Otro's eyes narrowed to slits. "Twenty-four warships. Missing."

"That's not all," Tarvox added, stepping forward. "The Kryntok yards show similar patterns. Nine ships reported complete, six delivered—except these were battleships. These missing vessels aren't in transit, and they are not docked for modifications. They simply… don't exist in our records anymore."

The temperature in the room seemed to drop. Otro moved closer, his voice dropping to a dangerous whisper. "Where are these ships, Mavkah?"

Griglag met his leader's gaze directly. "I believe the Shwani shipyards are diverting production. Building warships that never reach the Malvari."

"For whom?"

"That's the question, isn't it?" Griglag's jaw clenched. "The Groff Directorate oversees those facilities. Director Vak'Atioth's clan controls Shwani."

Silence stretched between them, heavy with implication.

"You're suggesting," Otro said slowly, "that the Groff are building their own fleet."

"I'm reporting facts, Great Zon. The ships exist—the resources are consumed, the workers paid, the reactors installed. But they don't join our battle lines." Griglag's voice hardened. "The Groff's mandate is intelligence and civil order. Not naval construction. If they're building a separate fleet…"

"It would be treason," Otro finished. His hands extended involuntarily, his talon-like fingernails scraping against the table. "Or preparation for something worse."

Tarvox cleared his throat. "Great Zon, there's precedent to consider. During the Var'Soth Rebellion, certain clans maintained private fleets—"

"That was three centuries ago," Otro cut him off. "Before the Unified Fleet Doctrine. Before the Groff existed in their current form." He turned back to the display, staring at Shwani. "Vak'Atioth wanted to be Zon. He believed Utulf would appoint him to the Council, position him as successor."

"Instead, Utulf chose you," Griglag said carefully.

"After the Sol disaster." Otro's voice carried bitter memory. "A hundred thousand warriors lost because the Groff's intelligence failed us. They said Earth's defenses were compromised. They said the humans were unprepared." His fists clenched. "We lost the *Nefantar*, and hundreds of warships, because of that failure. That fool Vak'Atioth blamed me for surviving it."

Griglag chose his next words carefully. "If the Groff are building a shadow fleet, it could mean they're preparing for the Empire's collapse. Positioning themselves to seize control when the Malvari can no longer maintain order."

"Or," Tarvox suggested grimly, "they're preparing to force its collapse."

Otro spun to face them both. "Find those ships, Mavkah. Use whatever resources necessary. But do it quietly. If Vak'Atioth learns we're investigating, he'll either hide the evidence or accelerate whatever he's planning."

"I'll deploy reconnaissance teams immediately," Griglag confirmed. "Trusted warriors only. We'll track shipping manifests, reactor allocations, crew assignments. Ships that size can't simply disappear."

"What about the Council?" Tarvox asked. "Should they be warned?"

Otro considered this. "No. We don't know how deep Vak'Atioth's influence runs. The wrong word to the wrong councillor…" He let the implication hang. "Mavkah, I want you to double the guard details for myself and the Council. Use only Malvari troops whose loyalty is beyond question."

"The Groff will notice increased security," Griglag warned.

"Let them. Call it a response to the Kryntok raid. Additional precautions against Republic infiltrators." Otro's expression darkened further. "If Vak'Atioth objects, that itself will be telling."

Griglag struck his chest in salute. "It will be done immediately, Great Zon."

"There's something else," Otro said, his voice quieter now but no less intense. "If the Groff are building a fleet, they'll need crews. Warriors trained to operate those ships. Find out where they're getting them. Are they recruiting from the Malvari? Drawing from planetary militias? Creating their own training programs? I need to know."

"I'll investigate every angle," Griglag promised. "Though if I may suggest—we should also examine their reactor procurement. The shortage affecting our Victory ship program… perhaps it's not just about the *Plarix* battleships."

Otro's eyes widened slightly at the implication. "You think they're deliberately constraining reactor production?"

"Or redirecting it," Tarvox offered. "If they control both the shipyards and reactor supplies…"

"They control our ability to wage war," Otro finished. The full scope of the potential betrayal was crystallizing before them. "Mavkah, this investigation is now your highest priority. Even above the Tueblets defense preparations."

Griglag hesitated. "Great Zon, with respect, if the Republic invades while we're focused on internal threats—"

"If the Groff stab us in the back while we're fighting the Republic, it won't matter how well we've fortified Tueblets." Otro moved to the chamber's floor-to-ceiling window, looking out over the capital. "We're fighting a war on two fronts, Mavkah. One we can see, one we cannot. Both could destroy us if we're not careful."

The weight of that truth settled over the room. Griglag straightened, feeling the familiar burden of impossible duty.

"I'll have preliminary findings within three days," he promised. "If the Groff are building a shadow fleet, we'll find it."

"See that you do." Otro turned back to face them, his expression carved from stone. "The Empire stands at the precipice. External enemies mass at our borders while internal ones sharpen their knives. We cannot afford to be blind to either threat."

"What if we find proof?" Tarvox asked. "If the Groff truly are preparing for treachery, how do you want us to respond?"

Otro's response was immediate and cold. "Then we remind them why the Malvari, not the Groff, are the Empire's sword. And why that sword cuts both ways."

Chapter 30:
Death from Above

February 4, 2116
CNS *Bloodhawk*
Above Zinconia

    The magtube deployment pod sealed around Brigadier General Brian Royce with a pneumatic hiss. A red tactical light bathed the cramped interior as he formed a final equipment check. His HUD synced with the *Bloodhawk*'s targeting systems, letting him know they were on final approach. Through the narrow viewport, he caught glimpses of his Delta operators being loaded into adjacent tubes—human projectiles about to be fired into the heart of the enemy.

    "Alpha Team, sound off," Royce commanded through his helmet comm.

    "Alpha Two, locked and loaded."

    "Alpha Three, ready to drop."

    "Alpha Four, let's rain some pain."

    The confirmations rolled in—twelve Republic Deltas and four Humtar Special Forces soldiers. They formed the strike team he'd lead for the direct attack on High Council building. Somewhere else in the *Bloodhawk*'s belly, Bravo, Charlie, and Sierra teams were running through their own pre-drop sequences, getting ready to drop alongside him.

    Captain Rhan-Set's voice crackled over the command channel. "T-minus thirty seconds to launch window. Final systems check."

    Royce ran his fingers over his M-111 Slayer secured against his chest plate. The weapon's weight felt reassuring—the blaster and its 20mm grenade launcher were ready to rain hell on the enemy. He checked his HUD, all systems flashed green across the board: Star Wheel deployment mechanism, rocket boots, drag chute. Everything that stood between him and becoming a lawn dart on Zinconia's surface showed ready for action.

    "Attention. Attention. Twenty seconds to drop zone. Stand by…magcoils beginning to charge."

    Royce felt the pod vibrate as the electromagnetic energy built around the launch rails. Through his helmet's audio pickups, he heard the rising whine of capacitors reaching critical charge. His stomach tightened, not from fear but from anticipation. Fourteen days of bruising training had led to this moment. It wasn't enough, it never was. War was messy like that. You made do with what you had—the army you have, not the one you want.

"Stand by…ten seconds to drop—brace for launch."

Royce pressed his head back against the pod's cushioned restraint. Around him, the vibration intensified until he felt his teeth rattle. This was nothing like a HALO jump—no gentle roll out of a cargo bay into free fall. This was pure kinetic violence of action.

"Five… four… three… two… one…launch, launch, launch!"

The universe compressed around him as his pod was hurled down the tube. The g-forces slammed Royce deep into his restraints as the mag-tube shot him into Zinconia's atmosphere. His vision tunneled, peripheral darkness creeping in despite the suit's pressure compensation. The pod's ablative shell glowed cherry-red through the viewport as friction tried to burn them alive.

Mach one. Mach two. The velocity indicator on his HUD climbed relentlessly.

"Alpha Team launched." Rhan-Set's voice sounded distant through the roar of atmosphere. "Bravo Team launching in three… two… one…"

The pods screamed earthward in precise formation, forty-two Republic Deltas and eighteen Humtar operators wrapped in shells of superheated ceramic. Through gaps in the cloud layer below, the sprawling capital city emerged—a maze of towering spires and military compounds with the byzantine High Council building at its heart.

"Passing twenty thousand feet," Royce's suit AI announced with mechanical calm. "Shell separation in fifteen seconds."

His fingers flexed against the Slayer's grip. Below, the compound expanded in his vision—guard towers, defensive emplacements, the distinctive dome of the Council Chamber. Intel put at least two hundred Zodark warriors on-site. They were about to drop into a viper's nest.

"Ten thousand feet. Shell separation… now."

The pod's outer casing peeled away like a metallic flower blooming in reverse. Wind howled past as Royce plummeted free, the sudden transition from enclosed pod to open sky hitting like a physical blow. His suit's stabilizers fired automatically, arresting his tumble.

Terminal velocity. Two hundred meters per second straight down.

"Rocket burn in three… two… one…"

The boots ignited.

Royce grunted as his exoskeleton suit absorbed the deceleration, locking his feet and legs in position for the three-second burn. It felt like an eternity, slowing his descent. The ground rushed up—buildings, streets, individual vehicles becoming visible. As the rockets spent themselves, they fell away, his altimeter showing twelve hundred feet.

"Drag chute deployment," came the automated voice from HUD.

The chute snapped open with a violent jerk. Immediately after, the Star Wheel mechanism activated. The six blade-like wings extended from his back unit, catching the air and beginning their distinctive rotation. The spinning blades bit into the atmosphere, generating lift, transforming his plummet into a controlled descent.

His HUD populated with steering indicators. A gentle shift of weight sent him gliding left. The Slayer came up in a smooth motion as the High Council compound filled his vision. Guard towers sprouted from the walls like thorns. Through his rifle's optic, Royce spotted movement—a Zodark sentry on the northeastern tower's roof, weapon casual at his side.

The warrior had no idea death was descending from above. But he was about to find out as Royce brought his rifle up, zeroed in on the sentry and fired. The guard dropped before he knew he was under attack.

Dozens of shots rang out as the Delta operators ruthlessly engaged targets as they approached the ground.

The Star Wheel's blades bit into the air one final time as Royce's boots touched down on manicured grass. He hit the quick-release, the spinning mechanism detaching and tumbling away as he rolled forward into a combat crouch. Around him, Alpha Team landed in practiced sequence—Deltas and Humtar operators spreading into defensive positions among ornamental fountains and sculpted hedges.

The grounds were a stark contrast to the violence descending upon them. Crystalline ponds reflected the morning sky, alien water lilies floating serenely on their surfaces. Statues of ancient Zodark heroes stood watch over gravel pathways, their stone faces gazing eternally at gardens that were about to become a killing field.

Then the C300s arrived—his Tinmen.

They dropped from the sky like metallic angels of death, fifty-two of the C300 Combat Synthetic Humanoid Robots. They landed with ground-shaking impacts, their Star Wheel's disconnecting as they took in the situation. Eight feet of armored death, each one immediately transitioning from descent to combat mode. Their optical sensors glowed red as targeting algorithms engaged, M-111 Slayers snapping up with mechanical precision.

"Tinmen element, weapons free. Clear all hostiles," Royce commanded over the tactical net. He then pointed toward the High Council building's main entrance. "Tinmen One, Alpha One—time to go full Leeroy Jenkins on that building. We'll be right behind you!"

The fourteen combat synthetics of Tinmen One peeled off from the main group as they charged toward the ornate double doors with their rifles up, firing at targets the entire way. They rushed the enemy with zero tactical finesse—just overwhelming force and speed. The lead Tinman racing for the door didn't bother to slow its stride. It simply lowered its armored shoulder and smashed through the entrance like a battering ram. The giant sixteen-foot wooden-and-metal double doors exploded inward from the impact and the blaster shots to its hinges.

The roar of weapons fire erupted immediately—not the panicked shots of surprised guards, but disciplined volleys from elite Zodark warriors who'd likely drilled for this moment. The first C300 through the door fired relentlessly as volleys of blaster fire sparked across its chest plate like a jackhammer until it staggered and fell over.

Grenades flew into the building as a second Synth pushed past its fallen comrade, only to take a blaster shot to its optical array. It stumbled forward, firing blindly before a Zodark guard put three rounds through its CPU housing.

"Move, move, move!" Royce shouted over the roar of the battle. He charged after them, his team flowing around him like water.

The foyer had become a slaughterhouse. Two of his C300s were down, lying in sparking heaps near the entrance, their armored bodies torn apart by concentrated fire. But for every Synth down, seven to eight Zodark bodies littered the polished floor. The remaining Synths advanced relentlessly, absorbing punishment that would have shredded his Deltas.

"Contact left!" Tanner's voice crackled through comms.

A squad of Zodarks burst from a side corridor, energy swords humming to life—their distinctive whine letting everyone know its molecular disruption field was active. The lead warrior, moving with inhuman grace as he ducked under a Tinman's rifle burst, closed the distance. His blade swept upward, carving through the Synth's torso like it was made of butter. Sparks and hydraulic fluid sprayed as the C300 toppled to the floor in pieces.

Royce's Slayer tracked the Zodark, he squeezed the trigger, sending a trio of rounds into its center mass. The warrior's momentum carried him two more steps before he collapsed, sword clattering across the marbled floor.

"Alpha Team, watch those blades!" Royce barked. "Cover the Synths' flanks!"

The combined force flowed deeper into the building, Tinmen drawing fire while Deltas picked off threats with surgical precision. A Zodark warrior charged from behind a column, sword raised high. Corporal Jackson's 20mm grenade caught him midstride, the explosion painting the walls a gory blue.

Another elite squad attempted to flank through the east gallery. The Tinmen swiveled as one, laying down suppressing fire while Alpha Three and Four maneuvered for angle. The cross fire was devastating— disciplined bursts cutting down warriors before they could close to sword range.

"Stairs!" a Humtar operator called out as he cut loose a volley of fire, killing several Zodarks.

More guards poured down the sweeping staircase, some with rifles, others with those deadly energy blades. A C300 at the base of the stairs took a sword through its shoulder joint, the arm falling away in a shower of sparks. Before the Zodark could follow up, Staff Sergeant Chen put a burst through his skull.

The Tinmen adapted instantly, firing one-armed. Three synthetics formed a firing line, their Slayers creating a wall of death as they advanced up the stairwell. Behind them, Deltas lobbed grenades in high arcs, the boom balls exploding on the landing above, the explosions shredding defenders before they could attack.

"We gotta push through to the Council Chamber and offices!" Royce commanded. "Tinmen One through Seven, continue clearing the first floor. Tinmen Eight through Fourteen, clear the second floor. Alpha Two, you got the ground floor—Alpha One, you're with me. We're heading up!"

They advanced over Zodark bodies, and the sparking remains of four more of his C300s. The elite Zodark guards had fought well—better than any force they'd faced before. But against the perfect coordination of human operators and robotic killers, even their skill wasn't enough.

Royce saw a wounded Zodark tried to rise, energy sword flickering weakly. The nearest Tinman didn't hesitate—a single shot to the head dropped him.

"Council Chamber is on the second floor," Royce reminded his team, stepping over the carnage. Through his HUD, he could see the other teams' progress—Bravo sweeping the grounds, Charlie preparing for the inevitable counterattack, Sierra deploying their deadly drone swarm.

The fight was just beginning, and time was not on their side.

****

High Council Chamber
Drokanis, Zinconia
Zodark Home World

Zon Otro barely registered Governor Kalaxis droning about agricultural quotas when the first explosion shook the building. The crystalline chandelier above the Council table swayed, casting dancing shadows across the assembled officials' suddenly alert faces.

"What was that?" Councillor Drex demanded, rising from his seat.

Before anyone could respond, a second explosion—closer this time. Through the chamber's tall windows, Otro caught a glimpse of smoke rising from the eastern gardens.

A coup. The thought crystallized instantly in his mind. *Vak'Atioth has finally made his move.*

"Guards!" Otro barked, but his elite bodyguards were already moving, weapons drawn, forming a protective circle around him.

Captain Varix, commander of his personal detail, pressed a hand to his ear, receiving reports through his comm unit.

"My Zon." Varix's voice carried an edge of disbelief. "The grounds are under attack. Heavy assault, multiple breaching points—" He paused, his blue skin paling to almost gray. "Sir, it's... it's the Republic. Republic forces are inside the compound."

The words hit Otro like a physical blow. Not a coup. Not internal betrayal. The Republic had somehow reached the very heart of the Empire.

"Impossible," he breathed, then his voice hardened to steel. "Alert the garrison immediately! I want every warrior in the capital converging on this location!"

"Already done, sir," Varix confirmed. "But they're reporting it will take time to mobilize—fifteen minutes minimum before the first response units arrive."

Fifteen minutes. An eternity in combat.

The building shook again. Through the walls, they could hear the distinctive shriek of blaster fire growing closer. Screams echoed from somewhere below.

"Deploy every guard in the building to defensive positions!" Otro commanded. "They will hold the Council Chamber at all costs!"

His remaining guards rushed to comply, taking positions at the chamber's main entrance. But Otro could read the fear in their movements. These weren't frontline Malvari—they were ceremonial guards, trained for assassination attempts, not full military assault.

"Great Zon"—Councillor Zek's voice cracked with panic—"we should evacuate—"

"And go where?" Councillor Gorax snarled, though his hands trembled. "They're already inside!"

The blaster fire was definitely closer now. Otro could hear explosions, the crash of breaking stone, alien voices shouting in accented Zodark—no, not Zodark. English. Republic Standard.

"How?" Governor Kalaxis whispered, his administrative mind struggling to process the impossible. "How could they reach us here?"

Varix suddenly gripped Otro's arm. "My Zon, we need to move. Now."

"I will not abandon—"

A massive explosion somewhere below shook the entire building. Cracks spiderwebbed across the ancient stone walls. Through the doorway, they could see guards falling back, firing desperately at something advancing up the main stairwell.

"Sir!" Varix's tone brooked no argument. "My duty is your survival. We go now!"

The captain's hand found a seemingly decorative wall panel, pressing a hidden sequence. A section of ornate stonework swung inward, revealing a narrow passage Otro had never known existed.

"Inside, quickly!"

Otro hesitated for one heartbeat, watching his Council members mill in panic. Then training overrode pride. He dove through the opening, Varix following and sealing it behind them.

They plunged down steep stairs carved from living rock, the sounds of battle muffled but still audible above. Otro's mind raced—processing the impossible, calculating responses, burning with questions that had no answers.

Behind them, even through stone and distance, they heard the Council Chamber's doors explode inward.

"Faster, my Zon," Varix urged, guiding him through turns he'd obviously memorized.

They reached what appeared to be a dead end—a maintenance room on the building's ground level. Varix's fingers found another hidden control. The far wall parted, revealing a tunnel that smelled of age and careful preservation.

"Emergency evacuation route," Varix explained tersely as they ran. "Known only to the guard commander and the protective detail. It leads to—"

An explosion above sent dust cascading from the tunnel ceiling. The Republic forces were systematically destroying the building room by room.

They ran through darkness lit only by emergency phosphorescent strips. Otro's lungs burned, his ceremonial robes tangling around his legs. How many times had he sat in that chamber, believing himself untouchable? How many times had he dismissed concerns about security, trusting in the Empire's might to protect its heart?

"Here," Varix announced, stopping at a reinforced door marked with ancient Zodark symbols for sanctuary. His palm against a biometric scanner, a series of codes entered with practiced speed.

The door opened onto a room Otro had never imagined—a bunker deep beneath the capitol, stocked with supplies, communications equipment, weapons. Varix sealed them inside, engaging multiple locking mechanisms.

"Twelve hours," the captain said, finally allowing exhaustion to color his voice. "These walls can withstand direct orbital bombardment for twelve hours. By then, the entire Malvari will have responded."

Otro sank into a chair, his mind struggling to process what had just occurred. The Republic had struck at the Empire's heart. Not with fleets or armies, but with surgical precision that spoke of intelligence, planning, and an audacity he'd never credited them with.

"The Council?" he asked, though he already knew.

Varix's silence was answer enough.

Rage built in Otro's chest—not hot, but cold as the void between stars. The Republic had done more than attack a building or kill officials. They'd shattered the myth of Zodark invincibility, proven that nowhere in the Empire was beyond their reach.

And the Malvari—his vaunted military that consumed the Empire's resources, that promised security and strength—had failed utterly. No warning. No defense. Just Republic soldiers falling from the sky like divine judgment.

"Griglag," he whispered, tasting betrayal like acid on his tongue. The Mavkah had stood before him mere hours ago, promising victory, requesting resources, projecting strength. Yet Republic forces had waltzed through every defense like they didn't exist.

Twelve hours. Twelve hours to sit in this tomb while enemies desecrated the seat of Empire. Twelve hours to contemplate how thoroughly they'd been outmaneuvered.

When he emerged, things would change. The gloves would come off. No more measured responses or tactical withdrawals.

The Republic had wanted to humiliate the Empire? They'd succeeded.

But they'd also signed their own death warrant.

****

High Council Chamber
Drokanis, Zinconia

Brigadier General Brian Royce stepped through the shattered doorway into the Council Chamber, his Slayer sweeping the room one final time. The acrid smell of burnt ozone and scorched stone filled his nostrils. Bodies lay scattered across the ornate floor—Council members who'd chosen to die fighting rather than surrender.

The chamber that had witnessed centuries of Empire decisions now bore the scars of its final meeting. Blast marks scarred ancient murals. The Council table lay overturned, its polished surface pocked with blaster burns. Blue blood pooled beneath ceremonial robes.

"Any sign of the primary target?" Royce asked, though he already knew the answer.

Sergeant Major Tanner shook his head, frustration evident even through his tactical helmet. "Negative, sir. We've swept every room, every corridor. Zon Otro's not here."

"Secret passage," Royce concluded, examining the walls. "Has to be. Nobody just vanishes from a room with one exit while it's under assault."

"Want us to search for it?"

Royce checked his mission clock. They'd been on the ground eleven minutes. "Negative. We've overstayed our welcome already." He activated his comm. "All teams, this is Alpha Actual. Primary objective complete. Secondary target is a no-show. Execute withdrawal to extraction point."

"Copy that, Alpha Actual," came the responses. "Bravo moving to extract." "Charlie's holding but taking heavy fire." "Sierra confirms drone deployment complete."

Royce took one last look around the chamber—at the heart of an empire brought low in minutes. Not the complete victory he'd wanted, but devastating enough. The psychological impact would ripple through Zodark space for years.

"Let's move," he ordered.

They withdrew through corridors littered with evidence of the assault. His surviving C300s had been thorough—Zodark bodies lay where they'd fallen, caught between the mechanical precision of the Tinmen and the lethal expertise of his Deltas.

Exiting through the main entrance, Royce grimaced at their losses. Five Tinmen still functional out of fourteen. Their metallic bodies showed the price of leading the assault—armor punctured, limbs missing, optical arrays dark. But they'd done their job, absorbing damage that would have killed his human operators.

"Jackson and Reems?" he asked Tanner.

"KIA in the east stairwell," Tanner reported quietly. "Energy sword got Jackson. Reems tried to pull him clear, caught a burst from a Zodark heavy blaster."

Two more names for the wall. Royce pushed the thought aside—grief was for later.

"Three walking wounded," Tanner continued. "Nothing the C200s can't handle."

The medical Synths worked with mechanical efficiency, sealing wounds with bio-foam, administering stims to keep the injured mobile. One Delta sat against a decorative fountain while a C200 extracted shrapnel from his shoulder.

Across the grounds, Sierra Team's drones lifted into the air like a swarm of mechanical wasps. Each Killshot drone carried enough explosive to eliminate a squad of warriors. Hundreds of them spreading across the capital, programmed to strike at random intervals over the coming hours.

"Clear the EZ!" someone shouted.

Eight C300s from Sierra Team worked in concert, their enhanced strength making short work of monuments and decorative trees. Ancient statues toppled, thousand-year-old gardens became landing pads. The Zodarks would rage about the desecration—exactly as intended.

Royce's comm crackled. "Alpha Actual, this is Bloodhawk. Inbound hot, ETA three mikes. Be advised, multiple Zeek fighters converging on your position."

"Copy, Bloodhawk. We'll be ready."

The first Zeek appeared moments later—a sleek atmospheric fighter diving from the clouds. Its nose-mounted blasters opened up, stitching lines of destruction across the compound. Deltas and Humtar operators scattered for cover.

"MANPADS up!" Charlie Team's heavy weapons specialists were already tracking. The shoulder-fired missiles streaked skyward, their guidance systems locking onto the Zeek's heat signature.

The fighter jinked hard, deploying countermeasures. One missile went wide, but the second connected with its starboard engine. The Zeek transformed into a fireball, debris raining across the gardens.

Two more fighters screamed in from the east, their pilots learning from their wingman's fate. They came in fast and low, beneath optimal MANPAD engagement angles. Blaster fire walked across Delta positions, forcing them deeper into cover.

Then the sky darkened.

The *Bloodhawk* dropped from the clouds like an avenging angel, its stealth systems disengaging as weapons came online. Twin plasma cannons spoke with lethal authority. The lead Zeek simply ceased to exist, vaporized by converging beams. The second fighter tried to climb, presenting its belly to the Humtar vessel's point-defense lasers. It came apart in sections, burning wreckage tumbling earthward.

"That's our ride!" Royce shouted. "All teams converge on the EZ!"

The *Bloodhawk* settled onto the ruined gardens with surprising grace for something so large. Its boarding ramps dropped before the landing struts fully compressed. Deltas and Humtar operators streamed aboard, weapons still oriented outward.

"C300s, maintain perimeter!" Royce ordered. "Hold until we lift!"

The five surviving Tinmen from his team, plus others from the strike force, formed a mechanical wall between the extraction and the approaching Zodark response force. They would sell their synthetic lives dearly, buying seconds that meant survival for their organic operators.

Royce was last up the ramp, pausing to look back at the carnage they'd wrought. The High Council building burned, a final calling card they'd left behind as thermite grenades set fire to everything inside. He smiled, they'd killed hundreds of elite Zodark warriors, their bodies lying dead in their own sanctum. Soon, the chaos would spread throughout the capital, his drones prepared to spread their terror for hours to come.

"Ground team's aboard!" he announced.

The *Bloodhawk* lifted immediately, engines screaming. Through the closing ramp, Royce watched the remaining C300s engage the first wave of Zodark reinforcements. Outnumbered fifty to one, they fought with mechanical fury, making the Empire pay for every meter.

"Outstanding work, people," Royce said as acceleration pressed them into their seats. "We just kicked in the front door of the Zodark Empire and punch 'em in the face!"

Captain Maya Chen, Sierra Team leader, dropped into the seat beside him. Exhaustion lined her face, but her eyes sparkled with satisfaction. "We did it. Drones are fully deployed and operational. Randomized attack patterns active. The capital's about to have a very bad day, sir."

"Music to my ears, Captain. How long until the first strike hits?"

"We set the first strike for twenty minutes. Then random intervals between one and six hours thereafter." She smiled coldly. "Every Zodark warrior in the city just became a potential target. We'll have them jumping at shadows for days."

Royce nodded, allowing himself a moment of grim satisfaction. He had really wanted to capture Zon Otro. That would have been something, capturing the leader of the Empire. Even still, they'd done something perhaps more valuable—proved the Empire's vulnerability. If they could strike the Zodarks home world... nothing was safe from their reach. The psychological damage of this attack would outlast any physical destruction.

"Sir." Tanner approached, tablet in hand. "Preliminary BDA. Six confirmed Council kills, including six cabinet-level officials. Zodark military casualties—"

"Later, Sergeant Major," Royce interrupted gently. "We'll do a full debrief when we're back at Leatherneck."

He closed his eyes as the *Bloodhawk* climbed toward space. Mission complete, mostly. They'd lost good operators, but they'd achieved the impossible—struck the Zodark leadership in their own throne room and lived to tell about it. The war was far from over, but today they'd proven something crucial. The Empire could bleed. And if it could bleed, it could die.

He smiled, knowing this was the beginning of the end of the war. A war that had gone for decades was now closer to ending because of their actions today.

Chapter 31:
Ashes of Empire

Gardens Outside the High Council Chamber
Drokanis, Zinconia
Twenty-Four Hours Post-Attack

Zon Otro stood among the ruins of what had once been the Empire's most sacred gardens. It was a place to think, to reflect on the decisions and the responsibilities of running the country. Having emerged from the bunker, all he saw was scorched earth marked where ancient monuments had once stood for millennia. The smell of the garden used to remind him of conversations with Zon Utulf, his predecessor and mentor. In less than an hour, it had been replaced with the acrid stench of burnt vegetation mixed with the lingering smell of explosives and death. Glass from shattered windows crunched beneath his boots as he surveyed the devastation.

"My Zon," Captain Varix reported, his voice carefully neutral as he approached, "the sweeps of the capital are complete. Any remaining Republic drones have been neutralized. The aerial threat to our warriors is over."

"And the final tally—what did it cost us, Captain Varix?" Otro's voice was dangerously quiet, his eyes burning with barely contained rage.

Varix hesitated before answering. "Too many, Zon. We lost three hundred ninety-seven warriors in the secondary attacks following their withdrawal. The drones they left behind struck at random throughout the capital for sixteen hours before Malvari reinforcements were able to eliminate the last of them."

Otro's hands clenched, his fingernails carving grooves in the burnt remains of a decorative bench he'd sat on with Zon Utulf when he was Mavkah. Three hundred and ninety-seven warriors... their deaths another twist of the blade the Republic had plunged into the heart of the Empire. *How could this have happened...?* The thought continued to eat at him.

From the corner of his eye, he caught movement at the compound's entrance and looked up to see Mavkah Griglag approach. As he did, Otro noticed something on his scarred face he hadn't seen before—horror mixed with disbelief. The veteran warrior stopped at the edge of the garden, taking in the carnage with the practiced eye of someone who'd seen countless battlefields. Otro watched him as his gaze swept across the devastation—the blackened skeleton of the High Council building, the bodies of elite guards still being removed, rubble where centuries-old statues had been destroyed. He then moved with purpose, approaching Otro.

"Great Zon," Griglag began, then words failed him.

"Mavkah… explain this to me." Otro's words cut through the morning air like frozen razors. "Explain how Republic forces descended from our own skies. Explain to me how they could butcher the High Council in our own chamber. Explain how the Republic struck the heart of the Empire while the Malvari did nothing."

Griglag straightened, meeting his leader's fury without flinching. "We have been analyzing the insertion method, and it suggests this was done with either a Gallentine stealth frigate or"—he paused, weighing his next words carefully—"or the Humtars are directly helping the Republic or providing them with substantial technological assistance. Their technology, their tactics—"

"Yes, they are beyond our own," interrupted Otro, his voice rising. "Do you believe this is the work of these mysterious Humtars?"

"It's the only explanation that fits, given the evidence. We have checked our databases. There is no Republic vessel that could have penetrated our orbital defenses undetected. Either they've developed new stealth technology we're unaware of, or—"

"Or the Gallentines or Humtars are directly intervening in this war and it's over." The defeatist words escaped before Otro could stop them. He looked around nervously to make sure no one heard him, but the words hung in the air between them, terrible in their implications. This was the nightmare scenario they had talked about. If the Gallentines were committing their advanced fleets or if the mysterious Humtar were… how could the Empire stand against them?

Otro turned sharply, his ceremonial robes swirling. "Tell me, Mavkah. Was there anything, anything at all your forces could have done? Could you have intercepted this ghost ship? Could the Malvari have prevented this humiliation?"

The silence stretched between them as Otro watched Griglag's jaw worked as he struggled with the truth.

"No, we could not have prevented it," he admitted angrily. "Our warships failed to detect the vessel until it revealed itself for extraction. When it landed here in the gardens to recover their forces, that was when our ship first saw it. It was brief, and even then…" His voice dropped with his eyes. "Even then, our ships couldn't achieve a target lock to engage it. Whatever stealth system the vessel has and the countermeasures it uses were beyond anything we've encountered."

Griglag then dropped to one knee, his head bowed. "I have failed you, Great Zon. I have failed the Empire. I have failed to lead the Malvari. I offer you my resignation from command of the Malvari." His hand moved to the personal blade at his side. "I offer you, Great Zon, my life as consequence for this failure."

Otro was briefly taken aback by the gesture as he stared down at his oldest friend—the warrior who'd stood beside him through the Sol disaster, who'd helped him rebuild after that catastrophe. He knew at that moment, the smart move, the politically expedient move, would be to accept his offer. Take Griglag's head and pin the blame of this shame and dishonor on the Malvari's incompetence. But he couldn't, not now with Vak'Atioth circling him like a vulture.

No, the Groff Director would seize any weakness, any opening to advance his position. And Griglag, for all his failures, was still loyal. In a den of thieves and vipers, loyalty was more precious than competence.

"No. I do not accept your offer, Mavkah. You will not find release from this shame in death. You shall work to redeem yourself. Now stand up," Otro commanded.

Griglag looked up, confusion flickering across his features.

"I said stand, Mavkah. Do not make me repeat myself a third time." Otro's voice carried the weight of decision. "I cannot accept your resignation. Not with Vak'Atioth waiting to feast on our corpses."

"But, Great Zon—"

"No, Mavkah. You will find a way to defeat the Republic. I will attempt to contact the Collective—to find us a new ally. In the meantime, you will find a way to counter their new weapons and buy the Empire time. This is not a request."

Griglag rose slowly as his new orders sank in. "Yes, my Zon. I will do as you ask."

Otro began to pace, his mind already shifting from grief to calculation. "The Malvari failed to stop the attack, yes. But whose responsibility is it to know what capabilities our enemies possess? Whose duty is it to warn us, to warn the Malvari of new threats?"

"The Groff, of course," Griglag answered, catching on quickly.

"Exactly. The Groff." Otro's lips pulled back in a predatory smile. "If they had done their jobs—if Vak'Atioth's vaunted intelligence network had known about the Republic's new stealth vessels. If they'd warned us of Gallentine involvement or Humtar technology transfers— the Malvari would have prevented this dastardly attack."

"I... agree. Without the intelligence of what our enemies possess and their capabilities, the Malvari are blind. This attack, it's an intelligence failure that is the Groff's, and theirs alone," Griglag agreed, the confident steel returning to his voice.

"I think it's more than that." Otro stopped pacing, his decision crystallizing. "This attack succeeded because the Groff failed in their most basic function—protecting the Empire through information. They were too busy with their schemes and shadow games to notice the real threats surrounding us."

Otro turned to face the ruined Council building one final time. Six Council members dead. Hundreds of warriors slaughtered. The myth of Imperial invincibility shattered. But from these ashes, perhaps opportunity could rise.

"Spread the word, Mavkah," Otro commanded. "The Malvari fought bravely against an enemy using technology the Groff failed to warn us about. Ensure every warrior knows—we bled because Vak'Atioth's spies were too busy looking inward, chasing ghosts instead of uncovering our enemies' plans."

"Yes, Zon, it will be done," Griglag confirmed.

"And, Mavkah?" Otro's voice dropped to barely above a whisper. "Find me solutions. New weapons, new tactics if necessary. I don't care if you have to bargain with demons themselves. Find me a way to make the Republic pay for what they've done here."

As Griglag departed to carry out his orders, Otro remained among the ruins. The war had changed. Where had victory seemed possible a day earlier, now he wasn't so sure.

****

Groff Directorate Command Spire
Planet Shwani, Varkorion System

"Unacceptable! How could seventeen cells be compromised? We now have twenty-three operatives confirmed dead. This wipes out nearly our entire Gurista network. All of those leave behind forces, our operatives—gone," Vak'Atioth's voice railed as Heltet gave his report.

The holographic display between them showed the Orinda system, once riddled with Groff intelligence assets, now dark and silent absent one or two operatives still unaccounted for.

"The Republic's housecleaning has been thorough," Heltet continued. "They've turned the Guristas like they turned the Sumerians. What few remaining assets we have left are being hunted like animals. Those who haven't been executed have fled deeper undercover."

"Fled." Vak'Atioth tasted the word like poison. "The mighty Groff Directorate reduced to refugees in what has been our own territory for hundreds of dracmas."

"Director, we still maintain networks in—"

"In where?" Vak'Atioth erupted from his chair, looming over his subordinate. "Gravaxia? Lost. Orinda? Lost. Sumer? Lost. Sol? Not anymore. We have lost our eyes and ears across the frontier leaving us blind and deaf! How can we navigate this war with scraps of intelligence while the Republic seems to foresee our every move!"

The chamber's reinforced doors burst open. A courier rushed in, breathing hard, data pad clutched in trembling hands. The young Zodark's expression told Vak'Atioth something terrible had happened before he even spoke.

"Director... we received an urgent communication from Zinconia..."

Heltet snatched the data pad from his hands. His eyes scanned it, then widened as he read the report. "No. This... this cannot be accurate."

"What now?" Vak'Atioth demanded angrily.

"It's the High Council... the compound—it was attacked," said Heltet. "I don't know how this happened, but the report states that Republic forces... they attacked the capitol—the Council Chamber itself."

Silence engulfed the room. Even the distant hum of the spire's systems seemed to fade.

"Great Lindow... what kind of casualties are we talking about?" Vak'Atioth's voice was deadly calm.

"The High Council is dead—all six members were killed. The report says hundreds of warriors were killed defending the compound..." Heltet swallowed hard. "It also says the High Council building is in ruins. They struck from the sky—landing a raiding force that swept through the building, killing everyone in the compound before escaping."

"They managed to escape?" Vak'Atioth roared in anger. "And Otro? What fate did our great Zon share in all of this?"

"He survived," Heltet said in astonishment. "Apparently, his security detail rushed him to a hidden underground bunker during the attack."

Vak'Atioth turned slowly to face the massive windows overlooking the industrial sprawl of Shwani. When he spoke, his voice carried the weight of revelation.

"First they raid our mining systems with impunity. Now they execute Council members in their own chambers while that incompetent fool cowers underground." A harsh laugh escaped him. "Mavkah Griglag is proving his incompetence once more. The Malvari under his leadership couldn't protect a nursery from these humans."

"Director, surely this attack—"

"Is a sign." Vak'Atioth's eyes gleamed with sudden purpose. "Don't you see, Heltet? This isn't random misfortune. This is divine judgment."

Heltet shifted uncomfortably. "Divine judgment?"

"Think about it!" Vak'Atioth whirled to face him. "When in our history has the Empire suffered such humiliation? When have enemies struck at our very heart and lived to boast of it? This doesn't happen to the chosen of Lindow. This happens to the cursed."

Understanding dawned in Heltet's eyes. "Ah... I see what you mean..."

"Under Utulf, we conquered. Under his predecessors, we expanded. Under Otro?" Vak'Atioth gestured broadly. "Under Otro, we bleed. We retreated. He cowered in a bunker while aliens desecrated our sacred High Council."

"This will not go over well across the Empire. The people are already frightened from this latest string of defeats," Heltet said carefully. "But you might be right, Director. We could use this if we frame it correctly…"

"No, not frame, Heltet. The word you look for is reveal." Vak'Atioth's voice took on an almost prophetic quality as he continued. "Lindow speaks through action, not words, Heltet. And his message is clear: Otro was never meant to be Zon. He achieved his position through politics and maneuvering, not divine mandate. Lindow has withdrawn his protection to show us our error."

"Perhaps, but the priesthood might resist your interpretation—"

"My interpretation? No, the priesthood will see the truth when it's presented properly. That's our job, your job as Laktish." Vak'Atioth began to pace, his mind racing with possibilities. "Think about it. Republic forces just fell from our own skies like a divine punishment. Council members struck down while the false Zon hid instead of fighting, instead of leading his guard force in a heroic battle. We couldn't make the message any clearer if we tried."

Heltet nodded slowly. "What would you have me do?"

"You will spread the word—carefully, through our most trusted channels. This catastrophe is Lindow's warning. He is displeased with the Empire's direction, displeased with those who lead through trickery rather than divine right." Vak'Atioth's voice grew stronger with conviction. "If the Empire wishes to regain Lindow's favor, it must repent. It must cleanse itself."

"OK, and how will you have me frame this cleanse it must undertake?" asked Heltet carefully.

"New Council members to replace the dead—chosen by those who understand Lindow's will, the priesthood could be involved this time in their selection. And a new Zon, of course." Vak'Atioth's eyes burned with ambition barely concealed as religious fervor. "But it must be one whom Lindow has truly ordained, not a pretender who seized power through schemes."

Heltet bowed his head. "Give me a day to put together a plan, Director. Once you approve the message, I will make sure it spreads like wildfire through the faithful."

"Ensure it does. Let every believer know—our suffering isn't random. It's punishment for straying from Lindow's path. And redemption will require change."

As Heltet departed to begin his work, Vak'Atioth returned to the window. Below, the factories of Shwani continued their endless production, building ships for his shadow fleet. Soon, very soon, the Empire would understand that their salvation lay not with Otro and his failures, but with one who truly understood Lindow's will.

The Republic thought they'd struck a devastating blow. In truth, they'd given him the greatest gift imaginable—proof that the current regime had lost heaven's mandate.

Chapter 32:
Ghosts in Position

CDF Command Center
The Enclave, New Eden
Ninety Days after Technical Consultation

Admiral Veydris Korrath stood in his office, staring at the encrypted data packet that had arrived thirty minutes ago. Authentication codes matched Admiral Vesharuk's personal encryption keys. Classification header read: EYES ONLY—DAMOCLES DEPLOYMENT AUTHORIZATION.

Korrath had been expecting this, planning for it. But seeing the order made real—reduced to alphanumeric strings and authorization timestamps—made his chest tighten.

He opened the packet.

Orders were concise, written in clipped military language that turned civilizational extinction into logistics: deploy assets, secure positions, maintain operational security, and await further instruction. There was no drama, no philosophical hand-wringing—just the cold machinery of war turning over one more time.

Korrath pulled up the fleet manifests. Twenty-three *Shadowfang*-class stealth ships were prepped and waiting at dispersal points across three systems. There were eight hundred forty-seven autonomous probe swarms, each smaller than a human fist but packed with enough surveillance capability to map an entire planetary network. Then there were the payloads: quantum couplers, decoherence injectors, nanophage cartridges—all components needed to turn the Collective's consciousness infrastructure into a tomb.

The crews were elite. Humtar Reconnaissance Command didn't accept anyone who hadn't proven themselves in the worst situations imaginable. Korrath had handpicked the ship commanders himself—officers who understood that success meant no one would ever know they'd been there.

Compartmentalization was absolute. Each crew knew their specific targets, insertion vectors, exfiltration routes. But no single team knew the full scope of Operation Damocles. Only commanders understood they were seeding a weapon system capable of ending an entire civilization in seventy-two hours.

Korrath forwarded deployment authorization to his senior staff, then activated the secure channel for mission briefing.

Nineteen faces appeared on his display—ship commanders scattered across Republic and Humtar space, each waiting in ready rooms aboard vessels whose names were classified from most military personnel.

"Commanders," Korrath began. "Operation Damocles has been authorized for deployment phase. You are cleared to proceed."

He watched their expressions. None were surprised. They'd been expecting this too.

"Mission parameters are straightforward," Korrath continued. "Infiltrate Collective space and position assets at designated Arc Net nodes. Your packages contain quantum couplers, decoherence injectors, supporting hardware. Each device must be placed precisely at coordinates provided in your tactical packets. Variance tolerance is less than ten meters.

"Rules of engagement: passive operations only. No active scanning. No electronic countermeasures. No engagement with hostile forces unless directly compromised and exfiltration is impossible. Your mission is to remain invisible. If the Collective detects even one ship, the entire operation is blown."

Korrath let that sink in.

"Timeline: all assets must be in position within ninety days. Exfiltration will be staggered to avoid pattern detection. Once your package is delivered and confirmed dormant, you withdraw along randomized vectors and return to designated rally points."

One commander, Captain Seris Vaynor of the *Whispered Axiom*, raised a hand. "Admiral, what's our contingency if a package fails to achieve dormant status?" he asked.

"Retrieve if possible," Korrath said. "Destroy if retrieval is impossible. Under no circumstances can the Collective capture intact hardware. You have authorization to use any means necessary to prevent that outcome."

Including self-destruct, Korrath thought, though he didn't say it aloud. They all understood.

"One more thing," he said, his voice dropping. "You are placing the blade at the throat of an ancient enemy. You are seeding a weapon that could erase billions of lives in less time than it takes to finish a cup of tea. Make no mistakes. Check your work twice. Verify your positions three times. Because if this weapon is ever triggered, there is no margin for error."

The commanders nodded, faces grim.

"Questions?"

Silence.

"Then Godspeed. Korrath out."

The channel closed. Faces vanished.

Korrath sat alone in his office, staring at the tactical display. Tiny icons represented *Shadowfang* ships—each one a potential trigger for civilizational extinction. He thought of his own family, scattered across rebuilt Humtar worlds: his daughter on Velora, studying xenobiology, and his son commanding a patrol frigate near the Neythar Nexus.

He thought of Tannel. That broken man-machine hybrid, stripped of humanity by the Collective's philosophy of transcendence. The Orbots had volunteered for mutilation, believing it was evolution.

Korrath would die before allowing that fate to befall his children.

If the order came to trigger Damocles, he'd give it without hesitation because someone had to make the hard choices.

But he hoped desperately—with an intensity that surprised him—that he'd never have to.

****

CNS *Silent Theorem*
Edge of Collective Space
Fourteen Light-Years from Chor'vyn

Captain Lyrana Dovrek felt the *Silent Theorem* drop out of FTL like a stone falling into still water. One moment, they were riding at faster-than-light velocities. The next, they were back in normal space, coasting on momentum at a fraction of light speed.

"Phase-stealth engaged," her helmsman reported quietly.

"Confirm status," Dovrek said.

"All systems nominal. Thermal signature suppressed to background cosmic radiation. EM emissions zero. Gravitic distortion within acceptable parameters. We're a ghost, Captain."

Dovrek nodded. The *Silent Theorem* was one of the most advanced stealth ships in the Humtar fleet—it had a composite hull layered with metamaterials that bent sensor waves around it. Quantum-shielded reactors made power generation nearly invisible. Coolant systems bled heat so slowly that the ship could run for weeks without detection.

But nearly invisible wasn't invisible. And weeks of silent running through contested space meant weeks of holding their breath, hoping the Collective's sensors weren't better than intelligence suggested.

"Helm, plot approach vector," Dovrek ordered. "Passive sensors only. I want a complete catalog of Legion patrol patterns, Arc Net emissions, entanglement trunk signatures. Nothing active. Nothing that could give us away."

"Aye, Captain."

The bridge settled into whispered efficiency. Dovrek watched her crew work—analysts parsing sensor data, navigators plotting microcorrections to trajectory, engineers monitoring every system for anomalies. They moved like surgeons, precise and deliberate, because a single mistake meant detection.

And detection meant failure.

****

Three Weeks Later

The *Silent Theorem* reached its first designated target: a trunk splice point where three Arc Net branches converged in a junction node the size of a small station. Energy signatures bloomed across Dovrek's tactical display—quantum entanglement traffic, data packets moving at relativistic speeds, the constant hum of consciousness flowing through superconducting pathways.

"Tactical, confirm positioning," Dovrek said.

"Position confirmed, Captain. Variance within two meters of target coordinates. We're in the envelope."

"Deploy the package."

The weapons bay opened silently—no hydraulics, no sound, just magnetic clamps releasing their grip. The quantum coupler drifted free, a diamondoid cylinder half a meter long and thirty centimeters in diameter. Cryo-cooled to near absolute zero, armed with decoherence injectors pretuned to the Collective's qubit basis—it was a masterpiece of covert engineering, designed to kill gods.

Dovrek watched on her display as the coupler maneuvered itself toward the Arc Net trunk using microthrusters that burned colder than the void. It latched on to the superconducting busline, its surface morphing to match the texture and thermal signature of standard maintenance hardware.

Within seconds, it was indistinguishable from the legitimate nodes surrounding it.

"Package deployed," Tactical reported. "Dormant status confirmed. Quantum masking active."

The device began listening—sampling the Arc Net's quantum heartbeat, measuring error correction thresholds, mapping data flows. All passively, invisibly.

Dovrek allowed herself a single breath of relief.

"Helm, prepare for departure. Compress telemetry and prepare squirt transmission."

"Aye, Captain."

The *Silent Theorem* withdrew slowly, drifting away from the junction node at velocities that mimicked debris. Once it was clear by five thousand kilometers, the communications officer sent the transmission—a compressed data burst less than a millisecond long, encrypted and tightbeamed toward a relay drone waiting three light-days away.

"Package One delivered. Dormant and masked."

****

The near miss happened during exfiltration.

Dovrek had just completed her final deployment—quantum coupler number seven, positioned at a critical Arc Net relay near Chor'vyn's inner system. They were withdrawing along their planned vector, systems cold, moving at barely a crawl.

Then the proximity alarm pinged—once, softly.

"Contact," Tactical whispered. "Legion patrol. *Harvester*-class destroyer. Bearing one-seven-three mark four-five. Range: forty-two thousand kilometers and closing."

Dovrek's stomach dropped. "Intercept vector?"

"Unclear, Captain. They're on a standard patrol route, but if they maintain current heading…"

"They'll pass within four thousand kilometers of us," Dovrek finished.

Close enough to detect. Maybe.

"All stop," Dovrek ordered. "Kill everything except life support. Minimal power to phase-stealth only."

The ship went silent. Systems died. The gentle hum of reactors faded to nothing. Even air circulation shut down, leaving them breathing recycled atmosphere that tasted like copper and fear.

Dovrek watched the tactical display as the Legion destroyer approached. It moved with lazy confidence of a predator that owned its territory, scanning in wide arcs, searching for threats that probably didn't exist.

Except this time, they did.

Four thousand kilometers… three thousand five hundred… three thousand.

Dovrek's knuckles were white on her command chair. Her crew sat frozen, barely breathing, as if movement itself could give them away.

The destroyer passed. Two thousand eight hundred kilometers at closest approach.

And then it continued on its patrol route, sensors sweeping past the *Silent Theorem* without detecting anything more suspicious than cosmic background radiation.

Dovrek held position for thirty-eight hours after the patrol departed. Her crew breathed recycled air that grew increasingly stale, ate cold rations, waited in silence.

Only when absolutely certain they were clear did she give the order to resume exfiltration.

"Helm, take us home. Slow and steady. Let's not give the universe any more chances to kill us."

"Aye, Captain."

****

Quantum Operations Center
The Enclave
Ninety Days after Initial Deployment

Dr. Zeralleh Myrathi stood in the Quantum Operations Center, watching status boards update in real time. This was the Enclave's most secure facility—buried three hundred meters beneath the Central Research Tower, shielded against every known form of surveillance, accessible only to personnel with clearance so high most government officials didn't know it existed.

The final status update arrived at 0347 hours: "All assets in position. Damocles active."

Myrathi read through the consolidated report:

- 340 quantum couplers active and masked
- 187 kinetic munitions pre-positioned in holding orbits
- 42 nanophage seed points confirmed
- Backup site reconnaissance: 89% confidence on all major locations
- System diagnostic: nominal across all nodes
- Trigger readiness: 28-second synchronized strike window confirmed

Every piece was in place. Every system tested. Every fail-safe verified. They'd just armed an existential weapon.

Myrathi composed the transmission to Admiral Korrath, Admiral Vesharuk, President Gudea, and Viceroy Hunt. She kept it brief:

Subject: Damocles Active. Sword Suspended.

Message: All deployment objectives achieved. Assets in position and dormant. Weapon system operational.

Awaiting authorization for trigger or stand-down.

She sent it via quantum-encrypted channel, then sat back in her chair and let the enormity wash over her.

No one beyond this room knew. Not the Republic citizens. Not even most of the military. The Collective continued their expansion, their probing attacks, unaware that their entire civilization now balanced on a knife edge.

All it would take was one command, twenty-eight seconds, and trillions of lives would end.

Myrathi ordered standing watch rotations. The Quantum Operations Center would never be unmanned. Dual-key authorization protocols would be tested weekly. *Shadowfang* ships would maintain perpetual rotation, monitoring for Collective countermeasures or hardening efforts.

Every report would be analyzed. Every anomaly investigated. Every sign of treaty violation or preparation for renewed offensive would be cataloged and assessed.

They were guardians now of a doomsday clock.

****

Later That Day

Myrathi found Dr. Walburg, Sam, and Tannel in their workshop—a repurposed lab space in the Enclave's civilian wing where they'd been developing new therapeutic protocols for awakened Orbots. It was life-affirming work—work that built instead of destroyed.

Walburg was adjusting neural interface calibrations while Sam ran diagnostic scans. Tannel sat nearby, mechanical legs folded beneath him, reviewing data on a holographic display.

They looked up when Myrathi entered.

"It's done, isn't it?" Tannel asked. His eyes were dark, knowing.

"Yes," Myrathi said. "All assets deployed and active."

Tannel was quiet for a moment. "Has the order come?"

"No," Myrathi said. "And with luck, it never will."

Sam's optical scanner swept toward her, amber light pulsing slowly. "Hope is the only weapon that doesn't kill."

Walburg stood and moved to a small heating unit in the corner, where a kettle of water was already steaming. He poured tea into four cups—a ritual of normalcy against the shadow of apocalypse.

They sat together in silence, drinking tea, saying nothing.

Myrathi finished her tea and set the cup down gently.

We built a weapon to end those who think they have become gods, she thought. *Now we pray we never meet one arrogant enough to prove they aren't.*

Chapter 33:
Will We Ever Know Peace?

Allied Headquarters
Operation Center
Alliance City, New Eden

Viceroy Miles Hunt sat patiently in the operations center as they waited for the return of the *Bloodhawk*. It had been a risky decision to send the ship in alone, without escorts or a raiding force to clear them a path to the planets surface. He was relying on the stealth capability of the Humtar frigate to deliver the raiding force and recover them once the mission was over. If everything worked, the entire operation should take less than twenty minutes.

One of the things Hunt learned during the decades of war was that few things went according to plan. The enemy was always going to get a vote, and it seldom went your way. For this plan to work, they needed complete surprise, he hoped they'd achieved it. As the hours ticked by, he prayed he'd made the right decision.

Hunt looked at the main tactical display. The projection showed New Eden and the steady accumulation of Republic, Altairian, Humtar, and Tully warships in orbit. The buildup of forces for the invasion of Tueblets was well underway. The only thing he needed now was a signal from the *Bloodhawk* that the mission had succeeded.

"You're brooding, Viceroy." Admiral Korrath approached, his voice hushed so only Hunt could hear. The Humtar admiral lowered himself into the adjacent chair, his face a mix of concern and confidence. "You know the *Bloodhawk* has to maintain a comm blackout until they're clear of Zodark space. It's standard protocol, especially for a mission like this."

"I know the protocol. Doesn't mean I like it," Hunt replied calmly, his gaze never shifting from the display. "I've been fighting the Zodarks for twenty-three years, Korrath. No matter how many missions I've ordered, this part... the waiting, it never gets easier."

Korrath settled back in his chair as he pulled his Qpad from his pocket. "It's the burden of command—the decisions we have to make as commanders," the Humtar replied. Holding his Qpad in his hand, "I just finished reading your book. *Burden of Command*—good book, and an apt title. From one commander to another, the book does a good job of capturing the challenges of having to make decision that may cost hundreds, maybe even millions of lives, yet they are decisions that must be made. It's not an easy decision, but it is our decision, and ours alone to bear. I can see why it's required reading for your senior officers."

Hunt turned slightly. "I try to prepare them as best I can for the decisions they'll have to make—especially ship captains."

"I can see that. Let me ask you something. In chapter seven— 'The Cost of Victory'…" Korrath's eyes held steady. "You wrote it after losing your ship. The *Rook*, right?"

Hunt's jaw tightened as he thought back to that day. The battle replaying in his mind, the decisions he made or should have made that haunted him to this day. "Yeah, I did. It was during our second major battle with the Zodarks. Back then we didn't know about the alliance we are now part of. We were battling the Zodarks on our own." Hunt paused, his eyes staring into the distance as the memories of that flooded forward. He could feel his heart quicken, beads of sweat forming on his head. "The battle was at a tipping point. If I didn't maneuver the *Rook* into position to draw enemy fire off Admiral Halsey's ship, the *Voyager*, we would have lost it. In the end, we saved our flagship, destroyed a pair of Zodark warships but lost the *Rook* in the exchange. I lost hundreds of spacers that day. It was the worst day of my life. That evening, after we abandoned ship. We landed on the surface of New Eden. I managed to organize most of our survivors into a defensive position while we waited for recovery. Mind you, this was before we had captured the planet and removed the Zodarks from it.

"As darkness descended, they pounced on us—the Zodarks. They picked us off one at a time. They'd snatch someone before we could react. Shortly afterwards… we would hear their screams. Those bastards would torture them. Make them cry out in agonizing pain and leave us wondering who would be next. We lost dozens of people that night. Waiting for the dawn to come knowing they would likely finish us off," Hunt recounted somberly, a slight tremor in his right hand as he reached for a glass of water.

"That's awful, Miles. I am sorry you had to go through that," Korrath offered. "I suspect you questioned that decision for some time afterwards too?"

Hunt sized him up for a moment, then replied calmly, "You're damn right I did. I hated myself for it. But eventually, no matter how many times I replayed that day, the decisions I made and the actions I took, I still came back to the realization that no matter how grisly things turned out, I made the only call I could. The only call that could win—and I'd do it again in a heartbeat." His voice was hard as steel.

"That was going to be my next question—would you still make the same decision?" Korrath replied, his tone softened. "You have been through a lot, Viceroy. Made decisions no one should have to make. I like that about you. Despite everything this universe has thrown at you, you remain solid as stone. You didn't crumble under the pressure like most would have in your position. Instead, that pressure hardened you. Made you into the leader this alliance needs."

Hunt grunted at his comment. "Thank you for the vote of confidence, Korrath. But what's your point in all of this?"

Korrath's expression darkened as he leaned forward. "My point, Viceroy, is that in the coming days, regardless of the *Bloodhawk*'s mission, a decision as to when and how to end this war will have to be made, and that decision—once it's made—is going to cost the lives of tens of thousands whether it succeeds or fails. But you, Viceroy"—Korrath pointed at him, his voice growing stern—"are the leader this alliance needs. This war with the Zodarks, as brutal as it has been, as long as it has gone on—this is just the pregame to the war that will decide the fate of all living and sentient beings—the war to stop the Collective. They are a cancer that must be stopped."

"That's what Emperor SuVee says," Hunt acknowledged. "He calls it the greater war. The one he wants us to join them in fighting." He paused for a second before looking Korrath in the eyes, his stoic veneer disappearing for a moment. "I am tired of war, my friend... everyone is. We long for peace... to raise our families, to grow old with our wives or husbands... to watch our kids grow old and have kids of their own. Will we ever know peace, Korrath? Is that even possible for us, or is this all we have—to wage war after war without end... only the dead to know true peace?"

Korrath's weathered face softened—the practiced stoicism of command giving way to something rawer. He leaned back, studying the ice water in his glass before meeting Hunt's eyes.

"Peace. You want peace?" The words came out like gravel. "In the Ark Galaxy we retreated to—your astrographers know it as Messier NGC 205 (M110)—we fought wars on our side of the gate that you have yet to learn of. I commanded fleets for two centuries before your people left Earth, Viceroy. I have seen empires rise—I have conquered worlds. Two hundred years of watching civilizations bloom and burn. You want to know what I learned?"

He took a slow sip, condensation dripping onto the table as he let the silence hang.

"The dead don't know peace—they know nothing. It's the living who carry the weight. Every commander tells themselves the same lie: *just one more war, one more enemy to defeat, then we rest.* But you know what? There's always another threat waiting in the dark. Always…"

Korrath's jaw tightened. "My people hid for millennia, thinking isolation would bring us peace. We thought we had destroyed the Collective. We had won the war. Then we discovered that in their final moments, the Collective had unleashed the Neurocyte-7 virus. We saw our entire civilization wiped out—'not with a bang, but in a fevered whimper,' to paraphrase your Earth poet, T.S. Eliot. What remained of our ancestors retreated behind the gate leading to the Ark and sealed themselves off. You know what that bought us? Shame. And the Collective—they revived themselves the moment someone discovered our ruins. Now they are stronger than ever, spreading like a cancer while we played dead for thousands of years."

He leaned forward, his voice dropping to barely above a whisper. "You asked if we'll ever know peace? Here's the truth, Miles— we're already dead men walking. Every day we wake up, every battle we survive, that's borrowed time. The question isn't whether we'll find peace. It's whether the next generation gets to ask that same question, or the Collective turns them all into mindless drones, devoid of free will."

A bitter smile crossed Korrath's face. "But you know what keeps me moving? Same thing that kept you going after the *Rook*. We make the call no one else can make. We burn ourselves on the altar of war so maybe—*maybe*—our grandchildren get to die of old age instead of plasma fire."

Korrath raised his glass slightly. "To the burden of command, Viceroy. To being the blade others are too weak to wield. And to hoping we're both wrong about peace—even if we know better."

Hunt wished for something stronger than water to toast with, but that was all they had. "To the burden of command. May we know peace in this life or the next." Hunt tilted his glass toward Korrath.

A soft chime sound, interrupting their conversation. Both turned as Lieutenant Chen looked up from her station, eyes wide.

"Viceroy, Admiral—incoming transmission. It's the *Bloodhawk*."

Hunt's breath caught. Korrath placed a steadying hand on his shoulder as they both stood.

"Decrypting now," Chen continued, fingers flying across her interface. "Authentication confirmed. Message reads..." She paused, rereading. "Mission complete. All secondary objectives achieved."

The operations center erupted in controlled celebration. The mission had succeeded, and the ship returned. Hunt remained still for a moment, absorbing the implications.

"Secondary objectives," he said quietly. "That means they couldn't capture anyone."

"True. But it also means the High Council was eliminated." Korrath's voice remained steady. "You wanted to sow chaos across the Empire—it'll begin now."

"Signal Captain Theruun, and General Royce," Hunt ordered, voice steady. "Tell them well done. Have them proceed to the station for debrief."

As his staff rushed to comply, Hunt caught Korrath's eyes. The admiral offered the slightest nod—understanding without absolution.

The burden of command, Hunt had written, was knowing which decisions were necessary. Living with them—that was the lesson still being learned.

****

Office of the Viceroy
Alliance City, New Eden

A week had gone by since the *Bloodhawk* had returned from its mission to decapitate the leadership of the Zodark Empire. Standing over the conference table in the room adjacent to his private study, Viceroy Miles Hunt looked at the status reports of the various allied fleets as they continued to marshal in the Primord system of Pfeinstgard and the Republic system of Rhea—New Eden. The various pieces on the chessboard were nearly in position, ready to strike once he gave the order.

"You look troubled, Miles," said Senator Handolly from his seated position across the table.

Hunt looked up at the Altairian. They had known each other for two decades. Handolly was one of the few Altairians he genuinely considered a friend. "No, not troubled. Just wondering how ready one can be to start the next battle versus continuing to prepare and prepare some more."

"Ah yes. The question of when is enough, enough," Handolly replied.

Admiral Vesharuk smiled at them. "One can never be too prepared, but one must wary of paralysis through analysis. It can keep one in a doom loop of inaction and indecisiveness that can ruin even the best-laid plans."

"Hear, hear to that," commented Admiral Bailey, the Republic Fleet Commander. "Vice Admiral Lee's Task Force 28 reports his force and the Primords are ready for action."

"As does Task Force 20," declared Vice Admiral Rosentreter from his seat next to Handolly. "Near as I can tell, the only piece we're waiting on is Admiral Korrath and his task force."

"And they're nearly ready," interjected Commander Zalira Namtar, the Humtar's Head of Strategic Planning. "The *Razorwind* is finalizing repairs as we speak. Admirals Ithis and Korrath are firm about waiting for them to join the fleet before things begin. The *Razorwind*'s firepower is more than worth the wait," she reminded them.

"That it is," confirmed Hunt, settling the issue. "Gentlemen, when this operation begins, we have to push fast and push hard if we're going to break the Malvari. The intelligence we're receiving from the *Bloodhawk* and her sister ships, the *Voidraven* and *Ironwing*, shows massive unrest across much of the Empire. Some worlds are demanding that Zon Otro resign. Others are demanding the Groff Director, Vak'Atioth, be replaced for his intelligence failures. This division is grinding them to a halt—something we plan to take full advantage of.

"For now, we wait until the *Razorwind* rejoins the fleet. We let our eyes and ears inside their territory continue to report on what they are seeing as we prepare to strike. Admiral Dobbs, I want your plan ready to brief by 0900 hours tomorrow," Hunt directed as he looked at Rear Admiral Amy Dobbs before turning to Admiral Takmahl, the *Freedom*'s starfighter commander.

"Admiral Takmahl, the mission to neutralize the Nargulon fuel extraction facility above Nargulon had better be tight. You'll brief your plan after Dobbs. If we do this right, we're going to smash Tueblets, and end this war once and for all. Dismissed."

Chapter 34:
The Gilded Cage

Malvari Command Center
Velkryn, Moon of Xyrvannis
Tueblets System

Zon Otro pressed his palm against the reinforced viewport, feeling the faint vibration of a fortress alive with activity. Beyond the thick barrier, the massive blue-green sphere of Xyrvannis dominated the sky, its continental masses and sprawling oceans visible even from the moon's fortified command center. Three smaller moons traced their orbits around the planet like dutiful attendants, their trajectories precisely calculated millennia ago.

It was beautiful, orderly—everything his Empire was not.

The viewport was set into three meters of reinforced durasteel and composite armor, part of the command center's outer shell that had been carved directly into Velkryn's largest mountain range. The entire facility sprawled across forty square kilometers—some sections buried hundreds of meters beneath rock and hardened bunkers, other portions camouflaged by native vegetation and terrain features that made orbital targeting nearly impossible. Plasma cannon batteries dotted the surrounding peaks, their barrels tracking the sky in endless vigilance. Missile silos hid beneath false rock formations. Point-defense grids covered every approach vector.

Griglag chose well, thought Otro. *If the Republic wants to take this facility, they'll pay in blood and warships.*

His reflection stared back from the glass—older than he remembered, with new lines etched around his eyes. The ceremonial robes of his position as Zon draped across his frame like a shroud, the weight of his position crushing him. Otro had worn the same robe for two weeks now, ever since Mavkah Griglag had forced him to flee Zinconia under the cover of darkness. He'd been forced to abandon his home world like a coward, while religious fanatics screamed for his blood in the streets and attempted to attack his personal residence.

Zon Otro had ordered the executions of nearly ten thousand followers of that religious sect for their attempted insurrection—the decision gnawed at him like a parasite. He'd happily given the order himself and watched as Malvari warriors systematically purged the zealot sect from the capital. But the fact that he'd had to do it at all was what angered him most.

Outside the capital, the bodies filled the Gardens of Caution, a place where Zon Utulf had once taken him to discuss philosophy and the burden of leadership when he had appointed him Mavkah. Now the site held mass graves, a warning of what happens to insurrectionists. It frustrated Otro to no end that this had happened, and worse, the schism between the Groff and the High Council had only grown.

Otro had hoped the executions would end this notion of insurrection, but they hadn't. The unrest had spread like a plague. There'd been more protests and more violence. Then there were the attempts on his life—crude, poorly planned, but terrifyingly close to succeeding. If his personal guard hadn't detected the infiltrators breaching the outer walls of his residence...

Otro's hand curled into a fist against the viewport.

Vak'Atioth. The name tasted like poison. He couldn't prove it yet, couldn't trace the conspiracy directly back to the Groff Director with the certainty he needed to charge him, but he knew it was him. The timing was too perfect, the coordination too precise. Vak'Atioth had been the Groff Director for too long. He was too powerful to remove, yet too powerful to leave in place.

The door behind Otro hissed open. He was about to turn when he recognized the heavy footfalls of Mavkah Griglag crossing the converted conference room that now served as his temporary High Council Chamber. The space had once hosted tactical briefings for sector commanders—walls lined with holographic displays, a central planning table, reinforced doors designed to withstand direct hits from orbital bombardment. Now it was draped with the trappings of authority: the Zon's ceremonial banners, the Circle of Truth recreated, and seats arranged for clan representatives.

"My Zon," Griglag began, his voice carefully neutral. "The clan representatives are arriving. They'll be ready for your address within the hour."

"Good, let them wait. You and I have much to discuss." Otro's words came out sharper than intended. He took a breath, forcing his tone to soften. "Forgive me, Mavkah. These past weeks have been... difficult."

"Difficult does not begin to describe it." Griglag moved to stand beside him at the viewport. The scarred veteran's reflection joined his own in the glass. Beyond, a squadron of Zeek fighters banked across Velkryn's reddish sky, their atmospheric engines leaving contrails against the twilight. "If I may speak plainly?"

"Ha-ha," chuckled Otro. "When have you ever needed permission to do that, my old friend?"

A ghost of a smile touched Griglag's lips before his expression turned serious. "I know you aren't comfortable with the optics of relocating here. It was unfortunately necessary. The Malvari intercepted three more assassination plots in the final days before we evacuated you. We are assuming they are Vak'Atioth's operatives. What's surprising is their increasing boldness. Here on Velkryn, the Malvari control every access point, every transport, every communications node. Mavkahs before you and me designed this facility to withstand a full-scale assault. Even if the Republic somehow penetrated our orbital defenses, they'd lose tens of thousands trying to breach the walls of this fortress."

"Mavkah, all of that is true, but a fortress is just a gilded cage." Otro gestured at the mountain peaks visible through the viewport, their slopes covered in dark vegetation that masked sensor arrays and weapon emplacements. "No matter how well defended, I'm trapped here while our Empire burns."

"Better trapped and alive than dead in your own home." Griglag's tone hardened. "The zealots nearly succeeded in capturing you. If we hadn't intervened when we did—"

"I know." Otro cut him off. He didn't need the reminder of how close death had come. "You saved my life, old friend. Again. But that doesn't change our strategic reality. Vak'Atioth has gone too far this time. I've known the man despises me, but this...wanting me dead?" Otro shook his head in sadness and disgust. He looked up at his friend. "It would seem that since his attempt has failed, he's settling for making me and you appear weak. And look at us, Griglag. We stand cowering in a fortress on a moon while he spreads his poison across the Empire."

"Cowering? No, I don't think so." Griglag's voice carried an edge to it. "You are not cowering, my Zon. You are commanding from the most secure location in the Tueblets system. Even now, clan leaders continue to arrive here to hear *your* words, to speak with *you*, not Vak'Atioth. Here, the Malvari operate from this facility, coordinating our entire military structure. This isn't a retreat—it's consolidation of power into a defensible position."

Otro nodded. He wanted to believe that—desperately wanted to feel the certainty Griglag projected. But standing here, watching Xyrvannis turn slowly against the void, he felt more like a prisoner than the leader chosen by Zon Utulf to succeed him.

"You speak wise words, Mavkah. Let me ask you this: was it boldness or desperation on the part of Vak'Atioth?" he asked quietly. "I am struggling to understand the motivation of this move against me. Which do you believe drives him?"

Griglag's jaw worked as he considered the question before answering. "I cannot know the mind of Vak'Atioth, but I suspect it was both—bold desperation in an attempt to seize power. I believe the Groff Director overplayed his hand with the religious zealots, warping their minds and beliefs to take actions that would only benefit him and his desire for power. The killing of your security detail in the wake of the Republic raid coupled with dracmas of Frockings and public executions among anyone who questions the Groff has turned public opinion against him more than it has against you.

"It is no secret that Vak'Atioth believes he should have been Zon. Had you not been rescued from the disaster in Sol, he would have become Zon. He is a cunning politician. He creates chaos because in chaos, he creates opportunity. Look at what he has done to the Empire— he has left us deaf, blind, and mute in this war as our enemies circle us like a wounded animal. He's gambling the Empire, betting that he can seize power before you can stabilize the situation," Griglag explained. It was a rare moment of open honesty that Otro had desperately needed.

"Mavkah… that is an astute assessment of our current predicament. Let us discuss now how precarious his position truly is and what we can do about it." Otro moved to the conference table, where holographic projections flickered to life at his approach. Star systems materialized in blue light, some pulsing green, others angry red. The tactical display, a three-dimensional map of the Empire's current disposition, dominated the room. "This was compiled by the Malvari. It shows us the loyalty of the clans and tribes across the Empire, correct?"

Griglag nodded, then activated his data pad. The holographic display shifted, systems reorganizing by allegiance. Otro was surprised by how many systems showed green—more than he had thought.

"Unsurprisingly, the Shwani clan remains firmly with Vak'Atioth," Griglag began, gesturing to the amber icon representing the Varkorion system. "That's expected, given the fact that their clan dominates the system. The Dralkeg and Rithak clans in the Orrvek system have declared neutrality, but Malvari intelligence suggests they're waiting to see which way the wind blows before committing."

"Cowards and opportunists." Otro studied the map, noting the clusters of green spreading across imperial space. "And the rest?"

"The rest stand with you, my Zon." Pride crept into Griglag's voice. "Twenty-three of the major clans, representing sixty-seven percent of our military strength and seventy-two percent of our industrial capacity. They've formally denounced the Groff for the intelligence failures that led to the High Council attack, the loss of the Gravaxia system, and the raid the Republic pulled on the Kryntok system."

Otro felt something unfamiliar stir in his chest—hope, perhaps, or at least the shadow of it. "Hmm, explain that further to me."

"Your framing of the Council attack as a Groff failure resonated deeply." Griglag expanded the display, showing communication intercepts and clan council recordings. "The warrior caste despises Vak'Atioth. His heavy-handed methods, his use of fear and surveillance—they go against every principle of honor our society was built upon. When you gave them permission to blame the Groff for failing to warn us about Republic capabilities, you gave voice to decades of resentment."

Otro watched the data streams flow past. Intercepted messages between clan elders, transcripts of heated debates, recordings of tribe warriors swearing renewed oaths to the Zon. The narrative he'd crafted in the ashes of the Council attack had taken root deeper than he'd imagined.

"The Groff has made many enemies over the dracmas," Griglag continued. "Their intelligence network infiltrated every clan, every tribe, reporting on internal matters that were none of their concern. They blackmailed honorable warriors, extorted clan elders, used secrets as weapons against our own people. You've given the clans justification to hit back."

"So Vak'Atioth's isolation is complete?" Otro leaned forward, studying the amber glow of Varkorion on the display. "He controls only his home system?"

"Effectively, yes. Our reconnaissance confirms his shadow fleet—the vessels he's been building in secret—numbers approximately eighty ships. Significant, but not enough to challenge the combined might of the loyal clans." Griglag paused, his expression darkening. "However, there's a complication."

Of course there was. There always was. "And what is this complication?"

"The religious issue hasn't disappeared. Vak'Atioth's zealots may have failed to overthrow you, but their message still resonates with certain factions in the Veythar system. It was always a bit more of a religious world. They claim Lindow has withdrawn his favor, that your ascension to Zon was illegitimate. Every defeat against the Republic gives them ammunition."

Otro felt the anger surge again, hot and familiar. "So I'm damned either way. If I focus on crushing Vak'Atioth, the Republic gains ground. If I focus on the Republic, Vak'Atioth continues to erode my legitimacy from within."

"That's the strategic reality we face." Griglag's tone was grim. "Which brings me to the more pressing concern." He pulled up new tactical data—ship movements, battle reports, casualty figures. "The Republic just conducted another raid on one of our mining systems. They hit the Tavrix system hard, destroyed significant infrastructure. But more concerning than the raid itself is *how* they did it."

Otro's tone sharpened. "Explain."

Griglag zoomed in on a rotating hologram of debris fields and weapon-impact models. "We recovered fragments from our orbital sentries. The energy resonance doesn't match any Republic or Gallentine weapon. It's older... cleaner. The harmonics carry a recursive phase pattern we've only seen once before—on recovered Humtar relics."

Otro froze. "You're certain?"

"Yes, my Zon." Griglag's expression was grave. "The Gallentines use linear pulse arrays. This was something else—an adaptive beam lattice, self-modulating mid-flight. No known Republic ship could carry such a weapon, and the Gallentines have never fielded it in the Milky Way. Our analysts are unanimous: the technology is *Humtar*."

He switched the display again, revealing ghostlike outlines of ships. Their hulls were smooth, angular, designed to absorb both light

and   sensor   emissions.
"We've also identified three new vessel signatures during the engagement," he continued. "No registry, no emissions, but their profiles match structural principles found in archived Humtar schematics— gravity-damped hulls, photonic absorption layers, and quantum-jump distortion traces. These weren't Republic ships, my Zon. They were built *by* the Humtars—or *for* them."

Otro leaned against the table, knuckles whitening. "So the Gallentines are not behind this."

"No," Griglag said firmly. "Their vessels broadcast distinct field harmonics—loud and proud. These ships ghosted through our perimeter without tripping a single alarm. The Gallentines don't have that kind of stealth. It has to be the Humtars."

The words seemed to drain the air from the chamber. Otro stared at the slow advance of red icons across the map—Republic forces, multiplying, consuming worlds one by one. Each now backed by a power older and far more dangerous.

"So, it's true," he murmured. "The Humtars are now fighting alongside them."

Griglag nodded once. "The evidence leaves no room for doubt. Their technology has shifted the balance completely."

Otro's voice dropped to a whisper. "Then tell me plainly, Mavkah—can we win?"

Griglag hesitated. "When the Gallentines intervened at Sol, it crippled us. This..." He gestured toward the glowing battlefield. "This is worse. The Humtars have joined them. They're *rewriting the rules of war.* I don't believe we have a chance in Hark of survival...not without a similar intervention and help from an equally powerful ally."

"You mean Legion?"

Griglag nodded slowly, his expression unreadable.

"Legion is as much a threat to us as they are to the Republic." Otro turned back to the viewport, his reflection staring back at him with haunted eyes. "We'd be trading one enemy for another. Possibly a worse one."

Neither warrior spoke. The question hung in the air between them, unanswered and perhaps unknowable. Outside, Velkryn's fortifications stood ready, weapons charged, sensors sweeping the void.

But all the armor and plasma cannons in the galaxy wouldn't matter if they were facing enemies on all sides.

"If I pursue Vak'Atioth aggressively," Otro said finally, breaking the silence, "if I commit forces to crushing the Groff and securing Varkorion, I leave our frontiers vulnerable—the Republic will sense weakness and strike." He gestured at the display, highlighting the system marked in angry red. "The loss of Gravaxia unfortunately places us in a precarious position right now. Vak'Atioth knows this. The Malvari can't really commit to bringing the Groff to heel, because it would leave Tueblets vulnerable to the joint Primord-Republic fleet in the neighboring system."

Griglag's shoulders sagged slightly, the first sign of true weariness Otro had seen from his friend. "I won't lie to you, my Zon. Gravaxia's loss is a strategic setback. That system was our buffer, our early warning post. Now the Republic sits on our doorstep—and, yes, it places us in a very tough position regarding what we can do to handle the growing insurrection from the Groff."

"Then perhaps direct confrontation isn't the answer." Otro moved back to the conference table, his mind working through alternatives. "What about approaching this politically? I could speak with Heltet, the Groff's Laktish. His position is supposed to be more neutral—the Empire's enforcer of the High Council, even though the position is within the Groff and under Vak'Atioth's control. Perhaps he might see reason. Perhaps he could broker some sort of reset with Vak'Atioth to avoid civil war and prepare to fight back against the Republic."

Griglag considered this, his scarred face thoughtful. "Heltet is…complicated. He's served the Groff faithfully for dracmas, but he's also shown independence when it matters. During the Sol disaster, he was one of the few who questioned some of Vak'Atioth's more extreme actions." He paused. "But approaching him directly would be risky. If he reports the contact to Vak'Atioth, it could be seen as weakness. Or worse, as an attempt to suborn one of the Director's key subordinates."

"Everything is risky now." Otro's voice carried the weight of exhaustion. "The question is which risks are worth taking."

"Then I'll arrange a secure channel. Make it appear routine—a Council matter requiring the Laktish's input. If Heltet is willing to talk, we'll know soon enough." Griglag made notes on his data pad. "And if he reports it to Vak'Atioth?"

"Then at least we'll know where he truly stands." Otro studied the loyalty map again, its colors swirling like the politics they represented. Green for loyalty. Amber for opposition. Gray for the neutrals waiting to see which side would win.

Too much gray, he thought. *Too much uncertainty.*

"Against their current strength, how long could we hold Tueblets if the Republic committed to a full assault?" Otro asked, pulling up defensive schematics of the system.

"Depends on how much they're willing to commit." Griglag expanded the tactical display, showing fleet dispositions and defensive platforms. "If they bring everything—their full battle fleet, the Gallentines, the Humtars, the Primord—I have no idea how long we could hold, but likely not very long. Our plasma batteries can engage targets in low orbit. Missile silos provide area denial across multiple vectors. The asteroid fortifications we've been positioning create overlapping kill zones. But ultimately, if they're willing to pay the price, they'll break through."

"And how many ships would they lose in the attempt?"

"That is hard to say, especially if the Gallentines or Humtars join them." Griglag's expression darkened. "But that assumes we're fighting them with our full strength. If Vak'Atioth's forces join the battle—on either side—the calculations change dramatically."

Otro closed his eyes. Behind his eyelids, he saw the faces of those who'd shaped his path. Utulf, his mentor, had taught him that leadership required vision beyond mere survival. His clan elders had drilled into him that honor and duty were the foundations of Zodark society. The High Council members, now dead, had trusted him to guide the Empire through this crisis.

All of them had believed in him. And he was failing them all.

"I need to address the clan representatives," he said finally, opening his eyes to find Griglag watching him with an unreadable expression. "They're waiting for guidance, for some sign that the Zon has a plan to salvage this disaster. What do I tell them, Mavkah? That their choices are between a slow death of attrition or a humiliating surrender?"

"You tell them the truth." Griglag's voice hardened with conviction. "That we face the greatest crisis in our Empire's history. That our enemies are strong and our internal divisions threaten to destroy us. But we have not lost yet and will not so long as we stay unified. We have the majority of clans standing with their rightful Zon and our warriors remain the finest in the sector. Our industrial base is strong, and our might has not been broken."

"It's not that I disagree with you, Griglag, but we had better make sure our words are backed up with action. We have to make it clear to Vak'Atioth that his attempts to seize power have failed, and that his continued insolence threatens the very survival of the Empire. Our enemies are closing in on us, and instead of focusing our efforts on preparing to fight them, we are fighting among ourselves," he replied angrily, his patience exhausted.

Otro studied his friend's face, searching for doubt, for hesitation. He found none. Griglag believed what he was saying, truly believed they could still salvage this catastrophe. But was that belief rooted in strategic reality, or was it simply the stubbornness of a warrior refusing to admit defeat? Was he refusing to admit defeat out of his own pride, or could he salvage the situation?

"When Zon Utulf appointed me Zon, I never envisioned it would be like this—gambling the fate of the Empire on the success or failure of one or two battles." Otro shook his head, feeling the weight of the decision pressing down on him like a physical force. "Vak'Atioth and the Groff's intelligence failure during the Sol invasion may well have cost us the Empire. I feel that every choice, every decision I have made since that day could be the one that ends everything."

"We can't change the Groff's failure. What is done is done. You were chosen to make the decisions that will decide our fate. That's what it means to be Zon." Griglag's expression softened. "Utulf used to say that you'll never have perfect information, never have ideal circumstances. You can only act on what you know, and pray to Lindow that you've chosen wisely."

A proximity alert chimed softly from the tactical display. Both warriors turned to see a cluster of new icons appearing—transport ships dropping out of FTL transit, beginning their approach to Velkryn. It was the clan representatives, arriving for the assembly.

Otro returned to the viewport one final time. The planet Xyrvannis filled his vision, blue and green and seemingly peaceful. Somewhere beyond the planet's curve, he knew, lay the other worlds of Tueblets—each one vital, each one vulnerable.

This system was the Empire's heart. If it fell, everything fell with it.

"Once the remaining clan representatives have arrived, ensure they are gathered with the others," Otro said quietly as the final transports approached. "I'll address them within the hour. It's time we steel their resolve for the coming battle. It's only a matter of time until our enemies attack. When they do, the outcome will decide the fate of our people."

Griglag saluted, then turned to depart, leaving him alone with his thoughts. As decisions loomed, the remaining choices grew less appealing by the day. Both paths would lead to ruin. The only question was which ruin would inflict the least damage on his people, and which one he would choose. He prayed that once he made the decision, he'd have the strength to follow it through to its bitter end.

In the mountain depths of Velkryn, surrounded by enough armor and weapons to hold off an army, Zon Otro had never felt more vulnerable or alone in his life.

Chapter 35:
A Monster's Calculus

Bridge of ZNS *Harvex's Vengeance*
Departing Planet Shwani, Varkorion System

"Jump sequence initiated. Thirty minutes to transition point."

Director Vak'Atioth stood on the bridge of the *Harvex's Vengeance*, hands resting against the tactical rail as he surveyed his command. The *Plarix*-class battleship hummed beneath his feet—2,100 meters of warship built in secret at the Tarkun shipyards, hidden from Zon Otro's spies, the High Council's auditors, and even most of the Groff's own operatives. Blue-white light gleaming from tactical displays cast harsh shadows across the bridge crew's faces. Twelve Zodarks worked their stations with quiet efficiency, each one handpicked, each one sworn to absolute silence.

The low thrum of the battleship's massive reactors vibrated through deck plating, a constant reminder of the ship's power. Recycled air carried the faint metallic tang of new construction—sealant compounds not yet fully cured, hull plating still settling into its final molecular configuration. The *Vengeance* had completed her shakedown trials only six dracmas ago. Her weapons had never fired in anger. Her armor had never tasted enemy fire.

Let us hope it stays that way, Vak thought, studying the tactical hologram floating above the command deck. Three contacts accompanied his flagship: the heavy cruiser *Dralkeg's Wrath*, and frigates *Nulvox* and *Rithak*. It was a minimal escort for a battleship of this class, but Vak wanted no witnesses beyond those he controlled absolutely.

"Director," called NOS Kelvoth from the helm station, "scout frigates report no contacts along approach vector. Space is clear to the transition point."

Vak's ears rotated toward the officer, processing the information. "Maintain sensor sweeps. Legion does not announce its presence until it chooses to."

"Understood, Director."

Silence settled across the bridge, broken only by the soft chirp of sensor arrays and the whisper of environmental systems. Vak pulled a data tablet from his belt, calling up the encrypted message he'd received three days prior. The text was brief: coordinates and a time window—nothing more. There were no reassurances, no protocols, and no indication of what awaited him at the rendezvous point along the contested border between former Orbot territory and Zodark space.

A border that shouldn't exist, Vak reflected bitterly. *The Orbots were supposed to be our allies, our partners in resisting the Gallentines' expansion. Instead, they surrendered—laid down their arms like cowards and accepted subjugation.*

That failure had created the void Vak now sought to fill. The Collective had lost its proxy in the Milky Way. Legion would need a new proxy to bleed the Republic, to tie down Gallentine allies, to keep the alliance distracted while the Collective prosecuted its war in Andromeda. The Zodark Empire—desperate, weakened, facing invasion on multiple fronts—could serve that purpose.

The only question is, What price will we be asked to pay?

Vak's hands tightened around the tablet. He thought of Tueblets, the Empire's strategic heart. Eight stargates connected to every major system. Without Tueblets, the Empire fractured into isolated territories. The Republic knew this. What limited intelligence he had suggested their next offensive would target that very system, severing the arteries that kept the Empire alive.

The Malvari fleets were weakened by defeats at Gravaxia, Orinda, Kryntok. The reserve fleet Vak had built—the *Plarix* battleships and Thoraxian destroyers hidden at Tarkun—might delay the inevitable, but delay wasn't victory. The Empire needed more than ships. It needed time.

Or a devil's bargain… Vak thought.

"Director," Kelvoth announced, "thirty seconds to FTL engagement."

"Proceed."

The bridge lights dimmed as power surged to the FTL drives from the Arkanorian reactors. Vak felt the familiar sensation of reality bending, space-time compressing around the hull. Through the forward viewport, stars began to stretch—pinpoints of light elongating into brilliant lines as the *Vengeance* accelerated beyond conventional physics.

"FTL drive engaged. Transit time: four hours, seventeen minutes."

Four hours until he met with the Collective. Four hours until he offered his people's service to something utterly alien—something that converted living beings into Legion, their cyborg slaves, consciousness trapped in mechanical bodies that did their bidding.

Vak stared at the streaking starfield, his reflection ghosting across the viewport glass. Three eyes looked back at him—Director of the Groff, master of the Empire's intelligence apparatus, architect of countless covert operations that had shaped Zodark policy for decades.

What am I becoming?

He dismissed the thought. Doubt was a luxury he couldn't afford. The Empire's survival demanded action, demanded sacrifice. If that meant trading honor for existence, so be it. The Zodarks would endure. They would fight. And when the war ended—*if* it ended—history would judge whether his choices had been necessary or monstrous.

The *Harvex's Vengeance* and her escorts plunged deeper into quantum space, racing toward a rendezvous that would damn or save the Zodark Empire.

Vak just wasn't sure which.

****

Bridge of ZNS *Harvex's Vengeance*
Orbot–Zodark Neutral Zone

"Contact! Designate Alpha One. Configuration unknown— mass signature equivalent to a vessel in our libraries. It looks to be a Legion warship."

The bridge of the *Harvex's Vengeance* erupted in controlled chaos. Sensor operators hunched over their displays, fingers flying across controls as they attempted to refine readings. Weapons officers looked to Vak, awaiting orders that would determine whether the next moments brought dialogue or destruction.

Vak's hands tightened on the tactical rail. "Tactical display. Full magnification."

The hologram flickered, resolving into sharp clarity. Before them hung the rendezvous coordinates—a dying red dwarf star casting sickly crimson light across empty space. There were no planets, no asteroid fields...nothing but void and fading stellar radiation. They were in perfect isolation and perfect secrecy.

Floating at the coordinates was a cylinder-shaped structure, barely thirty meters long, dull gray metal that seemed to absorb light rather than reflect it. No weapon emplacements were visible. There was minimal power signature—just enough to maintain life support and basic systems. It was a meeting place, nothing more—utilitarian architecture stripped of all pretense.

But three thousand kilometers beyond the outpost, holding position with predatory stillness, waited something that made Vak's blood run cold.

The *Harvester*-class destroyer.

"Magnify that contact," Vak ordered, voice steady despite the ice forming in his gut.

The hologram zoomed in. What appeared on the display defied every principle of warship design Vak had studied across fifty dracmas of service. The Legion vessel was *wrong*. Its hull wasn't constructed—it looked like it was *grown*. A combination of iron and bio-forged carapace plating covered its 1,300-meter length in what resembled segmented like insect chitin, overlapping in patterns that suggested both armor and living tissue. It was unlike any design Vak had seen before. Even its weapons, hidden in ports along its hull, pulsed in faint life.

The ship had no running lights, no identification markings, and no aesthetic considerations whatsoever. It just sat in silent patience, a menace radiated from every meter of its hull.

"Director," NOS Kelvoth whispered from the helm, his voice carrying the tremor of instinctive fear, "that ship… by Lindow's grace, what *is* that thing?"

Lindow… what have I summoned? Vak thought but kept the words internal. Aloud, he projected calm authority. "It is our contact. Maintain defensive posture but do not power weapons. We are here to talk, not fight."

A chirp from the communications station. "Director, incoming transmission. Text only. No audio, no holographic component."

"Display it."

Words appeared on the main viewscreen, stark white letters against black background:

VAK'ATIOTH. PROCEED TO CONFERENCE FACILITY. ALONE WITH MINIMAL GUARD COMPLEMENT. DO NOT DEVIATE.

"Commander, two of your guards will accompany me and no more," directed Vak. "And, Commander—if I don't return within two hours, take the fleet back to Shwani. Inform Heltet of what transpired here. He'll know what to do."

"Director—"

"Two hours, Commander. Not a moment longer." Vak straightened, forcing his spine rigid, his posture projecting confidence he didn't feel. "Ready my shuttle."

****

The shuttle's maneuvering thrusters fired, adjusting angle and velocity. Magnetic docking clamps extended, seeking purchase against the outpost's port. Metal scraped against metal—a shriek that transmitted through the shuttle's hull, setting Vak's teeth on edge.

Clang.

Docking complete.

"Atmospheric seal confirmed," the pilot reported. "Pressure equalized. You are clear to disembark, Director."

Vak stood, his legs steadier than he expected. Behind him, Kravex and Julthar rose in synchronization, weapons held at ready positions. Professional. Prepared. Terrified beneath their disciplined exteriors.

"Stay close," Vak ordered. "But do not fire unless I give the command or we are fired upon first. Am I clear?"

"Yes, Director," they responded in unison.

The airlock cycled. Pressure equalized with a hiss of rushing atmosphere. Cold air flooded the shuttle—colder than regulation, carrying no scent Vak could identify. Not the recycled staleness of ship air. Not the chemical tang of industrial atmospheres. Just... nothing. Sterile. Lifeless.

The inner door opened.

Beyond lay a short corridor, ten meters of bare tritanium walls and harsh overhead lighting. No decorations. No viewports. Just function stripped to its most brutal essence.

And at the corridor's end, a door stood open. Waiting for him to talk through.

Vak lifted his chin in a posture of confidence and stepped into the outpost. Kravex and Julthar followed, their footsteps echoing against the metal flooring behind him.

****

The corridor stretched before Vak like a tunnel to damnation. His breath misted in air colder than regulation—cold enough to make his scales prickle, cold enough that each exhalation formed visible clouds that dissipated slowly in the recycled atmosphere. He walked forward. The door's threshold beckoned like a mouth ready to swallow him whole.

Vak crossed it into the conference room. When he entered, he saw a round table occupied the center, utilitarian metal surface reflecting overhead lights. Four chairs surrounded it, simple constructions without padding or comfort considerations.

That was when he saw him, or rather… it. One chair was already occupied. When the figure looked up, Vak's breath caught. *What in Lindow's name is that…?*

The figure sitting in the chair looked like it had been Zodark once, now a cyborg, an abomination. He could see the remnants—cranial ridge structure running from forehead to the back of the skull, skeletal frame proportions that matched his own species, posture that suggested familiarity with bipedal movement. But everything else was… *wrong*.

Half its face was metallic plating fused directly to bone, seamless integration that suggested surgical precision beyond anything Zodark medicine could achieve. The plating wasn't bolted or grafted—it was *merged*, metal flowing into organic tissue like two substances that had been melted together and allowed to cool as one.

One eye remained natural—milky yellow iris surrounding black pupil, the same as any Zodark's. But it didn't blink. Didn't move. Just stared with predatory focus that never wavered.

The other two eyes—where Zodark physiology placed secondary visual organs above and to the side of the primary—had been replaced with glowing optics. Mechanical constructs that tracked independently, rotating in their sockets with faint servo whirs. One focused on Vak's face. The other swiveled to track Kravex and Julthar as they entered behind him.

The cyborg's arms rested on the table. Segmented metal fingers—too many joints, articulation points that bent at angles organic anatomy couldn't achieve—lay flat against the surface. As Vak watched, one finger tapped experimentally. *Click.* The sound was sharp, precise, utterly devoid of warmth.

But worst of all was the chest cavity.

Transparent alloy covered the torso where armor or clothing should have been, revealing what lay beneath. Pulsing biomechanical organs—some clearly organic, others obviously artificial, many a nightmarish fusion of both—worked in rhythmic synchronization. Vak glimpsed what might have been lungs, except they were reinforced with metallic struts. A heart, except it beat with mechanical precision rather than organic variability. Tubes and wires threaded through tissue, carrying fluids he couldn't identify.

The cyborg didn't breathe. Its chest didn't rise and fall. Those hybrid organs cycled, but not for respiration—for something else. Power distribution? Coolant circulation? Vak didn't know, couldn't guess, didn't want to understand.

It wore no uniform. No insignia. No clothing beyond the necessary components that held its hybrid anatomy together. Just raw, functional horror.

The cyborg sat motionless. Watching. Assessing.

Behind Vak, Kravex made a strangled sound—half gasp, half whimper. Julthar's rifle rose slightly, instinct overriding discipline.

"Hold, you fool," Vak commanded, voice barely above a whisper.

The cyborg raised one multijointed hand. Pointed to the chair opposite it with a finger that bent at four distinct joints between knuckle and tip. No words. Just the gesture.

Its facial expression—what remained organic on the half-flesh side—shifted. Muscles pulled in patterns that suggested a smile. Or a sneer. The boundary between welcome and threat was impossible to read on features that were more machine than living tissue.

Vak walked to the chair. Each step felt like wading through deep water, resistance building with every movement. He reached the chair, lowering himself into it. The metal was cold even through his robes, leeching the warmth from his body.

Behind him, Kravex and Julthar remained standing, weapons kept low.

This is what Legion does, Vak thought, staring at the thing across the table. *They break you down and rebuild you. Strip away everything that makes you an individual and reconstruct you as a tool. A slave wearing a shell of what you used to be. And here I am. I'm asking them to save us.*

The cyborg sat motionless. Its natural eye never blinked. The mechanical optics whirred softly as they adjusted focus, studying Vak with the detached curiosity of a scientist examining an interesting specimen.

Ten seconds passed. Twenty. Thirty. Then the cyborg spoke. "You requested this meeting—do not waste our energy, speak."

The voice sounded Zodark. It spoke with perfect grammar. Flawless pronunciation. No accent, no hesitation, no hint of mechanical modulation or translation artifacts. But something about it was *wrong*. Vak swallowed. His throat was dry despite the humid air his species preferred. He met the cyborg's gaze—natural eye and mechanical optics both—and forced words past the horror threatening to choke him.

"The Orbots, they were your proxy in the Milky Way. They were defeated by the allies of the Gallentines. I have come to offer the Zodark Empire's service in its place, if you will help to preserve the survival of our Empire from the allies of the Gallentines."

The cyborg tilted its head forty-five degrees. A gesture that might have indicated curiosity in an organic being, but in this hybrid nightmare, Vak suspected it meant something else. Calculation. Assessment. The weighing of value against cost.

The silence was unnerving. Vak felt compelled to speak, to further press his case.

"The Orbots failed you. They surrendered to the Republic rather than fight. They laid down their arms when victory still remained possible. The Zodarks value honor over one's life. We would die before dishonor. We can continue this fight against the allies of the Gallentines," Vak explained, then paused, gathering his thoughts, forcing confidence into words that felt like ash on his tongue.

"We have the industrial base to fight a protracted war— shipyards across a dozen systems, foundries that can produce weapons and vessels at scale. And we have something the Orbots lacked." Vak leaned forward slightly, meeting that horrible trifold gaze. "We have a warrior culture. We are bred for combat. We raise our young from birth to view death in battle as the highest honor. We can accomplish what the Orbots could not—contain the expansion of the Gallentines' allies, bleed the Republic, the Altairians, keep the Gallentines distracted while you prosecute your war in Andromeda."

The cyborg stared. Just… stared. Ten seconds passed. Twenty. Thirty. The silence pressed down like atmospheric pressure at crushing depths. Then the cyborg's expression shifted. Its posture straightened slightly.

When it spoke, that layered voice carried new harmonics—satisfaction mixed with anticipation, like a merchant who'd just found a buyer willing to overpay. "We have evaluated your proposal. We will accept it. But we demand tribute."

Relief flooded through Vak so powerfully his vision blurred until the cyborg's last words sank in. *Tribute… what kind of tribute could he mean…?* The words crashed down like falling stone, crushing relief beneath cold reality.

A pause stretched across the cold air. Studying Vak's reaction. It was measuring how much he'd pay. Calculating the precise threshold between acceptance and rejection.

Vak forced himself to speak. "What kind of tribute do you have in mind?"

"Director, you bioengineered something you called the perfect foot soldier—a species crossbred with the DNA of your former human pets, Zodark genetic traits, and an animal from your home world, Zinconia. You call them Gurgorra. That is your tribute—you will give them to us—all of them without question."

Vak felt his chest tighten and a shiver run down his spine. *The Gurgorra… this is impossible… how could they know…?*

"Who told you about the Gurgorra?" The words escaped Vak's before he could stop them.

"Who told us is not important. How we know is not important. This line of questioning is a waste of energy. Tribute is demanded. What is your answer?" the cyborg asked in its clinical way.

Vak's mind raced. This was happening too fast, their demand steep. The Groff had spent a century perfecting the Gurgorra. They had genetically bred the Gurgorra to replace their warriors, to absorb the high casualties of conquest. The Zodarks were not known for high birthrates, and the expansion of the Empire had come at a cost. The Gurgorra were going to be the foot soldiers of the Empire while the Guristas, their human pets, would be the spacers that crewed the ships delivering them. This was Vak's long-term strategy for sustained expansion and conquest of the Milky Way while mitigating the sacrifice generations of his people would otherwise have to make.

The cyborg sensed Vak's hesitation and spoke more plainly. "Director, you have asked *us* to intervene and preserve your Empire," it said, voice dropping half an octave as deeper harmonics layered beneath the primary tone. "Service to us comes with a price. In addition to your tribute, going forward, half of all systems and worlds the Zodark Empire conquer with our aid and technology will be ceded to us—to aid in our establishment of a base of operations within the Milky Way. This is nonnegotiable. This is the price for your survival."

A pause stretched between them. The organic eye narrowed— an expression that suggested satisfaction, or perhaps contempt for prey too weak to resist the trap closing around it.

"Director Vak'Atioth, you agree to the terms, yes?"

Vak couldn't speak. He simply nodded in acquiescence, not trusting his voice. Inside, he raged at the terms being offered. He knew what it meant to be handed over to the Collective, to Legion for those who failed to bend the knee of submission to become one with the Collective, to forgo all individuality and freedom of thought, choice, and future. Yet what choice did he have if he wanted to snatch victory from the jaws of defeat?

The cyborg spoke once more, its demands yet sated.

"Your military situation is bleak—you were smart to have contacted us. To restore balance in your favor. You will work with Legion to establish a trap." The voice dropped another octave, harmonics deepening until it sounded like an entire choir speaking in perfect synchronization. "You will lure the Gallentines and their proxies—the Altairians, the Republic, the Primords, the Tully—to a location of our choosing, where Legion will devour their fleets. The scales will rebalance in your favor—your enemies crippled. You will have the time you desire to rebuild your forces, to resume the expansion of your Empire."

The nonmechanical iris fully opened, its pupils dilating to the available light as the cyborg spoke. "You will replace the Orbots as our caretaker of Milky Way. Do not fail us as the Orbots did, or you will face the same fate."

Vak stared at the thing across the table from him, his mind racing through implications and consequences faster than he could process them. The price he had agreed to was staggering. *But what's the alternative?*

He thought of Tueblets under siege. Eight stargates connecting the Empire's vital systems, now threatened by Altairian, Republic, and Primord fleets the Malvari had proven incapable of destroying. He thought of the raid on the High Council, how exposed Zinconia was. Their capital world vulnerable to outside invasion for the first time in history. He thought of the Empire fracturing into warring clans as their enemies burned system after system—and the return of the Humtars… how their weapons carved through Malvari armor like tissue.

Vak's voice came out barely above a whisper. "I… accept your terms." The words felt like vomit the moment he spoke them. Like poison forcing its way past resistance, contaminating everything they touched. Each syllable a betrayal. Each breath that carried them damnation.

The cyborg's expression shifted—that horrible half smile widening into something that might have been satisfaction. Or triumph. Or the mechanical equivalent of pleasure at prey accepting the trap they had willingly walked into.

The cyborg rose from its chair and turned toward the door without further acknowledgment. Without further details about how the terms would be implemented. Then Vak remembered something. The Humtars… he'd forgotten to mention them.

Vak called out, "Wait… there is something more."

The cyborg stopped midstride. It didn't turn immediately. Just halted, perfectly still, like a machine awaiting a new input. A new order for what to do next. Then it rotated slowly—servos silent now, movements deliberate. Both mechanical optics locked onto Vak first, then the organic eye followed with that unsettling delay before waiting to speak, or waiting for Vak, he couldn't tell.

"Something more…" it repeated. "Do not waste our energy asking for more." Its voice sounded annoyed, menacing. "Speak now. Do not waste our energy further."

Vak swallowed hard. His throat was suddenly dry. "The histories tell us of an ancient society, a highly advanced society, the ones who built the stargates—the ones they call Humtar," Vak said, his confidence returning. "Are you aware of their return? Are you aware that this enemy we battle, the Republic—they are Humtar descendants?"

The organic eye widened the moment he mentioned the word Humtar. It was the first time Vak had seen anything he considered an indication of surprise in the cyborg's demeanor. Its body turned to face Vak, then walked toward the chair it had left moments earlier, leaving Vak to wonder if he should have stayed silent.

The cyborg's hand rested on the back of the chair, its eyes narrowing, seeming to bore through him. Then it spoke. "Director, you should have mentioned this first—more energy you have wasted. This enemy power... the Republic. They are descendants of Humtar? Do they possess Humtar vessels—technology, weapons... of what value are they to us?"

The voice was different now. Deeper layers emerged from beneath the primary harmonics—as if dozens of consciousnesses spoke simultaneously, overlapping by microseconds. Its tone wasn't anger. It was something older. Something that predated emotion and transcended it into pure calculation of threat and response—fear.

"Forgive me. You are right. I should have led with this information." Vak's voice came out raspy as he tried to mask the growing fear he felt whelming up within him. "Yes, the Republic are Humtar, a former colony long lost to the histories, but they survived. They do not possess the level of Humtar technology their ancestors once possessed," he explained. He noticed the cyborg visibly relax before he continued, "Nearly four years ago, a starting discovery was made. The Humtars whom you previously fought... they have returned—"

"Returned?" interrupted the cyborg, concern in its voice. "Explain, Director—and do not waste our energy or there shall be consequences."

Vak reached into his robes with trembling hands, withdrawing a data drive the size of his thumb. The device contained all of the information the Groff had collected on the Humtars. Extending his hand, Vak held the drive for the cyborg to take.

To his surprise, it didn't reach for it. It just stared with its mechanical eyes. Then Vak felt something begin to happen. The drive in his hand vibrated, as though it was being remotely accessed as he held it for his guest.

When Vak looked at the device, he saw a green light blinking on it. It blinked a few times, then went dark, the warmth fading quickly. *Great Lindow... it just extracted the data while I held it...* What kind of technology did they have that they could extract encrypted data from a drive remotely? It was beyond what Vak had thought possible.

"This changes the calculus...Director Vak'Atioth—we miscalculated. We have underestimated the threat posed against your people...against us." The cyborg's cut through the tension like a blade.

It reached into a compartment on its torso and retrieved a small device, holding it for a moment as Vak stared at it. It was obsidian in color, smooth exterior and edges. It was featureless, like the drive still in Vak's hand, only somehow it seemed more menacing.

"Keep this device on you at all times," the cyborg said, extending it for Vak to accept. "I will be traveling to the Nexus to share this discovery. Once I return, I will contact you with instructions on how to lure your enemies into a trap Legion will set."

The cyborg still held the device in its hand as Vak's fingers gripped it tight. "Before I leave, Director—you will render a payment," it explained. "The guards behind you... they will accompany me. This is nonnegotiable. Our deal is contingent on their compliance."

Vak's blood ran cold. He imagined Commander Julthar and Kravex protesting behind him. He raised a hand, silencing their objections before telling them, "You have been chosen by Lindow. Duty. Honor. Sacrifice—this is the path of the warrior. Do you accept this great honor from Lindow?" It was a rhetorical question, but Commander Julthar answered for them both.

"We accept this honor Lindow has bestowed upon us. Let the young sing praises of our sacrifice," he replied as he began to disarm himself, his partner joining him.

"The terms are... accepted. Thank you for bestowing this honor on my people," Vak replied to the cyborg. There was nothing he could say or do in that moment other than agree to its demands.

The cyborg smiled as it released the device. It had received what it wanted—compliance, surrender.

Vak accepted the object. It felt heavier than its size suggested. Dense. Compact. Yet somehow it felt *alive*—a faint vibration against his touch.

The cyborg turned without another word. Walked toward the exit—movements precise now, mechanical efficiency without the earlier predatory fluidity. Mission accomplished. Terms agreed. Tribute extracted.

It paused at the threshold. It rotated its head one hundred and eighty degrees, vertebrae clicking like ratchet gears engaging one tooth at a time. The organic eye found Vak across the chamber while the mechanical optics tracked his disarmed guards, their faces accepting whatever fate had just befallen them. "The two of you... follow me... and, Vak'Atioth—do not fail us as the Orbots have done."

Vak watched as his guards walked past him, their eyes low, their shoulders slumped forward as they followed the cyborg to the uncertain fate awaiting them. Then they were gone. The door hissed shut with pneumatic finality as it sealed him off from the cyborg and the guards he was leaving behind.

They were a sacrifice I would gladly make again if it meant saving the Empire, Vak thought selfishly, arrogantly, as he walked to the shuttle waiting for him.

Chapter 36:
Vak'Atioth's Détente

Bridge of ZNS *Harvex's Vengeance*
Departing Planet Shwani, Varkorion System

"Malvari boarding party inbound. All security protocols active."

Laktish Heltet stood in the transport's passenger cabin, watching through the viewport as the *Executioner's Wrath* filled his field of vision. The Malvari dreadnought was a monument to martial power—3,200 meters of armor plating, weapon batteries, and reactor cores capable of reducing lesser warships to ash.

The transport shuddered as magnetic clamps locked onto the hull. *Clang. Clang. Clang.* Each impact reverberated through the deck plating, a rhythmic percussion that reminded Heltet he was entering enemy territory. Not officially, of course. The Groff and Malvari served the same empire, answered to the same High Council, worshipped the same teachings of Lindow.

But trust? That commodity had grown scarce between the intelligence service and the military caste.

"Docking complete," announced the pilot. "Atmospheric seals confirmed. Malvari security is requesting you disembark immediately, Laktish."

Heltet stood, no weapons, preparing himself to exit the shuttle. The airlock cycled open with a hiss of equalizing pressure. Four Malvari warriors stood in the docking bay, muscles rippling beneath combat armor. Blaster rifles held at ready positions—not aimed at Heltet, but the message was clear. *Do not try anything.*

The lead warrior, NOS Tarvox judging by the rank insignia, stepped forward. "Laktish Heltet. You will follow us to the war council chamber. Do not deviate from the designated route. Do not attempt to access restricted areas. Your compliance is mandatory."

"Of course, NOS Tarvox," Heltet replied, keeping his voice neutral, deferential, although he outranked the NOS. "I am here at Zon Otro's invitation. I have no desire to cause difficulty."

Tarvox's expression suggested he didn't believe that for a moment. "Move."

They walked through corridors that gleamed despite the ship's battle scars. Polished deck plating reflected overhead lights. Bulkheads bore no scratches, no wear—maintenance crews kept the *Executioner's Wrath* in immaculate condition. But between the polish and the cleanliness, Heltet noticed the trophies.

Primord battle standards hung at intersections, captured during the conquest of Intus and Rass decades ago. Fabric emblazoned with alien script, stained with blood that had long since dried. Republic hull fragments mounted on display pedestals—twisted metal from destroyed warships, each piece labeled with system name and date of victory. Gravaxia. Orinda. Myrkarian.

They celebrate their triumphs, Heltet thought. *How long until those trophies include fragments of Groff ships if Vak'Atioth gets his way?*

The rhythmic thrum of the ship's massive reactors vibrated through the deck with each step. Power cores large enough to fuel a small city, channeled into weapons systems. The *Executioner's Wrath* was Otro's mobile fortress, his symbol of Malvari supremacy.

And Heltet was about to walk into its heart, unarmed and alone, to negotiate with a Zon who despised his Director.

They turned a final corner. Ahead, massive double doors carved from dark stone loomed—the entrance to the war council chamber. Ancient Zodark script ran along the door's edges, quoting from the teachings of Lindow: *Victory flows to those who strike without hesitation. Defeat comes to those who deliberate while enemies advance.*

NOS Tarvox gestured to the two guards flanking the entrance. They pulled the doors open, revealing the chamber beyond.

The room was circular, fifty meters in diameter, its ceiling lost in shadows high above. He saw the faces of the six new High Council members as they sat in tiered seating that ringed the chamber's perimeter. Flanking the Council members were Malvari commanders, clan representatives, and senior NOSs whose names carried weight across the Empire. Perhaps thirty warriors total, all regarding Heltet with expressions ranging from curiosity to open hostility.

But Heltet's attention fixed on the man seated in the middle of them.

Zon Otro sat elevated above the council, his massive frame dominating the space. He'd once led the Malvari as the Mavkah himself.

Loyalties across the military ran deep, many commanders having served with him throughout the dracmas. Otro's eyes narrowed as Heltet entered, studying him with the focus of a hunter evaluating prey.

Flanking Otro's throne stood NOS Griglag, the Mavkah who commanded the Malvari. He was shorter than Otro but no less dangerous, with a reputation for tactical brilliance and ruthless efficiency that preceded him. Other commanders occupied positions of honor near the throne—warriors Heltet recognized from intelligence briefings. Hardliners. Traditionalists. Zodarks who viewed the Groff as parasites feeding on the Empire's strength.

Otro's voice cut through it, deep and resonant, carrying to every corner of the chamber. "Laktish Heltet." He let the title hang in the air, heavy with contempt. "The Groff finally deigns to kneel after Vak's scheming has failed."

Heltet walked forward, forcing his stride to remain steady despite the hostile gazes boring into him from all sides. He stopped at the chamber's center—the Circle of Truth, where those seeking the Council's ear must stand to speak. Ancient tradition held that blue flames of Lindow's judgment would consume liars who entered the circle, though Heltet had never witnessed such divine intervention.

Today might be the day, he thought darkly.

He bowed, lowering his head in formal deference. "Great Zon. Esteemed Council. I come bearing words from Director Vak'Atioth. Words I believe you will wish to hear."

Otro leaned forward on his throne, hands scraping against stone armrests. "Then speak, Laktish. But choose your words with care. My patience for Groff schemes has worn thin."

Heltet straightened, meeting Otro's gaze. Around him, thirty Malvari warriors waited to hear whether the Groff came offering peace or plotting more treachery.

The weight of the Empire's future settled onto his shoulders as he began to speak.

"Great Zon. Esteemed Council." His voice carried across the chamber, steady and clear despite the tightness in his chest. "I come bearing an offer from Director Vak'Atioth. An offer I believe addresses the threat our Empire currently faces."

Otro's expression remained carved from stone. "Speak plainly, Laktish. The Groff are masters of words. I prefer facts."

"Facts, then." Heltet met Otro's gaze without flinching. "Under the direction of Director Vak'Atioth, the Groff has been building a reserve fleet to defend the interior of the Empire. This was done to protect our people should the fleets of the Malvari fail to keep our enemies from penetrating the outer edges of the Empire. Vak'Atioth has directed me to make it known to the Malvari and the High Council that this reserve fleet will be made available to defend Tueblets should it be invaded."

"As we suspected, my Zon, the Groff has been withholding critical warships from the Malvari," criticized Mavkah Griglag before asking Heltet, "And how many ships has the Groff kept from the Malvari?"

Heltet answered without hesitation. "The reserve fleet stands at one hundred and sixty *Plarix*- and *Thoraxian*-class heavy destroyers. The ships were built in secret at the Tarkun shipyards over the past eighteen dracmas. I want to clarify that these ships were constructed to ensure that the interior of the Empire would not fall should the Malvari face… unforeseen setbacks."

The chamber erupted in angry accusations and shouts the moment Heltet finished speaking.

"Outrageous!" shouted Councillor Gorax from his seat, surging to his feet. "The Groff built a *fleet* without Council authorization? Without Malvari oversight?"

"Secret shipyards!" another councillor yelled. "Secret fleets! How long has Vak'Atioth been preparing to usurp—"

Bam.

Zon Otro slammed the Rock of Order against his armrest. The crystalline impact echoed like thunder, silencing the chamber instantly. "Councillor Gorax. Sit. The rest of you, remember where you stand. The Laktish speaks under Lindow's protection within this circle. You will hear his words before passing judgment."

Gorax settled back into his seat, face flushed with barely contained fury. Others followed suit, though hostile muttering continued in whispers around the tiered seating.

NOS Griglag, standing at Otro's right hand, stepped forward. The Mavkah's scarred features twisted into something between contempt and grudging respect. "Convenient timing, Laktish." His voice dripped sarcasm like acid. "The Groff hoards ships while we bleed in battle—

while Malvari warriors die at Gravaxia, Orinda, Kryntok—and now Director Vak'Atioth offers assistance when defeat looms at our gates? Forgive my skepticism, but this reeks of political opportunism."

Heltet had expected this. Griglag was no fool, and the optics *were* damning. He chose his next words carefully, weighing each syllable for maximum impact.

"Mavkah Griglag, you are correct that the timing appears... calculated. But consider the alternative explanation. Director Vak foresaw that our enemies possessed technological advantages we did not fully understand. The appearance of stealth capabilities we saw used in the attack on the High Council. We cannot dismiss the theory that Humtar weaponry has likely been transferred to the Republic. Look at the campaign in Sol. When the Gallentines intervened, destroyed our fleet and the Orbots, it tipped the balance irrevocably against us."

Heltet gestured toward the chamber's displays, where tactical plots showed Zodark territory shrinking like diseased flesh. "The Groff's mandate is intelligence and strategic planning. When we saw the internal security of the Empire compromised by a diminished Malvari presence, when the balance of power move permanently against us, the Groff built a reserve fleet to—"

"To what? Further weaken the Malvari and diminish our ability to win?" Griglag snarled.

"No, to ensure the Empire's survival." Heltet's voice hardened. "If the Malvari fall—if every battleship is destroyed, every warship eliminated—the Empire would need a reserve force to prevent total collapse. That is what Director Vak created. Not a tool of usurpation. A contingency against a catastrophic defeat." Heltet could feel the chamber's atmosphere shifting, councillors recalculating their positions, weighing pragmatism against principle.

Otro leaned forward in his chair, his massive frame looming over the council. His three eyes studied Heltet with predatory focus, searching for deception, measuring sincerity. When he spoke, his voice was dangerously quiet.

"Tell me, Laktish. Why should I trust Vak'Atioth? A shadow fleet, built in secret, commanded by warriors loyal to the Groff rather than the Malvari..." Otro's arms scraped against his stone armrests, the sound grating against Heltet's nerves. "His ships could just as easily be aimed at my throat. His stirring of religious zealots has already threatened to overthrow the High Council. How am I to know he will not try to install himself as Zon when he sees the chance to do so?"

And there it was, the question Heltet had prepared for, dreaded. If he hoped to live beyond the next few minutes, he had to answer carefully. He took a breath, centered himself, and spoke the truth wrapped in careful presentation. "My Zon, trust does not bely the fact that we are surrounded by our enemies, who even now prepare to invade. Simply put, you need the Groff's fleet, and the Groff needs the Malvari to win, if the Empire is to survive."

Heltet felt his voice carried no deception, no artifice. Just stark reality delivered with brutal honesty. He hoped Zon Otro would listen. He then added, "My Zon, Tueblets is the heart of the Empire. Eight stargates connecting every major system. Without Tueblets, we fracture into isolated fiefdoms. The Republic knows this. Intelligence indicates their next offensive will target this system for that very reason—to sever the arteries that keep our Empire alive."

He gestured toward the viewport, where the planet Thrakkon's orbital infrastructure glittered against the black—shipyards, defense stations, supply depots that fed the war machine.

"Director Vak knows this. He has no illusions about what happens if Tueblets falls. Neither the High Council or the Groff can govern an empire that doesn't exist. Our influence, our power, our very survival depends on the Empire enduring. So he offers these ships because survival outweighs personal ambition," Heltet explained, his gaze sweeping the Council, meeting eyes that ranged from hostile to calculating to reluctantly impressed.

Heltet then added, "One hundred and sixty battleships and destroyers. Crews already trained. Weapons systems operational. Ships that can be deployed to Tueblets the moment the enemy makes their move. The Malvari may doubt Director Vak's motivations, may question his methods, may despise his secrecy—but can you afford to refuse the help?"

Murmurs rippled through the chamber. Councillors leaned toward neighbors, whispering furiously. Some faces showed anger at the Groff's presumption. Others showed calculation—pragmatists tallying ship counts, running mental simulations of Tueblets' defenses with and without Vak's reinforcements.

NOS Griglag's expression remained skeptical, but he didn't interrupt. A sign, perhaps, that even he recognized the strategic value being offered.

Zon Otro sat motionless on his throne, processing. His hands tapped against the armrest—once, twice, three times. A rhythmic percussion that measured thoughts too complex for words.

The silence stretched until Heltet felt his nerves fray. Had he pushed too hard? Revealed too much about Groff intelligence capabilities? Insulted Malvari pride by suggesting they needed rescuing?

Finally, Otro leaned back. The movement was slight, but in the council's hierarchical language, it signaled a shift from confrontation to consideration. "Laktish, I have listened to your words. I have heard Director Vak'Atioth's offer and... I accept," replied Otro in an authoritative tone, his decision final.

Relief flooded through Heltet so powerfully his knees nearly buckled. He locked his legs, maintaining posture through sheer willpower, but couldn't suppress the exhalation that escaped his lips—a breath he hadn't realized he'd been holding.

"You and Director Vak'Atioth will be held to your word, your commitment now unbreakable, your punishment Frocking should you fail to uphold your agreement," ordered Otro before he continued, his voice carrying across the chamber with final authority. "As of this moment, the Groff's ships are hereby integrated into the Tueblets Defense Command under Mavkah Griglag's operational control. We will coordinate deployment schedules and tactical doctrine to maximize defensive coverage."

NOS Griglag stepped forward, his expression skeptical but professional. "Great Zon, I recommend we inspect these vessels before full integration. Verify their combat readiness, crew competency, weapons systems—"

"Agreed," Otro said. "Laktish Heltet will provide manifests, inspection access, and liaison officers to facilitate integration. The Groff will cooperate fully with Malvari oversight. Am I understood, Laktish?"

"Perfectly, my Zon." Heltet bowed, relief still coursing through him. "Director Vak anticipated your requirements. Full documentation is ready for transfer."

"Excellent." Otro surveyed the Council, his gaze sweeping across assembled warriors and politicians. "This session has concluded.

You are all dismissed. Return to your duties. Prepare for the Republic's inevitable assault. And remember—the Empire's survival depends on unity of purpose, not petty rivalries between clans."

The dismissal was clear. Councillors rose from their seats, filing toward exits in small groups. Conversations erupted immediately—some praising Otro's pragmatism, others complaining about Groff presumption, most simply calculating how this development would affect their own positions and patronage.

NOS Griglag gathered tactical data pads, preparing to leave with his staff officers. But as Heltet turned to follow the exodus, Otro's voice cut across the chamber. "Remain, Laktish Heltet. We have much to discuss."

Heltet froze midstep. "Yes, of course, my Zon. As you wish."

The chamber emptied quickly after that. Warriors who moments ago had been eager to linger now hurried toward exits, unwilling to risk Otro's displeasure by appearing curious about private matters. NOS Griglag hesitated at the doorway, catching Otro's gaze with an unspoken question.

Otro's three eyes narrowed slightly. A warning. A command to leave.

Griglag nodded once, then left. As he left the room, the massive doors slid shut with a thud that echoed off the vaulted ceilings. Heltet noticed Zon Otro disabled the recording system within the room, giving the two of them an added layer of privacy.

Once it was just the two of them, Zon Otro walked toward him, toward the Circle of Truth where Heltet stood. He stopped three meters away from him. Close enough for conversation. Close enough to kill with bare hands if he chose.

"You did well, Laktish." Otro's voice was quieter now, stripped of formal authority, carrying instead something more dangerous—personal intent. "Your presentation was masterful. Framing Vak's fleet as contingency rather than conspiracy. Playing to the council's pragmatism while acknowledging their concerns. That was very... skillful."

"I speak only truth, my Zon. Director Vak—"

"Director Vak is a fool and a schemer." Otro cut him off with a gesture. "He's a brilliant schemer, I'll grant you. He saw threats I ignored, prepared for failures I refused to acknowledge. In another life, he would have made an excellent Zon. But this is not another life, and I am Zon now, not him."

Heltet's hearts accelerated. This wasn't the direction he'd expected this conversation to take, but he was open to seeing where it went.

Otro circled slowly, studying Heltet from multiple angles like a predator evaluating wounded prey. "I can forgive Vak's transgressions, Laktish. For now that is. The Empire needs his ships, and I am pragmatic enough to accept gifts even from those who meant to use them as leverage. But do not mistake my acceptance for trust."

He stopped directly in front of Heltet, looming over him, eyes boring into Heltet's soul.

"When this war ends—when the Republic is defeated or driven back, when the immediate crisis passes—I want you to know that I fully intend to remove him as the Groff Director."

The words hung in the cold air like a death sentence. Heltet's mouth went dry, unsure what to say next or what Vak'Atioth's removal would mean for him. "My Zon, I—"

"I want to offer you the position of Groff Director, Heltet," interrupted Otro, his voice quiet, conversational, devoid of any doubt. "When Vak is removed, Laktish, you will succeed him. You will have full authority over our intelligence apparatus—rebuild what Vak has lost," Otro explained as he circled Heltet. He stopped in front of him, staring him in the eyes. "I am taking a risk sharing this with you—there are those who would object, but I am Zon, and they will do as they told.

"Listen, Heltet, I value loyalty and service to the Empire. If you will swear fealty to me—your Zon—I will also ensure you are rewarded with a seat on the High Council once you have cleaned up the Groff, should you so desire. There is but one condition I ask of you." Otro leaned closer, voice dropping to barely above whisper. "You must keep Vak in check until it is time to remove him. You report any future attempts by him to usurp my authority or the High Council's power. He mustn't know you are reporting to me, and you must ensure he understands that should he attempt to cross those limits again… it will result in his removal from office and Frocking as punishment."

Heltet's mind raced. *Could this be a trap? It had to be.* This must be a test… Otro was testing him, seeing whether he'd betray his

Director for personal advancement. Except… this offer felt genuine. The Zon's expression carried no hint of deception, just cold calculation.

If he refused the offer now, it could mean losing Otro's trust. Possibly his own life. The Zon couldn't allow someone who had rejected such an offer to return to Vak's service—the risk of Heltet warning his Director about Otro's intentions was too great.

But accepting meant betraying Vak, who had trusted him, elevated him to Laktish, shared secrets that could destroy careers and end lives. And now Otro asked him to become a spy within his own organization, reporting on the very leader he'd sworn to serve.

What choice do I have?

Otro stared at him, studying him. "Heltet, if Vak steps out of line again—if he plots more schemes, makes any move that threatens the stability of my rule or the High Council's authority—it will be on you to ensure his Frocking. You will read the charges. You will strip him of position and power. You will place his fate in Lindow's hands through the traditional rites."

Heltet's hands trembled. He clenched them into fists, hiding the physical manifestation of the internal turmoil raging within him. Thoughts cascaded through his mind faster than he could process— loyalty versus survival, honor versus pragmatism, the oath he'd sworn to Vak against the oath Otro now demanded. He nodded slowly, deciding then and there his path.

Heltet lowered himself to one knee. Submitting to Otro's demand. This was the moment he chose survival over honor. Duty to country over loyalty to Vak.

"I renew my loyalty to you, Zon Otro, and to the High Council."

The words came out steadier than he felt. Each syllable was a betrayal, a knife sliding between Vak's ribs, a choice that would haunt him for however many dracmas remained of his life.

Otro's smile widened. "Rise, Laktish. You have made the wise choice."

Heltet stood, a sense of purpose and hope replacing the unease he'd felt moments earlier.

"Return to Shwani, Heltet," Otro commanded, voice returning to formal authority. "Inform Director Vak that I accept his offer. Coordinate the fleet transfer with Mavkah Griglag's staff. And remember—I will be watching. Those loyal to me will report your actions, your words, your loyalties should you waver. Serve me well, and you will be rewarded beyond measure. Fail me…"

Otro didn't finish the sentence. He didn't need to.

"Yes, my Zon." Heltet bowed deeply, then turned toward the exit.

He walked through the corridors of the *Executioner's Wrath* in a daze. Malvari warriors passed him without acknowledgment, focused on their own duties.

Heltet's transport detached from the *Executioner's Wrath* and returned to the *Harvex's Vengeance*. Within minutes of his return, they accelerated to the Varkorion stargate. It was time to return to the Groff and report the outcome of the meeting to Vak.

As he thought about the director, he had a bad feeling in his gut. *Vak never should have met with the Collective… I just hope he didn't sell out the Empire to save his own skin…*
****

Following Day
Groff Directorate Command Spire
Shwani, Varkorion System

Vak'Atioth sent the summons within an hour of the *Harvex's Vengeance* docking at Shwani's orbital platform. He needed answers. Had Otro accepted the fleet? Had they averted civil war? And more importantly—he needed to share Legion's instructions with someone he trusted.

He stood at his office window, watching shuttles rise and fall between surface and orbit. Three hundred meters below, Shwani's capital district sprawled—temples, government buildings, monuments to an empire that might not survive the next dracma.

The door chimed. "Enter."

Heltet stepped through, robes disheveled from travel, data pad in hand. He looked exhausted but steady.

"Director." Heltet bowed. "I trust your meeting was productive?"

"It was. Sit, we have much to discuss." Vak gestured toward the chair opposite his desk. Between them, a holographic star map materialized—Zodark territory in red, contested zones in amber, enemy holdings in blue.

The red had shrunk dramatically the past couple of dracmas. Territory conquered over decades, slipping away.

"Did Otro accept the fleet?"

Heltet's expression remained neutral. "He did. The reserve fleet will defend Tueblets under Mavkah Griglag's command."

Relief flooded through Vak. "Good. That buys us time."

Silence stretched. Vak studied Heltet—the way he averted his eyes to stare at his data pad. He could sense tension between them where none had been before his trip to meet Otro. But Heltet's service record was impeccable. Fifty dracmas of loyalty. Paranoia could be a useful tool. But not if you let it control you.

"The Collective agreed to help us," Vak finally acknowledged.

Heltet's eyes widened fractionally in genuine surprise. "They did? And what did they demand in exchange for this help?"

Vak considered his answer, weighing how much to share. Trying to guess how Heltet would respond to the loss of the Gurgorra. The pair of guards he'd had to sacrifice during the meeting, or how the Collective had demanded half of the territories of any future conquests they made. Vak knew each detail was leverage someone could use against him... someone like Otro... maybe even Heltet.

Grunting before responding, he finally said, "Less than I feared, but more than I wanted to give." He'd given him truth without specifics and hoped it would be enough. "They are going to work with us to lure our enemies into a trap where they will destroy them."

"Really. What kind of trap?" Heltet leaned forward, his interest piqued.

Vak paused, recalling the conversation from this morning. The device Legion had given him had activated shortly after he'd woken up. That strange layered voice from that cyborg had spoken instructions over the device. The instructions had been brief, specific, and terrifying in their simplicity.

"It told me that when the Republic attacks Tueblets—and they will attack—our reserve fleet fighting alongside the Malvari are to hold as long as possible, inflict maximum casualties, then retreat to the Varkorion stargate and return to Shwani," explained Vak.

"Whoa, wait a second… did you say retreat?" Heltet stiffened at the idea of withdrawing during battle. "No, the dishonor, Director, we couldn't abandon Tueblets—"

"No, you are mistaken, Heltet. We are not abandoning it. We are luring the enemy into our trap." Vak activated a section of the star map, highlighting the path between Tueblets and Varkorion. "The reserve fleet falls back here, to Shwani. To the planetary defenses we have spent dracmas preparing."

Heltet stared at the map. "I don't understand. You want to draw Republic fleets into Groff territory?"

"I want them to follow us through the Tueblets stargate into the Varkorion system. Once they commit—once their fleets are inside our defensive perimeter around Shwani—that is when Legion will appear and the battle to end this war commence."

The words hung between them, no one saying anything as Heltet took it in and Vak waited for his response.

Vak watched Heltet's expressions cycle through calculation, concern, and eventually reluctant understanding. "I see… the ambush is where Legion will be waiting to pounce."

"Yes, exactly," Vak confirmed, his voice hardening. "This is where Legion will eliminate their fleets. The Republic, Altairians, Primords—crippled in a single engagement. This is where the strategic balance will tilt back into our favor and give us the breathing room we need to rebuild our fleets and reclaim our lost territories—and seize new ones."

Heltet nodded slowly, then asked, "And if Legion fails? If the trap doesn't work?"

"Then Shwani burns, and the Empire dies the death it was already going to," replied Vak as he met his gaze. "It won't fail, Heltet. The Collective doesn't make promises it can't keep."

"I see. When did they contact you and how do you communicate with them?"

Vak reached into his desk. Withdrew the communication device Legion had provided. Placed it on the surface between them. It was black as the void. Smooth as glass, and featureless.

"They contacted me this morning. Through this device they gave me during the meeting," explained Vak.

Heltet stared at it before asking. "Huh. What is it?"

"I don't know. Communication relay of some sort? Legion didn't explain it. It just... gave instructions." Vak's hand hovered over the device but didn't touch it. "When the battle begins, they'll know. They'll arrive at the precise moment our fleets retreat into Varkorion."

"How can they possibly—"

"Enough, Heltet." Vak's voice cut through the speculation. "You ask questions neither of us can answer. What I *do* know is Legion has fought the Gallentines for centuries. Clearly, they possess military capabilities beyond what we currently have. If they're confident they can defeat the Gallentine proxies—the Altairians, Republic, Primords, and Tully—I believe them."

Heltet opened his mouth to respond, then closed it. Nodded slowly.

Vak continued, his tone shifting to operational. "We need to prepare our forces for the battle we know is coming. Ensure we have enough V-boats for the engagement at Tueblets. And keep a hundred or so aside for the defense of Shwani should it come to that."

"Understood, Director." Heltet's fingers moved across his data pad, already logging the directives. "I'll coordinate with the shipyards immediately. Production has already been accelerating—we should have sufficient numbers within two weeks."

"Good." Vak gestured dismissal. "Coordinate with Griglag's staff. Ensure fleet integration proceeds smoothly. And, Heltet—" He paused. "Tell no one about Legion's plan. Not Otro. Not the High Council. Not anyone. Operational security is absolute."

"Understood, Director."

Heltet bowed. Turned. Paused at the threshold. "Director... I hope it was worth the price," he said, and then he left.

Vak stood alone, staring at the device on his desk. Outside, Shwani gleamed in the afternoon light—ignorant of the role it would play, the bait it would become, the trap that would save or doom them all.

He thought of Julthar and Kravex, taken by the cyborg as tribute. The Gurgorra, all of them, handed over to Legion, along with half the Empire's future conquests. Prices paid and yet to be paid for the privilege of serving the Collective.

You know you never see the monster in the mirror... you stop looking...

Vak returned the device to his pocket and began drafting the operational orders that would position Shwani's defenses for Legion's arrival. *Whatever it costs, we will survive.*

Chapter 37:
The Trap

CNS *Voidraven*, *Shadowfang*-Class Stealth Ship
Outer Kuiper Belt, Tueblets System
Seventy-Two Hours Before Allied Invasion

Captain Theron Kylis stood in the *Voidraven*'s signals intelligence suite, watching data streams scroll across multiple holographic displays monitoring the system. The *Shadowfang* stealth ship hung motionless in the black, phase-stealth engaged, passive arrays drinking in every electromagnetic whisper from the battle preparations unfolding millions of kilometers away.

In seventy-two hours, the allied invasion of Tueblets would begin. Seventy-two hours until the Republic, Altairian, Primord, and Humtar fleets converged on the most important and strategic heart of the Zodark Empire and ended this war.

And for their part, her ship, the *Voidraven*, was the eyes and ears of the allied fleet, watching. Listened. Recorded everything and passing it along to allied intelligence.

"Captain, we're detecting unusual quantum signatures," Lieutenant Seris Navon reported from the cryptanalysis station. "It's a tight-beam transmission, highly encrypted. Origin point... huh, that's interesting. It matches Legion communication protocols."

Kylis raised an eyebrow, then walked to her station. "Legion, you said. That is interesting. Show it to me."

The display shifted, isolating the signal. It had originated from deep space—somewhere beyond the system's heliopause where nothing should have. Then the destination coordinates resolved into something recognizable: Zodark space. Specifically, the Varkorion system they were presently surveilling.

"Interesting. They appear to be talking to someone. See if you can't decrypt it. Let's figure out who they're talking to," Kylis directed. She knew if Legion was talking to someone in Varkorion this close to the allied invasion, it likely had something to do with it.

"Aye, ma'am. Attempting decryption now," Navon replied, fingers flying across her interface. "Signal architecture matches patterns observed from Legion Arc Net nodes. Wow, multiple encryption layers, quantum-entangled keys… I'll bet it's some high-level stuff."

Kylis leaned forward. Before the *Voidraven* had taken up station in the Varkorion system, they had been working with the *Bloodhawk* and a few of the other stealth frigates for months, monitoring Collective communications—part of the reconnaissance phase of Operation Damocles. During their time behind enemy lines, they cataloged transmission patterns, mapped Arc Net topology, and analyzed quantum error correction thresholds. But intercepting active command traffic? Now that was a gold mine if they could crack the encryption.

"You might be right, Lieutenant. How long to crack it?"

Navon shrugged. "I couldn't tell you. Could be minutes. Could be days," she replied before pausing, her expression shifting. "Wait a second. I think we found something. I'm getting partial plaintext. The fusion cell at the Enclave found some encryption protocol flaws during their analysis a few weeks ago. We just found them here, in this message. If the adaptive algorithms don't properly compensate for quantum decoherence, the message degrades during transmission, creating an opening we can exploit."

"Um, OK, Lieutenant. Explain that to me like I'm a first-year cadet at the academy," Kylis half joked, barely understanding what Navon had said.

"In short, I think we cracked the encryption. Here, I'll pull up the parts of the text that've been decoded so far," Navon replied with a chuckle. The data populated the screen. Fragments at first. Then sentences. Then entire paragraphs.

As Kylis read it, she did a double take and asked Navon to verify it twice.

"Lieutenant, package this up and get it sent to the Enclave, Priority Alpha—Eyes Only to Admiral Vesharuk," Kylis ordered. She turned to her communications officer. "Send a flash message to Admiral Vesharuk and Admiral Korrath. Tell them we have a problem with the invasion."

******

Sixty-Eight Hours Before Allied Invasion
Humtar Intelligence Fusion Cell
CDF–Sol Command Center

The Enclave—New Cambria, New Eden

Admiral Veydris Korrath entered the secure briefing room to find it already packed. Admiral Vesharuk was already seated at the head of the table, his weathered features showed him deep in concentration. Captain Lyrana Dovrek stood beside a holographic display showing the intercepted transmission. Dr. Zeralleh Myrathi sat opposite, data pad in hand, head shaking in disbelief.

"Admiral Korrath has arrived," someone announced.

Korrath waved them down. "As you were. I got here as quick as could. What do we have?"

Dovrek activated the display. Text appeared—clinical, precise, translated from Legion's layered machine language into something humans could read and understand.

TRANSMISSION INTERCEPT – LEGION COMMAND TO ZODARK CONTACT

ORIGIN: *Harvester-Prime Omega-0001, Devourer-Class Star Carrier* **Eternal Harvest**

DESTINATION: *Director Vak'Atioth, Groff Intelligence Directorate*

SUBJECT: *Directive Z-0001 – Operational Parameters – Destruction of Allied Fleet*

Korrath read the key section aloud:

"Invasion plans for the Gallentine proxies allied fleet confirmed. Proxy leader Viceroy Miles of the Republic will lead an allied fleet composed of multiple hundreds of warships from the Altairian Kingdom, the Primord Kingdom, and a minor contribution from the Tully Federation. An unknown contribution of Humtar vessels have been confirmed and will participate in the action. The target of the invasion is the Malvari Command Center at Velkryn, in the Tueblets system. Objective is the elimination of Zon Otro, Malvari leadership, and Malvari fleet to force the capitulation and surrender of Zodark leadership—to end the war.

"Director Vak'Atioth of the Groff. Omega-0001 of Harvester-Prime aboard the *Eternal Harvest* is ordering you to comply with the following directions:

270

"Phase One: Upon arrival of the allied fleet, you are directed to dispatch the Groff's fleet in the Varkorion system to attack the allied fleet.

"Phase Two: At your fleet commander's discretion, the Groff fleet will withdraw from the battle to the Stargate Two Alpha and wait. The Groff fleet must entice the allied fleet to pursue Groff vessels into the Varkorion system.

"Phase Three: Upon the return of Groff forces to the Varkorion system, travel back to orbital defenses around the planet Shwani and await the arrival of the allied fleet. Upon arrival of enemy forces, Omega-0001 aboard the *Eternal Harvest*, a *Devourer*-class star carrier, will initiate the quantum bridge to facilitate the arrival of Legion forces and initiate the destruction of Allied Forces in the Varkorion and Tueblets systems.

"Phase Four: Upon the destruction of the allied fleet and the preservation of the Zodark Empire, Legion will implement the agreement—payment will be made in full.

"End of Directive Z-0001."

Korrath felt his chest tighten. "Well, that settles that. Not only does the Collective know when and where we're launching this invasion of Zodark space, they've apparently cut some sort of deal with them."

He shook his head as he met Admiral Vesharuk's gaze. "Not only have they partnered with the Zodarks, it appears Legion has also penetrated the communications of at least one of the allied partners participating in the invasion. It could be the Republic, the Tully, the Primords, Altairians—hell, it could even be the Gallentines for all we know. In either case, someone's security has been compromised at the highest strategic level."

"Yeah, this is a problem we're going to need to address," Vesharuk agreed.

Dr. Zeralleh Myrathi set down her data pad. "You both are right. We have a significant intelligence failure days before the start of a battle. Legion obtained the operational details—timing, force composition, objectives of the allied fleet—and shared it with the enemy we are invading."

Captain Dovrek's expression darkened as the gravity of the situation set in. "Admirals, if the Zodark and Legion know our plans ahead of time, they'll position assets accordingly. Pre-position ships where they'll be needed most. Optimize defensive arrangements based on our fleet compositions. Every advantage we thought we had—"

"I know, Captain... becomes irrelevant," interrupted Vesharuk, his voice calm, but Korrath caught the edge beneath it. "Legion wants the Zodarks to retreat so we'll follow them to where they want to spring their trap. That's why they want us to follow them to Varkorion... so let's give them what they want," Vesharuk said, to the chagrin of the others.

Korrath laughed, unable to contain himself. He knew exactly what his friend was implying.

"Oh, that's brilliant, my friend. They'll never see it coming," said Korrath, his laughter subsiding. "For those who haven't figured it out yet, let me explain. For months we've been deploying Damocles across Collective space. What we hadn't figured out yet was how to contact the Collective so we could deliver our ultimatum and put an end to this war and the persistent threat they pose to us and sentient beings everywhere.

"Now, according to this message, in less than three days' time, we will know the location of a Collective vessel—Varkorion—and who to give the ultimatum to—Omega-0001. All we have to do now is show up and follow the plan that we've already devised and they've confirmed. We couldn't have asked for a more perfect opportunity to deliver Damocles," Korrath finished. "Admiral Vesharuk, I'd like to add some firepower to our contingent since the enemy knows our plan and fleet composition, if that's possible?"

Vesharuk raised an eyebrow. "That sounds reasonable. What are you thinking?"

"I'd like to add some of our heavy hitters, especially if Legion decides to fight. I was thinking we could add another five *Voidhammer* heavy battleships and three *Warclaw* light battleships," Korrath replied, then paused. "I'd love to have the *Solvaris*—the Keeper of Worlds—as our flagship... that's the ship to deliver the ultimatum to Omega-0001."

A smile formed on Vesharuk's face. "The *Solvaris*, you say... you're right, old friend. That is the ship we should deliver the ultimatum from—approved. I'll have additional warships dispatch from home immediately. Oh, one more thing. The *Solvaris*, she'll arrive to deliver the ultimatum. I don't want her involved in the fight in Tueblets, not unless it becomes absolutely necessary. Once Legion sees her in action, her tactical and strategic advantage is gone forever. I don't mind them seeing her, but not her capabilities, not unless we have to fight Legion, understood?" Vesharuk replied firmly.

"I can live with that." Korrath smiled. "It'll be nice to take the hangar queen for a stroll, stretch her legs and show off her guns, even if we don't use 'em."

"I'll send a message to Fleet Command and inform President Gudea we're taking the *Solvaris* for a stroll," confirmed Vesharuk before walking toward his office. He stopped at the door and turned to look at Korrath. "I'm going to brief Viceroy Hunt on these developments. Include the additional *Voidhammers* and *Warclaws* to our fleet plans, Korrath—and make damn sure Damocles is ready. We're only going to get one shot at this. We can't screw it up."

Chapter 38
The Endgame

Office of the Viceroy
Alliance City, New Eden

Forty-eight hours until the *Razorwind* cleared the dock. At least, that was what the latest report told Hunt as he stared at the amber status light on the tactical display. He turned to look out the floor-to-ceiling windows at the forested mountains just beyond Alliance City. It was peaceful—cathartic, even—to see the beauty of nature. Four weeks had gone by since the raid on Zinconia. Four weeks of watching allied fleets converge in orbit above like storm fronts building on the horizon.

Behind him, the viewport framed New Eden's capital sprawl: government towers rising from the planned grid of downtown, transit tubes threading between districts, the distant peaks of the Founder's Range catching the afternoon sun. Beyond the city limits, farmland stretched toward the horizon in geometric patterns. Above it all, pinpricks of light marked the orbital shipyards and the growing fleet.

Breathing in deeply, Hunt could smell air mixed with the climate control's recycled output with a hint of pine from the plaza gardens below. His reflection ghosted across the holotable's surface— older now, lines deeper, the kind carved by decisions that sent people to die. Three hundred and thirty-four Altairian warships. Seven Humtar dreadnoughts. The Republic's entire expeditionary force. All converging in orbit for Operation Downfall.

If this fails, he thought, *we may lose more than a battle. We might lose the war.*

The door chimed behind him. Pandolly entered without waiting for acknowledgment, his compact frame moving with the clipped efficiency of a career officer. He stopped at the holotable, his jet-black eyes scanning the fleet disposition projected above the surface. The Altairian's white skin caught the blue glow of the hologram, making him look almost spectral.

"You have assembled a fleet capable of ending empires, Miles." No triumph in Pandolly's voice. Only the weight of command.

Hunt gestured at the display. Ship icons floated in organized clusters—Republic blue, Altairian silver, Humtar aqua, Primord gold. "I don't know about that, but if we break the spine of an empire, like Tueblets, we just might win this war."

"Three hundred and thirty-four warships." Pandolly's six-fingered hand traced through the Altairian formation. "King Grigdolly placed nearly half our fleet under my command. This is more than a gesture of support, Miles. That is a declaration of faith and confidence in your plan."

"And I appreciate that support." Hunt pulled up the Humtar contingent. Seven massive icons dominated the display—*Voidhammer*-class heavy battleships, each 3,200 meters of layered organic and composite armor and massive laser cannons. "These arrived in-system this morning. *Stormbreaker, Iron Requiem, Doombringer*—" He stopped himself before reciting the full list. The names alone carried enough weight. "Seven *Voidhammers*. Admiral Vesharuk calls them 'empire killers.'"

The holotable updated in real time as Hunt expanded the Humtar formation. Five *Warclaw*-class light battleships joined the display—sleek, predatory vessels built for pursuit and flanking maneuvers. At 2,600 meters, they were anything but light, but compared to the monstrous *Voidhammers*, the designation fit.

Pandolly leaned closer, studying the formation. "I have read the intelligence reports on Humtar warships. Their armor specifications exceed our own by fifty percent. Their laser cannons generate temperatures capable of liquefying Zodark Bronkis5 plating in sustained fire."

"They should." Hunt zoomed the display to focus on the *Stormbreaker*'s schematic. "The Humtars built these ships to fight the Collective. Everything else is just practice to them."

The Altairian's expression remained neutral, but his fingers drummed once against the table's edge—a tell Hunt had learned to recognize. Uncertainty.

"Why are you troubled, Pandolly?" Hunt asked.

"I am not troubled, just pragmatic." Pandolly straightened. "With the Pharaonis defeated and the Orbots no longer a threat, our border regions no longer require heavy defensive concentrations. We are no longer fighting on three fronts. But if we fail here—"

"We won't fail," interrupted Hunt.

"If we fail here," Pandolly continued, his voice patient, "we lose our forward momentum. The Altairians lose half their offensive capability. The Humtars lose credibility with the very allies with which they seek to rebuild relationships. And the Zodarks…" He gestured at the holodisplay, at the enemy force estimates clustered around the Tueblets system. "The Zodarks could rally. They might remember they are an empire, and they remember how to win."

Hunt met his friend's gaze. The weight of it settled between them like a physical thing.

"Then I guess we'd better not fail," Hunt countered.

The door chimed again. Admiral Helixar entered, the Gallentine's towering frame making even Hunt's spacious office feel smaller. The angular ridges along his temples caught the light as he moved to join them at the table. Behind him, Admiral Vesharuk followed—the Humtar commander's presence carrying the same quiet authority Hunt had come to respect.

"Gentlemen." Helixar's voice rumbled. "I see we are contemplating the stakes of what comes next."

"We were discussing our chances," Pandolly replied.

"I'd say our chances are pretty good." Vesharuk tapped the holotable, pulling up a new data overlay. Tactical projections bloomed across the display—engagement zones, firing solutions, probability matrices. "With the added strength of the Humtar Confederation, this fleet possesses the firepower to shatter the Zodark defensive positions at Tueblets and lay waste to their fleet. The question is not whether we can break them. The question is whether we can do so decisively enough to end their will to continue this war."

Hunt studied the projections. Red zones indicated optimal firing positions for the *Voidhammer*-class vessels. Blue zones showed Republic magrail effective ranges. Silver zones marked Altairian turbo laser coverage. Where they overlapped, the display was painted deep purple—kill zones where nothing could survive.

"The Zodarks have fought us for decades," Hunt said quietly. "They watched us destroy the Pharaonis. They've seen their Orbot allies collapse. They know we're coming for Tueblets. If they break here, they break everywhere."

"I agree, which is why we hit them with everything we have." Vesharuk's jaw set, the muscles along his neck tightening. "We can have no half measures. No holding back our reserves. We must demonstrate the full weight of this alliance and make them understand that continued resistance is futile."

Helixar nodded slowly. "Our war with the Collective taught us Gallentines a hard lesson about half measures. When facing an existential threat, you must commit everything to that fight, or you lose everything." His gaze shifted to Hunt. "I know you understand this, Viceroy. I have seen it in how you have prosecuted this war."

Hunt said nothing. The holotable hummed between them, projecting futures written in ordnance and blood.

"I will admit," Helixar continued, "we had thought we were gaining ground against the Collective. What the Humtars showed us sadly removed that illusion. Without their help, without the full commitment of our forces…" He trailed off, leaving the conclusion unspoken.

"Then it is good we are joining this fight with you," Vesharuk confirmed. "We thought we had defeated the Collective once. We were wrong. We will not make that mistake again."

The office fell silent except for the omnipresent hum of the building's systems. Through the window, Hunt watched a transit tube streak past, carrying workers from the industrial sector to downtown. Somewhere below, in the plaza gardens, citizens went about their lives—unaware of the storm gathering in orbit, of the hammer about to fall on the Zodark Empire.

His wrist comm chimed. He glanced down at the notification, and something shifted in his chest.

"Admiral Vesharuk," Hunt said, looking up. "I believe you have news for us."

The Humtar commander allowed himself a thin smile. "Ah, it would appear that I do. Admiral Korrath reports that CNS *Razorwind* has completed her repairs. She will rejoin the fleet in two days."

The amber light on Hunt's display finally shifted green.

Pandolly exhaled slowly. "Well, then we have our timeline to launch the attack."

"Yes, we do. I propose we launch in three days." Hunt straightened, his hands flat against the holotable. The projections continued to rotate above the surface—ships, trajectories, kill zones.

"Three days should be more than enough to make final preparations. Then we launch Operation Downfall."

"I like it. The battle to end the war," Helixar said confidently.

Hunt met each officer's gaze in turn. Pandolly, who carried the weight of half the Altairian fleet. Helixar, whose people had fought the Collective for generations. Vesharuk, whose ancestors had built the stargates and paid for their hubris with extinction.

"The battle to end *this* war," Hunt corrected. "What comes after…" He trailed off, thinking of the Collective, of Legion, of the storm gathering beyond the Milky Way.

"What comes after," Vesharuk finished, "we face together after *this* war is over. As it will be going forward."

The holotable pulsed once, updating with new fleet arrivals. More ships. More firepower. More lives that would be committed to the battle.

Hunt pulled up the master operations timeline. Departure windows, jump coordinates, formation assignments—all of it converging on a single date, a single system, a single moment when decades of war would either end or metastasize into something worse.

"Gentlemen," he said, his voice carrying the finality of command. "Inform your fleet commanders. Operation Downfall launches in seventy-two hours. Make sure everyone is ready."

They nodded, each man understanding what that readiness meant. Ships prepped for battle. Crews at war stations. Weapons armed. Reactors hot. Every soul in the fleet pointed at Tueblets like a spear aimed at the heart of an enemy.

As the admirals filed out, Hunt remained at the holotable, watching the fleet icons pulse in their formations. Outside the viewport, Alliance City continued its evening rhythm—lights flickering on across the skyline, transit tubes weaving their luminous paths, the distant glow of the spaceport where shuttles ferried personnel and supplies to orbit.

His reflection stared back from the darkening glass. Older. Harder. Ready for this fight.

Three days, he thought. *Three days and we end this war.*

He grabbed his cover and headed for the door. A shuttle waited at the government spaceport to take him to orbit. The RNS *Freedom* hung among the gathering fleet, and there were final preparations to oversee. Captains to brief. Doubts to bury, and a war to end.

****

Three Days Later
RNS *Freedom*
High Orbit, New Eden

The shuttle's docking clamps engaged with a hollow thunk that vibrated through the airlock. Hunt felt the magnetic seals lock home, equalizing pressure with a hiss of recycled air. Four weeks of planning, Four weeks of watching the fleet assemble, and now the moment had arrived. He stepped through the hatch into the *Freedom*'s port hangar bay.

The smell hit him first—a mixture of lubricants, ozone from plasma conduits, and the metallic tang of a warship preparing for battle. The hangar deck thrummed with activity. Deck crews swarmed over F-19 Hellcats lined in precise rows, running final systems checks. Ordnance teams loaded JATMs and plasma torpedoes onto bomb carts. The sound of pneumatic tools, shouted orders, and humming repulsor sleds created a symphony of controlled chaos.

"Viceroy on deck!" someone called out.

Hunt waved off the announcement. "As you were. Keep working."

He moved through the organized mayhem, his boots ringing on deck plating still warm from a recent scrub cycle. A young ordnance tech—couldn't be more than nineteen—fumbled with a plasma torpedo mounting bracket. Hunt paused.

"First time loading live ordnance, son?"

The kid's eyes went wide. "Sir, I—yes, sir. Viceroy, sir."

"It's OK, take your time. Best to do it right. With some luck, that torpedo's going to wreck a Zodark battleship's day."

"Yes, sir!" The tech's hands steadied as he resumed his work.

Hunt continued across the hangar, feeling the deck plates vibrate as the *Freedom*'s massive Quantum Fusion Reactors cycled to combat readiness. Fourteen thousand souls aboard this ship. Tens of thousands more across the fleet. All of them depending on the plan he'd put in motion three days ago in that quiet office overlooking the mountains.

The lift to the command deck took forty-five seconds. Long enough to feel the weight settling on his shoulders again. Long enough to remember every decision that had led here. Alfheim. Sirius. Zinconia. Decades of war compressed into the next few hours.

The doors opened onto the command deck—a two-hundred-meter corridor of controlled intensity. Officers moved with purpose between stations. Data streams scrolled across holographic displays. The low murmur of tactical updates filled the air. At the far end, the bridge doors stood open, light spilling from the command center like a beacon.

Hunt stepped through. "Viceroy on the bridge," announced the duty officer.

The command center of the RNS *Freedom* was a symphony of war, and he was the conductor. The main viewscreen dominated the forward bulkhead—twenty meters of high-resolution display showing New Eden's orbital infrastructure and the gathering fleet beyond. Tactical holotables flanked the command chair, projecting real-time fleet disposition in three dimensions. Workstations ringed the space in tiered levels—sensors, weapons, communications, engineering—each manned by specialists who'd trained for this moment.

Admiral Wiyrkomi rose from the captain's chair. The Gallentine's angular features remained impassive, but Hunt caught the slight tension in his shoulders. "Viceroy. The *Freedom* is at Condition One. All departments report ready for combat operations."

"Outstanding work, Admiral." Hunt took his position at the command chair, feeling the familiar contour of the seat. Designed for long engagements, with integrated displays and a direct neural interface capability he rarely used. The chair's armrests held tactical controls, fleet communications, and override commands for every system on the ship should he need it.

He settled in, letting the bridge activity wash over him. Third Officer Arvexian—the Gallentine sensor specialist—worked his console with precision. Commander Kryvion monitored weapons status, his muscled frame bent over the tactical display. Lieutenant Rosales sat at the helm, young but steady. The crew Hunt had assembled over months of operations, now about to face their greatest test.

"Status of the fleet?" Hunt asked.

Commander Rowe looked up from the operations station. "All vessels report ready, sir. Four hundred and sixty warships in formation.

Republic contingent holding position at grid seven-niner. Altairian fleet maneuvering to final deployment zones. Humtar forces anchored at grid eight-two."

Hunt pulled up the master display. Icons filled the hologram—each one representing a warship, a crew, a weapon aimed at Tueblets. The Republic contribution showed as blue markers: three *Constellation*-class carriers, six *Victory* battleships, forty-eight heavy cruisers, thirty-two destroyers, twenty-four frigates. The Altairian contingent appeared in silver—three hundred and thirty-four ships, the largest single deployment in their history, ranging from star carriers to battleships to light cruisers. The Humtar forces glowed aqua—thirty-four vessels led by twelve *Voidhammer*-class heavy battleships, their 3,200-meter hulls bristling with weapons that could tear through any Zodark armor.

"Admiral Pandolly signals ready," Rowe continued. "All Altairian commands report weapons hot, crews at battle stations."

"Admiral Vesharuk confirms Humtar readiness," added Admiral Ithis from his coordination station. "The *Voidhammer* battleships are in attack formation. *Oathbreaker* has deployed its advance sensor net."

Hunt nodded slowly. The pieces were in position. Every captain knew their role. Anvil Strike would hit Nargulon's fuel infrastructure. Hammer Strike would wreck the Thalyss shipyards. And the main fleet—his fleet—would tear the heart out of Zodark High Command.

"Commander Rowe, open a fleet-wide channel," ordered Hunt in a firm voice, his mind readying what he wanted to say.

"Aye, sir. Fleet channel opened," Rowe confirmed seconds later.

Hunt nodded, then stood, his hands folded behind his back as he prepared to speak. In that moment, as he prepared to give the final order that would commit the Republic and the entire alliance to what he felt would be the battle to end the war. He suddenly felt the weight of decades of decisions, decades of loss, sorrow, and the elation of victory pressing down on him. Every battle he fought, every loss he had endured, every decision he had made, it all brought them to this very moment. He looked one last time at the planet they called New Eden as its curves fell away into the darkness. This was what they were fighting for. The preservation of the Republic, a future for humanity among the stars.

"Attention all ships, all commands—this is Fleet Commander Viceroy Hunt speaking." His voice was transmitted to nearly five hundred warships. "When we left Sol for the Rhea system, we came as peaceful explorers looking to colonize our first world beyond Earth. What we found instead was the Zodarks. For a quarter century, we have fought these blue devils and their allies across space and on numerous planets. We have liberated the oppressed, freed those enslaved, and brought hope to the hopeless.

"In thirty minutes, the greatest fleet ever assembled will bridge to the heart of the Zodark Empire—Tueblets. What we do there, each and every one of you will echo across this galaxy for generations. The Zodarks have fought us for decades. They have occupied worlds, enslaved populations, and challenged our very right to exist. Today, we end that threat."

He paused, letting the words settle. As he looked around the bridge, he saw the officers surrounding him had paused their work to listen to him.

"The Tueblets system is their stronghold. Their command center. The heart of everything they've built. When we emerge from that quantum bridge, every Zodark commander in the system is going to see us. They will know we've come for them. And they will fight with everything they have to try and defeat us."

Hunt's jaw tightened. "And that's exactly what we want. Let them bring everything they have to this fight. Let them throw every ship, every weapon, every ounce of strength at us. Because while they're focused on the *Freedom*, on this fleet, our strike wings will be systematically destroying the engine that has powered their Empire. We are the anvil, and Task Force 28 is the hammer. Today, we break them, and we end this war once and for all.

"Every one of you knows your duty. Every captain knows their target. Trust your training. Trust your shipmates. Trust the plan. And when the shooting starts, remember why we're here. We fight for people next to us and for those we love behind us. We fight for the Republic. For every world that lives in fear of the Zodark Empire. Today, we end that fear."

He paused one final time. "I want to wish each and every one of you good luck today. Good hunting. And I'll see you all on the other side. Hunt out."

As the channel closed, the bridge erupted into motion with officers returning to their stations with renewed intensity. Hunt caught Wiyrkomi's eye—the Gallentine nodded once, respect clear in that gesture.

"Admiral Takmahl," Hunt called to his Chief of Flight Operations. "What's the status on our strike wings?"

The Gallentine flight commander and fighter pilot looked up from his console. "All squadrons report ready, Viceroy. Rear Admiral Hunt's Thunderjacks are standing by for Anvil Strike launch. All strike packages are armed and ready."

Hunt allowed himself a moment of paternal concern. Ethan would be leading the strike force heading for the Nargulon refineries. He couldn't have been more proud as a father and more scared for his son than he was right now. He'd grown over the years into one hell of a pilot and commander. *Come back safe, son. Come back and tell me about it over that beer you promised.*

"Viceroy," Admiral Ithis interrupted his thoughts. "Priority signal from CNS *Oathbreaker*. Captain Naram-Suen reports their tachyon scanners are operational and ready to monitor quantum bridge activity across the system once we cross."

"Excellent. We'll need that early warning if the Zodarks try to bring in reinforcements." Hunt settled back into his command chair. Twenty-eight minutes to bridge insertion. Twenty-eight minutes until they ended this war or proved they never could.

"Third Officer Arvexian, activate long-range sensor suite. I want a complete picture of Tueblets the moment we emerge."

"Aye, Viceroy. Configuring sensor protocols now."

"Commander Kryvion, weapons status?"

The tactical officer's hands flew across his console. "All batteries report ready. Primary magrails loaded with armor-piercing rounds. Turbo lasers at full charge. Torpedo tubes loaded with plasma warheads and ready to launch. All point-defense gun systems are online and green across the board. We're ready to deliver hell, sir."

"Outstanding." Hunt pulled up the mission timeline. Thirty seconds after bridge insertion, fighters launched. At sixty seconds, the fleet began to move into a battle line formation. Ninety seconds, Anvil and Hammer Strikes separated from the main formation and launched their attacks. Five minutes after arrival, they'd be in optimal weapons range to begin their attack. That was when the real dance began.

"Viceroy," Lieutenant Rosales called from the helm. "Navigation confirms jump coordinates locked. Quantum bridge generators charging. We're green across the board."

Hunt felt the deck plates vibrate as the *Freedom*'s exotic matter generators powered up. The quantum conduit bridge was the pinnacle of Gallentine technology built into the *Freedom*. It had proven more than once to be a game-changing gift from the Gallentines. The ability to bend space and time, connecting to points hundreds of light-years away to deposit hundreds of warships directly into the enemy's home system, was beyond comprehension.

"Commander Rowe, what's the final fleet status?" Hunt asked.

"Primed and ready. All vessels standing by to jump," Rowe confirmed. "All formations locked. All groups ready."

"Admiral Vesharuk signals the Humtar contingent is prepared," Ithis added. "He wishes you 'honor in battle and victory in purpose.'"

Hunt smiled thinly. Vesharuk had a way with words. "Tell him the honor is ours."

As the minutes crawled by. Hunt watched the countdown timer on his display, each second bringing them closer to the jump. Around him, the bridge had settled into the focused calm of professionals about to execute a complex operation. No panic. No uncertainty. Just the disciplined readiness you would expect from seasoned veterans.

"Ten minutes to bridge insertion," announced Rosales.

Hunt stood, moving to the forward viewport. Beyond the reinforced transparisteel that protected the window, he took a final glimpse of New Eden as it hung in space—blue and green and white, a world being remade and colonized by the Republic. When a soldier or spacer left for war, there was always a chance they might not return. All the training, all the planning in the world, wouldn't save you in the end if it was your time to go. Instinctively, Hunt knew that. Still, he hoped to return home from this battle and see his wife, his daughter and his son once more.

As he took in the view of the fleet he had assembled, he felt an immense amount of pride fill him. Through grit, determination, and force of will, he had managed to assemble the largest fleet of warships he had ever seen. Hundreds of warships from the Altairians, the Tully, and the

Humtars all assembled for what they all believed would be the climactic battle to end the war. This didn't even include the ships of Task Force 28 in the Gravaxia system next to Tueblets. Hunt's longtime Primord friend and ally, Admiral Stavanger, was leading that fleet along with Vice Admiral Ripley Lee. When he ordered this second force into the system, it would add nearly two hundred warships to the already enormous fleet.

This is simply incredible what we have built, Hunt marvelled as his thoughts drifted back to the very first battle he had fought against the Zodarks from his battle cruiser, the *Rook*. *From that first desperate battle at Rhea to this moment. Every sacrifice, every loss, every hard-won victory has led us to this moment.*

"Five minutes to bridge," Rosales announced.

Hunt returned to his command chair, having bidden a final farewell to New Eden, to his wife, Lilly. His hands rested on the armrests, feeling the slight vibration as the quantum generators reached full power. On the tactical display, formation icons glowed steady—all ships in position, every captain ready to execute.

"Miles," Wiyrkomi said quietly as he leaned over from his chair next to Hunt. "For twenty years we have worked together. I have been your Gallentine advisor, and commander of the *Freedom*. I am proud to call you my friend, and I know I have said so before. But on the eve of our greatest battle, I want to say it again. It has been an honor serving with you."

Hunt smiled warmly at his advisor. "This position of Viceroy is a lonely one. One I am not sure I would have navigated nearly as well without your continued guidance and friendship. The honor's mine, Wiyrkomi. Now let's go end this war."

The bridge lights dimmed slightly, power redirecting to jump systems. Hunt felt the familiar tingle in his teeth as exotic matter fields built up around the hull. The *Freedom* was preparing to tear a hole in reality itself.

"All hands, this is the bridge," Hunt transmitted across shipwide comms. "Stand by for quantum bridge insertion. Thirty seconds to combat zone. Make your peace, check your gear, and get ready to fight. Hunt out."

Hunt pulled up a private channel. "Admiral Dobbs, good luck with Hammer Strike. We're counting on you to make that shipyard disappear for us."

"Roger that, Viceroy. *Draco* out," Dobbs replied, tension in her voice.

Opening another channel, he connected to his Strike wing commander. "Hey, Ethan, I know you can't respond. I just wanted to say… I'm proud of you, son. Fly safe, and burn those fuel depots to the ground."

"One minute to bridge," Rosales said as the clock moved closer to zero.

Around the *Freedom*, the fleet began to glow as the quantum fields enveloped each hull. On the main screen, space itself started to shimmer and distort.

"Thirty seconds. QCB generators at maximum output," announced Commander Rowe.

Hunt gripped the armrests as he mentally prepared to jump.

"Fifteen seconds. Quantum tunnel forming."

On the main display, Hunt watched reality bend. The stars stretched and twisted, pulled toward an impossible point directly ahead where the quantum bridge was opening.

"Ten seconds. All systems nominal," updated Rosales.

The bridge had fallen silent except for the rising hum of the generators.

"Five seconds."

Hunt took a breath, holding it as he waited for the jump.

"Three. Two. One."

"Execute," Hunt ordered, his voice carrying the weight of command across the entire fleet.

A flash occurred as the space in front of them tore open. A brilliant white tunnel yawned before them, edges writhing with exotic energies. The *Freedom* surged forward, two million tons of warship accelerating across hundreds of light-years.

"QCB insertion complete. Transit in progress."

The viewscreen showed nothing but white light and quantum distortions. The tunnel stretched ahead—a gateway of twisted space and time connecting New Eden to Tueblets.

"Ten seconds to exit," Rosales reported, his voice steady despite the g-forces pressing everyone into their seats.

Hunt felt his command chair compensate, inertial dampeners working overtime. Around him, the bridge crew maintained their posts, eyes locked on displays that showed fleet cohesion holding despite the quantum transit.

"All vessels maintaining formation," Rowe confirmed. "No stragglers. Fleet integrity at one hundred percent."

Five seconds. Half the tunnel traversed. On the other end, Tueblets waited—unaware that hundreds of warships were about to arrive.

Hunt breathed deeply, settling his nerves as he sat forward. "All hands, battle stations! Combat alert! Set Condition One throughout the ship!"

Klaxons wailed. Red lights flooded the bridge. Throughout the *Freedom*, fourteen thousand crew members waited for whatever would happen.

The white light at the tunnel's end grew brighter, resolving into the familiar black of space dotted with stars. Hunt's jaw set. *Here we go.*

"Two."

"One."

"Emergence!"

The *Freedom* burst from the quantum bridge into the heart of the Zodark Empire like a shooting star. Reality snapped back into focus. The viewscreen filled with an alien sun, unfamiliar constellations, and the massive olive-hued world of Xyrvannis hanging in space. Above its curve, the five moons orbited the planet in stately procession.

"Navigation confirms position," Rosales announced. "Forty-three thousand kilometers above Velkryn's northern pole. Exactly as planned."

"Sensors active," Arvexian reported, his console erupting with data. "Detecting multiple Zodark signatures. Velkryn command center at bearing two-seven-zero, distance thirty-nine thousand klicks. And there they are, the Zodark Defense Fleet is reacting to our presence. I count one hundred and thirty-three capital ships in orbit. Their engines are powering up—they're moving to break orbit."

Hunt allowed himself a predator's smile as he listened to the reports coming in. They'd emerged exactly where they'd planned—close enough to threaten the command moon, far enough to maneuver. And like clockwork, the Zodarks were reacting exactly as predicted.

"The full fleet has emerged," Rowe called out. "Republic vessels reporting in... Altairian contingent reporting all present... Humtar forces are emerging now."

On the tactical display, friendly icons bloomed into existence as the allied fleet poured through the quantum bridge. Blue, silver, aqua— a rainbow of death materializing for one purpose, to the kill the enemy and end this war.

"Fleet emergence is complete," Rowe confirmed. "All four hundred and sixty vessels accounted for. All ships report ready and moving to battle formations."

Hunt stood, his eyes on the main screen where the Zodark command center gleamed like a fortress against Velkryn's surface. If their intelligence was right, Zon Otro himself might be there.

"Attention all gun and missile batteries," Hunt ordered, his voice carrying across the bridge, across the fleet. "Prepare to engage the command center on Velkryn."

Hunt had barely finished speaking when he felt the *Freedom*'s weapons come alive. The turbo lasers and magrails charged to fire, torpedo tubes opening like the maw of a primordial beast.

Hunt fixed his eyes on the enemy who had terrorized the galaxy for too long. He raised a hand, then shouted, *"Fire all weapons— weapons free! Let's kill 'em all!"*

Chapter 39:
Overwhelming Odds

2116
RNS *Freedom*
Velkryn Orbital Command Center, Northern Polar Axis
Zeta Gas Giant, Tueblets System

The *Freedom*'s weapons spoke first.

Turbo lasers lanced out in brilliant emerald streams, carving across forty-three thousand kilometers of the void. Volleys of magrail rounds followed—tungsten-jacketed death accelerated to relativistic speeds. Waves of antiship missiles followed, warheads streaking toward Velkryn's surface like falling stars.

Around them, four hundred and sixty allied warships opened fire in near-perfect synchronization. Space erupted in violence.

Viceroy Hunt gripped the armrests of his command chair as the *Freedom* shuddered with each weapons discharge. On the main display, the Zodark command center sprawled across Velkryn's northern pole— a fortress moon turned military nerve center, exactly where Humtar intelligence said it would be.

"Direct hits on the command center's outer armor plating," reported the weapons officer, Commander Sarah Chen, her voice cutting through the bridge's controlled chaos. "Turbo lasers burning through reinforced sections—thermal blooms confirm deep penetrations. We're seeing magrail impacts showing structural deformation across the northern defensive ring."

"Heads up, the Zodark fleet is breaking orbit," Third Officer Arvexian called out, his capable hands flowing across the sensor console. "Sensors are showing one hundred and thirty-three capital ships on the move. They're forming a battle line. I'm reading multiple battleships to include those new *Plarix* battleships, cruisers, and frigates. Their weapon systems look to be charging—they're moving to engage."

Hunt's jaw tightened. The enemy was reacting faster than projected. "Admiral Wiyrkomi, fleet maintains bombardment formation. Every gun stays on that command center until it's slag. I want it destroyed before we have to shift our focus to those ships."

"Aye, sir," Wiyrkomi responded, his fingers dancing across the tactical network relay. Orders rippled outward through the allied fleet to maintain the bombardment.

"I guess we'll have to teach them a new lesson, Wiyrkomi." Hunt turned to his CAG. "Admiral Takmahl, we have their attention. It's time to deploy our strike packages—initiate Anvil Strike."

Admiral Takmahl straightened, his olive features set with determination. The Gallentine flight commander's bright blue eyes blazed with anticipation. "Affirmative. All wings standing by, Viceroy. The 4th Fighter Wing reports ready to maintain CAP around the *Freedom*. They're launching now. Rear Admiral Hunt's Thunderjacks are ready to initiate Anvil Strike."

"Very well. Execute Anvil Strike."

"Aye, Viceroy. All wings, this is Takmahl. Execute deployment pattern Hydra. Anvil Strike is a go. I repeat, Anvil Strike is a go."

The *Freedom*'s massive hangar bays opened like the maw of some primordial beast. Strike craft poured forth in disciplined waves— sleek F-19 Hellcats and heavy B-19 Devastator bombers. More than four hundred fighters and bombers emerged from the dreadnought as the various squadrons formed up before heading off to their objectives.

"Thunderjacks are clear and accelerating toward Nargulon," Takmahl confirmed. "Time to target, seventy minutes."

The *Freedom* trembled again as another magrail volley fired from the main guns. Hunt's eyes fixed on the command center below, watching the Fleet's relentless fire hammer into heavy armor plating and the rock face carved deep into Velkryn's crust. Explosions blossomed across the facility's surface—orange fireballs and debris clouds erupting where missiles detonated against reinforced bunkers and gun emplacements.

I've waited for this moment for years, Hunt thought grimly. *Years of planning, politicking, convincing the Altairians and Gallentines that this strike was necessary. A billion souls might still be alive if we'd struck when I first proposed it a decade ago.*

Somewhere down there, buried beneath layers of armor and rock, intelligence suggested Zon Otro himself might be coordinating the Zodark response. Hunt wanted that facility obliterated—and the monster inside it dead.

Lieutenant Dumeris leaned toward his superior, speaking rapidly before addressing the bridge. "Rear Admiral Ithis recommends repositioning our *Ironveil* cruisers to better support the Altairian left flank."

"Approved." Hunt nodded. "Make it happen."

"Viceroy, Admiral Dobbs signals ready," Rowe reported. "Her detachment is standing by for your order."

Hunt studied the tactical display, watching as the picture continued to change. Rear Admiral Amy Dobbs was commanding the third prong of his attack force from her star carrier *Draco*. Her strike force—six *Victory* battleships, eight Kraken heavy cruisers, and four Humtar *Warclaw*-class light battleships—would break off from the main fleet to go after the Zodarks' Thalyss shipyard. If they could severely damage or wreck the facility, it could cripple their ability to replace ships lost in battle. The Thalyss shipyard was the Zodarks' most complex facility in the Empire, with nearly two hundred construction slips, all of them with a warship in various stages of construction. Its destruction would utterly hamper the Malvari.

"Very well, signal Admiral Dobbs. Hammer Strike is a go. Execute Hammer Strike. Tell her good luck and happy hunting," ordered Hunt as he set the third element of his plan into motion.

"Viceroy, the command center is returning fire," Arvexian announced, his bright blue eyes narrowing at his displays. "Multiple plasma cannon batteries activating across the surface. They're targeting our lead ships."

Hunt watched as crimson bolts erupted from Velkryn's pockmarked surface, reaching up toward the descending allied fleet like claws grasping for prey. The first shots splashed against the *Freedom*'s forward armor, scorching ablative plating in brilliant flashes but failing to penetrate. More followed—dozens, then hundreds—a constellation of angry red death climbing toward them.

"Damage report," Hunt ordered.

"No damage. Forward armor holding," Chen reported. "We're too far out for their cannons to ablate our armor. They can't penetrate it."

"Sounds like we got lucky. All batteries maintain fire," Hunt commanded, his voice iron. "I want that facility reduced to rubble before we have to shift and engage their warships."

The *Freedom* shuddered again, her weapons singing their song of destruction. Around them, the allied fleet poured fire downward in relentless waves. Velkryn's surface was beginning to glow with impact strikes, the Zodark command center disappearing beneath a curtain of fire.

This was what Hunt had come for. To destroy the enemy. To end this war.

****

Observer Unit 4471-Theta
Assimilator*-Class Scout *Eternal Vigil
Outer Kuiper Belt, Tueblets System

The *Eternal Vigil* hung motionless in the black, wrapped in silence and shadow.

Its stealth plating—adaptive alloys grown from harvested materials and Legion biotech—drank in electromagnetic radiation across every spectrum. No active sensors. No engine emissions. Just passive observation arrays drinking in photons and gravitational distortions from the battle unfolding ninety-seven million kilometers away.

Observer Unit 4471-Theta processed the incoming data streams with cold efficiency, its consciousness one small node in the vast neural network of the Collective. The war-body it inhabited aboard the scout ship had once been something else—someone else—but those memories were suppressed, irrelevant to current function.

Republic fleet strength: four hundred sixty vessels. Composition: mixed human, Altairian, Gallentine construction. Primary target: Zodark Command Center, Velkryn.

The data flowed through 4471-Theta's processors and into the quantum tether linking it back to the Collective's main consciousness nodes light-years distant. The Zodarks and Republic were tearing each other apart with predictable ferocity. Both sides hemorrhaging resources, technology, lives—all of which would eventually be harvested when the Collective moved to assimilate whatever remained.

Then 4471-Theta detected something unexpected.

New signatures. Ship configurations unlike Republic or Zodark construction. Scanning the hull profiles against archived databases yielded a match that sent a cascade of priority alerts through its neural pathways.

Humtar vessel classification confirmed. Count: eighty-three capital ships. Weapons systems: advanced beyond Republic baseline. Threat assessment: extreme.

The Collective had theorized about Humtar return vectors. Ancient warnings in recovered data suggested they might come back. But this was the first confirmed military sighting in fifty thousand years—a full battle group operating alongside Republic forces.

4471-Theta flagged the report with the highest-priority encryption and transmitted it through the quantum tether. The Collective had to know. The calculations would require updating. The timeline might need acceleration.

The Humtars had returned to the Milky Way. And they had brought warships.

Aboard the *Eternal Vigil*, 4471-Theta continued observing, recording, transmitting. Its stealth plating rippled slightly, adapting to a minor gravitational fluctuation from a passing asteroid. It would remain here until recalled or until the battle concluded.

Silent. Patient. Watching.

The Collective always watched.

******

1st Carrier Strike Wing "Thunderjacks" (JACKAL)
Nargulon Fuel Extraction Infrastructure
Orbit of Nargulon, Tueblets System

Rear Admiral Ethan Hunt checked the time on his HUD. Forty-two minutes had passed since Anvil Strike launched from the decks of the *Freedom*. Two hundred and seventy-two allied warships had anchored themselves around the *Freedom* as it sat in high orbit above the moon Velkryn's northern pole. While the Fleet focused on destroying the Zodark command center and Hammer Strike vectored toward the Thalyss shipyards, Ethan's wing—the spear tip of Anvil Strike—would go after the Zodark fuel giant of Nargulon, the logistical heart pumping fuel into the veins of the entire Tueblets sector.

The only downside to Anvil Strike's objective was the distance—seventy minutes from the rest of the Fleet at cruise speed. His strike wing had been flying dark for over forty minutes at seventy percent power, slipping through the system's outer orbital layers in tight formations under full EMCON. No communications, no active sensors, no weapons activation. Nothing that might betray Anvil Strike's position or vector.

While the Thunderjacks closed on their target, the RNS *Freedom* and her battlegroup remained thousands of kilometers behind them, locked in brutal combat near the moon Velkryn's orbit. But that engagement was the matador's cape—a blinding sword stroke meant to fixate the Zodark High Command while Anvil Strike slipped between their ribs. Hammer Strike would deliver another blow to their shipbuilding capacity at Thalyss. Together, the three-pronged assault would cripple the Zodark war machine in its own stronghold.

Nargulon was Anvil Strike's kill zone.

Suspended in high orbit around the swirling storm-churned gas giant was a sprawl of infrastructure that looked more like a city than a refinery—multikilometer fuel processing rings, orbital tank farms, and monolithic sky stations tethered to atmospheric collection arrays that plunged down into the planet's violent cloud bands. These arrays harvested raw hydrogen and helium-3 in a constant cycle, pumping it skyward via kilometers of reinforced conduit lines into orbital processors where it was converted into refined fusion propellant. From there, it was transferred to storage blisters, ready to replenish Zodark warships across a dozen star systems.

This was no simple supply depot. Nargulon was a strategic nerve center—the critical refueling nexus that enabled the Zodark fleet to project power from Tueblets to the fringes of the sector. Take it out, and their offensive momentum would grind to a halt. Without fuel, warships were nothing more than stationary gun platforms and monuments. The towering collection arrays presented a critical opportunity. If they could be severed before emergency protocols kicked in, the strike would achieve two objectives. First, it would cripple the supply side of the operation. Second, it would prevent the arrays from dropping into the gas giant's gravity well, limiting or even eliminating recovery operations for months to come.

This was Anvil Strike's mission—strike deep, fast, and without mercy. Wound the beast behind its shield wall. While the Fleet burned Zodark cruisers near Velkryn, Ethan Hunt's Thunderjacks would take a scalpel to its spine. The trickiest part of the mission was crossing the distance between the fleet and the target while maintaining their cover for as long as possible. The Thunderjacks flew under EMCON discipline, their F-19 Hellcats and B-19 Devastators running silent through the void. No active sensors, no communications beyond tight-beam laser bursts—nothing to betray their approach to Nargulon's fuel infrastructure.

Looking through his canopy, Ethan could see periodic flashes in the distance illuminating the darkness. The *Freedom* and her escorts were engaged with the Zodark fleet. He saw a brilliant explosion bloom. It was too far to identify the victim, allied or Zodark. The urge to break EMCON gnawed at him, but discipline held. His father commanded the *Freedom*, and if he knew one thing about his father, it was that Miles Hunt had survived worse.

"Jackal Lead, flash traffic," came the whisper-quiet laser comm from Commander Eiran Vos. The Gallentine's voice carried its usual clinical precision. "Ghost Rooks painting massive EM signatures ahead. It's confirmed, the Nargulon defenses are fully activated. They probably did so the moment they saw the Fleet arrive."

Ethan acknowledged with a double click. Vos's B-19E Spectres—eight modified Devastators crewed entirely by Gallentine EW specialists—were the eyes of his strike force. Their Quantum Ghost Net suites could detect a metallic whisper at fifty thousand kilometers.

Lieutenant Mattison "Matti" Danseen held perfect position off his starboard wing. Even through EMCON, her eagerness radiated through precise stick work. The kid had that rare mix—raw talent married to relentless hunger. If they survived this war, she'd wear oak leaves soon enough.

He checked the clock, twenty-eight minutes to target. He could see Nargulon swelled from a distant marble to a looming giant. Orbital infrastructure glittered like deadly jewelry—processing stations, storage depots, collection arrays drinking from the planet's atmosphere. The lifeblood of the Zodark war machine.

His tactical display populated with faint returns from the Ghost Rooks' passive sensors. The picture it painted wasn't pretty. Point-defense towers created overlapping kill zones around primary facilities. Vulture patrols swept predetermined routes. Six frigates held station near the main processing hub.

"Strike Lead, Anvil One-One," Commander Kenneth Vosler's voice came through on laser comm. "Ruin Fangs standing by. Confirming four flights for initial strike?"

"Confirmed, Anvil Lead. Stand by for sprint." Ethan referenced the attack plan. Four bomber flights would hit primary targets while fighters cleared the path.

Fifteen minutes out. More ghost returns—Vultures vectoring toward their general approach. The enemy couldn't pinpoint them yet through the jamming, but they smelled trouble in their direction and that was enough to put them on their trail.

"All Thunderjack elements, Strike Lead," Ethan transmitted. "Phase line Alpha in ten mikes. Weapons hot at my signal. Valkyrie, your Talons have point."

"Copy, Strike Lead." Commander Julius Holden's Australian accent carried controlled aggression. "Black Talons ready to draw blood."

As they continued to close the distance, the fuel infrastructure resolved into distinct targets. The main processing station hung like a metal metropolis, kilometers of pipes and storage tanks. Secondary stations ringed it, connected by transfer conduits. Below, collection arrays extended into Nargulon's atmosphere—massive scoops feeding the entire operation.

His threat receiver chirped. Search radar painting them.

"Wraith Lead, begin jamming sequence," Ethan ordered. It was go time.

"Ghost Rooks engaging," Vos confirmed. "Phantom Torch activating now."

The Gallentine EW pilots executed with surgical precision. Eight Spectres lit up their jammers simultaneously, flooding local space with electromagnetic chaos. Zodark channels dissolved into static. Targeting radars struggled against the interference.

Through his HUD, Ethan watched the Ghost Rooks deploy their Echo Racks. Dozens of mimic drones scattered, each broadcasting the signature of a Hellcat or Devastator. To Zodark sensors, the strike force had just multiplied threefold, and in the wrong place.

Five minutes raced by as individual Vultures became visible, twin-tail silhouettes probing the jamming field's edges. Behind them, frigates maneuvered, weapons tracking toward the electronic storm.

"Strike Lead, Talon Two. Count forty-plus Vultures, more vectoring from that far-side facility that intelligence suggested might be a flight hangar."

"Copy, Talon Two. All fighters prepare to engage. Bombers, attack runs on my mark."

He lifted the master arm switch, activating his weapons and their targeting systems. All around him, two hundred Hellcats began arming their weapons. In the bomber formations, crews ran final checks on plasma torpedoes and Havoc missiles. Years of training compressed into minutes.

Minutes ticked by like seconds as the two forces closed in on each other. Suddenly, a Vulture stumbled into visual range of Matti's Hellcat. Both pilots reacted instantly—the Zodark rolling inverted, afterburners blazing.

"Contact! Bandits, two o'clock!" Ethan's voice alerted.

"Holy crap! He must have ghosted in on us for our sensors not to have spotted him," Matti countered as she reacted swiftly to the presence of the enemy fighter.

The dancing in the dark was over. The forces were merging and it was go time.

"All Thunderjack elements—weapons free! Light 'em up!"

Hoots and hollers of excitement followed Ethan's announcement as two hundred Hellcats erupted from the void. In an instant, sensors blazed active, illuminating every fighter, every tower, every target. The tactical display on Ethan's dashboard exploded into red.

"Tallyho!" Holden roared. "Black Talons engaging!"

"Anvil Lead, Strike Lead—execute! Send them in!"

"Copy, Strike Lead! Ruin Fangs, attack pattern Delta!"

In seconds, the forty-eight Devastator bombers rolled into attack runs. With bomb bays opened, revealing death waiting to be unleashed. They followed the Hellcats in as they surged ahead, lasers carving through Vultures and sentry towers alike.

The Hellcats began launching their JATM missiles in salvos, blue exhaust trails etching faint lines across the blackness of space.

Ethan zeroed in on a Vulture angling for an attack on one of the bombers. He'd achieved a lock with a JATM and fired, watching as the enemy fighter desperately tried to evade the missile closing on him. A flash erupted—a cloud of expanding debris appeared where the fighter had been moments earlier.

"Splash one!" he announced while rolling his Hellcat left, lining up for another target.

"Jackal Lead, Ghost Rook Three," a Gallentine pilot reported calmly. "Deploying Blackout missiles at defense grid, sector seven— stand by for flash."

Ethan caught a glimpsed the EW craft's work as the specialized missiles detonating in brilliant flashes aimed directly at the remaining point-defense towers. The sudden flash of blinding light blinded and overpowered most targeting systems, at least until they could reboot. With targeting sensors down, the volume of defensive fire slackened, creating gaps in their coverage. With the EW crews neutralizing the enemy guns, the Hellcats finished them off while the bombers closed in for their kill shots.

"Beautiful work, Wraith!" someone called out. "Towers six and nine destroyed."

"The first wave of torpedoes are about to hit," Matti announced as her Hellcat pulled alongside Ethan's.

Ethan watched the first volley of plasma torpedoes hit their targets. Explosions rippled across the main processing station before culminating in a brilliant white flash before collapsing in on itself. Secondary explosions soon cascaded through the structure as stored fuel found oxygen pockets. The station began breaking apart into several sections, each trailing fire as it burned up the remaining atmosphere.

"Hot damn! Now that's what I'm talking about!" Vosler shouted. "Second flight of bombers rolling in now!"

More Devastators dove on the secondary and tertiary targets. Plasma torpedoes and JATM missiles slammed into storage tanks and nearby refueling vessels, rupturing their tanks as they vented their contents into giant clouds waiting to be ignited. A flurry of laser shots zipped into the clouds, a flash erupting into a giant spherical fireball for a second before dissipating to nothing.

One of the Zodark frigate's point-defense guns fired relentlessly in the direction of the bombers closing in on it and another part of the refinery. It looked like a firework celebration as red laser fire zipped through the void toward the attacking bombers. Ethan watched in horror when a Devastator's wing got clipped by the frigate's PDGs. The bomber veered off course as the pilot desperately tried to evade the hailstorm he'd flown into.

A flash erupted where the bomber had been, then a trio of explosions rippled across the frigate before it blew apart in spectacular fashion. Three of the bomber's torpedoes had nailed their target, seconds too late to save the Devastator.

"Damn, we lost a bomber," Ethan said aloud to no one in particular.

"Paladin—watch out for that sentry tower. Its guns are still active!" Matti warned just as streaks of light zipped around his Hellcat.

Ethan jerked the flight stick, sending his Hellcat into a tight roll through defensive fire, his Hellcat's agility keeping him barely ahead of its AI tracking systems. Hitting the reverse thrusters as he realigned his guns, he fired his lasers, walking a string of fire across a defense tower until it exploded. Next he hit the booster on his engines, accelerating him rapidly as laser bolts flew through the space he'd just occupied.

"Damn, cutting it close there, Paladin," Matti called out as her Hellcat pulled alongside him.

"Oh, you know me, adrenaline junkie," he jokingly responded.

"Jackal Lead, be advised," Vos's voice cut through. "Ghost Rooks detecting power surge in collection arrays. Emergency detachment sequence initiated."

"Oh no, you don't. Not happening," Ethan replied. "Third and Fourth Attack Groups, new priority—kill those arrays!"

Ethan was determined to stop the atmospheric scoops from attempting to drop into Nargulon's gravity well for later recovery. Thanks to the quick heads-up from Vos's people, the bombers were already adjusting their attack runs to make sure that didn't happen.

Plasma torpedoes and Havoc missiles began slamming into connection points. One by one, the massive collectors tumbled out of control into the crushing atmosphere.

"Scratch six arrays," someone reported. "They won't be processing jack."

The Ghost Rooks continued their deadly ballet. Ethan watched one Spectre launch a cloud of mimic drones that drew an entire Vulture squadron away from the real bombers. Another used its jammers to ghost three Devastators through a frigate's point-defense envelope. The Gallentine EW pilots flew with an almost artistic precision, turning electronic warfare into a symphony of misdirection like a skilled magician.

"Anvil Lead to all Ruin Fangs," Vosler's voice came through, breathing hard. "Weapons expended. Repeat, we are Winchester on stores."

"Copy, Anvil Lead." Ethan checked his tactical display. The fuel infrastructure was thoroughly wrecked and devastated. Everywhere he looked he saw burning stations, ruptured tanks, arrays tumbling into Nargulon's depths. *Yeah, mission accomplished.* "All Thunderjack elements, Strike Lead. Objective complete. Execute retrograde. Let's RTB to the *Freedom*—first round of beers is on me!"

The strike force began its turn, Hellcats maintaining defensive screens as the remaining bombers accelerated clear of the target. Behind them, Nargulon's orbital infrastructure was a floating wrecked ruin. It would take the Zodarks months if not a year to repair it and restore fuel production operations.

"Ghost Rooks, excellent work today," Ethan transmitted to the Gallentine crews.

"Acknowledged, Strike Lead," Vos replied with typical understatement. "Acceptable performance parameters achieved."

Ethan smiled behind his oxygen mask. Acceptable performance—the Gallentine had just helped orchestrate the complete destruction of a major logistics hub. But that was Vos and his crews—clinical precision wrapped in professional detachment.

Seventy minutes back to the *Freedom*. Seventy minutes hoping his father's ship was still there to receive them. Ethan settled into his seat, eyes scanning for a pursuit that never came. The Zodarks were too busy dealing with the hammer blow they'd just delivered to try and chase after them. His Thunderjacks had earned their pay today. He just hoped the other strikes had earned theirs too.

****

RNS *Vanguard*
Thalyss Orbital Rings, Moon of Kar'Thon
Tueblets System

Captain Joe Wright stood in the center of *Vanguard*'s CIC, watching the tactical plot with the intensity of a chess grandmaster.

300

Eighty-six minutes had passed since Hammer Strike separated from the *Freedom*'s main fleet. His detachment—commanded by Rear Admiral Amy Dobbs from her star carrier *Draco*—consisted of six *Victory*-class battleships, eight *Kraken* heavy cruisers, and four Humtar warships racing toward their objective: the Thalyss Orbital Shipyard Rings.

While Viceroy Hunt kept the Zodark High Command fixated on defending Velkryn and his son, Rear Admiral Ethan Hunt led Anvil Strike against Nargulon's fuel infrastructure, Hammer Strike would deliver the third blow. The shipyard complex orbiting Thalyss—five massive concentric rings containing over two hundred construction slips—represented the industrial heart of the Zodark Empire's war machine. If they could succeed in destroying it, it could cripple their ability to replace ship losses for months, perhaps years into the future.

"Captain, we're forty-three minutes from the target," announced Lieutenant Godley, his helmsman. "Maintaining flank speed."

Wright stared at the tactical display, studying the details of the target. They were deep in contested space now, six AUs from the relative safety of the *Freedom*'s guns and the protective cover of the allied fleet. Each AU or astronomical unit they had traveled placed them about one hundred fifty million kilometers further away from support and deeper into the enemy's defensive envelope. But that was the beauty of the Viceroy's three-pronged assault—the Zodarks couldn't be strong everywhere. They would have to choose where to commit, and once they had, it would be next to impossible to disengage when they suddenly had to reinforce a position somewhere else.

"Captain, receiving an update from *Freedom*," reported Lieutenant Waldman, his comms officer. "They're reporting the main Zodark fleet has fully engaged them now. That second force that entered from Gate Two Alpha, the one that connects to the Shwani system—it's just arrived in orbit of Velkryn. It's engaging them. They don't appear to be headed in our direction thankfully."

"Outstanding. I'll admit I was a little nervous that other fleet might have tried to interdict us. It looks like they're taking the bait—focusing everything on the *Freedom*," commented Wright, a visible sigh of relief on the faces of his bridge crew. He turned to his weapons officer. "Lieutenant Latter, what's the status on our strike packages?"

Lieutenant Latter's fingers danced across his console. "All tubes loaded with penetrator warheads. Primary targeting solutions locked on Shipyard Rings Two through Five. Secondary targets plotted on the molecular foundries in the inner rings."

Wright nodded. Those shipyards had taken the Zodarks decades to build—massive zero-g construction facilities where their next generation of warships took shape. Intel showed at least forty vessels in various stages of completion, including several of the new *Plarix*-class battleships. Half-built warships that would never taste vacuum if Hammer Strike succeeded.

"Sir, long-range sensors just detected a Zodark picket squadron," called out his TAO, Commander Thomas Hill. "It looks to be two destroyers and three corvettes advancing toward us on an intercept course."

"Very well. Maintain heading." Wright's jaw tightened. He expected to run into some resistance. Hopefully this picket force might be the extent of it. They were about to learn what happens when you get between a *Victory*-class battleship and its prey. "Comms, signal Admiral Dobbs, let her know we're engaging a forward picket screen. We'll look to hammer them as we pass through them, but if any survive. Her cruisers will have to clean 'em up."

Within minutes the space ahead of the *Vanguard* erupted in fire as Wright's lead ships opened up with their forward batteries. Magrail rounds and turbo laser bolts zipped across the void, the battleships' superior firepower quickly overwhelming and pummeling the smaller Zodark vessels. Wright barely spared them a passing glance as one of the corvettes exploded after taking multiple direct hits from the main guns. A frigate exploded next when half a dozen magrail slugs ripped the vessel in half before it blew apart. His ship barely registered the enemy fire, their lasers not nearly strong enough to penetrate the Bronkis5 armor as the *Vanguard* sailed past them.

"Thalyss rings now on long-range sensors," Commander Hill reported. "Confirming five operational rings, heavy industrial activity. I'm reading... good Lord, there's got to be at least fifty ships in those construction berths."

"Wow, that's incredible. Let's make sure they stay there permanently, shall we?" Wright keyed the squadron channel. "All Hammer Strike vessels, this is *Vanguard* Actual. Thirty minutes to primary weapons range. Prepare to execute Attack Pattern Typhoon once you see us fire the first shots."

Wright watched as the shipyard continued to grow in size the closer they got to it. He had to admit, it was impressive. Behind each construction slip looked to be multiple factories and ore foundries. Their close proximity to the ships being built likely cut down on the production time needed to build them. Say what you wanted about the Zodarks, they weren't stupid, even if they were savages in the way they treated anyone they encountered.

"Sir, we're approaching optimal range to begin firing the primary and secondary turrets," announced Lieutenant Latter, waiting for him to give the order and initiate the attack. The moment the *Vanguard* opened fire, the rest of the squadron would join in.

Turning to face his helmsman, Wright directed, "Lieutenant Godley, bring us to starboard three-five degrees and reduce engines to fifty percent."

The plan called for them to reduce their approach speed while executing a gradual starboard turn, presenting their port battery to the shipyard rings. This would allow their squadron to deliver a sustained, devastating broadside as they passed the facility. By timing their approach with Thalyss's gravity well, they could use the moon's pull to assist their turn and maintain momentum, slingshotting around it and back toward their original vector without burning excessive fuel or sacrificing the speed they'd built up during their attack run.

"Lieutenant Latter, commence firing—all gun turrets are weapons free. Let's wreck the place," ordered Wright with a devilish smile.

No sooner had Wright given the order than he felt the deck plating beneath his feet shudder violently. The *Vanguard*'s thirteen portside twin-barreled thirty-six-inch magnetic railguns spoke in thunderous sequence, each barrel accelerating multiton projectiles to relativistic velocities. Between the magrail salvos, seven triple-barrel turbo laser turrets added their own fury—brilliant lances of coherent energy that painted the void in shades of crimson and gold.

On the main monitor, Wright watched the devastation unfold in real time. The magrail slugs—dense tungsten-carbide penetrators tipped with delayed-fuse warheads—crossed the intervening space as barely visible streaks of displaced particles. Where they struck Shipyard Ring

Two, massive sections of hull plating crumpled like aluminum foil. The kinetic impact alone vaporized metal in expanding spheres of superheated gas before the warheads detonated seconds later, erupting from within the ring's structure in volcanic gouts of flame and debris.

The turbo lasers painted a different kind of destruction. Ruby beams sliced through the shipyard's skeleton with surgical precision, melting through support struts and docking clamps. Where the magrails smashed and shattered, the lasers cut and burned. Wright watched one beam track across a half-completed destroyer caught in its construction berth—the ship's unfinished hull glowed white-hot before splitting open like overripe fruit.

"Secondary batteries engaging," Latter reported as the smaller guns joined the symphony of destruction.

The monitor filled with a storm of fire. Eleven quad-barrel sixteen-inch magrails spat streams of smaller but still devastating projectiles, their higher rate of fire turning sections of the shipyard into swiss cheese. The eighteen portside antimissile turbo lasers, freed from point-defense duties, added their rapid-fire pulses to the barrage. It was controlled chaos—alternating waves of kinetic hammers and energy scalpels dissecting the Zodark facility with methodical brutality.

"My God," someone whispered. Wright couldn't tell who—his eyes remained fixed on the screen as a massive fuel depot took a direct hit from a thirty-six-inch slug. The explosion bloomed outward in perfect silence, consuming three construction bays and the corvettes they'd been birthing.

The *Vanguard* continued her stately turn, bringing fresh gun batteries to bear while the port weapons cycled through their reload sequences. Behind her, the rest of Hammer Strike added their own fire to the apocalypse. Through the tactical overlay, Wright could see the devastating effectiveness of their attack pattern—overlapping fields of fire that left no section of the shipyard untouched.

"Ring Three is breaking up," his tactical officer reported. "Structural integrity failing across... wait. Sir, I'm reading massive secondary explosions in Ring Four's antimatter storage!"

The main screen flared white as a new sun briefly bloomed where the storage facility had been. When the filters compensated, Wright saw Ring Four had simply ceased to exist—only an expanding cloud of ionized gas and tumbling debris marked where thousands of Zodark shipwrights had been working moments before.

Wright finally turned away from the destruction of the shipyard to catch up on the battle continuing to rage in the other areas of the system. Behind him, his tactical plot showed the larger picture he was looking for. Velkryn's defenders had fully committed to engaging the *Freedom*, while Ethan's strike wings approached Nargulon unmolested. The Zodarks were reacting exactly as Viceroy Hunt had predicted—defending what they thought mattered most while their real vulnerabilities burned.

"Whoa, Captain!" exclaimed Commander Little, his XO, her voice cracking with urgency. "I don't know where they came from, but we have six Zodark battleships emerging from behind Thalyss's shadow. They must've been hiding in the moon's sensor blind spot!"

Wright spun to the display. The enemy battleships—older *Drovak*-class vessels—accelerated hard toward his squadron's flank, their weapons already tracking. A classic ambush, using the moon's mass to mask their presence.

"All ships, emergency turn to starboard!" Wright barked. "Bring main batteries to bear—"

"Sir, the Humtar ships!" his tactical officer interrupted. "They're breaking formation!"

On the display, the CNS *Razorwind* and CNS *Dark Omen*—the two *Warclaw*-class light battleships assigned to Hammer Strike—suddenly surged forward with impossible acceleration. The Humtar vessels, each only 1,400 meters long, looked like minnows compared to the 2,100-meter Zodark battleships. But what happened next defied everything Wright knew about naval combat.

The *Razorwind* fired first. Its turbo laser batteries—only eight twin mounts compared to a *Victory*'s twenty-six—spoke with a violence that made Wright's breath catch. The coherent beams of energy didn't just strike the lead Zodark battleship's armor—they punched through it like tissue paper. The *Drovak*-class vessel's reinforced bow plating, designed to withstand Republic magrail bombardment, simply ceased to exist.

"Mother of—" someone whispered over the comm.

The *Dark Omen* joined its sister ship, both Humtar vessels accelerating to attack speed that should have torn their hulls apart. Their turbo lasers fired in perfect synchronization, each shot placed with surgical precision. No wasted energy, no suppression fire—every beam found a critical system.

The lead Zodark battleship's reactor containment failed catastrophically. The explosion should have damaged the Humtar ships at that range, but their armor—that strange iridescent material that seemed to drink in energy—barely showed scorch marks.

"Sensors, what am I seeing?" Wright demanded. "How are their weapons doing that?"

"Unknown, sir! Energy readings are off the charts. Their turbo lasers are outputting nearly three times what our models predicted!"

The five remaining Zodark battleships tried to respond, concentrating their fire on the *Razorwind*. Dozens of plasma bolts and turbo laser beams converged on the smaller ship. The impacts should have been devastating. Instead, the Humtar vessel's armor seemed to shimmer, dispersing the energy across its hull in rippling waves of light.

"Their armor's... it's not ablating," the science officer reported, voice filled with awe. "Jesus, it's somehow redistributing the thermal load across the entire hull matrix."

The *Razorwind* and *Dark Omen* split, executing a maneuver Wright had only seen in fighter combat. They curved around the Zodark formation in opposite arcs, their turbo lasers never stopping. Where Zodark weapons splashed harmlessly against Humtar armor, the return fire carved through battleship hulls like a plasma torch through ice.

A second Zodark battleship died as the *Dark Omen*'s guns found its torpedo magazines. The explosion chain-reacted through its hull, breaking the massive vessel into three burning sections. The Humtar ship flew through the debris field without slowing, its armor deflecting multiton chunks of wreckage.

"Captain, the Zodarks are trying to concentrate fire," tactical reported. "They're—no, wait. The Humtar ships are jamming their targeting sensors!"

Wright watched in amazement as the two light battleships systematically dismantled their opponents. They moved like predators, using their superior acceleration to maintain optimal firing positions while denying the Zodarks clean shots. When enemy fire did connect, that impossible armor absorbed or deflected it.

The third and fourth Zodark battleships died within seconds of each other. The *Razorwind* put a full turbo laser salvo through one ship's engineering section, carving out its power systems. The *Dark Omen* simply deleted another vessel's bridge superstructure, leaving it a headless hulk drifting without control.

"This is impossible," Wright muttered. "Those are light battleships. They're half the displacement of their targets."

"Sir, the Humtar vessels are closing on the remaining Zodarks," Commander Hill reported unnecessarily—Wright could see it clearly on the display.

The last two Zodark battleships tried to flee, pouring emergency power to their engines. It didn't matter. The Humtar ships accelerated effortlessly, their superior speed allowing them to maintain perfect firing solutions. Turbo laser fire walked across the fleeing ships' engine blocks with contemptuous ease.

One Zodark battleship's drive section detonated, sending the forward two-thirds tumbling end over end. The other simply... stopped, its engines carved away by surgical fire, leaving it a powerless hulk. The *Razorwind* finished it with a single salvo to its reactor complex.

The entire engagement had lasted less than four minutes. Six Zodark battleships—over twelve thousand crew—reduced to expanding debris fields by two ships that shouldn't have survived the first salvo.

"Captain..." His communications officer's voice was subdued. "Captain Naram-Suen from the *Razorwind* is hailing."

"Put him through."

The Humtar commander's voice was calm, almost bored. "*Vanguard* Actual, this is *Razorwind*. Enemy flank neutralized. Resuming escort position."

Wright found his voice. "Acknowledged, *Razorwind*. That was... exceptional work."

"Standard engagement protocol, *Vanguard*. *Razorwind* out."

Standard. The Humtar considered that slaughter standard. Wright turned to his bridge crew, seeing his own shock reflected in their faces.

"Sir." His weapons officer finally spoke. "If two of their light battleships can do that..."

Wright nodded slowly. The implications were staggering. The Humtar weren't just allies—they were operating on a completely different technological level. Thank God they were on our side.

"Captain, urgent flash traffic from *Freedom*," comms reported, breaking the spell. "Zodark reinforcements jumping in from Gate Two Alpha. Estimated eighty-plus heavies, mostly *Plarix*-class."

Wright smiled grimly. Even with Humtar technology in play, those were daunting odds. More ships pulled from other critical locations, drawn by the *Freedom*'s threat. Every Zodark vessel converging on Velkryn was one less defending their logistics network.

"Acknowledged. Signal Admiral Dobbs—we continue the attack." He turned back to the tactical display as Shipyard Ring Five erupted in flames. "We've got them singing to our tune now. Let's see how they like the music."

In the distance, the Humtar ships had returned to formation, showing no sign of the devastating power they'd just unleashed. But Wright would never look at them the same way again. The battle for Tueblets had begun—not with the crushing fleet engagement the Zodarks expected, but with precise strikes at the tendons and arteries that kept their war machine functioning.

And as Shipyard Ring Six joined its siblings in fiery destruction, Captain Wright knew they were just getting started. But now he also knew they had guardian angels—angels with impossibly advanced armor and weapons that could carve through enemy battleships like a Thanksgiving turkey. The real question now was, What other surprises did the Humtar have waiting for them?

Chapter 40:
The Gathering Storm

Task Force 28
RNS *Vega*
Gravaxia System

The admiral's ready room aboard the star carrier *Vega* had quickly become Vice Admiral Ripley Willis Lee's favorite place aboard his flagship. He'd spent two and a half decades in the Navy, twenty-five years living aboard warships. The *Vega* was his home, and the ready room was his command center. From here, he commanded fifty-six Republic warships alongside the Primord Admiral Stavanger's fleet of one hundred and twenty-seven battle-hardened ships from the previous campaigns they had fought together. The combined combat power of Task Force 28 was immense, and about to be unleashed upon the enemy. As he stood in front of the viewport, he could see the expanse of one hundred and eighty-three ships waiting around the stargate leading into to Tueblets.

Here we are… on the eve of the battle that should end the war. Lee's mind raced with a million ways this could all go sideways on them.

Continuing to stare into the black of the Gravaxia system, he thought back to the multiple battles he'd fought to conquer this system. The lives he'd lost, the ships now nothing more than floating debris where frantic battles had once raged. The wreckage was a monument to the struggle of the men and women who fought there, the destroyed hulls and the frozen corpses of the dead still uncollected. It galled him not to police their dead, to give them the proper honors and military burials they deserved. But while his forces now controlled the vast majority of the space within Gravaxia, they still had yet to subdue the planets within it. Until the threat of planetary raiding parties was eliminated, it was too dangerous to conduct salvage operations without deploying considerable naval forces to protect the salvage and recovery ships.

Lee had heard the Primords were preparing ground forces to eventually subdue the planets and moons of the system. He had no idea if the Republic Army would get involved, but he suspected they would. The RA had fought like savages alongside the Primords in nearly every campaign of the past two decades. He didn't see that changing anytime soon.

Giving credit where credit was due, the Zodarks had fought like devils to hang onto the system. Lee was still chiding himself over the actions of that Delta team that had gotten him into trouble with the Viceroy. That was before the arrival of the Humtars, of course; things were different now. To the shock of everyone, especially the Republic, the Humtars—the elder race that had conquered the stars—were humans, and the Republic were in fact their direct descendants, a lost colony of their former empire.

Closing his eyes, Lee recalled the meeting with Admiral Bailey shortly before leaving for this campaign.

"Ripley, I'm sorry about what happened with Captain Haas, and the Viceroy effectively ending your career after this war is over. I want you to know that I spoke with him about this, and he has agreed the calculus that demanded this action has changed—you will not be retired at the end of the war unless you so desire. When this war is over, Ripley, I intend to retire. It's time for new blood and new ideas to lead Space Command. Admiral Fran McKee is next in line to replace me. Should she turn it down, I want to recommend you as my replacement."

Lee opened his eyes, the conversation having replayed a million times in his head. He'd known Fran his entire career. He couldn't think of a better officer to replace Chester than her. The fact that Chester thought so highly of him still surprised Lee, especially after the disciplinary hearing.

Reflecting on that day, he could see in the Viceroy's eyes how it pained him to punish everyone involved in the whole affair. The Gallentines wanted someone to be held accountable. In all fairness, Lee realized he'd probably gotten off lucky compared to the immediate sentence that had followed for the Delta captain.

Lee had decided that if Fran chose not to accept the role as Head of Space Command, he would. If she did, then her role as Chief of Naval Operations, a role he had come to covet once he'd pinned his first admiral's star, would become his. Very few rose to those lofty ranks. He intended to be one of them.

"Admiral, we received a message from Admiral Stavanger," announced Commander Steve Miller, his senior aide and operations officers. "He reports all Primord ships are ready to jump into Tueblets once the order is given."

He turned to his aide. "Acknowledged. Inform him Task Force 28 stands ready to jump. It shouldn't be long now until the party starts," Lee jested, injecting a little humor to cut through some of the tension.

"Aye-aye, Admiral," Miller acknowledged with a slight smile.

Lee scrolled through the current fleet status. His flagship, the star carrier RNS *Vega*, dominated the formation, thirty-two hundred meters of Bronkis5 armor and enough firepower to devastate a fleet on its own. His former command, RNS *Cassiopeia*, along with the RNS *Rass* and *Majestic*, were the only *Victory*-class battleships in his formation. They comprised the bulk of his heavy-hitting combat power outside his space wings. The *Cassi* and *Rass* were thirty kilometers on his starboard flank, while the *Majestic* was to his port.

Flanking his capital ships were the battle cruisers *Invincible* and *Resolute*. For escorts, he had ten corvettes interspersed between his capital ships for antifighter support with fifteen heavy cruisers and twenty-five frigates spread across the edges of his formation. He had the heavy cruiser *Nebraska* positioned with the Primord contingent, her captain serving as his liaison with Admiral Stavanger. This was by far the largest fleet action he had been a part of since the Intus Invasion.

Lee's hand reached up to his chest, touching the cross beneath his uniform collar. He took a deep breath and closed his eyes for just a moment. That was when he would hear the voice of his mentor speak to him. Captain James Oldendorf's voice echoed in his mind: "*Command means you hold the steering wheel of other people's lives, Lieutenant. They are trusting you to drive them home. To protect them, to lead them. That trust placed in you—never forget that trust is earned one decision at a time. That's a weight that never gets lighter, but your shoulders will get stronger.*"

The old man had understood something about leadership that couldn't be taught in academies. Lee felt damn lucky to have had the man as his first captain. Lee fought to retain every word the old man had spoken, as if by pure determination he could keep Captain Oldendorf's voice alive in his mind. So many years had passed, but somehow— maybe by grace, or by the relentless will of a student who refused to forget his teacher—that old captain's wisdom surfaced exactly when Lee needed it most. And every time, it arrived like answers to prayers he hadn't known he was praying.

The door chimed. Lee heard it, his eyes focused on the void. "Come in," he called, waiting to hear who it was.

He turned when he heard steps approaching and saw Commander Lucia Rodriguez. She carried a secured data pad and that serious expression of hers. He guessed she was about to give him the news that he, Commander Miller, and Captain Noriko Sato had been waiting for. Truth be told, he felt damn lucky he had been able to reconstitute many of the officers he'd served with over the years. He trusted them implicitly, and trust was what he needed when commanding a fleet of this size.

Behind him, Sato had been sitting at a small table, her face buried in a tablet for the past fifteen minutes. She'd been reviewing some information from the upper brass. She was quiet as ever, focused as usual. While Lee commanded the fleet, she commanded the *Vega*. It felt right that she should command his flagship. She'd been his XO on and off for a decade and a half. She'd earned this command, and he was proud to have recommended her for it.

Rodriguez cleared her throat. "Admiral, Captain, Commander, we received the final defensive analysis of Tueblets from the CNS *Bloodhawk*. I'll bring it up for you," she announced as she activated the room's tactical action map. A holographic display floated between them. Lee studied the projections intently, looking for changes from the previous intelligence reports.

Several planets orbited a yellow star, with the gas giant Zeta and its moon network forming the center. Velkryn, the largest moon, was home to the Zodark Military High Command. Tueblets was the heart of the Zodark Empire, a hub system with eight stargates that stitched the Empire together. Its capture thereby cut the Empire into eight segments that could be picked off at their leisure.

"What's their strength at in the system?" Lee asked, his eyes fixed on something else.

"Still formidable, but predictable. Humtar surveillance ships have given us a detailed breakdown of what to expect. The Zodarks continue to concentrate their heaviest units around Velkryn and the orbital command facilities. It's rumored their Zon might even be there," explained Rodriguez as she highlighted the enemy positions.

"Intelligence counts four hundred and seventy warships in the primary defensive zone."

Commander Miller let out a soft whistle. "That's a lot of ships..." His voice trailed off.

The numbers were significant. Lee had faced tough odds in the past, but these might prove to be the toughest yet. As with most military plans, the key to success lay in the timing and positioning of their joint fleets—Gravaxia and the Viceroy's in Rhea. "Any change to their patrol patterns?"

"Negative. No change to their routine sweeps—still six-hour rotations. Humtar intelligence estimates their response time from outlying positions to Velkryn, around forty-five minutes at maximum acceleration." Rodriguez expanded the display to show the predicted algorithmic movement patterns based on weeks of observation.

Lee nodded. The *Freedom*'s arrival with the largest allied fleet in history would trigger every defensive instinct the Zodarks possessed. "Excellent. Thank you, Rodriguez."

She dipped her head. "Sir, ma'am, I'll be on the bridge if you need me," she said and left the room.

"Admiral," Sato said, her tablet still resting in her palms, "I've reviewed the operational plan with the senior staff again. With Task Force 28's role as the mallet to Hunt's anvil, the timing has to be damn near perfect for this to work."

"And it will be, or near as it can be. Don't forget, Sato—everyone has a plan until they get punched in the face. This is no different. We'll adapt and improvise if we have to." He grinned and winked at her, knowing it would drive the perfectionist nuts.

She wasn't wrong about the complexity of the plan. During briefings, the slides and diagrams made it sound simple. Phase One—the *Freedom* would jump into Tueblets with the Humtar fleet. They'd then engage the primary defensive force, drawing the enemy to them like a moth to a flame. The Zodarks would respond by committing their reserves to the engagement, and that was when TF 28 would join the fray.

Phase Two—his element would jump into the system once the enemy had fully committed. Lee's joint task force would hit the enemy formation from the rear, causing the Zodarks to focus on the *Freedom* and the Humtar ships.

Sounded easy, but as Sato was also seeing, as many times as Lee went over it, everything that could go wrong stacked up like dominoes. Jump too early, and the Zodarks would spot Task Force 28's arrival before committing their reserves. If that happened, the reserve force camping on the other side of the gate would greet them upon entry. It would tie his forces up, keeping them stuck at the gate instead of pinning the Zodark main force between Hunt's fleet and his own. If they jumped too late, Hunt's fleet might get torn apart before Lee could relieve the pressure.

The stargate jump calculations alone required split-second coordination across light-years. If it wasn't for the Quantum Beamlink upgrade in their comms network, he doubted they could have coordinated such a complicated plan. Like all battles, there were other variables you couldn't always account for, like Zodark response times, fleet positioning, communication delays between systems. A single missed signal, one navigation error, or an unexpected enemy maneuver could collapse the entire operation. Lee just hoped Hunt knew what he was doing. This wasn't just another battle. They were betting the house, going all in on a single battle in hopes of ending the war.

With his finger, Lee traced the projected courses of their two fleets. Part of the plan relied on Zodark predictability and Hunt's ability to absorb punishment while maintaining offensive capability. Task Force 28 would exploit the tunnel vision that came with the enemy's desperation and shock that comes when being invaded. Then the enemy's hesitation and confusion with their sudden need to defend the sector would expose the enemy in a myriad of ways.

His personal communicator buzzed with an encrypted priority message. He walked over to his desk and activated the holographic display. Admiral Stavanger's face materialized above the desktop.

"Admiral Lee, my friend… we have received word from Viceroy Hunt. It's official. They have begun the invasion of Tueblets. The Altairians and Humtar Fleets crossed into the system with the *Freedom*. This is going to be a fight for the ages, Lee. The battle to end the war. Stand by for orders to jump, and I'll see you on the other side," relayed the Primord admiral excitedly before ending the call.

Sato checked her data pad. "Admiral, he's right. We just received the same message from Admiral McKee. We're to stand by for orders to jump."

Lee acknowledged the order, then returned his gaze to the fleet assembled before him. Tens of thousands of spacers were about to jump into whatever was waiting for them in Tueblets. He also knew some of them wouldn't come home from this fight. That was a reality of war. Good people had to die. You tried to minimize it as best you could, but in the end, good people would have to die to win the day and, if they were lucky, end the war and the Zodark threat once and for all.

This was one aspect of command he hated the most—knowing his spacers were going to die once the order to invade was given. It was a hard reality, but it came with the burden of command, or at least that was the guiding philosophy Viceroy Hunt instilled in all of them.

He touched his cross again. Captain Oldendorf had worn an identical cross through fights that became legend and choices that rewrote fleet doctrine long after he died. The old man had known what it meant to sign death warrants with the stroke of a pen, to sleep each night knowing you'd traded lives for objectives.

Faith doesn't make the burden lighter, Lee thought, *it just makes it more bearable.*

The door chimed again. Lee looked over his shoulder. "Enter."

Commander Connor Rhom stepped inside. His data pad showed priority intelligence markers. At the same time, his expression told Lee that complications were about to make everything worse.

"Admiral, we have a problem," Rhom announced as he brought up the latest report they had received. "The Humtar ship, *Voidraven*, in the Varkorion system, reports a large fleet movement toward the gate leading into Tueblets. They are reporting sixty-plus ships approaching the gate. We also received a message from Admiral Wiyrkomi, aboard the *Freedom*. The Zodark fleet camping at the Gravaxia gate has left. They're en route to link up with the main Zodark fleet engaging the *Freedom*."

"Really?" Lee asked in surprise. He had thought the Zodarks would take more time before committing their reserves, but apparently not. Before Lee could respond, his communicator buzzed again. He saw it was a priority transmission from Allied Fleet Command.

He opened the message to the order he knew was coming. "Admiral Lee, Task Force 28 is ordered to jump immediately into the Tueblets system. Proceed to coordinates Gamma-One-Nine and engage Zodark forces as planned," came the message from Viceroy Hunt.

Lee looked at his officers. They knew what had happened without him voicing it. "We have our orders, people. It's time to earn our pay and go kick some ass."

Chapter 41:
The Brotherhood

Flight Deck Operations
RNS *Vega*

Three hundred meters of flight deck sprawled before Blake "Coop" Cooper. Floodlights glared brightly, giving maintenance crews enough illumination as they crawled over the parked Gripen IIs. Tools clanged against hull plating. Pneumatic wrenches whined while techs torqued down engine mounting bolts. Missile racks scraped against metal as crews loaded fresh ordnance. Somewhere a tech cursed as he cleaned plasma residue from laser cannon barrels. Another ran diagnostics cable through a cockpit access panel. And on and on it went, and all to prepare the fighters for combat.

Coop walked the perimeter, then paused beside a tech crouched under a Gripen's underbelly. The kid couldn't have been more than twenty. From the expression on the young man's face, the guy was flushed with frustration. He'd been fighting with a railgun pylon that had apparently jammed mid-calibration. As Coop looked the spacer up and down, the man's hands shook as he tried to force the mechanism. It meant the ensign had been at this for far too long, overstraining his muscles. It was probably like the kid's mind right now—overstrained.

"Breathe, kid. It's not biting back today." Coop rolled up his sleeves and knelt in the deck grime beside the fighter. "What's the problem?"

The tech looked up, eyes wide. "Sorry, sir, this mount's been giving me hell. The shear pin keeps slipping every time I try to lock it down."

Coop examined the weapon's housing. Standard-issue headache, but a no-brainer. He'd seen this a few times. "Twist from the shear pin, not the mount, or you'll strip the threads like I did on my first tour with these birds."

Together, they worked the mechanism. Coop guided the young tech through the process, showing him the proper angle and pressure. The pylon clicked into place with a *thunk*.

The spacer grinned and wiped his forehead with his sleeve, leaving a grease mark. "Thank you, sir."

Coop rubbed his hands together. "No problem, son. You've got the hands for this deck, Spacer. Keep them steady. Keep what you learn in your head at all times, OK? You never know when the right solution might pop up, at the last minute and in the nick of time. Seen it often. Also, next time you have an issue, ask for help, don't struggle like that, understand?"

"Understood, sir."

"Good."

He left the tech and headed for the ladder well. As he descended toward the tactical operations center, his mind drifted to other decks, other wars. Flashes of his maverick days surfaced. Barrel rolls and going rogue against Zodark troop transports on New Eden. Uncovering an enemy spoof op on planet Intus and drowning the hostiles' base in missiles and lasers. Glory-chasing dogfights where he'd broken formation to rack up kills, both in training and during real combat. Now those memories felt like watching someone else's life. Used to be about the kill count. Always the tally. Competition against his own squadron. Now it was about getting his pilots home to chase skirts on the next Earther world over.

What a career it'd been.

The tactical op center was busy when Coop sealed himself inside. Holodisplays flashed on the bulkheads, the screens flowing with data streams. He pulled up the fresh Fleet intel dump.

His shoulders fell a few centimeters.

The displays in front of him showed Zodark reinforcements jumping in from the Varkorion system—Shwani's sector, where the Groff secret police had their headquarters. Word on the street was the those shadowy bastards had been creating their own ghost fleet. Now it was vectoring straight for the *Freedom* and Humtar anvil. He wasn't sure how, but he was certain this new development was about to change things. He wondered when orders would ping through, telling to *Vega* jump through sooner rather than later, to link up and prosecute the attack.

When he clicked on the details of these new battleships the Zodarks had built, he whistled softly at the sheer size of them. They were beasts. Then he saw something else, a new ship intelligence said the Zodarks were calling Victory boats—V-boats for short.

Huh, what in the world are those for?

Coop zoomed in on the threat assessment. *Oh, Badger would love this*, he thought. The pilot had the reflexes for Gripens.

Commander Riggs stepped into the room, salt and pepper across his hair and growing stubble. The commander's flight jacket hung loose over one shoulder like he'd just crawled from a cockpit.

"Captain, these flyboys are primed, but we're staring down a meat grinder." Riggs leaned against the display table, studying the tactical data. "Last sims had us losing eight birds."

Coop paced around the holographic Tueblets system, its gas giant and moon network rotating slowly between them. "Readiness status?"

"Ninety-six percent quals green, but fatigue's creeping in. Three pilots nursing significant pain from the last battle we'd just had." Riggs scratched his jaw. "Losses projection? Twenty to thirty percent attrition if these death boats, or whatever the hell they're called, deploy a strength we don't yet know and hit us across the side of our damned faces... sir. Can't sugarcoat it. Tell them straight, or we'll have mutiny in the bays."

Riggs ran hot on everything. Casualties, timelines, threat assessments. Most of the time his numbers landed somewhere in the ballpark of reality, but he always padded them like he was planning for the apocalypse. The problem was those rare times when his worst-case scenarios played out exactly as predicted. Smart money said you prepared for his calculations regardless, because the man was a walking stim pill who'd never met a problem he couldn't multiply by three.

"We shield the anvil, Riggs. Your wingmen hold the line. Simple is as simple does."

"Aye, Captain."

They clasped hands briefly. It was a gesture rarely performed in the military, but these two had shared years of combat, and luck. You didn't fix what wasn't broken, or in other words, you didn't change what worked, and these handshakes somehow kept them alive to help humanity for yet another day. At least, that was how they squared it with one another.

Minutes later, the squadron leaders filed into Tactical Ops. Seasoned pilots carrying data pads and serious expressions. Captain Hamilt led the interceptor group, already studying the holographic display. Other fighter leads and two bomber squadron leads flanked her.

Coop wasted no time. "*Freedom* and the Humtars drop the mallet. They're through the gate and in combat now. As you know, they draw the Zodarks' teeth to Velkryn. We are the anvil's edge." He motioned at the display, highlighting key positions. "Your squadrons screen the fleet, vectoring combat space patrol to shred inbounds before they kiss our hulls. Reserves commit? That's our window. Peel off flights, prosecute runners. No escapes, ladies and gents. We've briefed this before. You know this like the back of your hands. Tueblets falls on our blades. We do this right, the war ends here."

The leaders nodded. Quick. To the point. No questions. The leads had this locked down and airtight in their minds after multiple briefings. There wasn't any time to brief more, as they'd be pushing through the stargate very soon.

As they filed out, Coop pulled up Badger's file on his data pad. The hotshot lieutenant junior grade stared back from his service photo. The guy had the most kills, and his sim scores had spiked fifteen percent during the most recent sessions. The pilot was shedding his glory itch, had even nailed a four-on-one Vulture takedown in yesterday's drills. But Coop still saw those stars in the young pilot's eager eyes. *Can't let him chase them into the dark.* Protecting the squadron meant reining in echoes of his past self.

Minutes later, the ready room came alive with nervous energy as pilots crammed into the space. Holoscreens looped Tueblets overlays while countdown clocks ticked toward jump time. The room felt smaller with all of them packed inside. Shoulders touched as they settled around battered tables.

Coop stood on the small podium, a patched leather chair serving as his throne. He spoke over the chatter. "This might be the last big dance, folks. Tueblets is their Alamo. We jump now, link the anvil, and swing." They, too, like the leads, had been briefed multiple times on what to expect once the invasion got underway. "But hear this... we're not here for medals or epitaphs. The age-old adage is true, that dead heroes can't fly home. Keep your six clear, buddy up, and return to base with war stories to tell your grandkids... all of you."

A pilot in the back raised his hand. "Captain, what about those Humtar allies? Their tech specs are off the charts?"

Coop managed a grin. "Twenty-two warships. *Voidhammer*s and *Ironveil*s with armor that can take a beating more than anything else out there. You've probably heard about their infiltration frigates mapping targets down to the last rivet, eh? That's outstanding. Get inspired, ladies and gentlemen. We've got their tactical data feeding our systems right now, and it's looking good."

He turned to the holo. "Those Humtar battleships hit like freight trains and move faster than anything their size should. Take notes, people. If they can bend physics, we can learn from it. Use their example to push your birds harder. Got it?"

"Yes, sir!" they replied in unison.

Next, he fielded quick questions about tactics—"Jink high, laser arcs low"—then broke the group into element briefs as the squadron leaders took over their subgroups.

As the room erupted into smaller planning sessions, Coop lingered at his locker. He pulled out a faded holoframe, its edges cracked from too many combat deployments. A grainy squad picture from his old squadron, the Jolly Rogers, showed grinning faces, half now long dead. Ninja. Ghostdog. Lucky. And others. Gone to Vulture swarms, some during Rass, some during Alfheim, and others elsewhere on missions he couldn't talk about, even behind closed doors. Even his old best bud, someone he still cringed when thinking about. What would have been if that old bear of a man was still alive?

He touched the scars on the glass. They should have wings, not coffins. Every damn one of them.

Badger paused nearby, offering a silent nod of respect. The brotherhood moment hung between them before the young pilot rejoined his element. That grin was still too wide, too eager. Give it a side of arrogance, and it would be way too much, and if that was the case, he'd sit the fellow pilot out. But it wasn't, and all for the better.

Coop pocketed the frame and steeled himself for the storm of battle ahead.

The alert klaxon cut through the planning sessions. Harsh tones echoed off the bulkheads as red lights pulsed overhead.

"Captain Blake Cooper and all senior officers to the admiral's conference room. Jump sequence initiating."

Pilots scattered toward the flight deck. Coop strode toward the bridge levels with Riggs at his flank, wondering what this was about. Sure, he'd thought they'd up the jump time, but now? Their boots clacked against the deck plating.

"Anvil's set, Captain," Riggs said. "Let's hammer."

That's Riggs for you, Coop thought. The man's solution to every tactical problem was to hit it harder until it broke.

The conference room filled quickly with the senior staff. Admiral Lee stood at the head of the table, both palms on the tabletop, leaning forward and eyeing every single person in the room. The holoscreen showed Task Force 28 in formation. One hundred and eighty-six ships preparing for the jump into hell.

"Gentlemen," Lee said. "The situation has changed. Zodark reinforcements from Varkorion are already en route to Tueblets. We jump immediately to support the *Freedom*."

Lee looked at Coop from across the table. "Captain Cooper, your wing runs fleet defense. No enemy fighters get through to our big guns."

"Understood, Admiral. My birds are your umbrella. We'll keep the rain off."

The briefing lasted eight minutes. Orders cascaded down the chain like falling dominoes, each link in the command structure adding their piece to the puzzle. Coop was back on the flight deck before the reverberations of Lee's final words faded.

The Gripen IIs sat in perfect rows. Each fighter carried eight JATMs nestled in their weapons bays and four laser cannons mounted on the fuselages. They were nothing but beautiful death machines waiting for their moment in time.

Pilots jogged past him toward their birds, flight suits zipped and helmets tucked under arms. The deck crews moved fast, final checks completed in minutes. Badger caught his eye from across the deck, offering a sharp salute before climbing into his cockpit. That grin was still there.

Damn that grin.

After he stepped up the ladder into his Gripen II's cockpit, Coop ran through his preflight checks. The stargate loomed ahead, a doorway to extreme mayhem. Soon the fleet would slide through that portal and into whatever nightmare waited on the other side. He'd led his pilots through dozens and dozens of battles, but this felt different. This felt final. And for the sake of humanity, and for the sake of the galaxy, he hoped this was indeed the battle to finally end the war.

Chapter 42:
Into the Maelstrom

Task Force 28
RNS *Vega*
Tueblets System

The stargate spat Admiral Lee's task force into the void of empty space. Once his fleet had fully emerged, they jumped to the coordinates they'd been given and braced for impact. They'd dropped out of FTL directly into hell. What he saw through the main viewport made his stomach churn. They'd landed in a cauldron, a killing field of hundreds and hundreds of warships.

Everywhere Lee looked, he could see weapons fire shooting across space. Fire clouds blasted here and there against the starfield, ships finding their demise quickly—cracking in half, listing starboard or port as they vented atmosphere or lost power, knocked out of the fight.

Unfolding before Lee was the largest fleet battle in human history.

My God... that's a lot of ships... how in the hell are we going to survive this? he thought.

"Jesus, Admiral, would you look at that?" said Commander Miller as the main display showed the grandeur of the battle before them.

Lee could see several massive allied formations engaged in combat. Anchored around the RNS *Freedom* were more than a hundred Republic warships, from a handful of battleships to dozens and dozens of battle cruisers and heavy cruisers, trading salvos with Zodark defenders.

The Altairians, true to their word, had arrived with a fleet of a hundred and forty-two ships, the largest allied deployment in their history. He watched their battle lines press the attack on the enemy flanks, moving to envelop them.

In the center of it all was the Humtar contingent, twenty-two warships led by their massive *Voidhammer*-class heavy battleships. He marveled at the sheer power of these warships as they fired volleys that melted through Zodark armor like it was nothing. The Zodarks, for their part, were laying into the Humtar ships, desperately trying to slow them down or stop them from decimating their ranks.

It didn't take long before contact reports began littering the tactical display. Hundreds and hundreds of vessels in battle across several sectors of the system. In the distance, the Nargulon refueling depot burned brightly under a swarm attack of Gallentine starfighters and bombers. In another sector, the Thalyss shipyards were being savaged by a squadron of Republic battleships and a pair of Humtar vessels. At Velkryn, the main fleet traded barrages with the Zodarks in a running battle stretching across half the moon's orbital zone with a spectacular display of lasers, missiles, plasma torpedoes and magrail projectiles.

"Admiral," Commander Rhom said from his station. "Fleet Command is ordering us to engage the rear elements of the Zodark reinforcement fleet. They're vectoring in from the outer system."

The tactical holo materialized above the command deck. Eighty-plus contact markers moved in formation toward the main engagement. Each one larger than anything they'd faced before.

Lee swallowed hard. "Ship class analysis?"

"At least forty of them are those new *Plarix*-class battleships, sir. Significantly larger than standard Zodark vessels."

"Specs?" Lee demanded.

"Pulling up the intelligence files now, Admiral."

Lee leaned over the tactical display as the data streamed across his screen. Twenty-one hundred meters long. Forty-five million metric tons. Thirty percent larger than the *Drovak*-class battleships they'd faced before. He read down the readout. Twelve main laser batteries instead of ten. Eighteen secondary batteries. One hundred and twenty point-defense guns.

Fifty percent more defensive fire than anything in their database.

The armor specifications made it worse. Layered Bronkis5 composite plating that could absorb thirty to forty percent more punishment than previous Zodark classes. Advanced thermal-masking systems. Multispectrum chaff launchers.

Lee straightened. The Zodark reinforcements had positioned themselves to flank Hunt's forces. If they reached the main battle, they'd roll up nearly three hundred allied ships from behind. The Republic, Altairian, and Humtar fleets were fully committed to their frontal assault. They couldn't turn to face this new threat without exposing themselves to the primary Zodark defensive positions.

And now he knew exactly what kind of monsters his ships would face.

"Signal all ships," Lee ordered. "Form a battle line abreast our position and prepare to engage the enemy."

Captain Sato looked up from her captain's chair. "Admiral, we dropped in near them at forty thousand kilometers. That's not a lot of time for long-range maneuvering."

"Then we don't maneuver. We hit them hard and fast." Lee pressed the fleet comm. "All ships, this is Admiral Lee. We've dropped directly behind their formation at forty thousand kilometers. Maximum deceleration on my mark. Weapons free the moment your ships achieve lock."

The minutes stretched as Task Force 28 adjusted course for the attack run while the Zodark reinforcements maintained their advance toward the main battle, unaware of the incoming threat from their rear.

Lee counted down the minutes as the battle continued to rage. Task Force 28's hundred and eighty-six Republic and Primord warships cut the distance to thirty thousand kilometers.

"Weapons free!" Lee shouted as he saw Rhom's gun crews achieve lock.

The fleet's magrails, missiles, and turbo lasers brightened the expanse, with concentrated firepower focused on the rear elements of the Zodark formation. A pair of *Plarix* battleships trailing the formation were caught completely off guard. The ships were hammered with a thunderous barrage of more than a dozen warships. In seconds, armor plating was being vaporized as giant holes were being cut into the guts of the ships. As magrail slugs hammered home, internal explosions rippled across their hulls, secondary explosions tearing the ships apart.

"Pour it on!" Lee commanded. "Don't give them time to turn those guns on us!"

The Republic *Virginia*-class battleships main batteries started cutting loose. Their sixteen-inch magrails started punching holes through Zodark armor. The battle cruisers *Artemis* and *Orion* flanked the formation. Their numerous weapons systems took chunks out of enemy exteriors.

For ninety seconds, it looked like the surprise attack might shatter the enemy formation completely.

Then Commander Rhom ended the illusion. "Sir, I'm reading small emerging from near those enemy battleships—oh wow, they look to be those V-boats we were warned about."

Hundreds of tiny contacts that had been hugging the larger Zodark vessels started separating from the shadows they'd been hiding within. Each ship was no larger than a shuttle, but accelerating at incredible speeds.

"What's their intercept time?" Lee asked.

"Forty seconds at current velocity," Rhom replied. "Admiral, they're weaving through our defensive fire like it's not even there. A few of them took direct hits and seemed to shrug it off."

Through the main viewer, the first wave of small craft approached RNS *Longbow*, a frigate holding position on the formation's starboard flank. The frigate's point-defense systems opened up, filling space with laser fire and kinetic rounds.

The first impact came suddenly. A single small craft punched through *Longbow*'s hull amidships and detonated inside. The frigate broke in half. Her forward and aft sections spun away from each other in a brilliant flash. Hundreds of lives gone in seconds.

"What in God's name are those things?" Lee whispered. He knew their nickname—death boats—but it was the first time he'd seen those little demons in combat.

Another impact. RNS *Stalwart*, another frigate screening the formation's port side, took a direct hit from one of the craft. The entire forward section vaporized in a ball of plasma. The remainder of the ship tumbled away. Atmosphere bled from a dozen hull breaches.

"Analysis, Commander!" Lee demanded.

Rhom's mouth moved as he silently read the scrolling text on his console. "They're like some kind of torpedo, sir. Maybe manned? I'm not sure. I can't get a clear energy signature on that. Velocity thirty kilometers per second and climbing. They're maintaining attack vectors despite our defensive fire, but they're using microcorrections to avoid point-defense targeting solutions. Each impact registers equivalent to three torpedo warheads." He paused, eyeing the readouts. "Sir, telemetry indicates these may indeed be manned craft executing deliberate ramming attacks. They're carrying some kind of high-yield warhead that detonates on impact. Their small profile and speed are making them nearly impossible to track with our standard fire control systems."

"Kamikaze runs?" Lee asked incredulously.

Rhom hesitated before responding. "I never would have thought so, but it appears that way. Most likely some sort of suicide attacks."

The little atrocities began hitting all across Task Force 28's formation. RNS *Kraken*, a heavy cruiser, took two impacts within seconds of each other. Massive internal explosions gutted her engineering section. The ship began to drift out of formation, her main guns falling silent.

"All ships, target those small craft!" Lee shouted into the fleet comm. "Point defense, maximum rate of fire!"

He switched to the flight operations channel. "Cooper! Get your fighters out there now! We need them targeting those suicide craft!"

Captain Cooper's voice crackled back immediately. "On it, Admiral! Launching now!"

Through the viewport, Gripen fighters streaked from *Vega's* launch bays. The interceptors engaged the incoming swarm right away, their laser cannons picking off individual targets. But for every death boat destroyed, three more slipped through the defensive screen.

The Primord ships adapted faster than the Republic vessels. Their alien point-defense systems seemed better suited to tracking multiple smaller targets at a time. A partial window on the main viewscreen showed a Primord cruiser shred a cluster of incoming craft with weapons firing in rapid patterns.

The Republic ships struggled. Their defensive systems had been designed to engage large targets at long range, not swarms of suicide craft at knife-fighting distance.

Another cruiser died. RNS *Portland* took a single impact near her reactor compartment. The explosion tore through half the ship before the automatic containment systems could respond. She rolled away from the formation, her hull glowing orange and red, reminding Lee of embers from a dying campfire.

"Loss count, Commander," Lee ordered.

"Twelve ships destroyed, fifteen damaged," Rhom responded.

Lee cringed. *And in the first five minutes of engagement.*

The swarm of death boats moved fast around Task Force 28's formation. Each impact meant hundreds of dead crew members. Each loss weakened their ability to hold the line.

The massive *Plarix* battleships began their turn and brought their main armaments to bear on the allied formation. Lee realized that Task Force 28 was caught between the suicide craft and enemy battleship guns. In minutes, those heavy weapons would start blasting away.

"Admiral," Sato said, "recommend emergency withdrawal. We can't sustain these losses."

For a moment, Lee hesitated. The seconds seemed like ten minutes as possibilities tumbled through his mind. Run now and save what remained of Task Force 28. Or hold position and watch his command get torn apart by hundreds of suicide craft while Hunt's three hundred ships faced annihilation from behind. It could mean losing eighty ships to save three hundred, or losing all three hundred and eighty when the Zodark reinforcements rolled up the entire allied formation. Lee saw the faces of his bridge crew, the thousands of spacers trusting his decision, the wider consequences rippling across the entire sector if they failed here. The choices. Run now and save what remained of Task Force 28, or hold position and prevent the Zodark reinforcements from flanking Hunt's main force.

In truth, his decision was easy.

"All ships maintain attack!" Lee commanded. "If we run now, they'll turn on the flank of the main fleet!"

The bridge shuddered when something slammed into *Vega*'s starboard hull. It shook again, this time more violently. Damage reports flooded in from across the ship. A death boat had managed a glancing blow. It tore through two decks before its warhead detonated against the secondary armor.

"Minimal damage to primary systems," Sato reported. "Hull breach sealed."

It felt like time stopped, at least for Lee, anyway.

He locked his fingers across his stomach and closed his eyes. In the middle of hell, with death boats screaming toward his ships and suicide pilots ready to tear his fleet apart, there was only one thing left to do. The most strategic move in any battle. The most important weapon he had—prayer.

At the end of the day, Lee didn't serve the Republic Navy. He didn't serve Viceroy Hunt or the war machine or even humanity itself. He served God. The same God who'd given him the guts to face down impossible odds before. The same God who'd carried him through years of this nightmare war.

Lord, help us hold the line. Give me wisdom to see the path through this mess. Give my crews steady hands and true aim. If today's our day to die, let us die well. Let us buy Hunt the time he needs. Let us stand between evil and the innocent one more time. Give me strength, Lord. Give us all strength.

Lee turned back to the tactical display. The death boats continued their assault. But his ships were adapting. Fighter screens tightened. Point-defense patterns improved. The Primord vessels shared targeting data with their Republic counterparts.

The *Plarix* battleships completed their turn. Their gun ports opened along their massive hulls, and they took aim.

"All ships, emergency evasive maneuvers!" Lee ordered. "Present minimal profiles!"

Two more *Plarix* battleships succumbed to the sustained bombardment, but the remaining enemy vessels pressed their advance.

"Cooper, status report!" Lee called to his fighter commander.

"We're holding them off, Admiral, but barely! These death boats keep coming!"

A few of the dogfights opened up on a window on the main viewer. Gripen fighters engaged the suicide craft at point-blank combat. The pilots had learned to target the small vessels' guidance systems, sending them spinning away to detonate harmlessly in space.

The bridge trembled. Another near miss rattled *Vega*. Lee braced himself against his command chair, tightening his grip on the chair's arm. His formation continued to take losses.

Lee touched the cross beneath his uniform collar. "Stand fast!" he called to his crew. "We hold here, or everything we've fought for dies!"

Chapter 43:
Kamikazes

Tueblets System
RNS *Vega*

The catapult flung Coop's Gripen from the *Vega*'s flight deck into a maddening conflict. Within fractions of a second, his radar scope was filling with hundreds of contacts, his HUD becoming saturated with targets.

"Sweet mother of..." Coop murmured as his eyes narrowed taking it all in. "All Thunderjacks, weapons free! Priority targets are those kamikazes and keep 'em from hitting our ships! Let's do this, Thunderjacks!"

There are too many targets... I can't focus like this, Coop's mind raced before he directed his targeting AI to filter only the priority targets his wing was responsible for engaging. In seconds, the hundreds of targets dropped into a few dozen, making it easier for him to see and prioritize which of those V-boats he needed to go after first.

Everywhere he looked, his HUD was showing him swarms of Vulture starfighters, Glaive bombers, and dozens upon dozens of V-boats racing toward Republic and Primord vessels. Some of the red dots winked out before he could maneuver to engage, while friendly blues were snuffed out faster than he could count.

Looking to his right through his canopy, Coop saw a V-boat push through a myriad of flak before slamming into the hull of the RNS *Neptune*, the explosion obliterating the corvette. *Damn, if they keep nailing our escorts like that...* Coop knew if they didn't find a way to stop the suicide attacks against the *Vega*'s escorts, the carrier would become extremely vulnerable to these kinds of attacks.

He rolled his fighter hard to starboard, pulling eight g's in the process. It crushed him back into his seat even with his suit's compensation. His squadron quickly formed up around him as he led them toward a wave of V-boats heading toward them.

"Alpha Squadron, finger four formation!" Coop transmitted. "Tommy, you're my three o'clock. Stay tight on the weave."

Alpha Squadron dove into the swarm of charging kamikazes.

The V-boats were about the size of a transport shuttle, but they seemed to have an overabundance of forward-facing armor, and a thruster able to move them quickly. What set these deadly little terrors apart from a missile or plasma torpedo was the bang in whatever kind of warhead they were using. One hit in the right spot against a corvette or frigate and the ship was gone. Thankfully, the heavy cruisers and larger seemed to fare a little better, but not by much.

"Seven o'clock—three leakers... I can't get a lock on them," cursed one of Coop's pilots as three of the V-boats zipped past them faster than he thought possible.

Coop turned in time to see the frigate *Stalwart* taking evasive maneuvers as the ship's point-defense guns lit up the space around the V-boats bearing down on them. He found himself shouting for joy when two of the V-boats blew apart, then swearing moments later when the third scored a hit. It flashed, causing him to squint. A second later he saw nothing but debris as the ship broke apart. One moment it was there, the next it was nothing more than twisted, charred metal.

Coop's targeting computer kept losing acquisition. The V-boats were fast, small, and flying evasive patterns that made no tactical sense until you realized they didn't plan on going home. Traditional fighter doctrine assumed your enemy wanted to survive the engagement. These bastards had thrown that assumption out an airlock. His Gripen's four laser cannons weren't designed for anti-small-craft work. The weapons had been built to punch through Vulture armor, not swat flies.

A missile lock alarm screamed in his cockpit. Vulture fighters were using the V-boat swarms as cover, picking off Gripens while the Republic pilots tried to intercept the suicide craft. The aliens had turned the death boats into psychological warfare, forcing Republic fighters to choose between protecting the fleet and protecting themselves.

"Omega Lead, I've got six on my tail!" Badger's voice burst through the comm chatter.

Coop checked his tactical display. Badger was three kilometers off *Vega*'s port beam, six Vultures closing fast. At the same time, his proximity alarm chimed. Four V-boats had broken from the main group, vectoring straight for *Vega*'s bridge section. Save Badger or intercept the suicide craft. This choice made life a special kind of interesting.

He chose *Vega*. Had to, and he would hope Badger would do the same thing in his position. But who knew with that young hotshot?

Coop rolled inverted and dove toward the approaching V-boats, the negative g's forcing blood into his head until his vision tunneled. His laser cannons spat and spat, but the tiny craft jinked away from his targeting solution. Behind him, he heard Badger screaming over the comm as Vulture fighters closed the range.

Coop closed his eyes for a millisecond, holding in a cringe. Ultimately, he liked Badger. Didn't want the kid to die. Not like this. Well, hell, not ever—he felt that way about everyone in his wing.

Still, out of anyone, Badger reminded him the must of himself at that age. Young, naive, a natural stick and rudder man but dumb as rails when it came to everything else. The kid had tons of upside, could be one of the best if he lived long enough to learn. It pained Coop that he couldn't do right by him, couldn't be there to pull his butt out of the fire right now. But that was command. Watching good kids take it on the chin for the wing, for *Vega*, for the Republic. Some lessons you had to learn alone. Bloody. Scarred. Scared, too. Or you didn't learn them at all.

Two Gripens appeared on Coop's peripheral display. They flew hard toward Badger's position. The communication link came alive as the pilots worked to bracket the Vultures. Relief flooded through Coop for just a moment. Maybe Badger would get his chance to learn after all.

"Coop, I'm seeing something here," Riggs's voice came through the comm. "These things fly predictably once they lock onto a target!"

Coop watched the lead V-boat for ten seconds. It had committed to its attack run, heading straight in toward *Vega*'s command tower. No more evasive maneuvers. Just a ballistic trajectory toward his target. The realization hit Coop quickly, like jumping straight into Antarctic waters. Wait for commitment, then strike.

"All squadrons, new ROE!" Coop said. "Let them commit to attack runs, then light them up! They fly straight once they pick their target!

"Beta Squadron, wall formation on my mark!" he continued. "Charlie, break into fighting pairs! Delta, hold reserve at grid four-two, off *Vega*'s starboard quarter!"

A Vulture exploded two hundred meters off his port wing. Debris slapped his canopy as another Gripen streaked past, already banking toward the next target. The tactical display showed friendly contacts converging on multiple threat vectors.

In a way, good. In a way, this was nuts. Too much going on, but he'd seen this multiple times throughout all the battles he'd participated in, and he'd get his squadrons through this, hopefully all in one piece.

The space around Task Force 28 had become an absolute nightmare. Gripen squadrons wove through V-boat clusters while Vultures picked off distracted Republic fighters. Zodark frigates laid down defensive screens, their weapons fire adding another layer to the mix. Debris from destroyed ships created navigation hazards that could shred a fighter's hull at combat speeds. Ships were massing together now, overlapping their point-defense fields, adapting under fire.

Coop's weapon warning system kept screaming constantly. He pulled a high-g maneuver, pushing his suit's compensation to its limits, the twelve-g turn threatening to tear his fighter apart as structural stress warnings flashed red across his HUD. A Vulture missile detonated fifty meters off his port wing. His craft shuddered, his teeth clacking together.

One V-boat had broken clear of the main engagement, streaking toward *Vega*'s bridge. Thing was, Coop couldn't let anything touch that part of the vessel, no matter what. You take out Admiral Lee, you slice the dragon's head clean off.

Coop rolled his fighter and gave chase, diving into the debris field of a destroyed cruiser. Gnarled hull plates and frozen atmosphere created a deadly path. The chase stretched through wreckage that could kill him as easily as enemy fire. The V-boat's pilot was good, using the debris to mask his approach, weaving between chunks of armor plating.

Coop caught him five hundred meters from impact. Two laser cannon bursts and the suicide craft came apart, its warhead detonating harmlessly in space. Before he could savor the moment, three Vultures rolled in from behind. Laser fire stitched so close to his canopy it made his butt clench.

Coop's target lock system shrieked. Yelled. Sounded like a female opera singer singing in his ear.

Laser fire grazed his port wing, then one hit hard, punching a hole through his armor plating. Sparks flew from his secondary systems panel. One more good hit would gut him.

Coop threw his Gripen into a barrel roll. The Vultures stayed glued to his six as laser blasts bracketed his cockpit. His starboard engine took a glancing hit. Temperature spiked. Power output dropped thirty percent. The stick felt sluggish in his hands.

He kept flying into the debris field, weaving between chunks of destroyed frigates. A laser blast vaporized a hull plate three meters from his canopy. Molten metal sprayed across his fighter's nose. The Vultures followed him, their expert maneuverability cutting off his escape vectors.

His port engine started stuttering. Warning lights colored his cockpit crimson. The Vultures closed the gap for what would no doubt be the killing shot.

That was when Tommy appeared from out of nowhere, the pilot's Gripen zipping vertically into the Vulture formation. Tommy's JATMs found two targets before the aliens could react. The third Vulture broke away, trailing plasma coolant from several hull breaches, its port engine compartment completely vented to space.

Holy hell! Coop's hands shook on the stick as his engines stabilized.

"Tommy… great flying," he said over the comm. "Thanks for the save."

"Roger that, Coop," Tommy replied. "You're clear. Where do you need me?"

"Form up on my wing. Got a ton more work to do."

Off his starboard, a death boat impacted a Primord vessel. The Prims' armor held better than Republic hulls. The suicide craft's warhead scarred the alien ship's surface, taking a chunk off, but it held together well. The Primords' point-defense systems tracked multiple small targets with incredible accuracy, their weapons firing in rapid patterns, hitting dozens of V-boats, sending them back to hell where they belonged.

"Lance is hit!" someone yelled over the comm.

Coop looked up to see Lance's Gripen tumbling out of control. A V-boat had clipped this fighter without detonating, tearing off the entire wing assembly.

"Control surfaces nonresponsive! Primary flight computer offline!" Lance said over the radio. "Can't—"

The ball of flames left a gash against RNS *Defiant*'s exterior. Lance had died in a blaze of glory.

Gulping down the reality of it all, that would never see Lance again, Coop made himself focus. Checking the hull damage, he assessed *Defiant*'s armor. There was a fifteen-meter breach in the vessel's port armor belt, no critical systems compromised.

"Boomer here, I'm Winchester!" The pilot's voice burst through the channel. "RTB for reload!"

Half Coop's squadrons were reporting ammunition critical. Eight JATMs and four laser cannons per fighter were never plenty, especially in a fight like this, against the bedlam of hundreds and hundreds of V-boats and Vultures. Like all combat, this one had turned super ugly, and fast.

"RTB if you're dry. Make it fast!" Coop transmitted. "We need reloads!"

A brief respite in the combat allowed Coop to check the tactical situation. Task Force 28 had lost fourteen ships, eight more showing critical damage on his display. RNS *Portland*: reactor containment failing. RNS *Kraken*: engineering section gutted, propulsion offline. RNS *Longbow*: total loss, no survivors. But they were holding the line, denying the Zodarks clean shots at Hunt's main fleet. Hundreds of V-boats had been destroyed, their wreckage spinning through space, but hundreds more still mobbed the joint task force.

Badger's tone boomed over the radio. "Multiple V-boats inbound, vector one-nine mark eight. I'm moving to intercept."

In quick succession, four V-boats were obliterated as Badger and his partner worked together, protecting a damaged frigate that had lost most of its point-defense systems. "Badger to all fighters, target priority: V-boats committed to attack runs on damaged vessels. Share targeting data through tactical net."

Coop couldn't help but feel an inner smile. Had the glory-hunting maverick become a team player? Maybe the kid finally got it.

Then Coop's jaw gaped slightly. What was coming wasn't good. Not even close. New contacts. Fifty more V-boats, maybe sixty, emerging from behind the wreckage of a destroyed battle cruiser. And twelve Vultures riding escort. All vectoring straight for *Vega*.

"Lord help us," he muttered. His ammunition display showed three JATMs left. Around him, his scattered pilots were probably running just as low.

The incoming wave would hit *Vega* in less than a minute. His carrier's point defense was already engaged with the current attack. No way those guns could handle this new threat.

"All available fighters near *Vega*, form up on me!" Coop ordered. "Big problem incoming! Sending coordinates."

His tactical display showed only twenty-eight Gripens in position to intercept. Twenty-eight fighters against sixty-plus suicide craft and a dozen Vultures.

Coop swallowed hard. He had to make the call that would cost lives to save lives. "Defensive screen formation! Overlap your fire zones!" His remaining fighters formed a screen directly in the path of the incoming suicide craft.

Three Gripens disappeared in bright flashes as pilots deliberately rammed V-boats to prevent them from impacting the carrier. Heroes with names Coop would remember if he lived long enough to file after-action reports. Tez, Luwan, Walski. The wash from an exploding V-boat nearly flipped his fighter as he jinked past another suicide craft.

Coop's target lock beeped. He fired a JATM and took out two suicide craft flying in tight formation. His second missile found a Vulture banking hard to port. Last missile gone. Now just laser cannons and whatever flying skills kept him breathing.

"Tango down!" Riggs called out. Her Gripen juked past a V-boat, guns blazing. The suicide craft exploded about a hundred meters from *Vega*'s hull.

Two Vultures bracketed a pilot named Camo from above and below. Missiles streaked toward his fighter. "Can't shake them!" Camo yelled. The first missile missed. The second one didn't. Camo's Gripen came apart in a ball of fire before it extinguished in the vacuum.

"Damn it!" Coop dove after the Vultures, his laser cannons spitting bursts. One alien fighter took hits across its starboard wing, rolling away.

A V-boat slammed into Bobo's fighter head-on. Both craft vaporized instantly. No time to mourn. No time for anything except killing the bastards before they killed *Vega*.

Coop's ammunition display showed zeros across the board. Laser cannons overheated. Around him, his remaining pilots were getting picked apart.

And he'd made the decision. The V-boats were kamikaze, but so would he, but to save lives, not to take them. He banked hard, heading toward a V-boat when it broke apart, flames scorching out its port.

Where did that come from?

Coop glared at his dashboard. The cavalry had arrived.

Seventy or more fresh Gripens streaked in from Hunt's main fleet. Delta Wing. Echo Wing. Bravo Wing. And others. Full missile loads and undamaged fighters. They tore into the V-boat formations like wolves hitting sheep.

"About damn time," Tommy muttered over the comm.

The fresh squadrons overwhelmed the remaining V-boats within minutes. Vultures tried to disengage but got hammered by concentrated missile fire. Space around *Vega* cleared of immediate threats. For now.

Coop sighed and inhaled deeply. He'd almost taken his own life to save the *Vega*. He stared at his ammunition counter for a beat too long, then snapped himself out of it, seeing zeros across the board.

Time to reload. *And time to get your head back into the game*, he told himself.

The approach to Vega's landing bay was uneventful. As his fighter settled onto the deck, Coop ran the numbers. Thirty-one fighters destroyed, seventeen more too damaged to continue operations. A lot of his wing gone in the first engagement.

The deck crew worked on his fighter, reloading missile bays and checking laser cannon alignment. "Captain, your starboard laser array is running at sixty percent efficiency," the crew chief reported. "Port engine shows stress fractures in the mounting assembly."

Outside, the battle continued. Ships died while he sat on the deck. People he'd trained, pilots he'd shared drinks with, good kids like Badger who'd finally figured out how to fight smart instead of stupid.

Coop took his helmet off and used a rag to wipe sweat off his face. He rested his face in his palm and shook his head. "How long can we keep this up?" he muttered under his breath.

Chapter 44:
Blood and Iron

RNS *Freedom*
High Orbit, Velkryn Tueblets System

Viceroy Miles Hunt gripped the armrests of his command chair as another shudder rippled through the *Freedom*'s superstructure. The main display showed Velkryn's Command Center reduced to a crater—a smoking wound carved into the moon's northern pole where Zon Otro's fortress had stood minutes ago. Plasma fires still raged across the facility's remains, visible even from forty thousand kilometers out.

One objective down. The hard part was just beginning.

"Viceroy, the Zodark Defense Fleet is closing to engagement range," Admiral Wiyrkomi reported from the tactical station. His Gallentine features remained calm, but Hunt caught the tension in his voice. "Confirmed one hundred thirty-three capital ships inbound. I'm reading thirty-four *Plarix*-class battleships leading their formation, forty older battleship hulls behind them, thirty-two cruisers providing screening elements, and the remainder frigates."

Hunt studied the tactical plot. The Zodarks had organized into a hammer formation—their new *Plarix* battleships forming the killing edge while older vessels provided weight and firepower. Smart. Aggressive. Exactly what he'd expect from warriors fighting for their home system.

"Fleet status?" Hunt asked.

"All four hundred sixty vessels maintaining formation," Wiyrkomi replied. "Altairian squadrons holding our port flank, Humtar battlegroup anchoring starboard. Primord cruisers scattered throughout for fire support. We're as ready as we'll ever be."

The *Freedom* trembled again as her forward batteries opened fire. Emerald turbo laser beams lanced across the void, joined by tungsten magrail rounds accelerating to relativistic speeds. Around them, the allied fleet erupted in coordinated violence—hundreds of warships pouring fire into the approaching Zodark formation.

"Enemy return fire incoming," called out Third Officer Arvexian from sensors. "Multiple plasma torpedo launches detected. Count exceeds four hundred projectiles."

"Point defense, engage!" Hunt ordered.

The *Freedom*'s antimissile batteries came alive, ruby laser pulses intersecting incoming torpedoes in brilliant flashes. Across the fleet, similar defensive fire created a lattice of light between the two formations. Most torpedoes died in the cross fire, but some punched through. Hunt watched an Altairian cruiser take a direct hit amidships, its hull buckling under the plasma detonation.

"Anvil Strike reports mission complete at Nargulon," Communications Officer Waldman announced. "Fuel infrastructure destroyed. They're RTB now, ETA seventy minutes."

"Hammer Strike reports Thalyss shipyards neutralized," Waldman continued. "Multiple construction rings destroyed. Admiral Dobbs requests permission to pursue fleeing Zodark garrison forces."

"Negative," Hunt replied immediately. "Tell Dobbs to consolidate and return to the main fleet. We need every gun here."

The range continued to close. Twenty thousand kilometers became fifteen, then ten. The Zodark *Plarix* battleships opened up with their magnetic railguns—a lesson learned from fighting Republic forces. Hunt watched the tactical display track incoming kinetic rounds, their velocity markers painting ugly red trajectories.

"Brace for impact!" someone shouted.

The *Freedom* shuddered violently as three magrail slugs hammered into her forward armor. Alarms shrieked across the bridge as damage reports flooded in.

"Forward armor holding," reported damage control. "Sections twelve through seventeen showing stress fractures. Ablative layers compromised but no hull breach."

Hunt felt sweat bead on his forehead. The Zodarks had learned well—their new railguns hit almost as hard as Republic weapons. "All batteries, target those *Plarix* battleships. I want them disabled before they can fire again."

The *Freedom*'s guns spoke in thunderous response. Her twenty-six twin-barrel turbo laser turrets tracked across the lead Zodark formation, each pair of beams focused on a single target. When a *Plarix* battleship's composite armor began glowing white-hot under sustained fire, the magrails followed—multiton penetrators slamming into superheated metal with devastating effect.

339

One of the *Plarix* battleships—Hunt thought it might be the *Drexol* based on hull markings—took a catastrophic hit. A magrail round punched through its weakened armor and detonated inside what must have been a magazine. The explosion tore the battleship in half, both sections tumbling end over end as secondary detonations rippled through the wreckage.

"Splash one *Plarix*!" someone cheered.

But the Zodarks weren't done. They kept coming, closing the range with suicidal determination. Their older battleships added their own fire to the barrage—plasma cannons and turbo lasers creating a wall of death between the two fleets.

"Viceroy, I'm detecting new launches from the Zodark formation," Arvexian called out, his bright blue eyes widening at his displays. "Small craft, dozens of them. No, wait—hundreds. They're accelerating toward our formation at attack speed."

Hunt leaned forward. "Fighters?"

"Negative, sir. These signatures are different. Thirty-eight meters, reinforced hulls, reading massive power spikes from their reactors." Arvexian's voice took on an edge of alarm. "Viceroy, those power signatures... they're configured to overload on impact."

The words hit Hunt like a physical blow. "Suicide boats."

"Confirmed," Arvexian said grimly. "I'm counting four hundred launches across multiple waves. They're targeting our capital ships."

Hunt's mind raced. Four hundred kamikaze craft, each carrying enough explosive yield to cripple or destroy a warship. The Zodarks had weaponized desperation itself.

"Admiral Takmahl, launch all reserve fighter squadrons," Hunt ordered. "I want every Hellcat we have engaging those boats before they reach our battle line."

"Aye, sir. Launching now," came the CAG's response.

On the main display, Hunt watched as blue icons—F-19 Hellcats—began pouring from the *Freedom*'s launch bays. Across the fleet, other carriers did the same. Within minutes, over three hundred Republic fighters were accelerating toward the incoming suicide craft.

The void between the fleets became a killing field. Hellcat pilots opened up with their JATM missiles and laser cannons, tracking the small, maneuverable boats with desperate precision. Hunt watched boat after boat explode under fighter fire, but there were so many. For every three destroyed, one slipped through the defensive screen.

"V-boat approaching *Steadfast*," tactical reported. "She's launching countermeasures—negative effect. Impact in five seconds."

Hunt watched helplessly as the small craft slammed into the Victory-class battleship's port quarter. The explosion bloomed bright enough to wash out the sensors momentarily. When the filters compensated, the *Steadfast* was trailing atmosphere and debris, a massive crater carved into her hull.

"*Steadfast* reports severe damage," Waldman announced. "Engineering section compromised, main reactor offline. They're maneuvering on auxiliary power."

Another V-boat reached an Altairian cruiser, detonating against its bow. The cruiser's forward section simply ceased to exist—vaporized in the fifty-megaton blast. The aft section tumbled away, already breaking apart.

"Get those fighters in tighter," Hunt ordered. "They have to stop more of them."

The Hellcat pilots fought with desperate courage, their laser cannons carving through V-boats at point-blank range. But the boats kept coming in waves, their pilots—*Exalted Riders*, Hunt thought grimly—committed to dying for their Empire.

A third V-boat reached the fleet, this time targeting a Primord heavy cruiser. The resulting explosion sheared away the cruiser's entire starboard side, sending it spinning out of formation trailing fire.

"We're taking serious losses," Wiyrkomi reported. "Six capital ships destroyed, fourteen more showing critical damage. The V-boats are tearing us apart."

Hunt's jaw tightened. The Zodarks had found an answer to numerical superiority—throw bodies at the problem until it bled. "How many boats left?"

"Approximately one hundred seventy still inbound," Arvexian replied. "Our fighters are accounting for most of them, but the leakers are doing catastrophic damage."

The *Freedom* shuddered again as her guns continued their deadly work. Hunt watched a Zodark cruiser explode under concentrated fire from three Republic battleships. Small consolation when his own fleet was hemorrhaging ships to suicide attacks.

"Viceroy, priority transmission from Admiral Stavanger," Waldman announced. "The Gravaxia stargate is clear. She's standing by for orders."

Hunt felt something shift in his chest. The moment of decision.

"Signal Admiral Stavanger and Vice Admiral Lee," Hunt ordered. "Execute Phase Two. Jump into Tueblets immediately and engage the Zodark reinforcement fleet."

"Aye, sir. Transmitting now."

On the tactical display, Hunt watched new icons appear—blue friendly markers materializing near the Gravaxia stargate coordinates. Stavanger's Task Force 41 and Lee's Task Force 28, over one hundred capital ships, flooding into the system to catch the Zodark reinforcements in a pincer.

"Sir, we have a problem," Arvexian called out. "New hyperspace signatures detected bearing zero-four-seven, range eighty thousand kilometers. Multiple Zodark capital ships emerging behind our formation."

Hunt spun to face the display. Fresh enemy icons bloomed into existence—the reinforcement fleet from the neighboring system, the one intelligence had warned about. He counted rapidly: at least sixty capital ships, maybe more.

"They're positioning behind us," Wiyrkomi said unnecessarily. Hunt could see it clearly—the Zodarks had just caught his fleet in a vise. Enemy forces ahead and behind, with his ships trapped in the middle.

"All ships, maintain firing on the primary target," Hunt ordered, forcing his voice to remain steady. "We breakthrough the force in front of us or we die here."

The *Freedom* trembled as another V-boat detonated against a nearby cruiser. The expanding fireball illuminated the bridge in harsh light.

"Viceroy, Admiral Vesharuk on secure channel," Waldman reported.

"Put him through."

The Humtar commander's voice carried across the bridge—calm, measured, utterly devoid of fear. "Viceroy Hunt, my sensors detect the enemy reinforcement fleet has positioned itself behind your formation. This is tactically disadvantageous."

"I'm aware, Admiral," Hunt replied dryly.

"I am detaching seven of my *Voidhammer*-class heavy battleships to engage this new threat," Vesharuk continued. "My remaining forces will continue supporting your assault on the primary target."

Hunt blinked. Seven ships? Against sixty-plus Zodark capital ships? "Admiral, I appreciate the gesture, but seven battleships won't—"

"You will see, Viceroy. Vesharuk out."

On the tactical display, Hunt watched seven aqua icons—the Humtar *Voidhammer*-class vessels—break from the main formation and accelerate toward the rear threat with impossible speed. Each battleship was massive, over two thousand meters long, but they moved like frigates.

"Viceroy, the Humtar ships are opening fire," Arvexian reported, his voice carrying an edge of disbelief.

Hunt turned to the secondary display showing the rear engagement. What he saw made his breath catch.

The lead Humtar battleship—the CNS *Darkstar*—fired its turbo laser batteries. The beams didn't just strike the Zodark formation—they carved through it. An older Zodark battleship took a direct hit amidships and simply broke apart, its hull unable to withstand the concentrated energy. A second battleship lost its entire bow section to another salvo, the metal glowing white-hot before exploding.

"Good God," someone whispered.

The other six Humtar battleships joined the attack, their turbo lasers firing with mechanical precision. Each shot found a critical system—reactors, magazines, bridge structures. The Zodark reinforcement fleet tried to respond, concentrating fire on the nearest Humtar vessel.

Plasma torpedoes and turbo laser beams converged on the CNS *Voidrender*. The impacts should have been devastating. Instead, the Humtar ship's armor shimmered with that strange iridescent quality Hunt had heard about. The energy dissipated across the hull in rippling waves, leaving barely a scorch mark.

"Their armor's not even ablating," Arvexian reported, voice filled with awe. "The thermal redistribution is... I've never seen anything like it."

Hunt watched the *Darkstar* put a full broadside into a *Plarix*-class battleship. The Zodark vessel's meter-thick composite armor—designed to withstand Republic kinetic weapons—lasted approximately three seconds before the Humtar turbo lasers burned through. The next salvo found the reactor complex. The *Plarix* battleship detonated with enough force to damage two nearby cruisers.

"Splash two *Plarix*, three older battleships, and four cruisers," tactical reported. "The Humtar ships are systematically dismantling the enemy formation."

The seven *Voidhammer*-class battleships moved through the Zodark reinforcement fleet like sharks through a school of fish. They accelerated, decelerated, and maneuvered with impossible agility for ships their size. Their turbo lasers never stopped firing—each beam placed with surgical precision, each target dying within seconds of being engaged.

A Zodark cruiser attempted to ram the CNS *Eternal Night*, pouring emergency power to its engines in a desperate charge. The Humtar battleship simply accelerated away, maintaining perfect firing distance while its aft batteries carved the cruiser into burning sections.

"Viceroy, Primord reinforcements entering the system," Waldman announced. "Admiral Stavanger and Vice Admiral Lee report they're engaging the Zodark reinforcement fleet from the opposite vector."

Hunt turned back to the tactical display. Fresh blue icons—Primord and Republic ships—were materializing near the Gravaxia stargate, exactly as planned. The Zodark reinforcement fleet that had tried to catch his forces in a pincer was now itself trapped between three forces: the Humtar battleships ahead, Stavanger's fleet behind, and Lee's forces moving to cut off their escape.

"The reinforcements are trying to break contact," Arvexian reported. "They're scattering, attempting to withdraw."

"Tell Stavanger and Lee to pursue," Hunt ordered. "Don't let them regroup."

On the secondary display, Hunt watched the Humtar battleships continue their slaughter. Another *Plarix*-class vessel died, its reactor containment failing catastrophically. An older Zodark battleship simply broke apart under sustained fire, its structural integrity collapsing. The Humtar ships showed minimal damage despite concentrated return fire—their impossible armor drinking in energy that should have destroyed them.

The *Freedom* shuddered again as another wave of V-boats reached the fleet. Hunt saw a Republic heavy cruiser take a direct hit, the explosion tearing through its engineering section. But the Hellcat pilots were adapting, learning to track the small craft more effectively. The number of leakers was decreasing.

"Enemy V-boat attacks diminishing," Arvexian reported. "I'm reading less than fifty craft remaining. Our fighter screen is achieving eighty-seven percent intercept rate."

Hunt allowed a grim smile. The Zodark suicide boats had hurt them badly, but the tactic was spent. Once the fighters learned the pattern, the boats became manageable targets.

"Forward Zodark formation is beginning to fragment," Wiyrkomi announced. "Multiple enemy vessels showing critical damage. Their *Plarix* battleships are attempting to cover the withdrawal of damaged units."

Hunt studied the primary tactical display. The Zodark Defense Fleet that had seemed so formidable minutes ago was now in disarray. Half their *Plarix* battleships were destroyed or crippled, their older vessels taking catastrophic losses from sustained Republic and Altairian fire. The suicide boat attacks had stopped their momentum, but hadn't broken the allied fleet.

"All ships, concentrate fire on the remaining *Plarix* battleships," Hunt ordered. "I want them eliminated before they can withdraw."

The *Freedom*'s guns spoke again, joined by three hundred allied warships. The combined firepower was overwhelming. Another *Plarix* battleship exploded under focused fire, its composite armor finally failing. A second lost power and began drifting, its hull glowing cherry-red from laser impacts.

"Viceroy, Admiral Vesharuk reports the enemy reinforcement fleet is in full retreat," Waldman called out. "The Humtar battleships are standing down to avoid overextending."

Hunt nodded. Seven Humtar ships had shattered a force ten times their number in less than fifteen minutes. The technological disparity was staggering—terrifying, even. But right now, he was grateful they were allies.

"Sir, Anvil Strike entering weapons range," tactical reported. "Rear Admiral Hunt reports his strike wing is combat effective and requesting orders."

"Tell Ethan to form defensive screen around our damaged vessels," Hunt ordered. "I want those V-boats kept away from our cripples."

The battle was turning. The Zodark Defense Fleet continued fragmenting, their cohesion shattered by relentless fire. The reinforcement fleet was scattering under pressure from Stavanger, Lee, and the Humtar battleships. Velkryn's Command Center was a smoking crater. The shipyards at Thalyss destroyed. Nargulon's fuel infrastructure in ruins.

Hunt watched the tactical display update continuously—red enemy icons winking out, blue friendlies repositioning, the geometric dance of fleet combat resolving in the allies' favor. The cost had been steep: eighteen capital ships destroyed, thirty-seven more showing critical damage. Thousands of warriors dead or dying in the wreckage.

But they were winning.

"Admiral Wiyrkomi, signal the fleet," Hunt ordered. "All ships pursue fleeing enemy forces but maintain formation integrity. I don't want anyone charging off alone into a trap."

"Aye, sir. That Groff Fleet from the Varkorion System we've been monitoring... they're fleeing for home. Should we pursue—"

"No, I want you signal Admiral Vesharuk and let him know the trap has been set," Hunt replied quickly. "He'll know what to do."

"Affirmative, will do."

The *Freedom* trembled one last time as her forward batteries fired another salvo. Hunt watched a Zodark cruiser break apart under the impact, its reactor detonating in a brief new sun.

He knew the tide of the battle had shifted in their favor. With the Groff's fleet returning to Varkorion. The trap Legion had set would soon be sprung, and the war would end, or it would continue and consume them all.

Chapter 45:
The Betrayal

ZNS *Harvex's Vengeance*
Velkryn Orbital Zone, Tueblets System

Laktish Heltet gripped the tactical rail as another shock wave rippled through the *Harvex's Vengeance*. The battleship's armor held, but the impacts were coming faster now—turbo laser strikes carving through Zodark formations with surgical precision.

A flash occurred on the surface of Velkryn, a scene of destruction Heltet struggled to accept. The once-mighty Malvari citadel fortress, the temporary seat of the High Council, had blown apart in a spectacular explosion.

"Laktish... the Zon... the High Council... they're gone," NOS Kelvoth exclaimed, in shock. The others on the bridge seemed equally taken aback by the death of Zon Otro.

"NOS Kelvoth, is there any sign the Zon or the other Council members might have escaped?" asked Heltet hopefully.

There was silence on the bridge, even as the battle raged around them, while one of the sensor operators tried to assess if escape shuttles or pods might have launched in the final moments.

"No, Laktish, it does not appear that any shuttles or escape pods left the facility before it exploded... wait, we are receiving a message from *Utulf's Sword*," announced Third Spear Tavak. The *Utulf's Sword* was one of the new *Plarix* battleships and the flagship of the Malvari.

"Mavkah Griglag is ordering all warships to consolidate around the orbital defense batteries of Char-Ti," Tavak relayed, passing along the Malvari's latest orders.

Heltet looked for Char-Ti, grimacing when he saw a trio of those Humtar battleships changing course to head for it. It pained him to watch red icons blinking out of existence with horrifying regularity. He knew each one represented a warship. Hundreds and sometimes thousands of Zodark warriors, gone.

"It's those Humtar warships... they're cutting us to pieces," NOS Kelvoth said angrily after the loss of another warship. "What are your orders, Laktish?"

Heltet released a heavy sigh. He knew what had to be done. He just didn't want to give the order. The battle was far from over, but its balance had tipped in the allies' favor when the Malvari fleet had lost more than half of its battleships.

I must save what I can before all is lost, he thought before issuing the order he dreaded. "It is time. Signal all Groff forces to execute withdrawal Two Alpha," Heltet said in a somber tone.

"Laktish… sir?" Kelvoth's voice carried disbelief. "The Malvari are still engaged. If we withdraw—"

"I know, Kelvoth! If we stay longer, we risk the complete annihilation of our fleet—someone has to survive. Execute the order," interrupted Heltet as he stared angrily at the faces looking back at him.

The helmsman hesitated for a heartbeat. Then his fingers moved across the controls. "Aye, Laktish. Plotting withdrawal vector. Ships are acknowledging the order and complying."

The *Harvex's Vengeance* along with the remaining Groff vessels broke formation from what remained of the Malvari fleet. What had started as a Groff fleet of one hundred and thirty vessels was now down to just sixty-three.

"Sir, we're receiving a transmission from the *Utulf's Sword*," the communications officer announced. "It's Mavkah Griglag."

Heltet's stomach churned. He'd been waiting for this. "Go ahead, put him through."

The holographic projection materialized a moment later. Heltet saw Griglag's scarred features twisted with fury, alarm bells blaring in the background as smoke drifted around him.

"Laktish… Heltet, what in Lindow's name are you doing? Tell me the Groff is not abandoning us?"

"Mavkah… Griglag, I have orders from Director Vak—"

"Orders?" Griglag's voice was raw. "Our Zon is dead—the High Council is dead, and now you abandon us!"

Heltet met his gaze. "No, we are not abandoning you. This is part of the plan—"

"The plan? What plan? This is cowardice." Griglag's voice became colder. "In the heat of battle, the Groff finally shows its true colors. When the battle turns—"

The transmission was cut before he could finish. Heltet turned to his communications officer, "What happened?"

"It's gone—*Utulf's Sword* is gone," replied Third Spear Tavak as the bridge monitor showed the *Plarix* battleship breaking apart.

"We're approaching the Varkorion stargate," announced the helmsman.

"Order the fleet to jump, and proceed to Shwani," ordered NOS Kelvoth.

Heltet felt like screaming in anger as rage and frustration washed over him. Everything about this deal Vak had struck with the Collective felt wrong. If the Collective was going to aid them, it should have done so before the vast majority of their fleet was destroyed.

"Jump complete—all remaining Groff vessels have returned to Varkorion," reported Third Spear Tavak. "The finally tally of returning Groff vessels is fifty-nine."

"Fifty-nine? We had sixty-three at the gate—what happened to the other four?" demanded NOS Kelvoth in surprise.

"A handful of those Humtar vessels intercepted them before they could jump," replied Tavak. "They nearly had us too, NOS Kelvoth. One of their battleships had a weapons lock on us when we crossed the gate. If we had been even a few seconds slower—"

"Then we have our helmsman to thank for ensuring we jumped when we did," offered Heltet before ordering, "All vessels are to report to Shwani. We join the defense of the planet now."

As the *Harvex's Vengeance* accelerated to Shwani, Heltet couldn't shake the feeling of betrayal. Griglag's final words echoing in his head. Tueblets was the heart of the Empire... and Legion had ordered them to abandon it... to lure the allies into a trap, a decisive battle they insisted would win the war.

You had better be right, Vak'Atioth... or you'll have cost us the Empire...

Chapter 46:
The Price of Survival

ZNS *Harvex's Vengeance*
High Orbit, Planet Shwani
Varkorion System

Laktish Heltet stared at the bridge monitor while the planet Shwani floated below them, its surface obscured by heavy cloud cover. One hundred and thirty ships, that was how many warships he had started the day with—fifty-nine was all he had left. That was all that remained of the reserve fleet Vak and the Groff had spent eighteen dracmas building. Seventy-one ships lost in battle, reduced to nothing more than broken wrecks in debris fields scattered across the Tueblets system.

The *Harvex's Vengeance* sat within the outer defensive ring with the remainder of his fleet, surrounded by the Eyes of Shwani—a series of twelve massive orbital platforms bristling with plasma turrets and magrail batteries. Below them, the planet's defense grid pulsed with guns ready to lay waste to the allied fleet when it arrived—if it arrived.

"Laktish, there is an incoming transmission from the surface— it's Director Vak'Atioth," announced Third Spear Tavak. "It's a Priority One message on an encrypted channel."

Heltet's jaw tightened. He had known this call was coming. "Very well. Put him through to my station."

A moment later, Vak's image materialized above the command table in front of Heltet's command chair. He could see in his expression the Director was not pleased as he angrily spat the words, "Laktish, what is your report?"

"Director, we fought as ordered. Once the battle had turned, we withdrew to Varkorion as planned," replied Heltet. "I returned with fifty-nine vessels. We stand ready to defend Shwani should the allies arrive."

"Wait—am I to believe that only fifty-nine out of the one hundred and thirty vessels that left this morning remain?" asked Vak in surprise.

Heltet fought to contain his anger, replying, "Yes, that is correct. I have fifty-nine Groff warships with me. I can't say what remains of the Malvari. You ordered us to abandon them in the middle of the fight."

"Is that what you think I did?" Vak shot back angrily. "You know the plan, Heltet. Your job is to lure the allies to Varkorion. Now put aside your anger and tell me what happened," he ordered with a bit of heat in his voice.

Heltet took a breath and held it, calming himself before responding further. Closing his eyes, he watched the final moments of the battle replay in his mind. He could still hear Griglag's final transmission before the *Utulf's Sword* had disappeared.

"We fought the allies hard. The V-boats performed better than we had hoped. They scored many kills, even destroying a handful of Altairian and Republic battleships—but those Humtar ships... their battleships in particular..." Heltet voice trailed off. He shook his head before continuing, "Their weapons technology, Director... it's beyond what we encountered even against the Gallentines. The way their ships moved, their ability to absorb plasma and even kinetic hits—it's beyond what our knowledge of physics and material science tells us is possible."

Vak narrowed his eyes as he leaned forward. "Come, Laktish, it can't be that bad. Even the Gallentine warships have vulnerabilities—Legion has won battles against them."

"If these Humtars follow us here, you may get your chance to witness them in battle for yourself," Heltet replied softly, his mood somber.

"Very well—you said the allies took losses. Were they bad? Did our *Plarix* battleships perform well against them?" Vak asked, changing the subject.

Heltet nodded. "If you exclude Humtar vessels, then, yes, the allies sustained heavy losses. We fought well—the Malvari and Groff both. Our *Plarix* battleships and the V-boats made a huge difference. Early in the battle, we inflicted significant losses on the enemy. If I had to estimate the Republic, Altairian, and Primord losses... I'd say at least a quarter of their ships, mostly heavy cruisers and battleships. That was what we told the V-boats to focus their attacks on. Another third to half of their remaining vessels sustained light to moderate damage. A few could be severe, but it's hard to say."

"Heltet, if the Humtars hadn't assisted them, would our forces have been enough to defeat them?" Vak asked, his voice unsure.

"Perhaps," Heltet answered quickly, his eyes meeting Vak's gaze through the hologram. "We had numbers on them, and we had positioning. But those Humtar battleships… they tipped the balance."

"And the balance will tip in our favor with the help of Legion," countered Vak.

Heltet shook his head. "I don't know, Director. This deal with Legion had better be worth it. If they fail to help us retake Tueblets…" He paused, choosing his next words carefully. "Without Tueblets, we have no empire. The stargates, the logistics, the connections between systems—everything depends on holding that system."

Vak's eyes narrowed. "Are you questioning my judgment?"

"No, Director. I am questioning whether the Collective will honor its promises."

"Enough." Vak's voice turned sharp. "The Collective honors its deals, Heltet. Legion will arrive when the allies do, and we will reclaim what was lost. Do you understand?"

Heltet bowed his head slightly. "Yes, of course, Director."

"Good. Maintain your position within the defensive perimeter and prepare for battle—the real battle. The one that will decide this war," Vak ordered, then ended the transmission.

As Heltet stood in the command center, surrounded by the hum of active systems and the quiet conversations of his bridge crew, he wondered if he would live to see the end of this day or if these were his final minutes, his final hours.

NOS Kelvoth approached from the tactical station. "Your orders, Laktish?"

"Good question. For now, all ships maintain alert status. We don't know when the enemy will arrive and the next battle will begin," replied Heltet, unsure what else to say.

Kelvoth shouted some orders to the others on the bridge, then turned to face Heltet and in a low voice asked, "And if Legion doesn't arrive?"

Heltet didn't answer immediately. He looked at the fifty-nine red icons on the tactical display—all that remained of Vak's grand fleet. "If that happens, Kelvoth, then we die defending our home world."

Chapter 47:
Sword of Damocles

CNS *Solvaris*
High Orbit, Planet New Eden
Rhea System

Admiral Veydris Korrath stood on the bridge of the *Solvaris*, watching New Eden's azure surface roll beneath them. The ship's name meant "Keeper of Worlds"—it was a star carrier the Navy had built to destroy the Collective. The 4,200-meter vessel carried eight hundred starfighters and four hundred bombers in her bays, with fabrication systems capable of replacing losses mid-battle. She housed three thousand six hundred spacers, twelve hundred pilots, three thousand maintenance crew, and four hundred and fifty security personnel and had berths for seven thousand five hundred soldiers.

Her armor was adaptive and regenerative. A dozen *Voidhammer* heavy battleships could hammer the *Solvaris* for hours before inflicting meaningful damage. Her primary turbo lasers would cut through a *Voidhammer*'s armor in a handful of hits. Her magrail slugs struck at near light speed with devastating kinetic force.

The ship was an energy hog, powered by four antimatter reactors. Its offensive weapons consisted of twenty thirty-six-inch twin-barreled magrails lined each flank of her armored hull, interspersed with twenty-six triple-barreled antiship turbo laser cannons. Because a ship could never have enough firepower, the *Solvaris*'s secondary armaments consisted of forty eighteen-inch twin-barreled magrails alongside fifty-two medium turbo laser batteries for added punch. For enemy fighters and missiles that strayed too close to the carrier, she was equipped with ten missile banks per side, each loaded with two hundred interceptors, giving the carrier the ability to intercept swarms of enemy fighters and missiles. Should those systems fail, the *Solvaris* boasted two hundred laser PDGs—point-defense guns—that covered every angle of the ship.

Three *Warclaw* light battleships held escort formation off the *Solvaris*'s flanks, supported by twelve *Ironveil* cruisers and fourteen *Daggerwind* frigates. They'd waited most of a day while the allied fleet had fought in Tueblets—their part in the battle was nearly complete.

"Admiral, incoming transmission from Admiral Vesharuk," announced Commander Thyrax from communications. "Priority channel, encrypted."

"Put him through," Korrath responded.

The holographic display materialized in front of his command chair. Admiral Vesharuk appeared, his demeanor calm despite the sounds of battle happening on the bridge behind him.

"Korrath, the battle here is nearly over. We have detected the Groff fleet withdrawing to Varkorion," Vesharuk announced. "It's happening just as we thought it would."

Korrath felt his pulse quicken, a smile forming on his face. "Outstanding. How many of their ships survived to retreat?"

"It looks to be fifty-nine of them. We nailed a few of them before they could jump. We suspect they'll have retreated to the orbital defenses around Shwani, likely waiting for our forces to appear and for Legion to spring their trap," replied Vesharuk. Then his expression hardened. "Here in Tueblets, Viceroy Hunt and the allied fleet are finishing off the remaining Zodark forces. Their Zon, Otro, is dead. So is their Mavkah, Griglag—the *Utulf's Sword* was destroyed minutes ago. What's left of their forces are scattered. A few are choosing to fight to the bitter end, others are surrendering. It shouldn't be long now before the system is secured."

"That's good to hear, my friend. This battle has gone better than we thought," Korrath commented. "Is it time to spring our own trap?"

"Yes." Vesharuk leaned forward slightly. "My task force is ready to join you. We'll rendezvous with you at Shwani and wait for Legion to appear."

Korrath glanced at his tactical officer. Captain Zerith nodded once—confirmation that the *Solvaris* and her escorts were ready.

"Affirmative. We're ready," Korrath confirmed. "We have the Damocles files ready with our ultimatum the moment we identify the Legion command ship."

Vesharuk's eyes narrowed. "Good. And remember, Korrath, the *Solvaris* doesn't engage unless Legion forces our hand. We show 'em our teeth. We deliver the ultimatum. But we don't reveal what we're capable of unless we have to. We only have the element of surprise once."

"I know. We'll show our teeth and growl, but we'll hold our bite unless necessary."

"Good." Vesharuk paused, then added, "Viceroy Hunt sends his regards. Says you missed out on one hell of a fight."

Korrath smiled. "Yeah, no need to rub it in. Tell him we'll see him on the other side when this is all over. First round of beers is on him. Out." The transmission ended, and Korrath gave the order for them to jump. It was time to punch the Collective in the face and see how they responded.

****

CNS *Solvaris*
High Orbit, Planet Shwani
Varkorion System

Admiral Korrath held his breath as the *Solvaris* emerged from quantum transit into the Varkorion system. One second, they were in New Eden's peaceful orbit; the next, they were in orbit of the rust-colored planet of Shwani with its hostile gleam of defensive platforms surrounding it.

"Admiral, jump complete," the helmsman reported. "All ships accounted for. Battle formation intact."

On the tactical display, they could see that Admiral Vesharuk's task force had arrived and was holding position twelve thousand kilometers to port. Their seven *Voidhammer* heavy battleships were a welcomed sight. The warships were arranged in a defensive formation flanked by three additional *Warclaw* light battleships and their supporting cruiser and frigate escorts. They quickly added their firepower to the *Solvaris*'s own escort vessels as the two Humtar forces took up screening positions around the star carrier.

Positioned some thirty thousand kilometers below them was a formation of Zodark warships—the Groff fleet that had withdrawn from Tueblets. The Zodark ships were positioned around the Eyes of Shwani defensive grid, a series of asteroids and planetoids turned into fortified gun emplacements.

"Admiral, sensors are coming online. We're detecting multiple hostile contacts," Captain Zerith announced. "Sensors have identified fifty-nine capital ships interspersed with at least twelve orbital defensive platforms."

Korrath smiled as he stared at the tactical display. Everything was in place; the Groff fleet was where Legion had told them to be. Now they just had to wait for Legion to arrive.

"Admiral, quantum bridge signatures detected," Captain Zerith called out, his voice sharp with excitement. "It's got to be Legion—we're detecting multiple contacts bearing zero-three-five, range twenty-two thousand kilometers."

Korrath felt his pulse quicken as the trap began to spring. "OK, this is it, people! It's go time. Give me visual on their formation, main monitor."

The main display shifted, showing space rippling like disturbed water. A massive vessel pushed its way through the ripple to emerge in the system with them. The vessel had an angular, predatory look, bristling with weapons.

That has to be it, Korrath thought to himself. The ship a little more than twenty thousand kilometers away from them had to be the *Devourer*-class star carrier *Eternal Harvest*. As the magnification zoomed in closer to the ship, its hull plating seemed dark as the void, absorbing the light around it.

"Admiral, visual sensors have confirmed it. That's Harvester-Prime's flagship," Zerith reported from his station. "We're scanning it now for details… confirmed. The ship is four thousand meters in length. Whoa, energy readings are massive. Its sensors are going active."

As data continued to roll in from the various stations around the bridge, more ripples appeared around their fleet. The Legion warships were emerging in waves around the *Eternal Harvest*.

Korrath continued to watch the tactical display light up with red hostile icons. "I need a count. How many Legion ships are we looking at?" he demanded.

"Thirty vessels… forty… fifty…" Zerith's voice remained steady despite the climbing numbers. "Seventy-two contacts and still climbing, sir."

Korrath turned to his comms officer. "Hail the *Eternal Harvest*. Priority channel. I want to speak with Omega-0001."

Commander Thyrax worked his console. "Aye, Admiral. Transmitting now."

The seconds stretched, feeling like an eternity. More Legion vessels continued materializing around the *Eternal Harvest*. Korrath counted eighty-five ships now, and the number seemed to keep growing. Legion had to fight, and they'd brought enough firepower to give them a run for their money.

"Admiral, they're not responding."

"Keep trying. Hail them again," Korrath pressed more urgently. The plan wouldn't work if they couldn't make contact to deliver the ultimatum. Meanwhile, the tactical display now showed ninety-two Legion vessels—a battle line was forming around the *Eternal Harvest*. A sick feeling grew in Korrath's stomach as he realized they might have to fight their way out of this situation.

"Wait, I'm getting something—it's from the *Eternal Harvest*," Thyrax announced, to everyone's relief.

"Put it through the bridge speakers. I want everyone to hear this," ordered Korrath, his mind racing in anticipation of what was about to happen.

When the speakers activated, the voice they heard was unnerving, unsettling. It wasn't a single voice but a layering of many voices mixed together—one becoming many, many becoming one. It was enough to make Korrath's skin crawl.

"We are Omega-0001 of Harvester-Prime—Humtar… you were defeated. Why have you returned?"

Korrath had stood when the audio message turned to a video. He stepped forward, boldly declaring, "Yes, Omega-0001, we have returned from exile. We have come to finish what started long ago—to end this war."

For a moment his statement was met with silence, a blank stare from the mechanical figure staring at him from the bridge of the *Eternal Harvest*. Then it spoke in that same unnerving, layered voice that made the hair on the back of Korrath's neck tingle.

"Humtars come to finish the war *you* started," replied Omega-0001. "We defeated you once. We can defeat you again."

While Omega-0001 spoke, the tactical display alerted them to the *Eternal Harvest* surging power to its weapon systems. Korrath saw energy readings spiking across the Legion vessels as they prepared for battle.

It's now or never, Korrath thought, then turned to Commander Thyrax. "It's time. Send the Sword of Damocles file," Korrath ordered.

The commander's fingers danced across his console, then he looked up at Korrath. "It's done, Admiral. The Sword of Damocles is sent, receipt confirmed—it's in Omega-0001's hands now."

Korrath gave him a reassuring smile. It was out of their hands now and in the consciousness of the Collective. A part of him hoped they'd choose to fight, to end this conflict. He knew it was a selfish thought, to want revenge for what the Collective had done to their ancestors. It would lead to the deaths of millions, possibly billions, if the Collective wasn't stopped here and now. For that reason alone, Korrath hoped this Sword of Damocles plan would be enough.

When the clock showed a minute had gone by without a response, Korrath cleared his throat. "Omega-0001, the Collective has received our ultimatum—our Sword of Damocles. What is the Collective's response?" he asked.

Korrath held his breath as they waited tensely to hear the words that would end or escalate this fight. Then he saw something that caused his spirits to lift. Energy readings across the Legion vessels were dropping.

"The message was received," said the layered voice of Omega-0001. It paused as though calculating its next statement. "We have analyzed the Sword of Damocles and found...no alternative—it is accepted. But, Humtar...this war is not resolved—this fight is not over."

Korrath smiled, breathing a sigh of relief as he answered, "Perhaps you're right, 0001—I would have used Damocles to eliminate you entirely, but that decision wasn't mine to make. You have received the terms of the deal. The consequences of not following it are clear. If the Collective deviates from this agreement...you will be erased from existence."

The figure of Omega-0001 stared at Korrath, not speaking. As the silence stretched between them, Korrath saw changes starting to happen on the tactical display. The space around the Legion vessels began to ripple like disturbed water. A handful of cruisers disappeared, then destroyers followed as the number of Legion warships dropped quickly.

The *Eternal Harvest* rotated slowly, the Legion flagship lingering a moment longer as the final ships disappeared. The figure of

Omega-0001 canted its head to one side as it spoke. "Humtar... you should have stayed in your exile... the Ark Galaxy of NGC 205 (M110) was previously unknown to us... perhaps one day we will finish what *you* started."

The ship disappeared before Korrath could respond. The remaining Legion ships followed seconds later, leaving the Groff fleet of fifty-nine vessels as the only hostile ships in the system.

"That's it! It's confirmed, all Legion contacts are gone," Zerith reported.

"My God, we did it!" exclaimed Captain Zerith as the bridge crew broke out in excited cheers of joy and laughter.

Korrath released a breath he hadn't realized he'd been holding. That last statement from 0001 still lingered in his head, but the immediate threat was gone. They had done it.

He raised his hands to get their attention, shouting to be heard. "I need everyone's attention now! We still have a hostile Zodark force to deal with, so this battle isn't over yet. Commander Thyrax, open a channel to the Zodark ship *Harvex's Vengeance*. Address it to Laktish Heltet."

The bridge crew returned to their stations and got back to business.

"Admiral, I have a channel open. They'll receive it," replied Commander Thyrax.

Korrath nodded, then straightened his uniform as he spoke. "Laktish Heltet, whatever deal your people struck with the Collective is over. As you can see with your sensors, Legion is gone." Korrath paused for a second, letting the words sink in before offering terms of surrender. "Heltet, your Zon is dead and your fleet has been defeated. We control access to your systems, and we control the space above your planets. We do not wish to slaughter your people or reduce your cities to ash. As one of the allied fleet commanders, I ask for your surrender. Will you save your crew and fleet...or must more warriors die for an outcome already determined?"

Korrath waited, giving the Zodark command a few minutes to decide.

"Admiral, we are receiving a text transmission from the *Harvex's Vengeance*," Thyrax announced as he brought it up on the main display.

Korrath read the message, smiling as he did: *Enough warriors have died today. I will order my fleet to surrender. Director Vak'Atioth will likely order us to fight to the end. I suggest eliminating him. I will assume command of the Zodark Empire and agree to end the war. Are these terms acceptable?*

Coordinates identifying Vak'Atioth's location followed.

Korrath looked at his tactical officer. "Captain Zerith, transmit those coordinates to Admiral Vesharuk. Tell him...we have a final target of opportunity that needs attention. Then send a reply to Heltet and tell him his terms are accepted. Tell him to order all Zodark forces to stand down and await further instructions."

"Aye, sir. Transmitting now."

Moments later, three of the *Voidhammer* heavy battleships fired their turbo laser on the provided coordinates. It was one final shot to end the war.

"Sir, Admiral Vesharuk reports target destroyed," Thyrax confirmed. "*Harvex's Vengeance* acknowledges. Heltet confirms he's sending the orders to all systems and vessels. Hostilities are to cease—the war is over—all Zodark forces are to stand down effective immediately."

Korrath watched as the tactical display showed Zodark weapon systems deactivating. Power signatures across all the defensive platforms powered down, and targeting radars turned off. The fifty-nine warships of the Groff fleet signaled their surrender.

"Thyrax, get me Viceroy Hunt. Priority channel," ordered Korrath excitedly.

Hunt's image materialized moments later. His face looked tired, but his eyes had a glimmer of hope in them as he spoke. "Admiral Korrath, I trust you delivered the Damocles ultimatum?"

Korrath allowed himself a genuine smile. "Yeah, we did... it's over, Viceroy. They're gone. The Collective... they begrudgingly accepted the terms of the deal and left. I just finished speaking with the Groff fleet commander, Laktish Heltet—he's assuming command of the Zodarks. He has accepted the terms of surrender and agreed to end the war. It's over, Miles... the war is over."

Hunt's expression shifted from disbelief to exhaustion, then realization as the words registered. "Wait, Korrath... are you saying it worked? The Collective agreed? They've left?"

"Yeah, they did. We sent Omega-0001 the ultimatum and that Orbot was right, they chose the certainty of survival over the risk of permanent death," Korrath replied. "When Legion abandoned the Zodarks, that Groff fleet commander, Heltet, he told us if we eliminated the Groff Director, Vak'Atioth, Heltet could take control of the government and end the war. So that's what we did—we eliminated Vak'Atioth. Now he's the one in charge."

Hunt leaned back in his command chair, a look of disbelief still on his face. "I'll be damned, Korrath. This plan actually worked. This is really going to end, isn't it?"

"Yes, it is, my friend." Korrath glanced at the tactical display, where blue friendly icons now outnumbered the neutral gray markers representing surrendered Zodark forces. "We're securing things here. How is Tueblets going?"

"We're nearly done finishing off the last of the Malvari. Once Heltet's message reaches the system... I guess we'll see who honors it and who wants to meet Lindow, their god," Hunt replied, still in shock. "I think we should have the system fully pacified before the end of the day if they honor Heltet's orders." He paused, then added, "Korrath, good work today. We owe you and Vesharuk more than we can hope to repay."

"No, Miles, you are Humtar—we are family. We all played our part in ending this terrible war. Now comes the hard part, figuring out how to make the peace stick."

Laughing at his comment, Hunt countered, "One problem at a time, my friend. Oh, and, Korrath, when we return to New Eden, dinner and drinks are on me."

Korrath smiled. "I'm going to hold you to that, Miles. In fact, I'm going to order one of those Andorran steaks I've heard so much about."

The transmission ended, like the war. A new battle began—the fight to maintain the peace.

But that was tomorrow's problem.

Chapter 48:
Epilogue

Miles and Lilly Hunt took their long-overdue second honeymoon, and this time, no one interrupted their vacation. Miles spent the rest of his working career training several potential candidates for viceroy, so that the Republic and the Galactic Empire would remain in steady hands. He especially focused on making sure that the relationship between the Republic and the Humtars was peaceful and enduring.
****

Captain Wiyrkomi initially struggled after the end of the war. The Gallentines had been at war for thousands of years, and all of that had suddenly and unexpectedly gone away. At first, he worried that Legion might return, but after some long conversations with Viceroy Miles Hunt, he accepted the reality of the situation. Wiyrkomi decided that it was time to retire and take his friend Miles up on his offer to teach him to fly-fish.

Realizing he was still wrestling with the sudden change of pace, he worked with the Gallentine military to create a network of support groups for former soldiers who were adapting to civilian life. This additional purpose gave him the will to keep fighting.
****

Chester Bailey retired from Space Command. He and his wife returned to Earth, to their home on Merritt Island, Florida, near the old Space Command Headquarters at Patrick Space Force Base. The two of them celebrated eighty years of marriage, and after his wife had followed him around for eight decades, it was now his turn to support her career.

She'd always enjoyed cooking and had dreamed of running a gourmet seafood food truck. She launched a high-end, fancy hover truck that became all the rave. When not helping her run the grill, Bailey was busy penning his memoir, *The Old Man—To Space & Beyond*. It portrayed a largely unglamorous life for a man who was arguably one of the most powerful figures of the past quarter century.
****

Fran McKee turned down the promotion to become the head of Space Command and instead took a teaching position on the main Humtar home world, Etlu, teaching Earth history of the last fifty years. She eventually met a Humtar, fell in love and got married, having four children. She stayed on as a teacher, passing along her knowledge and years of experience to the next generation.
****

Ripley Willis Lee accepted Bailey's promotion to Fleet Admiral and Head of Space Command. He then had the task of maintaining the peace, documenting the lessons learned from the Zodark wars, and preparing Space Command and the Republic for whatever came next.
****

Brian Royce was promoted to lieutenant general and took charge of Republic Army Special Forces. He and his wife went on to have eight kids, and he stayed in the Army another ten years after the war ended before retiring to Alpha Centauri, the only planet in the Republic he had never fought on. Finally, he had found a place where he was able to find peace with his past and grow old.
****

Paul "Pauli" Smith left the military and the Reserves after the war ended. He grew his businesses on New Eden, becoming one of the most successful land developers on the planet, as well as one of the richest people on New Eden. He led philanthropic charities across the planet, using his immense wealth to build affordable housing, provide job training, expedite veteran services, and help people rebuild their lives following the war. He and his wife went on to have six kids, adopting twenty more over the course of their lives, giving orphaned kids a chance they otherwise would not have had.
****

Yogi Sanders, Pauli's best friend, went on to become one of his business managers. The two stayed close friends the rest of their lives. Yogi eventually got married and, like his friend Pauli, had a large family, having eight biological children, and adopting six more over the years.
****

Amy Dobbs would eventually become the Chief of Naval Operations, helping Ripley Lee rebuild the Republic Navy as it grew in size, eventually surpassing more than a thousand warships. She became instrumental in building an expansive naval reserve force of warships that had been kept mothballed. With her efforts, they were once again ready should a threat like the Zodarks ever materialize in the future.
****

Joe Wright retired after receiving his second admiral's star, eventually forming a luxury cruise company that catered to adventure thrill seekers, exploring asteroid belts and other special anomalies.
****

When David and Catalina were released from the Kites, they retired to New Eden and bought an Andorra cattle ranch. Their four children learned the business, and were completely unaware of their colorful past, instead believing that Mom and Dad were just old and boring parents. David and Catalina were content to have a plain and boring existence in their retirement.
****

Jess initially struggled with her loss of purpose after leaving the Kites, until she found something to bring her life new meaning. She and Somchai decided not to have any kids of their own. Instead, they moved to Éire and fostered several children, eventually adopting twelve orphans of the war in Sol. Jess became active as a coach for sports teams, and Somchai opened a Thai restaurant, which she also helped with from time to time.
****

Amir moved to Alpha Centauri, where he opened up a trading post. However, within a year, he had fallen head over heels in love with a local woman and decided to join her family's business in botany. They had seven children and were wildly happy.
****

Dr. Alan Walburg spent the remainder of his life in pursuit of scientific discoveries that would build up and not destroy. He and Sam became an integral part of the Republic'ss efforts to improve treatments for PTSD, significantly improving mental health outcomes and reducing veteran suicide rates substantially.

****

Dr. Katherine Johnson actually ended up marrying her "fling" and was surprised by the birth of a baby girl. She doted on her late-in-life daughter, who became a medical doctor of great repute.

****

After further exploration of Lab Site X with the help of the Humtars, Jack and Sakura moved to Alpha Centauri to continue work on the site there. Jack started a tea company, which was enormously successful. They had five children.

****

From the Authors

Miranda and I hope that you've enjoyed this book and the end of this series. It's hard to believe that this is the last book in the Rise of the Republic series—what a wild ride it's been. When we released the first book, we were still in the middle of a worldwide pandemic. Things have certainly changed since then.

Although this portion of the series will be wrapping up with the twelfth book, we do have some additional content that may excite you. A new spinoff series, spearheaded by our friend and successful science fiction author, Brandon Ellis, has already debuted, which has three of four planned books already released. Battles of the Republic dives deeper into some of the campaigns you've already read about in our main series, adding to the richness of the universe you've come to love. To grab your copy of first book in the new series, *The Intus Invasion*, visit Amazon.

On other fronts, if you are a fan of our military technothrillers, we have started a new series, A World on Fire. The first volume, *The Gotland Deception*, is already available, and we expect to release the next volume before the end of the year. We are also excited to announce that Jeffrey Kafer is going to be the voice of the series, with the first audiobook available this December.

In case you hadn't heard, we also finished the ninth and final book in our military technothriller series, the Monroe Doctrine, this past February. If you haven't had a chance to start this series yet, we have a box set of the first four books for you to binge at a discount, which is available on Amazon.

We are also trying something new with our Patreon page, sharing unedited chapters of the books we're currently working on for free. This gives you, the reader, a chance to help us craft better, more realistic and interesting stories while they are in the developmental stages before moving into the editing process. This is free to join, but of course, if you would like to help support our work, we are grateful for that and have some unique benefits just for you. You can check out our Patreon page at https://www.patreon.com/cw/Frontlinepublishing.

As always, we appreciate each and every one of you that take the time to read our books. We definitely couldn't do this without you. If you've enjoyed *Into the Schism*, we would love it if you could take a moment and write up a review on Amazon and Goodreads. Early reviews really make a huge difference in new readers discovering our books, and that in turn helps us to continue writing full-time and bringing you the stories you love.

All our best,

James Rosone and Miranda Watson

Abbreviation Key

1MC	Shipwide Communication System
AO	Area of Operations
AOR	Area of Responsibility
APC	Armored Personnel Carrier
ASAP	As soon as possible
ATAC	Armored Transport Assault Craft
CAC	Combat Air Coordinator
CAG	Commander Air Group
CAS	Close-Air Support
CIC	Combat Information Center
CNS	Confederation Naval Ship
CO	Commanding Officer
COB	Chief of the Boat
CSB	Combat Support Base
CSW	Carrier Strike Wing
DEAD	Destruction of Enemy Air Defense
DM	Direct Message
ECM	Electronic Countermeasures
ENDEX	End Exercise
FAE	Fuel-air Explosive
ENVG-B	Enhanced Night Vision Goggle—Binocular
ETA	Estimated Time of Arrival
FITREP	Fitness Report
FRAGO	Fragmentary Order
FTL	Faster Than Light
GDF	Gurista Defense Force
HQ	Headquarters
HUD	Heads Up Display
IED	Improvised Explosive Device
IFV	Infantry Fighting Vehicle
INTSUM	Intelligence Summary
IRW	Intergalactic Rules of War
JATM	Joint Advanced Tactical Missile
JSOC	Joint Special Operations Command
KBR	Keller, Booth, and Root

KIA	Killed in Action
KPS	Kilometers Per Second
LMG	Light Machine Gun
LTV	Light Tactical Vehicle
LZ	Landing Zone
MW	Megawatt
NCO	Noncommissioned Officer
NOS	Zodark Officer
OAT	Orbital Assault Troop
ODA	Operational Delta Attachment (Special Forces)
OP	Observation Post
OPFOR	Opposing Force
OSA	Omni-Spectral Array
P2	Priority Pad
PA	Public Announcement
PACT	Pilot Adaptive Combat Training
PDG	Point-Defense Gun
PELS	Pulsar Echo Location System
PFC	Private First Class
PTP	Pallas Training Protocol
QB	Quantum Beam
QF	Quantum Fusion
QFR	Quantum Fusion Reactor
QRF	Quick Reaction Force
R & R	Rest and Recreation
RNS	Republic Naval Service
RP	Rally Point
RTB	Return to Base
SAM	Surface-to-Air Missile
SITREP	Situation Report
SNA	State of Northeast Africa
SOF	Special Operations Forces
TAO	Tactical Action Officer
TOC	Tactical Operation Center
TRADOC	Training and Doctrine Command
UAV	Unmanned Aerial Vehicle
VSR	Void Scientific Research

XO   Executive Officer

THE END

Printed in Dunstable, United Kingdom